BEARSKIN

BEARSKIN

JAMES A. McLAUGHLIN

An Imprint of HarperCollins*Publishers*

Portions of *Bearskin* appeared in *The Missouri Review* (Summer, 2008) and *Salt Lake City Weekly*.

HarperCollins books may be purchased for educational, business, or sales promotional use. For information, please email the Special Markets Department at SPsales@harpercollins.com.

FIRST EDITION

Designed by Renata De Oliveira

Library of Congress Cataloging-in-Publication Data

Names: McLaughlin, James A., author.
Title: Bearskin / James A. McLaughlin.
Description: First edition. | New York : Ecco, [2017]
Identifiers: LCCN 2017034531 (print) | LCCN 2017043411 (ebook) |
ISBN 9780062742810 (ebook) | ISBN 9780062742797 |
ISBN 9780062742803
Subjects: LCSH: Bear hunting--Fiction. | Poaching--Fiction. |
GSAFD: Suspense fiction.
Classification: LCC PS3613.C5755 (ebook) | LCC PS3613.C5755 B43
2018 (print) | DDC 813/.6--dc23
LC record available at https://lccn.loc.gov/2017034531

ISBN 978-0-06-274279-7 (hardcover)
ISBN 978-0-06-285378-3 (international edition)

18 19 20 21 22 LSC 10 9 8 7 6 5 4 3 2 1

For Rosa
and
for Nancy

THE BEAUTY OF THE RATTLESNAKE IS IN ITS THREAT.

—Jim Harrison, "Suite of Unreason"

PROLOGUE

That first night Rice held a section of cast-iron water pipe under his pillow and pretended to sleep. He'd paid for the pipe, wrapped at one end with skateboard grip tape, with the last flat damp C-note from under the insole of his boot, plus promises of more, his American girlfriend visiting soon, bringing cash, three hundred U.S. dollars all told. He knew he'd probably been fleeced.

His cellmate read a folded El Universal in his bunk, shuffling the pages every few minutes. Without taking his eyes from the paper he lit a cigarette and smoked it fast. In several hours he had not once acknowledged Rice's presence.

The light changed, shadows, two men coming through the open cell door. Sooner than he'd thought. Someone had already run the necessary calculations, weighed the risks, made this decision. Rice was unimportant except he was important to the young woman, which gave the DEA leverage with her if they offered to bring him back to the States. Preemptively removing that leverage was classic Sinaloa: shrewd, brutal expediency.

Afterward they would watch the young woman. She would have no more reason to give them up, and every reason not to—she was a professional, and she would keep her head.

These two, the ones they'd sent, they had to know he would be fresh, still scared, thrumming with adrenaline.

They may not have known about the pipe.

He waited until they were close, until one reached out to hold his head back, to expose his throat and chest and belly, the heat from the hand was there, almost touching.

Twelve seconds later he was wounded in several places but the shiv was more of an assassin's weapon than a defensive one and both men lay on the floor. His iron pipe had rolled under the bunk. He stomped once on the first man's neck, the one who had reached for his head. He'd never killed, never even seriously hurt anyone in his life. He seemed to be watching himself from some remove in this, the first of the dissociative fugues that would become so commonplace he couldn't imagine a time without them. Watching, knowing already that he had become unfamiliar—not another person, he would never make that claim—but rather a version of himself that he would come to believe was monstrous.

He'd raised up his boot to break the man's neck when a voice behind him said, "Stop."

He stopped.

His cellmate watched him over the top of his newspaper.

"They'll come back if I don't."

"More will come if you do. Cut their heels."

"What?"

"The tendons. De Aquiles."

He knelt beside the first man and hacked at the tendon with one of the shivs they had dropped: a long nail, sharpened on the concrete floor, embedded in a wooden handle. He held the leg and stabbed and scraped with the point of the nail and the man groaned and tried to roll over. The handle of the shiv was slick in Rice's hand. Blood trickled down from an ugly ripped stab wound in his forearm.

A metallic click behind his ear, the cellmate standing there with an open folding knife. He turned it and offered the black plastic handle.

"All four," he said.

Rice wondered idly at the status of a man who could carry a knife like this inside. The blade was strange-looking, like the curved, hooked beak of a cartoon bird. It had a serrated edge, and the tendons parted at its touch, the calf muscles reacting in spasm, leaping away to bunch and squirm.

The second man didn't react to the cuts, and he didn't bleed as much as the first.

"This one might be dead."

"He's not dead."

A guard came and the cellmate spoke to him at the door and he dragged the two men away, one at a time.

Rice wiped the knife on his pants leg and handed it back. His cellmate took it without a word, turned and sat on his bunk, picked up his newspaper.

He went to his own bunk, reached underneath for his iron pipe, cleaned it on the underside of his thin mattress. The gash in his forearm was still bleeding, so he tore off part of his sheet to make a compress. When the blood stopped seeping through he tore two strips and bound the compress to his arm. He slid his pipe beneath his pillow and he lay down but he didn't sleep. Later he would remember this night for the obvious reasons, plus another, which was the irony that his first lesson in CERESO was one of mercy, of restraint.

He lay in his bunk. Outside, the cool desert night scraped quietly against the concrete walls of the prison. He didn't sleep.

ONE

The bees in the wall attacked in suicide pacts of two, three, five at once. They flew at Rice's face, and he brushed them away with his gloves. He'd lost count of the stings. One landed on his lip and tried to crawl into his left nostril, and while he swatted at it, snorting like a deer, another stung him in the center of his forehead. He blinked hard and kept working, almost finished now. He jammed the claw of his crowbar under the thin panels and snapped them away from the studs, working from floor to ceiling. When the nails were loosened he reached back for the sledgehammer, smashed the whole section clattering to the floor.

He stepped away from the wall and rested the head of the sledge on his boot. A breeze blew in the open door of the cabin, stirring up dust. His eyes itched and his nose was running. Sweat ran down his cheeks. He'd started before dawn and now all he had left was this six-foot section of panels he'd saved for last because of the hive. Part of his job up here was eradicating invasive species, but these European honeybees had made it onto the protected list, probably because they'd been around for about five hundred years and were famously dying off from some new ailment.

That last sting above his eyebrows had begun to throb like an ice-cream headache. He blew his nose in a dusty paper towel and watched the bees crawling on the panels. They moved like a drunken marching band—ranks and columns that circled, broke apart, coalesced into new shapes. A couple hundred nervous defenders, vibrating with collective outrage, waiting to see what Rice would do next. Bees were purposeful creatures and they had no time for this impertinent primate with his bent iron and oversize hammer.

He exhaled a long breath toward the wall, wondering how he was going to get rid of the bees without killing them. At the least, he had to pull those last sections of paneling so he could see what he was dealing with. He tied a bandana over the lower part of his face and buttoned the sleeves and collar of his work shirt. As he approached, the humming in the wall increased in pitch, an unmistakable warning, but he set the crowbar in place and pulled. Nails snug in thick oak studs for the better part of a century screeched coming out, and then something broke and a piece of paneling snapped away and fell on the floor. A yellowish mass seethed there as the hive-mind paused to gather itself, then all the bees attacked at once.

He stopped running in the grass behind the cabin, brushing bees from his hair and off his shirt, his bandana fallen around his neck. A cloud of angry bees boiled in the doorway but hadn't followed, apparently content to eject him from the cabin. The hot sun pressed on his shoulders, the air outside clean and pleasant to breathe. Dragonflies swooped and hovered over a fecund riot of chest-high bluestem and orchard grass. This late in the summer, the crickets sang all day, and from the tall trees at the edge of the forest came the neurotic pulse and whirr of dog-day cicadas. Overhead, the long green wedge of Turk Mountain loomed like a great wave breaking northward.

No other human being lived within miles. Rice presided alone over seven thousand acres of private nature preserve: he was the caretaker, the science tech. He drove the John Deere tractor. He'd exaggerated his construction experience on the job application, probably one reason they'd hired a guy with his record. That and the fact that he was a qualified biological science technician who looked like he could take care of himself. He'd agreed to do the work on the cabin so the owners wouldn't hire a bunch of carpenters to drive up in the mornings and ruin his solitude.

His neck ached, and when he took off a glove and reached up to touch below his ear he felt another quick jab of pain, like getting stung again. Something came away under his fingernail. A bulb of bee guts, attached to a tiny barbed stinger. All these bees had jammed their stingers into his skin and pulled away, leaving behind vital organs, and flown off to die. What a system. The stinging bees were females, nonbreeders, kamikazes all—apparently their individual survival meant little enough. He held the stinger in the sunlight, close to his face, looking for his future there, extispicy in miniature.

A shadow rushed him from the right and he dropped into a crouch and took two quick steps toward the doorway before his mind caught up with his reflexes. A vulture careened overhead, its wings hissing in the air as its shadow slid over the grass and flashed up the clapboard cabin wall.

He stood straight and breathed, grinning at himself. His pulse slowed but the thing that wasn't quite fear—it always felt more like recognition: *there* it is, *here* it comes—took a few moments to pass.

Six months now, since he'd moved up here. He was sure no one knew where he was.

He picked up the glove he'd dropped, stepped back out in the grass. The vultures always showed up around this time, after the sun had warmed the earth, lifting like paper kites in the thermal boiling up from the meadow.

"Goddamn buzzard," he said, without malice.

Two more appeared, flying one behind the other in tight formation. They banked at the edge of the forest and beat the air with a dozen choppy wingbeats, sailed past the cabin again. They turned their naked black heads to look at him as they passed. He waved, thinking it was best to act friendly. They seemed impatient to be away and soaring, to put the world in proper perspective—four thousand feet up with the land unrolling like a map beneath them, a road atlas with thick, bloodred lines for the cornucopian highways, thin fuchsia for the secondaries. Certain pastures would be shaded pink for stillborn lambs or lightning-struck cows. These black vultures were smaller than the redheaded turkey vultures, and they tended to be less patient with the dying. Last month he'd seen a piece in the paper about a new suburb in northern Virginia where the local vultures were attacking house pets. A flock of the birds would spot a geriatric Pekingese hobbling too far from the house and swarm on it like flesh-eating beetles, pull it to pieces in its own backyard while the neighbors' kids gaped from an upstairs window.

He was watching the vultures, feeling his face starting to get puffy, remembering he used to be allergic to bee stings when he was a kid and maybe he ought to walk over to the lodge and take a Benadryl just in case, and what exactly was he going to do about the bees now anyway, when a large animal walked out of the woods at the far end of the meadow. It was a quarter mile away, contorted by quivering heat waves. He squinted, shaded his eyes against the glare from the sky.

He'd been seeing bears. At first it was just sign—tracks and piles of scat and overturned rocks and logs—but in the past few weeks the bears had started showing themselves. A female with two first-year cubs had been feeding mornings in a blackberry thicket at the bottom of the meadow, and over on Serrett Mountain he'd glimpsed a huge adult male that ran with a limp. Two days

ago a sleek juvenile with one scabby ear split in a fight had crossed
the driveway at dusk. Rice had found tracks in the old fire road not
thirty yards from the lodge, the rear print like a barefoot man's,
the front a big broad paw. Now he locked his garbage in the tractor
shed and carted it to the public Dumpster every few days instead
of letting it pile up.

The figure had paused in the open, cautious maybe, but now it
was moving again, coming down the long slope of the fire road. It
shimmered and shifted in the hot air, a bearish wraith floating just
above the earth. As it approached it gradually took shape: a person,
a man, a bearded man with a large rucksack on his back, his legs
hidden in the tall grass.

Rice jogged past the tractor shed and toward the back porch of
the lodge, keeping his eye on the intruder. He would've been less
surprised by a bear. The gate at the entrance was always locked, and
he'd never seen anyone walk out of that forest. He kept a loaded .45
in the drawer of his bedside table in willful violation of his employment agreement, and that's where he was headed.

At the top of the steps, Rice turned for one more look before he
darted inside for the pistol. Something was wrong with the man's
left arm—it was short, and it swung in a rhythm that didn't quite
match his stride, like a child's arm attached to an adult.

Then he was in the yard, as if he'd leaped forward while Rice
blinked. A moment before, he'd been out in the meadow, a wild
creature Rice could observe with detachment, but he'd crossed the
boundary so abruptly that Rice wondered if he'd blacked out for a
moment.

His legs felt solid, steady, his feet flat on the rough floorboards.
This strange man walking toward the porch.

Rice raised his hand, palm out, like a cop halting traffic. "Hey,
buddy," he said. "You lost?"

The man stopped and grimaced, bared his straight yellow teeth.
He was hatless, his face tan and deeply lined above the dark beard.

Probably in his forties, though guessing the age of mountain people was always chancy. His eyes were light green, flat and expressionless. For an instant Rice thought he might be blind, some sightless forest wanderer come to visit, a prophet, purveyor of miracles.

The man shrugged out of his pack, dropped it on the ground, and stood there with his hips loose and his weight on one leg. The left arm was a stump, ending just above where the elbow should have been. He wore dusty black boots and tattered fatigue pants, a torn sleeveless shirt wet and sticking to his flat belly. A sheath knife hung from a leather belt just behind his right hip.

He asked something in a raspy voice. It sounded like "Yowl spear in the otter?"

"What?"

He cupped his hand and tilted it to his mouth. The arm was long and tanned, with corded muscles working under the skin like snakes. High on the deltoid was the crude tattoo of a humanoid figure with the head of some carnivore, its mouth open and showing teeth.

Spare any water.

Rice was supposed to keep trespassers off the property, but the day was hot and he'd lived most of his life in the desert and he wasn't going to refuse anyone a drink of water. He'd also dispensed with the idea of the pistol. There were good reasons for keeping the .45 handy, but defending himself from a one-armed man with a backpack wasn't one of them. He found an old army canteen in the kitchen closet, rinsed and filled it at the sink, watching the man through the screen window. He stood in the yard with his head tilted back, following a bird or insect flying overhead, but as Rice watched he dropped his gaze and stared hard at the window, just for a second, as if Rice had called out. Then he turned his attention to the meadow, intent for a moment, now relaxing, watching the horizon again. He reminded Rice of an alert dog, perceptive of faint sounds and old scents, ghosts and phantasms.

The canteen filled and overflowed, wetting the felt cover, cool on Rice's hand. Sweat ran from under his arms, trickled down his sides to the waistband of his pants. He popped two Benadryl tablets from a blister pack and washed them down with a can of Coors. He felt disoriented—objects across the room seemed far away, the kitchen floor tilting under him. In the past year and a half he'd become increasingly prone to minor fugues and fits of reverie. He would pause in his outside work—biological data collection, hacking at multiflora rose with a sling blade, tacking up *Posted No Trespassing* signs—and awaken later from a long daydream, vacant and disconcerted, his butt asleep in the dirt and several species of insect crawling on his skin, bites itching his ankles, a dog tick embedded behind his knee. He never remembered what he'd been dreaming about, just a vague sense of relentless motion, of buzzing and humming, grass vibrating in the air.

You've been up here too long by yourself, he thought. Turning into a hermit. Greeting imaginary strangers. At the last minute he pulled another beer from the fridge and carried it out to the porch with the water.

He pitched the canteen underhand from the top step and the man caught it nonchalantly, held it between his legs so he could unscrew the top. He drank in long gulps with his eyes closed. When he'd finished, he wiped his mouth with the back of his hand, nodded thanks, and tossed the empty canteen back to Rice, declining the offered beer. He was completely unimpaired, his movements smooth and powerful, that Popeye arm more than adequate. His forehead rose straight and broad under a tangle of thick black hair. There was that odd, blind man's stare, and his beard obscured a heavy chin and lips that barely moved when he spoke. He burped quietly and rocked back on his heels. He seemed to have something else on his mind but was restraining himself, perhaps out of politeness.

"What're you doing way back here?" Rice asked, a fake Turpin

County twang in his voice. The accent had been coming to him unbidden whenever he talked to locals.

"Pickin' mushrooms." The man tapped a canvas satchel hanging from his belt. "Chanterelles, 'seng, bilberry."

"Did you know this is private property?"

The man shook his head and said something Rice couldn't understand.

"What's that?"

He repeated himself exactly, but Rice caught it this time: "Din pick none hyar." His drawl was beyond anything Rice had heard in the county—he swallowed his consonants, the syllables rich with inflection but hard to group into words.

"You got those mushrooms up in the national forest and then walked all the way down here for a drink of water?"

The man only looked at him. Like he didn't understand how Rice's statement could work as a question.

"Trouble is," Rice began, "there's those 'Posted' signs up at the gate, about five miles back, I know you saw 'em."

"They's somethin' to show ye." The man turned at the waist and jerked his head back the way he had come, back up the mountain. "Sup thar."

"What is it?"

"Y'orta see't y'self."

Rice huffed through his nose. He still had to deal with those bees today, and clean out the cabin. He had a schedule. The porch rail creaked as he leaned forward to peer up at the weather. Above the mountain, a handful of cumulus humilis clouds hung lifeless and inert as god's laundry, refusing to develop into storms or to even provide much shade. It would be a hot hike to see this thing on the mountain, which could turn out to be the face of Jesus on a lichen-covered boulder, an albino rattlesnake, a single-engine plane crash. Maybe a group of compadres waiting in ambush over the ridge. The beer he'd brought out for his guest stood sweating on the railing, and after a moment's hesitation Rice went ahead and opened it for himself. He took a long pull and held the cold can against a bee-sting lump on his forehead.

"'S your place, ain't it?" The mushroom picker swept his arm in an arc that included the old hewn-log lodge with its massive stone chimney, the clapboard tractor shed, the freshly gutted summer cabin, the big meadow.

"No. I'm the caretaker."

A clamor started in the forest, and a red-tailed hawk shot out over the tall grass on stiff wings, heckled by a gang of crows diving and dipping. When they reached the lodge, the crows all flared and scattered back into the trees, leaving the hawk to glide downhill. The mushroom picker had turned to watch, but now he stared up at Rice with those eyes like pale stones, standing in the heat without seeming to notice it.

"I don't think you're real," Rice said, but the man didn't reply. The crickets ticking in the grass made a pervasive sound that could have been coming from the air itself.

TWO

By the fourth switchback Rice had fallen behind, his legs heavy, his breathing ragged. Sweat soaked his eyebrows and dripped into his eyes. The fire road was rough and overgrown with yellow pine saplings smelling of turpentine in the heat, their sharp needles pricking his skin. He caught a glimpse of the mushroom picker far ahead, waiting where he knew he'd be skylined, showing himself. Then he vanished again.

At the crest of the ridge, the road turned one last time and ran northward along the spine of the mountain. No sign of the mushroom picker. Rice stopped to catch his breath, arms akimbo, cooling in the faint breeze that rose out of the deep canyon to the west. A mile farther down, sheer limestone cliffs fell away to a broad creek bottom, the sanctum sanctorum of the Turk Mountain Preserve, a thousand acres of primary forest passed over by eighteenth- and nineteenth-century loggers and protected by the Traver family ever since. On the far side lay Serrett Mountain hazy and plump, and after that the wild Appalachians went on and on, folded blue-green ridges one after the other all the way to the horizon.

The road wasn't as steep from here and he thought he should be able to catch up. He shook his head. With the beer and Benadryl he was too loopy for a hike up the mountain, and this was probably a fool's errand anyway, but after a moment he turned and started jogging.

Halfway to the mountain's peak he stopped again, high on the exposed spine of the ridge where the oak and pine forest was stunted and the road more open, unshaded, paved with shards of broken purple sandstone that slipped and rolled under his boots. The air smelled of hot rock. Fence lizards skittered into dry leaves. His throat felt raw and was so dry it threatened to close up every time he swallowed. Should've brought that canteen. He hadn't seen the mushroom picker for nearly an hour and he thought the guy might've changed his mind and drifted off into the forest.

Suddenly dizzy, he bent over with his hands on his knees, watching sweat drip from his nose and chin onto the sandstone, darkening it from purple to blue-black.

"She ain't far now."

He stood too quickly, almost blacking out. The man hunkered on the side of the road not twenty feet away.

She?

Before Rice could ask, the mushroom picker walked due west into the thicket, following no trail Rice could see. They pushed downslope through oak saplings and scaly-barked rhododendron tangled with mountain laurel tugging at their thighs, cat's-claw vines pricking their shins.

Vultures flushed from a grove of big yellow pines. The man walked to the base of one of the trees and dropped to one knee as in supplication beside something lying in the pine needles, blocking Rice's view. Rice slowed, more cautious now and not sure why. Noisy, twirling swarms of bluebottle and greenbottle flies smacked like BBs into his legs. The rich, coppery smell was vaguely familiar—blood and viscera, sun-warm meat.

The mushroom picker rose and stepped away from a headless body lying on its side. At first Rice thought it was a woman. His breath caught and his skin tingled even as he recognized what it was.

"Done skint this'n," the mushroom picker said. "Ah seen more'n a dozen. Some's skint. Most times he don't take nothin' but they hands and they galls." He began to pace back and forth under the tree, muttering to himself. The creature was skinned naked, its muscles red and wrinkled where the fascia had started to dry. The abdomen had been slit, and the vultures had pulled out pale, ropy loops of intestine. All four limbs ended in polished white condyles at the wrist and ankle joints. Rice stared, struck by the human resemblance. After a few moments he felt able to speak.

"It's a bear?"

The man started, as if he had forgotten about Rice.

"'S'bar." He spoke through his teeth, his voice strange, lower and harsher than before. He seemed angry. "She-bar."

He kept his head lowered, mumbling gibberish, and he wouldn't meet Rice's eyes. He hunched his shoulders against the weight of his pack and shifted from foot to foot, stepping forward, then back, almost dancing, his movements jerky and powerful. Rice backed away. He was about to ask the man if he was all right when he turned and ducked and vanished into the rhododendron hell.

THREE

A warm shower fell on the forest as Rice made his way down the mountain, just enough rain to make the already muggy air intolerable when the sun came back out. This was his first summer in the Virginia mountains, and he found the humidity surreal and enervating. The air was palpable, buzzing with insects, and day or night the slightest breeze carried some fragrance: wet grass, honeysuckle, putrefaction.

Walking down was easier than climbing up, but his boots landed hard on the rocky trail and his strides were long and rubbery, every step a gamble on shaky knees and weak thighs. He recognized the lightheadedness that followed mild trauma. Explanations were available: the bee stings, beer and Benadryl, mild heat exhaustion, dehydration, too little sleep, too much time alone. A combination of all those things, for sure, plus something else.

She-bar, the mushroom picker had said: a wild female American black bear, *Ursus americanus*. Killed illegally on the preserve, bizarrely mutilated, and left for the scavengers. Disturbing enough, though it was the momentary apparition of a murdered woman that had recalled images buried in the far reaches of his imagination.

He was putting those things away again now as he hiked down the fire road, but the shock lingered. The dead bear had reminded him that what he had fled could still come here. He'd grown to imagine the Turk Mountain Preserve as the perfect refuge for him and for all the other creatures who resided there, a romantic idea indeed for a half-trained biologist. That sense of security, always fragile, had now vanished as surely and completely as the mushroom picker himself. Rice had tried to follow the man, and he was not an incompetent tracker, but after a hundred yards it was as if he had dissolved into the air.

A shrill, clattering call burst from the forest nearby. He stopped to watch, thinking *pileated woodpecker*, but the bird didn't appear. He knew most of the bird species now. His first log entries from back in March and April said things like *big-ass black woodpecker w/red crest*. While he watched, a fresh breeze brushed against the big tulip trees, red oaks, sugar maples. Heavy branches rose and fell in slow motion, and a million leaves twisted on their stems, showing silver underneath. The forest was eerily animate, a gigantic green beast dreaming, its skin twitching and rippling. Not quite threatening, but powerful. Watchful.

For a moment he imagined the forest was angry, disappointed, that this intrusion by the bear poachers was his responsibility. He felt some of the mushroom picker's outrage at what he seemed to regard as a murder. But he pushed those thoughts away. Recently he'd noticed in himself a slant toward excessive anthropomorphism. It was something he worked to keep in check.

Still, even if he focused only on the facts, he surely had new troubles. The rupture of his inviolate refuge, a sudden sense of encroachment and vulnerability. Potential law enforcement implications. And there was the affront to his professionalism as caretaker: at least one bear, and probably others, had been poached on his watch. It demanded a response.

Ever since he'd moved to Virginia, Rice had engaged in a nearly religious practice of keeping himself to himself, employing a human analogue to the behavioral strategies of certain prey species: drab coloring, quiet habits, never leaving cover, avoiding conflict. A change in strategy would be risky in a number of ways, not the least of which was the danger of unleashing his own tendency to push things further than he ought to. He wouldn't call the law—that would expose him far too blatantly—but he also knew he couldn't sit back and wait for more intrusions. Turpin County harbored an active and outspoken tribe of bear hunters, and the few he'd encountered had been openly hostile toward him. Unfortunately, he couldn't think of anyplace else to start.

At the lodge, he changed out of his sweaty clothes and, hiding his pistol as usual in a slit he'd cut in the passenger seat of his truck, started the engine and began the long drive down the mountain.

FOUR

Rice spun the round, padded seats of the old bar stools as he walked past, all of them tottering and squeaking in the near silence, one by one coming to a stop as he sat at the end of the bar. A game show flickered on a mute television perched above the register. An elderly couple, the only other patrons, sat immobile as mannequins at a table by the front window. The simple neon sign that gave the place its name wasn't turned on yet: *Beer & Eat.*

He waved to the bartender, a broadly built woman probably in her thirties. Her dirty-blond ponytail was tied back with a dark blue ribbon and the sewn script on her blue work shirt said "Karla." He wondered if the shirt was supposed to be ironic. Might not even be her name. She walked over and Rice ordered a Rolling Rock, but she hesitated, staring, like she was deciding whether to serve him. He remembered the bees and reached up to feel the lumps on his cheeks, his forehead. He leaned forward to peer at himself in the dark mirror behind the bar.

"Bee stings," he said, settling back on his stool, shrugging. "Got into a hive today."

"Why'd you come in here?"

He smiled and spread his hands palm-down on the cool wood of the bar top. He had been in the Beer & Eat only once before, back in the spring.

"I don't know what you mean."

She shook her head and walked to the cooler, stopping to draw once on the cigarette she'd left lit in an ashtray on the cash register. The statewide ban on smoking in restaurants apparently had no effect in the town of Wanless. On the television, an advertisement showed a shiny black SUV with its lights on, swinging fast around the curves on a cliffside highway in California. Smoke rose from the ashtray in a thin stream and curled and dispersed in front of the picture. Karla pushed the bottle toward Rice without looking at him and retreated to stand behind the register. She pointed a remote at the TV and turned up the sound. He tilted the beer and drank about half of it at once.

He'd been warned when he took the job, but the occasional flash of local hostility still surprised him. As the caretaker of the Turk Mountain Preserve, he represented wealthy outsiders and a preservation ethic that seemed nonsensical and elitist to the locals. The hostility apparently was bad enough it had driven his predecessor to leave the job. Sara Birkeland—he knew her name from the caretaker's logbooks and the junk mail that still came to the mailbox—was a real biologist, a postdoc herpetologist at Virginia Tech who was doing field research on a rare species of skink Rice had never heard of. She had moved back to Blacksburg, gone for several months by the time he arrived, but he'd lived with her lingering citrus scent in the bedroom, her handwriting in the field logs, long blond strands in the dust balls he swept out from under the furniture. He knew from her notes in the log that she had a particular and unscientific fondness for chickadees; he knew what kind of detergent and soap and toothpaste she used. She'd started showing up in his dreams, a faceless, petite blond stalking around inside the lodge, refusing to speak to him. For months she'd been the nearest thing he'd had to a human companion.

He squinted at his reflection in the bar mirror again. In this light his eyes were hooded, dark. He looked a little bit like a crazy person.

After several tries he got Karla's attention and ordered another beer. When it disappeared he ordered one more, with a glass of water. Mildly stupefied, he was content to watch television for a while. He knew most of the answers to the trivia questions until they got to current pop culture, where he failed miserably. Six months at the preserve, he thought, and I'm an ignorant backwoods hermit. A bee-stung Rip Van Winkle.

After six, sawmill workers started drifting into the bar in groups of three and four, ordering food and pitchers of beer. It was Friday and the place filled up fast, the air smelling now of sawdust and turpentine, creosote and sweat, the Wanless sawmill. Three young women stepped through the door with exaggerated bravado and descended on a table as though they'd rehearsed outside, gathering their nerve. They were dressed for the dance hall up in Clifford— tight jeans, cowboy boots, sculpted hairdos. The tall one with red hair stared hard at Rice, but when he grinned she turned away.

The kitchen in the back was bustling now, and greasy-smelling steam puffed through the swinging door each time the waitress went in or out. Rice ordered a hamburger and leaned back against the bar to watch the people in the room, middle-aged men in jeans, heavy boots, work shirts. Most had full beards or tough-guy goatees. They were dirty and tired, and they talked quietly in their small groups. The sharp clack of a break announced a pool game in the back room. Nashville country music drawled from an antique CD jukebox. He hated top forty, but this was the old stuff.

On the TV, a young woman in a tight beige suit pointed to a map of Virginia and West Virginia: "Weekend Weather." It would be clear and hot, more of the same, the drought dragging into its ninth week despite a few scattered thunderstorms. Most of the faces nearby had turned toward the television: men with gardens to water, maybe some skinny cattle to worry about, a meager second cutting of hay on the ground. Fishing trips to the reservoir over the weekend. They were regular folks with regular lives. No one was hunting them. Rice wondered how their days went, what they talked about at home over the kitchen table on Sunday morning. He permitted himself a flash of envy. He might as well be a separate species for all the day-to-day concerns he shared with these good people.

He slid off the stool and found the restroom, which smelled of the usual disinfectant and deodorizer, ammonia of old piss. Slurs and accusations on the walls. *Suzy is a whore. Johnny D. is a queer.* All with numbers to call. He reached to flush and there, printed in pencil on the wall next to the handle: *Will buy bear galls, paws Also jinsang.* He memorized the phone number.

When he returned to the bar, his hamburger had arrived and two men were sitting on stools nearby. Rice nodded and said "Evenin'" to the closer one, a gigantic lummox with a shaved head and bushy red beard. He ignored Rice and conversed with Karla about the long week, the hot weather. His voice was absurdly high-pitched for such a big man, almost a falsetto. The jukebox played a song about someone sitting in a bar listening to a jukebox. Halfway through his hamburger, Rice turned again to the giant sitting next to him.

"Y'all do any bear hunting around here?"

He swiveled around in no hurry, aimed his face at Rice like a satellite dish. Rice took this as a no.

"You know anybody who does? I'm looking to try, but I don't know much about it."

The big man nodded, pursing his lips. "Some folks like to hunt bar. They got dogs. Got to have dogs." He turned to the fellow he had come in with, raised his voice to a tenor screech. "Dempsey

Boger keeps hounds, don't he? This feller's lookin' to buy him a dog for huntin' bar."

The room quieted, and a palpable wave of public attention washed over them. Rice turned his face away. The caretaker of the Turk Mountain Preserve, a presumed ecofascist, was going bear hunting—it was interesting, but only for a moment. As the hubbub behind them resumed, the other guy shrugged without looking over.

"Yep, you go over see Dempsey," the man said to Rice. "Last place up Sycamore Holla fore the turnaround. Bunch a honeybee boxes and a big ole war kennel back a the house. He's got all kinda dogs." He nodded once and swiveled back to the bar.

Rice signaled Karla and ordered more beers for the three of them. When the bottles arrived, the big man next to him lifted his beer by the neck with thumb and forefinger, tipped it back to drink, smacked his lips, and gave a noncommittal grunt, but not a word acknowledging Rice's gesture of camaraderie. The other man ignored his bottle entirely. Free beer, Rice speculated, must magically appear in front of these two gentlemen on a regular basis.

Watching the mirror, he noticed three men slouched in a booth across the room, staring at him as they smoked cigarettes and nursed their beers. Probably in their early twenties, they were mill workers like the rest, but they lacked the poise and gravitas of the older men. One was skinny and pale, with a hard, thin-lipped mouth framed by an unfortunate attempt to grow facial hair. Rice recognized the other two. They were big, thick-chested fellows with freckled faces and crew-cut red hair—brothers, Stiller boys. The younger one's name was DeWayne, he thought, pronounced *Dee*-Wayne.

The Stillers were Turpin County gangster wannabes, small-time pot dealers and oxy slingers, part of the surly crowd that hung out weekends at their father's general store in the nontown of Stumpf, where Rice bought beer and milk and peanut butter when he didn't feel like driving fifty minutes to the real grocery store in

Blakely. The Stillers were also enthusiastic bear hunters, especially Bilton, the father, who enjoyed telling Rice how much he despised the Turk Mountain Preserve, the rich family that had excluded the locals for five generations, and every caretaker they'd ever had, apparently including Rice. The sons had tried to provoke him in the usual manner of alpha-male primates—aggressive stares, muttered insults, pushing into his space, that kind of thing—but conflict would bring attention and Rice had always pretended not to notice.

He turned to face the three men and raised his beer in salute, but their half-lidded, empty eyes were steadfast, their insolent mouths turned down at the corners, a practiced look of disdain. He grinned, drank from the beer as if he'd toasted their health. He kept an eye on the mirror, and when they finished their beers and got up to leave, Rice asked for his tab.

FIVE

Outside, a streetlight over the parking lot had come on early, low hum and blue-flicker in the warm, still evening. The three men were climbing into a black pickup truck, an older F-350 crew cab that looked like it had been in a wreck and salvaged by amateurs, bloated off-road tires and bright yellow shock absorbers to distract you from the Bondo and patches of flat black primer.

Rice called out and headed their way at a fast walk. They hesitated, their demeanor going defensive in an instant. He slowed and tried to smile, but it felt like a snarl. The smaller one said something to the others and they laughed and slammed the doors and drove off, big tires spinning in the gravel until they hit pavement with a short screech and the truck roared down the one street in Wanless.

"Well, shit." He watched the truck disappear into the forest at the far end of town. He could jump in his own truck and follow, but they'd probably get excited and take a shot at him before he could ask about the bears. Another pickup pulled into the lot, headed for the Stillers' empty space, and Rice turned away from the high beams. Someone opened the front door of the bar, ZZ Top on the jukebox now. The old couple by the window were long gone.

Cool air and smells from the river washed into the cab as he drove the narrow road curving through Dutch Pass. Sickly hemlock branches flashed overhead, adelgid-infested and diaphanous against the sky. He slowed on the bridge over Sycamore Creek, thinking, hell, it's still early, and turned right onto Sycamore Creek Road, a dead-end gravel tertiary winding through a small valley—a hollow—into the mountains. Tiny family compounds had sprouted like mushrooms in the damp blue air, always a weathered frame house close to the road, a clutch of trailer homes behind, fixer-up muscle cars and four-bys on blocks, a defunct, Brobdingnagian satellite dish covered with poison ivy and still aimed at the slot of sky overhead.

After a few miles, the valley opened up a bit, and narrow floodplain pastures appeared along the road, a handful of grazing Herefords, white faces turning to watch Rice pass. The dusky mountain slopes above were marked with a skein of zigzag logging roads through third-growth hardwoods, patchy clear-cuts coming up in rows of white pine.

Dempsey Boger's place was as Roy had described it, sitting at the end of the road in a half-moon lot bitten from the forest, a double-wide trailer home and three tall corrugated-metal sheds, a couple dozen white bee boxes arranged in a neat rectangle on the slope behind. The lawn was tidy, ornamented with a hopeful mélange: concrete sculptures of capering deer and bear, bird baths, and whitewashed tractor-tire planters spewing marigolds, chrysanthemums, violets. Two parallel lines of coarse gravel crunching under the tires led to a kind of courtyard behind the trailer lit by two mercury vapor floodlights. As Rice pulled in, a big woven-wire kennel tucked up against the overhanging forest exploded with leaping, howling dogs of mixed sizes and shapes. Next to the kennel were parked a gray Dodge pickup, a dented International log truck, and two yellow log skidders, one that looked newish, with a big articulated grapple. The other had seen some hard use, and metal kennel boxes were welded on the back where the winch was supposed to go. The guy must've retired the old skidder and decided it would make a fine hunting rig. Rice parked beside it, got out, and peered at the five-foot-tall tires with knobs the size of his fist.

More dogs barked in the house at his knock, and a man answered the door, frowning. He looked about fifty, medium height, with a compact paunch, and dark eyes far apart in a broad face tanned chestnut brown. In the room behind him, a skinny dark-haired woman sat in a chair with a girl child in her lap, looking to see who it was, two faces blue and shiny-eyed in the light of a television screen. An old bluetick standing next to them raised its head to aim a hoarse moaning bark at the ceiling. As Rice introduced himself—his local pseudonym was Rick Morton—the man stepped out and shut the door behind him.

"You're Dempsey Boger?" Rice finished.

The man nodded, peering at Rice's face. Rice was about to ask if he knew anything about people killing a bunch of bears out of season when some commotion in the kennel set all the dogs to howling and barking again. Both men turned to look, since the noise prevented conversation. Boger yelled "Shut the hell up!" but the dogs ignored him. Rice followed him out to the driveway, where he picked up a handful of gravel to hurl at the kennel without much force. When the dogs finally settled down, Boger turned to Rice. He looked amused, a grin twitching at the right side of his mouth.

"You got you a bee problem."

Rice reached up to touch his lumpy face again. "I was doing some remodel work. There's a big hive in the wall."

"Sure they ain't yella-jackets? I can't use yella-jackets."

"They're honeybees."

"Ain't many wild bees left. Varroa mites and spring dwindle done killed 'em off. The ones still around have got a resistance. You want me to come up there?"

This is serendipity, Rice thought, happening right before my eyes. "You know where I'm talking about? The Turk Mountain Preserve?"

Boger nodded, patting his breast pocket as if for cigarettes. Finding none, he folded his arms over his chest. There was a finality to the gesture, so Rice said okay and turned to walk back to his truck. He would ask about the bears tomorrow, after the bees had been taken care of. Somewhere down the valley several cows lowed together in a rough kind of harmony, hollow and melancholy.

"You leave that gate unlocked," Boger called out. "I'll drive up in the morning."

Rice thought about that on the way home. He hadn't left the gate unlocked since the night he arrived. A light squall had blown snowflakes in his eyes and he'd had to hold the frozen padlock between his gloved hands and breathe on it until his key would work. That had been the second day of March—his thirty-fourth birthday—and the weather had followed him all the way from Albuquerque, where he'd spent several days filing job applications, renting P.O. boxes, and pretending to settle down. After weeks of looking over his shoulder, snicking that cold padlock closed behind him had started the unwinding of a string in his mind pulled so taut it had been about to snap. As he made his way up the long driveway that night, two miles through forest, then another mile curving along the edge of the big open field, shifting into four-wheel-drive to get through the leftover snowdrifts, the corrosive stress of excessive vigilance had slowly drained away. He wouldn't have said he felt safe, but at the preserve he found he could envision more than a few days' or weeks' worth of personal future, and that had made all the difference.

Tonight he opened the gate, drove through, pulled it shut, and wrapped the chain around the latchpost as usual, but he left the padlock open for Boger. It nagged him all the way up the driveway. By the time he'd pulled into the gravel parking area in front of the cabin he was ready to turn around, drive back, and lock the damn thing after all—he could run down early in the morning and open it before Boger arrived. Might sleep better tonight.

He didn't cut the engine or the headlights. He just sat there, hands on the wheel, telling himself he'd been careful covering his tracks back in February, that he'd been living here six months without the slightest hint that anyone could have followed him, that the skinned she-bear had spooked him, sure, but let's be reasonable, bear poaching in Turpin County had no conceivable connection with the real source of his personal peril, saying this stuff to himself but not quite believing it, when a bear shambled out the open door of the cabin in the headlights, a bear coming out the door like a big hound dog rousing himself to see who'd driven up for a visit.

SIX

The bear was the young male with the hurt ear, the one he suspected had been sniffing around the buildings at night. Probably he'd been driven away by his mother in the spring and was working hard to survive on his own, hungry and clueless, watching over his shoulder for the larger males. His situation was not unfamiliar to Rice, and a surprising wave of interspecies empathy took hold of him. He felt he knew this bear. A skeptical voice insisted that the feeling was one sided, pure sentimentality, and yet he couldn't deny its power: a hitch in time's gait while the bear stood stunned by the headlights, his split ear twitching, nostrils dilating, eyes two bright green coins against the black hump of his body, a thousand bees orbiting his head like electrons. Then he wheeled and galloped around the side of the cabin and into the dark meadow.

Rice left the lights on and stepped inside to check out the damage to the hive, but the bees drove him away before he could see much. A lump of honeycomb the size of his hand lay where the bear had dropped it, a few angry confused bees still buzzing around. He picked it up and, seeing no bear slobber, pushed in with his finger, crushing the little wax hexagons, and licked a dollop from his fingertip. It was a stronger taste than store-bought. He took a bite, sucking out the honey and chewing the wax into a ball that he spit in the grass.

The bear's intrusion wasn't a surprise, exactly. This was nothing more than a new level of permeability in the boundary between wild and domestic, something he had come to accept while living up here. Last week, for example, he'd almost stepped on a corn snake lying in the doorway to his bedroom, stopped his bare foot inches above its back. The snake raised its head but otherwise didn't seem alarmed. It was a lustrous, ornamental-looking creature with a chain of rich orange and yellow ovals outlined in black along its length. He'd waited until it calmed, and he eased his hands under it, lifted it a few inches off the floor, cool and firm, sliding mysteriously across his skin. It moved and was gone, behind a door, into the dark hall, hunting the field mice, squirrels, chipmunks, and baby opossums that also found their way indoors. The lodge had been assimilated into the meadow over the past hundred years, and despite his efforts to keep the place up, an irresistible osmosis was always at work, the life outside inevitably forcing its way in. He kept the screen doors shut, and the windows were screened, but flies and moths and cicada-killer wasps got in anyway. In rainy weather he found inexplicable toads on the kitchen floor. Wolf spiders prowled the walls, and orb spiders spun webs in every corner, the ones closest to the lamps growing fat and minatory by late summer. Tiny stab-winged swifts flew down the chimney and out the open flue into the lodge. They vectored from windowpane to windowpane until they were so punch-drunk he could pick them up and carry them outside, light and fragile, coal-gray and smelling like stale ashes. When he opened his hands the birds would revive, rise and slide away in the air as if made of smoke.

Rice finished the honey the bear had dropped, and the sugar hit his bloodstream in about thirty seconds. Feeling manic, he shut off his headlights and slammed the truck door. What now? The gibbous moon had set, and the brightest stars glowed indistinctly. Blinking fireflies drifted past. A powerful cacophony emanated from the trees at the edge of the forest—lonesome trills and chirps, amphibian screams, the rhythmic shake-shake of katydids—a busy night in late summer, all the little creatures trying to have sex with each other before the season ended.

In the office, he plugged the old rotary phone into the wall socket. Inside the hard plastic moss-green shell there were two actual brass gongs that a striker rattled against when someone called. He'd taken the thing apart to check. He kept it disconnected to preserve the peace and quiet, not that anyone wanted to call him.

Cradling the heavy handset against his neck, he dialed the number from the restroom wall at the Beer & Eat and waited. The oscillating table fan on the desk clicked twice each time it changed direction, blowing on his face and whooshing in the phone every seven seconds. It was an antique, made back before they'd decided the screen over the blades had to prevent people from sticking their fingers in. He laid his palm lightly on the top wire, lowered three fingers toward the blades until he felt air vibrating on the pads. He wondered if the blades were sharp enough to chop the tips off.

A man answered on the sixth ring, and Rice put on his local accent.

"You the fella wants to buy bear galls?"

There was a pause, country radio in the background. The guy couldn't know where the call was coming from. Rice had made sure caller ID was blocked on outgoing calls, one of the first things he'd done after moving in.

"You got some?"

"I might."

"You might."

"Yep. You wan' talk?"

"You call me back when you got something you sonofabitch."

The man hung up, and Rice stared at the receiver for a moment before he hung up, too.

He stood on the back porch, bouncing on his toes, still amped from the wild honey. Something in the forest tugged at his mind: a new attraction, an enticement. Wan starlight, the dark forest speaking its night sounds. Where that bear had run, and where the mushroom picker had come from. For no good rational reason he could imagine, the forest was where he wanted to be. He jogged down the steps and headed up the fire road.

SEVEN

The clatter of a diesel outside, tires in the gravel, Rice waking in a rush, reaching into the open drawer beside his head, sitting up with the .45 in his hand before he remembered he'd left the gate open, that he was expecting the bee guy. He settled back into his pillow, rolled to face the window. He'd been having a vague, pointless dream about walking in the desert. Crows cawed, and a light breeze drifted through the screen, stirring the curtain. He reached and slid it aside and the sun came in like a shout. Too bright to see. He hadn't slept past sunrise in months. His dream was slipping away: a sandy wash, moonlight, thickets of cholla cactus making him careful; he was looking for someone.

A car horn honked three times. Locals did this, and it wasn't rudeness but a safer and more discreet alternative to walking up to a rural, isolated home and knocking. A door slammed. His eyes had adjusted now: a Dodge pickup was parked alongside his Toyota, Dempsey Boger in an orange Stihl cap reaching back through the open window to honk the horn again.

Rice wiped the pistol and replaced it in the drawer, draped with an old T-shirt saturated with gun oil. He'd found a couple of rust spots on the slide in May, and since then he'd worried about the thing seizing up in this Appalachian humidity and not working when he needed it. A full-size Colt Government Model 1911, it had been his father's, though he didn't think his father had shot it much. Certainly it wasn't Air Force issue. The 1911 was an old design but it was accurate and reliable if you kept it lubed and used good magazines. Rice appreciated the tactile pleasure of the thing: the flat, narrow steel slab, its cold heft solid and practical, like a well-balanced hammer, the satisfying slap as the slide racked forward, all of the parts locking into place, ready. The tubby cartridges themselves were proportioned like tiny round-topped beer cans of copper and brass, and they thunked together in his hand with a specific heaviness that made them seem precious.

His watch lay on the windowsill, stuck at one seventeen, but it started up again when he rapped it on the heel of his hand. He reset it, guessing seven fifteen, wound it, and put it back. When he moved his hand away, the sunlight reflecting from the metallic face projected a clear mirror image on the sun-bleached maple sill: the stick marks without numbers, the hour and minute hands, the sweep-second hand revolving counterclockwise. He watched, mesmerized, as it made one full rotation, a whole minute regained. It was a convincing hallucination of time going backward, and Rice felt an odd, weightless sense of relief. The headlong rush slowed, stopped. Reversed. His nose tingled and his eyes stung like someone had broken an ammonia capsule in his face. Everything would be undone.

A cloud passed in front of the sun and the reflection disappeared. He swung his feet out of bed onto the cool wood floor. Impossible fantasies depressed him and he shook this one off, tried not to think about it. He dressed and carried his boots out to the porch and sat on the top step to put them on.

"You want some coffee?" he called out. Boger was leaning into the bed of his truck, sliding boxes onto the open tailgate.

"Is it made?"

"Wouldn't take long."

"Nope, I got to get back. You a late sleeper, Mr. Morton?"

"Not usually. I went for a walk on the mountain last night."

Boger nodded as if he thought that was an acceptable explanation. Rice yawned, tying his boots, still wet from the night's dew. He didn't sleep much anyway, hadn't for a while now, but he'd fallen into bed only a couple of hours ago and he felt a powerful need for coffee. Maybe some more of that wild honey.

Last night he'd walked past the bear carcass to a rock outcrop near the peak of Turk Mountain. He'd sat there for hours, staring out over the dark canyon to the west, sweat cooling on his skin. Waterfalls hissed far down in the canyon, near where it emptied into the Dutch River. The attraction he'd felt back at the lodge had grown stronger, and it seemed to come from the ancient forest in the canyon. He wasn't supposed to walk around down there, one of the rules of the preserve. Near dawn, he'd thought he heard the baying of hounds, but it was just farm dogs waking up the cows in some hardscrabble hollow off to the east.

He carried Boger's white wooden bee box into the cabin while Boger stuffed dry grass into his smoker and lit it with a match. The bear had continued Rice's demolition work, ripping a torso-size hole in the paneling to get at the hive. He'd worried the bear might've driven away the bees, but hundreds were still buzzing around, and the damage to the comb didn't look bad. He must've surprised the bear before he had time to really dig in. Boger had walked into the cabin and was standing behind him.

"Bear got into it last night," Rice said.

Boger didn't reply, fussing with the lid to his smoker, which looked like a big tin can with a spout pointing forward and a bellows attached to the back.

"Set that box down here. We'll put the brood comb in it if your bear left us any."

Rice could tell Boger was restraining himself from commenting on the bear-in-the-cabin story. He gently worked the bellows once, twice, then he blew in through the open lid. Smoke lifted and swirled around his face. Finally he said, "It's no good when a bear starts acting that away. Crossing that line."

Rice cleared a spot on the floor, shoving broken paneling aside with his boot, and stood the bee box upright. He thought of the bear walking out of the cabin and standing there in the headlights, eyes glowing green.

"I'm not feeding them or anything."

"You don't have to. They just know. Bears are a lot like people, just wilder. Sometimes these back-to-nature types forget bears are wild animals, they want 'em to be like pets."

Rice wondered if Boger thought of him as a back-to-nature type. He lived up here away from other people, but he had no delusions: he bought his food at the store, the propane truck visited semiannually, and power from the grid arrived via three miles of buried line. His beer came from Colorado, his coffee from tropical countries he'd never even visited.

"The bears," Boger continued, "they ain't no better, you leave the door open they come right in and make themselves at home, but it always turns out bad. Bad for them, bad for you."

"Maybe this one was hiding out from the bear hunters. All that honey was a bonus."

Boger snapped shut the lid on his smoker. "There ain't no hunting allowed on you all's nature preserve. That's part of your problem, bears up here've lost respect for human beings."

"I don't know about that," Rice said. "A guy came by yesterday and showed me a dead bear he'd found up on the mountain. Somebody killed and skinned it, cut off the paws and took out the gallbladder, left the carcass to rot."

Boger stepped up close to the hive and slowly pumped the bellows, thick white smoke pouring out of the spout, filling the ragged hole the bear had made in the paneling. The smell of burning grass filled the cabin.

"I been finding dead bears, too, galls and paws gone like you said." Bees landed on Boger's arms and began crawling around, but he ignored them. "Six this year. One was skinned. Four of 'em was baited, still had popcorn and bread and such in their mouths, and they was shot with arrows, probably some sonofabitch with a crossbow, keeping it quiet. It happened before, back in the nineties. Folks killing bears for the black market. The mafia got into it, they'd pay two thousand dollars for one gall, grind up the bile salt and sell it to the Chinese for medicine. Now I reckon they're at it again."

"The mafia?" Rice pictured Italian guys in dark suits prowling the woods for bears. Toting their tommy guns. Lurking in moonshadows, smoking cigarettes and cracking their knuckles. "So you don't have any idea who's doing it."

"Hell, no. It ain't any houndsman. We don't kill no bears till they've done fattening up, 'round November."

"When the season's open."

"Meat's better then. I only kill one a year. Put up a lot more'n I shoot."

Rice was disappointed. He'd hoped it would be some nutjob the bear hunters could tell him about. A person Rice could find, and then . . . what? He would think of something.

Boger handed him the smoker and said to keep the smoke coming, to work the bellows gently so the fire wouldn't get too hot. Then he brought in a beat-up black and yellow Shop-Vac from his truck, plugged it into an orange extension cord Rice had run from the breaker box, and began vacuuming all the bees he could reach. The bees fetched up, apparently unharmed, in a shoe-box-size plastic container he'd duct-taped into the hose near the motor housing. Rice figured there had to be a screen in there to keep them from getting sucked into the machine.

"That's damned ingenious," he said over the noise.

Boger waved away the smoker. "You go on and pull the rest of that paneling off, and we'll see what we got. Who was this fella showed you the bear?"

"He didn't tell me his name." Rice realized he'd never thought to ask. "He said he picked mushrooms, ginseng, that kind of stuff. One of his arms was missing, cut off at the elbow."

Boger shook his head. "Don't know him."

Rice found his crowbar and worked his way around the ragged edge of the last section, prying the paneling away from the studs.

"Don't squash any. They'll get mean."

"They're not going to mind me crowbarring the wall off their hive?"

"They won't like that much either. But the smoke's took their mind off it."

The paneling broke into several pieces and by the time he'd cleared it away Rice had been stung half a dozen times. The hive filled the space between the studs and stood about five feet high, covered with unhappy bees.

"That's a lot of honey right there," Boger said. "I'll take enough for 'em to eat this winter, fill up the box, but the rest is yours. We can put it in that crate yonder." When he'd shut off the vacuum he glanced around the cabin, seemed to notice the demolition project for the first time. "What're you tearing this place up for?"

Rice explained that the owners—the Traver Foundation—wanted to turn the summer cabin into a guest house for scientists. They planned to start awarding residential fellowships: a graduate student or postdoc with a research project on the preserve would win the privilege of living there full-time for a semester or two. "It'll have its own bathroom, kitchen. I can do most of the work myself. I'm no carpenter but I worked construction for a couple of years, back before the crash."

"You're from Arizona?"

Rice nodded, thinking he would be a lot less conspicuous around here if he could score a set of Virginia license plates. Boger produced a kitchen knife and knelt on the floor, cutting the comb away from the studs, slicing pieces that he rubber-banded into frames that fit vertically in the hive box. He moved in an exaggerated slow motion, not brushing away the stray bees that landed on his arms and face.

"Born out there?"

"Born in New Mexico. Grew up in Tucson, mostly. My dad was in the Air Force. He died when I was in high school."

Boger paused, a tacit expression of sympathy, condolences. Then he said, "You came here to get away from something." It wasn't a question. The brood comb, filled with capped cells containing pupae, was heavy and fragile. Boger lifted it tenderly and secured it in a frame. "Usually it's the other way around, people head west to get away."

Rice dumped hand tools from an antique wooden soft-drink crate and lined it with wax paper. Boger cut a slab of what looked like pure capped honeycomb, and when Rice took it he bent his arm and a bee trapped on the inside of his elbow stung him. In that sensitive flesh it felt like an electric shock. He flinched but laid the comb in the crate without dropping it.

"Here she is." Boger held up a long, fat bee, a giantess with an abdomen extending far behind her wings. "You got to come with me, girl. Mr. Morton here is fixing up a fancy guest house." He pulled a plastic case from his pocket, a Rapala fishing lure box with tiny air holes drilled in the top, and shut the queen inside.

"I'm not sure how fancy it'll be."

"Fancy enough. If you're a scientist from the university they'll put you up on the place, but if you're a bear hunter from down the road you ain't welcome in the *old-growth forest*. You got Mr. Morton on your ass. They hired the muscle this time."

"Yeah that's me. Deppity Dawg." He wasn't sure how to handle this sudden turn in the conversation. Boger's tone was light, but Rice had learned that part of the caretaker's job was to be the focus of animosity toward the Travers and the preserve. "They have that deer hunt in the fall, don't they?"

Boger didn't even respond. The foundation sponsored an annual "nuisance hunt" in cooperation with the state game department and a local hunt club. The idea was to cull the whitetail herd, make a little peace with the neighbors, and provide venison for poor families. It was coming up in mid-November, something Rice dreaded—he imagined a weeklong Tet Offensive obliterating his precious solitude—but at least the hunters had to stay on the lower reaches of the property.

"I guess you don't think much of the idea. The preserve, protecting that old-growth forest."

"Old-growth is just good timber going to waste. Ain't right to lock up land and throw away the key like they done here. Ain't human beings part of nature?"

Rice grinned at that last bit. One thing they could sure as shit agree on.

"I reckon we are," he said. "The Travers decided a long time ago what they wanted to do with their land was to let it be. Hell, they can afford it."

"It don't seem right. Bible says man has dominion over the earth." This argument sounded perfunctory.

"The Bible says a lot of things. You a religious man?"

"Not really. You?"

Rice smiled and shook his head, remembering the psychotic Santa Muerte and Jesús Malverde cults that had sprung up among the cartels. In the pause that followed, he went ahead and asked his other question.

"You know anything about what happened with the last caretaker, the woman who was here before me?"

Boger's grin fell. He gave Rice a sharp look and turned away, set the Rapala box with the queen on top of the hive box. He acted like Rice had tricked him somehow and he'd just figured it out.

"Why you askin'?"

"I'm just curious."

Boger picked up his knife and went to work on what was left of the hive in the wall. "I know what everyone around here knows." He handed Rice another heavy rectangle of honeycomb and Rice laid it in his crate on top of the first, with another layer of wax paper in between.

"The lady who hired me said Sara didn't get along with the neighbors."

"Huh. I guess you could say that. She lawed folks she caught on the property, and she wrote letters in the paper, stood up at Forest Service hearings, saving the forest from the loggers, that kinda thing."

"A tree hugger. Lord have mercy."

Boger gave him another glance but turned back to his knife, cutting away the last fragment of honeycomb to stack in Rice's box. It looked like he would have enough honey to last a year.

"I know she's a nice gal," Boger said. "But people around here depend on the timber business, the sawmill. I heard some complaints. Not that anyone wanted what happened."

"Which was what?"

"You really don't know?"

Rice waited.

"She got kidnapped at those Dumpsters on Route 212, on the way to Blakely. They drove her up Sycamore Hollow to the hunter access road a half mile from my place, took her off in the woods. Beat her up and raped her and left her there. Damn near killed her, but she walked out, crawled, probably. A fella lives near us picked her up on the side of the road, took her straight to the hospital."

"Damn," Rice said. Boger had stood up and was peering at him. Rice realized he probably looked stupid, mouth open, a caricature of dumbfoundedness. "They catch who did it?"

Boger shook his head. Now he seemed grimly satisfied with the effect this news was having. "Bastards wore masks, put a blindfold on her. Sheriff's still lookin' into it."

EIGHT

Boger motioned for Rice to grab the other handle on the hive box and they lifted it together and carried it outside. Boger climbed into the bed of his truck and slid the hive box forward, snug against the toolbox behind the cab. A bright day, hazy sunshine, a light breeze cooling Rice's back where he'd soaked his T-shirt with sweat.

"I ain't surprised they didn't tell you what happened." Boger was securing the hive box against the toolbox with frayed bungee cords. "Now it's out of the frying pan and into the fire. You comin' here from out west, I mean."

Rice didn't respond right away. He had constructed a fairly complete identity for Sara Birkeland in his imagination, and Boger's story was too familiar. Unwelcome reflexes were firing. "You reckon I'm likely to get raped? That's what they do to the Turk Mountain Preserve caretaker?"

Boger hopped out of the truck bed without answering, and they walked back into the cabin.

"I'll tell you a story about the frying pan," Rice said. He gathered up the smoker and other items Boger had brought with him while Boger detached the bee-filled catch box from the Shop-Vac.

"This guy, Gutiérrez, was a big-time dealer, operated out of Phoenix, ran a Sinaloa distribution network in Arizona and Utah: pot, cocaine, black tar heroin, meth. About a year ago he got tagged by the DEA and agreed to testify against some of the top guys in the cartel." Rice hadn't talked to anyone about this, and he wondered why he was telling Boger.

"His testimony was important to a case the DEA, FBI, and the Mexican feds were all collaborating on. They hid him at some general's estate way out on the coast south of Tijuana, but somebody in the Mexican police gave him up and a team from Los Ántrax shot their way in and kidnapped him. Nobody heard anything for a couple of days, then he turned up at Phoenix Memorial, dumped at the emergency room entrance. Security cameras caught a couple of guys in gray hoody sweatshirts helping him onto a bench. His head was completely bandaged like the Invisible Man's, and he almost died of shock before someone noticed him and got him into intensive care. They found sutures all around his face and head, but nothing was missing, and the stitching was expert, done by a good surgeon. Gutiérrez remembered nothing; he'd been drugged the whole time. Nobody knew what it meant until the manila envelopes with glossy eight-by-tens started showing up in the hospital room and at the Gutiérrez family hacienda in Scottsdale: crisp, well-lit pictures of his bloody grinning skull, the slack bag of his face in someone's hands. Some fucker wearing it like a mask, fingers holding the eyelids open, his teeth laughing through Gutiérrez's mouth."

"They skinned his damn face?"

"And then sewed it back on."

"What the hell for?"

"The point was that they could do whatever they wanted. That they were holding back, being merciful. That nobody could imagine what else they might do. Gutiérrez recanted as soon as he woke up. Word spread, and other witnesses got forgetful. Pretty soon there wasn't enough left of the case to prosecute."

They were standing beside the truck now, and Boger had placed the catch box with the bees on the passenger seat, the lure box with the queen next to it. He took a deep breath and let it out slowly, and reached for a pack of Kools on the dashboard. "I better get on home before these critters start dying on me."

Rice pulled out his wallet. He had an expense account with the Traver Foundation. "I thank you kindly," he said. "What do we owe you?"

"Hell, you owe me these bees. I told you they got a resistance to whatever's killin' all the others, and I'm glad to have 'em. Ain't no charge. But I wish you hadn't told me about that fella's face. It's goddamn disturbing."

"It's no worse than what your local boys did to Sara Birkeland."

"The hell it's not." He held an unlit cigarette in his mouth, talking around it and making no move to light it. He'd become agitated and seemed eager to go. "I can't believe anybody would even think that up."

RICE LOADED THE DEBRIS FROM THE CABIN INTO HIS TRUCK AND DROVE TO the Dumpsters where Sara Birkeland had been abducted. He stood in the bed and tossed broken paneling and heavy plastic trash bags and tried to picture what had happened. The place was far from any house, and the Dumpsters were screened from the highway by a line of trees, but Route 212 was relatively busy and there was always a chance of someone driving in. Probably happened after dark, and they must have got her into a vehicle and out of here pretty fast. Were they waiting in ambush for someone, anyone, or did they follow her here? He started running scenarios and felt his pulse jump, told himself to quit thinking about it. He hadn't even met the girl.

Instead of heading back to the preserve, he turned left on 212 and drove another half hour into Blakely, parked on the street near the Blue Bean. Inside, college students slouched at tables and on the sofa, ignoring each other and staring into their phones; a long-faced guy about Rice's age with a frizzy ponytail sat by himself near the window; a fit-looking couple with matching shades of gray hair traded sections of the *New York Times*. He'd brought the slightly antiquated laptop from the office, and after buying an extra-large regular coffee—there were no pretentious size designations at the Bean—he set up at a small round table near an outlet in a corner. As always, he opened an onion-routing program to hide his IP address before he went online.

He sent an email to his boss, the board chair of the foundation that owned the preserve, attaching spreadsheets with August's cost accounting and the current and historical biological data he'd entered over the past month. He was supposed to report "immediately" any illegal activity on the preserve, so he noted offhand that he'd found a bear carcass and was looking into who might've killed it, hoping he wouldn't trigger any drama but knowing he probably would. After he sent the files, usually he would have a look at the *Arizona Daily Star* and check a handful of websites and blogs that reported on the Mexican cartels and violence along the border, but today he wanted to see about the bear poaching.

Within a few minutes, Boger's mafia theory didn't seem as far-fetched as he'd thought. As most markets legit and otherwise had globalized over the past few decades, illegal traffic in wildlife and their body parts had become the fourth-largest black market in the world, behind narcotics, counterfeiting, and human trafficking, generating billions of dollars every year and attracting the participation of terror groups and "traditionally drug-oriented criminal enterprises."

More searching turned up a post on a Virginia environmental blog about a recent surge in the poaching of bears for their gallbladders after years of low prices:

Bear bile is used in a variety of traditional Asian medicines, and the growth of a relatively affluent middle class in China and other Asian countries led to unprecedented consumer demand. News reports from the nineties and early aughts often compared bile and bile salt prices to that of cocaine and gold. Given the near-extinction of every Asiatic bear species, dealers looked to the American black bear, and a lucrative black market in their gallbladders briefly caught the attention of U.S. news media and law enforcement officials. Around the same time, the gruesome and inhumane practice of "bear farming" in China, Korea, and Vietnam began scaling up, eventually providing bear bile in industrial quantities. Poaching in the U.S. fell off, and black bear populations in Virginia have increased dramatically.

Recently, though, we've heard unofficial reports that hunters in some areas are being offered up to two hundred dollars for bear gallbladders and paws. The paws, which (unlike bile) can't be extracted on an ongoing basis from captive bears, are used to make soup and other delicacies—these are featured in trendy East and Southeast Asian restaurants popular with the newly affluent and a certain type of tourist.

A particularly troubling trend in some counties sees payment more often in kind than cash: meth, prescription opioids, and heroin are offered in exchange for bear parts as drug gangs move into the business. The game department officials we contacted declined to comment, citing ongoing investigations.

He also found a wildlife law forum where a professor from Montana was describing the counterfeiting of bear galls back in the 1990s, with a significant fraction of the "bear galls" confiscated in some markets turning out, upon testing at the federal wildlife forensics lab in Oregon, to be pig galls. Bear galls were either frozen or dried for sale, and while an expert might be able to identify frozen pig galls, desiccated pig galls looked identical to desiccated bear galls. This presented a problem for law enforcement and prosecutors, as apparently the laws in most states prohibiting trafficking in wildlife parts made it impossible to proceed with prosecutions when the evidence turned out to be counterfeit.

This gave him an idea. He found a discarded copy of the *Turpin Weekly Record*, opened to the classifieds page, and scanned the Agriculture section. Most of the ads were for farm fresh eggs and compost, but right there under "P" he found a simple listing, "Pork for sale." He tore out the ad and pocketed it.

He refilled his coffee and spent a few minutes studying the current hunting regulations online, then looked up the sections of the Code of Virginia relevant to poaching and trespassing. These he saved on the laptop. Before he left he checked his email account again. As expected, his boss had already replied, asking him to call right away. The Bean had an actual functioning pay phone in the back, meaning he could call now and get it over with. He closed the laptop and filled his to-go cup a third time before retreating into the dark-paneled back room where no one ever sat. He dropped a few quarters and dialed, turned and stood with his back to the wall.

"Where are you calling from?" No hello, no how are you.

"Coffee shop."

"You're feeding quarters into a pay phone again."

He didn't say anything.

"Even drug dealers have cell phones, Rice."

"I'm not a drug dealer."

"You know what I mean. Tell me about the bear."

This was Starr, of the unfashionably hyphenated surname Traver-Pinkerton. Back in February, he'd driven to her sprawling hacienda in the Catalina foothills for his interview after a particularly rough few weeks, and had hesitated at the massive carved mesquite doors, obviously antique, real Colonial Mexican. He was looking for a doorbell when both doors folded inward and there stood Starr, a rich old hippie, X-ray skinny in a flowered cotton dress, salt-and-pepper hair, clear blue eyes. She looked him up and down, introduced herself, and led him to a sandstone-paved courtyard where she'd set out iced tea, lecturing him along the way about the history of the property—her industrialist great-grandfather Marshall P. Traver had swooped down from Pittsburgh and assembled the property through a series of purchases in the late 1800s, the family had left the place untouched after he died until they'd contributed it to a family foundation in the 1970s, and so on. She'd already decided to give him the job, citing his impressive college transcript, his experience as a field biologist, his self-sufficiency. Now he suspected there were other aspects of his unique background she'd found attractive. Like Boger had said, they hired the muscle this time.

As briefly as he could he described the mushroom picker and the bear carcass, what Dempsey Boger had said about finding others, and what he'd just learned on the Web about the black market, the overlap with narcotics. When he'd finished, she suggested half-heartedly that he call the game warden. She knew of his allergy to law enforcement.

STP, as he'd come to think of her, had turned out to be a decent boss, idealistic and a little scatterbrained, but more than fair, tolerant of his idiosyncrasies, and willing to conspire in his disappearance. To avoid tax filings, she let him draw his pay in cash "for Turk Mtn. Preserve expenses" at the foundation's local bank in Blakely—he kept his savings in a small fireproof lockbox in the attic above his bedroom—and she put up with his usual state of incommunicado, contenting herself with monthly phone calls and emails from the Bean.

He told her he'd rather not call the game warden now. He had some ideas about who it might be, and after he'd looked around some, if he found anything, then they could involve the game warden, maybe the sheriff, too.

"Why the sheriff?"

"Because why didn't you tell me what happened to Sara Birkeland?"

She said "Oh," but then she took a long breath and exhaled before replying. Twice. It sounded like she was smoking. A Gila woodpecker chirred in the background. It was still morning out there in the shadow of the Catalinas, STP sitting in her courtyard with coffee and a newspaper, a thirty-foot saguaro peering over the wall.

"You think there's a connection," she finally said.

"I think it's possible."

"I should have told you before now. I'm sorry. I'm fond of Sara, and I was trying to respect her privacy. Also, believe it or not, I was trying to be sensitive. After what had happened to your girlfriend."

"Thanks. But it's common knowledge around here, and I just got blindsided." Another pause, filled with more evocative Sonoran birdsong. He missed the desert. He wondered when he would be able to go back. He'd still been traumatized the day he drove away from Tucson, and the landscape itself had come to seem tragic, a little melodramatic, tens of thousands of saguaro arranged there on the rocky slopes above the city, dusky green in the last light of a winter afternoon, tall, humanoid, resigned, holding up their arms. In his rearview mirror it looked like the people who lived in the city had climbed up on the hills and were just standing there watching, waiting for the end of the world.

"I flew to Virginia as soon as I heard," STP said. "She was unconscious for a few days. They had to induce a coma until the brain swelling went down. She still doesn't remember much about what happened, but she's better now, teaching classes, working on her lizard project again. You'll meet her soon. She wanted to stay on as caretaker, you know. As soon as she was out of the hospital, she was raring to go back. I'm not sure she was altogether rational at that point, and we had to insist. It wasn't safe." She stopped, probably realizing the implication of what she'd just said but unwilling to retract it.

"No idea who it was?"

"No," she said. "They wore masks. And all the likely suspects had alibis. Sheriff Walker thinks it was out-of-towners."

"Right."

She inhaled some more. He grinned, completing the picture.

"Starr, are you smoking?"

"No."

"A fatty-o on the patio?"

She actually giggled, but she got herself back under control quickly. He guessed she'd had a lot of practice. Now she sounded serious.

"You'll be careful with the bear hunters? They can be rough folk."

"I'm only going to talk to them. If I catch them I'll take their picture with that little camera you sent me. Criminals hate it when you take their picture. Then we can call the law."

She warned him again to be careful, and they said goodbye and hung up before he thought to ask what she'd meant when she'd said he would meet Sara Birkeland.

NINE

The directions he'd copied down from the pig farmer were vague to the point of nonsense, and he made several wrong turns and had to backtrack when a gravel road terminated at a washed-out bridge, crumbling concrete abutments clinging to the steep streambank, a single rusted cable strung across to keep drunkards and lost out-of-towners from driving into the creek. He stopped at a newish trailer home where a teenage boy knelt as if in supplication before an inverted dirt bike. His head was bowed, and a motley of engine parts, wrenches, bolts, and dirty rags had been scattered on the gravel in frustration. He looked up when Rice got out of his truck, brightening for an instant as if Rice were the wizard of motorcycle maintenance come to help, but he turned surly and taciturn when Rice began asking directions. After that, Rice tried a systematic approach, investigating every side road he came across, and thirty minutes later he stumbled upon the mailbox with the faded *SENS.* hand-painted in red.

He turned onto the rutted dirt driveway. The land in the southern part of the county was poor—patchy overgrazed pasture and cedar thickets, multiflora rose grown up in a ragged hedge along the drive. Past a warped wooden gate and over a weedy concrete cattle guard stood an old bank barn and several tin-roofed sheds. Beyond those, a two-story wood-frame house, its clapboard walls holding a faint wash of ancient white, as if it had been scraped for new paint and then left to weather.

He parked and got out of the truck. Nothing moved in the late-morning heat. A single cicada sang in a grove of sycamores leaning over the creek, its thin burr rising and falling hypnotically.

At one end of the barn, a wooden sliding door hung from its metal track by one rusted wheel. He shoved it open and stepped into the obscure aisle, waiting a few seconds for his eyes to adjust. The first stall was crowded with old motors and defunct farm implements, but in the next he found slop buckets and straw bedding strewn on the floor, a smell of urine and rancid garbage. Outside, a dead mule lay near a fence at the far end of a dry grassless paddock, one stiff hind leg saluting the sky.

Past the stall he opened a newer door, reached in and found a wall switch. Fluorescent lights flickered on and he entered a concrete-floored room with steel hooks hanging from the ceiling, the air too still and smelling of raw meat, a long table pushed against the back wall. Two pristine chest freezers flanked a white upright refrigerator from the 1950s, squat with rounded corners and a fat chrome door handle. In the fridge he found a hot dog bun bag tied at one end. He held it up to the light: three greenish, blood-streaked sacs, smaller than he'd expected, each tied at the end with thin white cord. Three might not be enough. The guy had said there would be seven. He had another job off the farm during the day but he'd said his dad would be here.

When Rice approached the house, a dog crawled out from under the porch and ran to the sagging woven-wire fence. It stood quietly, wagging its tail. Rice called out.

"Hello? Mr. Sensabaugh?"

The dog barked once and pranced its front paws. It was gaunt, long-haired like a collie, black with a white star on its chest. Through the screen door an excited male voice narrated a professional wrestling match on television. Rice unlatched the gate and the dog barked again and crept up to him whining and cringing, wetting dark puddles in the dust, a female. He let her sniff his hand, his pant legs and boots. He scratched her head, the ruff on her shoulders.

An old man walked out of the house and let the screen door slam. The dog ran to him.

Rice forced a smile, raised his hand in a slow wave. "Mr. Sensabaugh?"

"Yep." The man stood on the porch, working his jaw, mending a wad of tobacco in his bilged cheek without spitting. A line of brown sputum leaked from the corner of his mouth. He was short and bent and wore faded blue coveralls. The big skinny dog lay across his feet, her head on her paws.

"I'm John Tolley." He'd picked the name from the phone book because he didn't want to use his real fake name. "I talked to Wister, he said to come by today and pick up the gallbladders from some pigs he was butchering, and there was a bag of three in the refrigerator." He held up the bun bag by the tied end and it swung back and forth for a moment. This interested the dog. She got up and approached Rice, expectant. "But he said there was seven hogs y'all were butchering. Do you know if he saved out the other gallbladders?"

"How many'd ye want?" He gave a short cackle and moved his lips again, showing his gums, whitish and flecked with tobacco.

"Well, I thought he said seven?"

Mr. Sensabaugh nodded absently. "You don't want no piglings?"

"No, sir, just the gallbladders. Your son said y'all were butchering seven hogs this week."

"He kin butcher 'em. They a mite small."

Rice squinted at the man. He'd known this was going to be

a long shot. His telephone conversation with the son had been a comedy of miscommunication.

"I didn't see any pigs in the barn."

Mr. Sensabaugh considered, blinking slowly. His eyes were small, rheumy, set deep in his wrinkled face. He pointed a crooked finger toward the paddock.

"Go'n look about thet horse," he said.

Rice turned and glanced back the way the man was pointing. He'd parked his truck so it couldn't be seen from the house. A hot breeze, heavy with carrion stench, was beginning to move among the buildings.

"The dead mule?"

Mr. Sensabaugh nodded once, an almost imperceptible dip of his chin. Rice opened the yard gate to go, but the man called out. "Y'all kin to ol' Stevie? Come out Ar'sh Crick?"

Rice turned. "'Scuse me?"

"Your name's Tolley."

"That's right, but I'm not from around here. No relatives here at all."

He walked to the paddock and leaned against the unpainted board fence. The lot was empty except for the mule. He opened a gate and went in, breathing through his mouth. As he approached the carcass, greenbottle flies swarmed and then quieted. Yellow-jackets were working on the dried meat where the belly had been slit, tearing off tiny gobbets and flying with them toward the barn. There was a scuffling sound, and the upraised leg twitched.

He reached with his boot and kicked the mule's dusty back. A thousand flies lifted into the air with a noise like singing. Muffled squeals from inside. The mule's face was unreadable, its eye plucked out by crows and the lips drawn away from big square yellow teeth in an ambiguous expression, not grin or grimace but something else. As if some final, unexpected wisdom had come at the end. He kicked again, harder, and four shoats smeared with blood and shit came out shrilling as if birthed from the mule's open belly and ran across the paddock to the stall.

They quieted once they were inside and for a moment he stared after them, stared at the dark stall doorway as the flies settled again on the carcass.

When he returned to the house, the black dog came to the fence as before.

"Mr. Sensabaugh?"

There was no reply. Only the inane jingle from a television commercial. The dog sat panting and brushing her tail back and forth in the dirt. He reached over the fence and scratched behind her ears. The old man didn't appear. Rice wedged three five-dollar bills into a crack in the gatepost, though Wister had said he didn't have to pay, that he usually just threw out the galls. He hadn't asked what Rice wanted them for. When he turned his truck around and drove away, the dog was sitting at the gate, ears pricked forward, watching him go.

On the way through Blakely, he stopped at Marble Valley Rent-All to pick up a pressure washer and a portable construction heater. He didn't secure the equipment in the bed, so he was careful on the curves driving back to the preserve. He drove pretty slowly these days anyway. A speeding ticket or even a busted taillight could set off a chain reaction in the system—police reports, automobile registration, insurance records—that would turn into an expensive pain in the ass at best and a conspicuous broadcast of his location at worst.

A fixed wooden ladder led to the impossibly hot loft of the tractor shed, where he tied three lengths of monofilament fishing line to a beam, hanging a pig gallbladder from each. He let them swing back and forth, thinking they didn't look very impressive and wondering how long it would take for them to dry. He could move them to the cabin, hang them in front of the heater he'd rented, but someone might see them there. He plugged a long orange extension cord into the outlet near the tractor and brought the oscillating table fan from the office. For a while he sat sweating in the loft, watching the three galls twisting in the fan's zephyrs like bloody figs.

In the cabin, he balanced on the exposed floor joists and tried to shoo a couple dozen forlorn bees buzzing around the inside of the clapboard wall where their hive had been. He'd torn up the floor yesterday, and he'd called Boger in the evening to tell him there were still some bees flying around in here, and maybe he wanted to come back up and collect them.

"I don't need them stragglers," Boger had said, sounding a little hostile. Rice suspected he had a few beers in him. "You wash off that honey and wax stuck on the wall and they won't come back no more."

He hooked up the garden hose and started the pressure washer. It took about ten seconds to blast away the remnants of the hive. He'd forgotten how much fun these things could be—the cone of water scoured clean whatever it touched, like a magic broom. After he set up the heater to dry the wall before mildew could set in, something he wouldn't have to worry about in Tucson, he washed the cabin's front and back porches, the wood steps, the flat step-stones leading to the parking area. He stood in the gravel with the dripping nozzle, the compressor chugging behind him.

The clapboard exteriors of the cabin and the tractor shed had been restained within the past couple of years and didn't need washing. He'd stacked a half cord of firewood behind the shed anyway, and he didn't want to have to move it. Set in the front wall of the tractor shed was a tall sliding wooden door that revealed a big garage where the old John Deere resided. He backed the tractor out into the parking area and power-washed the concrete slab, left the door open so it could dry.

The compressor still chugging in the back of the truck, he carried the wand up the gravel path to the front porch steps. Had to be something on the lodge that needed cleaning. The central block and two bedroom wings were built on a dry-stack stone foundation naturally decorated with picturesque lichen, and the walls of thick chestnut logs—cut on the property before the blight—shone with a hundred-year-old silvery patina. STP would have him shot if he pressure-washed any of it. He gave up, shut off the compressor, and coiled the long hose in the truck bed.

Something was making him restless, probably that medieval scene earlier at the Sensabaughs'. Rice wasn't a squeamish person, but *piglets-emerging-from-mule-carcass* had been playing in the theater of his mind on a loop. A less sophisticated person, he thought, might look for portents and metaphysics in a thing like that.

Though he'd never pursued an advanced degree, he had studied in college to be a biologist, and he affected a scientific—or at least quasi-scientific—outlook upon the universe. Superstition, he'd always thought, was a story to explain what you haven't figured out yet, a capitulation to the human need for superficial existential comfort, a demonstrably unreliable tool for predicting cause and effect. And yet, since he'd moved to the preserve, his dreams had become as real as conscious experience, and he'd had to dismiss an unsettlingly high percentage of conscious experience as "hallucinations." The presence he'd felt emanating from the forest had become as constant and noticeable-on-demand as tinnitus.

He opened the storeroom under the porch and dragged the cranky gas mower into the ragged grass of the yard. It started on the seventh pull of the starter cord, possibly a record. The mowing didn't take long. Each time he cut the grass, he let the meadow encroach a little farther, and the squared-off acre he'd started with in March had shrunk to an irregular quarter acre barely encompassing the lodge and the outbuildings. He liked the unruly tall grasses better than the mowed yard, but come October, once the nesting animals were finished with it, he would have to bush-hog the fifty acres above the lodge, a couple of days mindlessly driving the tractor around in circles. The larger lower meadow had been established in native warm-season grasses, and apparently you burned that stuff instead of mowing it, once every three years, 150 acres of grass put to the flame. He guessed it would be an impressive thing to watch.

His boots were wet from the pressure-washing and covered with grass clippings. He pulled them off, socks too, and set them in the sun. He lay on his back in the cut grass, trying to relax. A turkey vulture appeared overhead, rising on the transparent thermal. The bird flew in circles, unreeling into the blue-white sky. A cloud of gnats swirled in what looked like Brownian motion until a breeze carried them away and the air was empty, without depth. After his boots dried, he would walk up the mountain and run a couple of scheduled transect surveys. While he was up there, he would keep an eye out for the bear poachers. One of the surveys, his favorite, crossed a section of the primary forest at the head of the big canyon on the far side of Turk Mountain. A survey entailed walking slowly along a particular compass bearing and recording observations in a number of prescribed categories: the status of certain plant species' flowering and leafing; presence of insects; animal tracks and direct sightings; bird calls; soil moisture. It was old-fashioned biology, but they'd been making systematic observations here nearly without interruption since the late nineteenth century, and the historical continuity of the data made it valuable, especially to scientists studying the ecological effects of climate change.

He opened the plank door creaking on its hinges and was about to push the mower back into the storeroom when motion on the floor stopped him—a copperhead uncoiling like a spring, striking the air three times in quick succession.

He felt the usual electric shiver, the ancient jolt of adrenaline. The snake didn't try to get away, just lay there in a block of sunlight from the open door, neck cocked in a tight S with its neat little viper's head pointed up at Rice. The strikes had looked more like a warning than a serious attempt to bite him. Its eyes were cloudy and its skin dull and dusty-looking, almost ready to shed, which made it nearly blind, vulnerable, and therefore truculent. It struck again as soon as his shadow fell on it. A copperhead wasn't going to kill you, but the bite of any pit viper could cause spectacular swelling, necrosis, tissue loss, and potentially gangrene, and was one of the more unpleasant things that could happen to you up here. He leaned into the doorway, reached around to where the shovels and rakes were stacked and pulled out a big aluminum grain scoop he'd used as a snow shovel last March. He would catch the snake, carry it out to the woods with the shovel, and let it go.

It struck again when he slid the shovel underneath it, pinging once on the metal. After a few seconds it seemed to settle down. He lifted it and started to back out the door, but the movement triggered a writhing panic, and though he tried to keep it centered, cradling the shovel like a lacrosse stick, the snake managed to launch itself from the end, landing on the floor with a dry slap. It headed for the back of the storeroom.

Without thinking about the likely result, he reached over with the shovel to block its path: the copperhead turned away from the blade and, still panicked, shot back toward Rice's bare feet. It was only trying to escape the shovel, but to Rice's sympathetic nervous system this looked a lot like an attack. He jabbed with the shovel and the snake was headless in an instant, its body thrashing and painting the floor with wild Pollockian sprays of blood. He cursed and stepped back out into the yard. His skin tingled. He wasn't supposed to kill native creatures up here, not even angry pit vipers.

The body was still twitching in the shovel as he carried it with the head out to the edge of the freshly mown grass and left the pieces there for the crows. When he came back to put away the mower, he crouched to examine the blood on the floor, the curved swipes and droplets already losing their bright red luster. Another portent, he supposed. The blood would dry and harden. He lifted the mower and stepped over so he wouldn't smear the patterns.

TEN

Sierra Vista, Arizona. Casita Cantina.

Apryl Whitson wore her hair in a thick black braid, a magnificent thing that just now rested on her left shoulder like a sleeping mamba. Over the past five days in the Coronado National Memorial, Rice had lost count of the times he'd wanted to hang her up in a cottonwood tree by that braid and leave her there for the javelinas.

"I don't think we should work together again," she said.

Rice pushed his empty plate to the edge of the table for the waitress, who was clearing things away. The rest of their party had left a few minutes before. Classic rock on the sound system. They used to play ranchera in here.

"Suits me," he said. "Dr. Warnicke told me I'd be working solo."

"Yeah, you by yourself, that might be best." She had dark blue, nearly purple eyes and heavy arching eyebrows. Her nose and mouth were almost too big and could come across as sensual when she wasn't smirking. At some point in the past she had embedded a fine silver loop in the flesh near the outside tip of her left eyebrow. She was ostensibly the team leader, but Rice was her senior by nearly a decade, and the two of them had clashed over everything from where to camp to how much water they and the four grad students should carry to how to hang the bear bags to how to conduct the soil and water tests and barking frog surveys that were the point of their little expedition. One of the doctoral candidates had told him Apryl got to choose the projects she led because she brought in a lot of anonymous funding. Nobody knew who her contacts were.

The look she gave him now was so comically baleful that he lifted his empty margarita glass and tipped it up to hide his smile. The ice cubes at the bottom hesitated for a moment before submitting to gravity and sliding down to crash against his teeth.

He rattled the ice in his glass. "You know, you're kind of a tyrant. Those guys"—he nodded toward the parking lot where the grad students had disappeared—"are terrified of you."

She shrugged. "They do their jobs." Her expression didn't change. "And you are a fucking know-it-all."

Rice hailed the waitress and pointed to their glasses, held up two fingers. She nodded and turned toward the bar. Apryl called out "Y dos sidecars por favor."

Rice stood up and raised an eyebrow at her crappy Spanish.

"Cuts the sweetness," she said.

He headed toward the back, looking for the restroom. When he returned, their drinks had arrived but both shot glasses were empty.

"I poured them in." She flicked a finger toward his glass. "You'd better stir."

He mixed in the extra tequila with a knife, the only silverware left on the table. Apryl watched as he took a long pull, crunched some ice, swallowed. It tasted like sweetened kerosene.

"The extra tequila helped a lot," he said.

"So why haven't you asked me?"

No pause, no windup. He drank again from the margarita, giving him time to compose his thoughts.

"So why are you so damn cryptic?" he asked.

Before sunrise on the third day, he'd been up having a piss away from camp when he saw her sneak off with her backpack. He followed for a couple of miles, all the way to the border, then across—in this remote area, the line between the United States and Mexico was barely marked. She dropped into a dry wash sloping off to the southeast. Rice had climbed up a slope nearby and used his binoculars. Two four-wheelers and three men in camouflage coveralls that looked like Mexican army uniforms waited on a graveled landing. Apryl approached, pulling a black dry bag about the size of a gallon jug from her pack, and handed it over. They opened it, looked inside, and resealed it. He couldn't hear if anyone said anything, and after a moment one of them nodded to Apryl, she nodded back, they all turned and separated, and Rice followed Apryl back into the United States. He'd been certain she'd never seen him.

She sat across the table waiting for an answer, head tilted forward so her eyes appeared even darker than usual, storm-cloud purple and peering out from under those big swooping eyebrows.

He set his glass down and slid it back and forth in the thin layer of condensation that evaporated as he watched. "Okay, what was in the bag?"

She slowly shook her head, just once, her elbow on the table now, pinching her lower lip between thumb and forefinger, watching him. After the passage of some period of time that, in retrospect, he found it impossible to gauge, the restaurant blurred around him. Then it began to move in a sickening shimmy, invisible thumbs pressing into his eye sockets.

He woke up in the front seat of her Jeep, wrists bound behind his back, ankles strapped together with plastic zip ties. Apryl stood in front of the vehicle, looking toward the horizon through Rice's binoculars. He vaguely remembered her paying the tab and apologizing to the waitress in bad Spanish as the two women half-dragged, half-carried him out to the parking lot. She'd parked up on a sandstone bluff and the country was shadowy blue all around but for a bright salmon blush in the west over unmistakable Baboquivari. They were a long way from the restaurant in Sierra Vista.

"Don't drop those." His voice came out weaker than he'd hoped. He cleared his throat and reached up with his feet to kick open the latch on the door. The door opened, but when he tried to get out he found she had secured his seat belt. He hitched himself sideways, trying to reach the buckle with his hands. He began to feel mildly nauseated.

She spoke without turning around. "How does a dirtbag like you afford glasses like these?" They were Leicas and he carried them in his pack whenever he was in the backcountry.

"Heirloom from my father. He couldn't really afford them either." The Leicas had been in the box of things his mother had saved for him, along with the .45 Rice kept in his truck and a steel Rolex GMT, a fancy pilot's watch his father had bought in the Middle East but had seldom worn. It was worth thousands, and Rice had given it back to his mother, told her to sell it and buy something she needed.

Apryl lowered the binoculars to rest on the strap around her neck and turned, walked to Rice's side of the Jeep, reaching behind her right hip as she came, producing the slim semiautomatic pistol she'd carried the whole trip in a flap holster, for rattlesnakes, she'd said. She leaned in and pressed it against his temple while he fumbled with his seat belt buckle.

He cut his eyes so he could watch her face. "That's a nice pistol, you know. Colt Woodsman. They don't make those anymore."

She stepped back when he disconnected his seat belt, let him hop to the flat rock in front of the Jeep. He stood unsteadily and admired the view for about three seconds before she kicked her heel into the back of his knee, forcing him down in front of her.

"You had these binoculars. You saw their faces."

"Not clearly. It was still pretty dark."

"You can't imagine how bad it is that you happened to see those particular guys. Of all the guys you could've seen, you saw those guys. I don't care if you're an undercover cop or just a slacker failed scientist who can't mind his business, which is what I think you are. If they found out you saw them they'd kill you, but then they'd kill me, they'd kill my sister." Her voice had started to quaver and she paused, then started again with more control. "They'd probably kill our parents too for good measure, though I could give a shit."

His head was still muddled from the roofie or whatever the hell she'd put in his margarita, but he was struck by both the gravity and the ridiculousness of the situation. Her feet shuffled on the rock, stepping backward, away from him. A reflex, unconsciously moving away from the bullet impact, the blood she might imagine would spray out. It was good that she didn't have much stomach for this, bad that she was so close to doing it. His knees were scraped and stinging from where he'd landed on the rough sandstone. He turned to look at her. Apryl Whitson was serious indeed, with frightening dark eyes like some Hindu god of the apocalypse.

He grinned. He had to admit he had a bit of a crush.

"Stop acting tough, Rice." Her voice was shaking again, and it was the first time she'd called him by his given name. "I really might have to fucking shoot you."

ELEVEN

Rice knelt at the peak of the cabin roof, poking with a screwdriver at the silicone caulking around the plumbing vent pipe jack. The plumbers and electricians had finished the rough-in yesterday, and the inspector from the county—bored and complaining about how far this place was from the road—had bestowed his official approval after barely a glance, so Rice had been looking over their work himself. The sealing around the vent was functional but ugly, and he'd decided he was going to have to cover the jack with metal flashing painted to match the roof. The rest of the work was acceptable, even careful, but the plumbers must've assumed no one would look too closely at the vent pipe.

Movement in his peripheral vision: a vehicle on the lower driveway, emerging from the forest. He vaulted over to the back side of the roof, gripping the metal seam at the ridge with his free hand, sliding backward until he was hidden from view. He crouched there and peered over. A blue wagon coming fast, still too far away to hear.

The day was overcast but bright, still hot well into September, and he'd neglected to put on a shirt this morning. The usual half-dozen cicadas wailed in the trees at the edge of the meadow. These insects were much louder than the western version, and most days they were a remarkable acoustic presence, Appalachia's howler monkeys. He still wasn't used to them. The plumbers had called them locusts, the same kind that came out every summer. Wait till next May, they'd said, when the seventeen-year locusts would swarm up out of the ground, billions of them, and it would be so loud in the forest you'd have to put your fingers in your ears. Not that Rice was sure he believed them. He'd had to stop the plumbers from killing a six-and-a-half-foot black rat snake they swore up and down was poisonous—their certainty had been absolute, their proof the pissed-off snake's tail vibrating against the dirt where they'd cornered it with shovels in the crawl space under the cabin. Them blacksnakes they mate with rattlers, they said. Rice had to catch the snake in his hands—the plumbers shaking their heads at his foolhardiness—and carry it all the way down to the forest to let it go before they'd get back to work. He found it puzzling that so many rural people were hostile to—even terrified of—the place where they lived. It wasn't just that hardworking country folk had no time for the precious concerns of effete urban environmentalists. What amazed Rice was how you could spend your whole life physically immersed in a particular ecological system and yet remain blinded to it by superstition, tradition, prejudice. Out west it was ranchers' holy war on predators and their veneration of Indo-European domestic animals they husbanded on land too dry to support them. Here in the Appalachians, you saw rugged country men who refused to walk in the woods all summer because they were scared of snakes.

He tucked the screwdriver into a pocket and settled back on his haunches, watching the car approach. Because the driveway was visible for a full mile as it climbed up from the forest below, the lodge and its two dependencies were almost impossible to sneak up on. He'd noticed that the first morning, back in March, when he'd stepped out on the front porch with a cup of coffee to see where he'd landed.

The car—it looked like an older Subaru wagon—raised a dust plume that hung above the meadow in the still afternoon air. He didn't expect his nemesis to arrive in broad daylight in a blue Outback, but whoever it was had made it past the locked gate somehow. He scrambled to the ladder he'd left leaning against the eaves on the back side of the cabin, climbed down, and ran past the shed to slip through the back door of the lodge. In the bedroom he threw on a shirt and opened the drawer beside his bed, reached under the rag, the pistol in his hand. He aimed the thing at the floor and pushed the safety lever down with his thumb, trigger finger straight along the base of the slide—all of this a cultivated reflex—reaching over with his left hand to grasp the slide and ease it back a little, just enough to see the brass glint of a round in the chamber. The slide snicked to battery and he levered the safety up into its notch. Cocked and locked is what people called it, "condition one": a round in the chamber, the hammer cocked, the safety on.

Back out the back door—he wouldn't want to be trapped in the lodge—retracing his steps to the cabin. This was the response he'd planned if a strange car appeared on the driveway: get the pistol and hide behind the cabin. If the visitor was innocuous, he could act nonchalant and saunter out the front door; if it turned out to be a carload of assassins, he would run to the forest. He stepped over the fresh dirt where the plumbers had ditched for the water and propane lines and kneeled in the moss at the base of the corner pillar, leaned down to where he could see the driveway through the crawl space underneath the cabin.

Glare on the windshield obscured the interior as the car pulled past the cabin and parked beside his truck. The driver got out, legs in jeans, feet in brown sandals, a woman standing in the gravel. He walked through the back door of the cabin, stashed the pistol in an empty cardboard box. Standing on the sheets of plywood he'd laid across the joists, he watched through a front window. She wore oversize dark glasses, white oxford shirt untucked, blond hair loose to her shoulders. She waited beside her car for a long moment, her hand on the open door, breathing deeply and looking around, absorbing, inspecting.

When he called out from the front door, she turned, startled. In his dreams, the few times when he could see her clearly at all, she'd been petite, bookish. The woman standing on the gravel path was tall and big-boned. Younger than Rice but not much. He wished STP had told him Sara still had a key.

"Why don't you answer the phone?" She had a slight southern accent, not local.

"I keep it unplugged until I need to call out."

That made her laugh, a pleasant sound, something he realized he hadn't heard in a while.

"Starr said you were odd that way."

He walked to meet her in the driveway. She was still smiling when she took off the sunglasses. Her left cheekbone was slightly flattened and marked by a fine vertical scar. Sky-blue eyes, freckles across the bridge of her nose. Broad mouth, whitened teeth. The transformation her smile wrought in her appearance was so dramatic it was like a behavioral display, a peacock opening its tail.

"What way?"

She held out her hand. "I'm Sara."

"Rick Morton."

She laughed again and he realized STP would have told her his real name. Her grip was strong, nearly mannish.

"Odd in the way of someone who would keep the telephone unplugged. Someone who would use a pseudonym. 'Don't make him talk about his past,' Starr says. So mysterious."

They walked together toward the lodge. She kept talking. She had brought him "something from Starr," and she needed to pick up some books and papers she'd left in the storage closet behind the office.

In his extended solitude he had developed a high degree of intimacy with his imagined version of Sara Birkeland, and it threw him to be in the presence of the real Sara, a substantial, talkative woman with pale feet in strappy sandals clacking up the board steps to the place that probably still felt like home. What had happened to her, what she'd survived, he couldn't push it out of the foreground. Not sure what to say—*Welcome back? How's the physical therapy coming?*—he kept his mouth shut. As he held the screen door open, his uncertainty must've shown on his face because the look she gave him was one of recognition but not invitation. It wasn't just him; people didn't know how to act around her.

She stepped inside and fired a series of breezy questions without giving him time to answer: how did he like the job, what'd he do with the TV and DVD player that she'd talked Starr into buying, maybe he didn't watch movies, was that how he had time to type in so much of the old logbook data, did he even listen to music, etc. It had been Sara's idea to digitize the historical natural history data from the logbooks so it could be made available to researchers. She and someone else at Tech had set up the software they were using to build a database portraying the phenology of several dozen plant and animal species. Rice didn't sleep well, and in addition to reading in the preserve's scientific and natural history library, he'd spent hundreds of late-night hours typing the observations of long-dead caretakers and Traver family members into the laptop. It filled sleepless nights with something other than his own thoughts, his own memories.

He wasn't going to explain his insomnia to Sara, so he led the way to the office, trying to make conversation about the yearling bear that had walked out the front door of the cabin, the honey in the wall, the guy vacuuming the bees. He hit the light switch and instantly he regretted bringing her in here, though there was no other way to get to the closet.

"This is nice." She glanced around half-smiling. Halfway, he figured, between laughter and alarm.

Three of the walls were lined with bookshelves, leaving space for a small desk next to the north-facing window. The preserve's laptop lay on the desk next to the current volume of the logbook, open to this week's entries. The bookshelves were the problem, in that the books were gone, replaced by his growing collection of found objects. It had become a minor obsession, bringing things home from the forest. He thought of them as fetishes, in the shamanistic sense: a defunct hornets' nest the size of a watermelon, translucent snakeskins, more than a dozen animal skulls ranging from hummingbird to coyote, Indian spear and arrow points, quartz crystals, rodent-gnawed deer antlers, turtle shells, mollusk fossils, feathers of turkey, hawk, owl, vulture.

"It's not a very scientific collection." He reached up to slide the key from the top shelf. He was supposed to keep the closet locked because the preserve's Winchester Model 52—a fine old .22 target rifle with peep sights and a leather military sling, for shooting rabid skunks and feral cats—was stored inside.

"I like it." She lifted a papery segment of shed snakeskin, held it up to the lamp. "This is a timber rattler."

"I thought so. Nothing else would be that thick."

"I saw a lot of big rattlesnakes here, the kind that people feel it's their civic duty to kill on sight everywhere else. The biggest ones all seemed to be yellow-phase, for some reason. Really beautiful. It was weird that I never found any of their den sites."

He'd already decided he wasn't going to admit he'd recently murdered a copperhead. Boxes were stacked just inside the walk-in closet, the books he'd moved from the shelves. He'd read most of them in the spring: treatises, essay collections, reference works, and back issues of technical journals—*Nature, Science, Conservation Biology.*

"I saw a big yellow one way up on the fire road in August." He started dragging the boxes out of the way. "It acted like a western diamondback, mad at the world, wanted to run me off the mountain. I thought timber rattlers were supposed to be mellow."

Sara replaced the snakeskin on the shelf, and stepped over to the wall beside the window where he'd taped up a composite of USGS 7.5-minute topo maps. The boundaries of the property were outlined in red, and Rice had marked with a pencil where he'd seen bears and other interesting phenomena—bold springs, a salt lick, cave entrances. Two timber rattler dens he'd found when the snakes had come out in May.

She played her fingertips over the markings.

"You've spent a lot of time up there."

He pointed to a penciled "TR" next to the dotted line of the fire road. "It was right here. The big rattler."

The closet was the size of a small room, about half as big as the office, fluorescent lighting overhead, its back wall lined with gray metal shelves from floor to ceiling. The long-barreled target rifle leaned in a corner.

"I've found they have surprisingly individualized personalities."

"Rattlesnakes?" He stood aside so Sara could get into the closet.

"Yeah, supposedly king cobras are even more that way, very individual. My little skinks, not so much."

She hesitated, and seemed to steel herself. As she brushed past he recognized the scent of her shampoo, a quarter bottle of which he had finished up himself when he'd first arrived at the lodge in March and couldn't afford to waste anything. He wondered what it had been like for her here, back in January, boxing up her belongings in a daze, hardly recovered from the assault, snow and sleet scratching at the window panes.

She reached up and put her hand on a shelf at shoulder height filled with cardboard boxes. "Everything on this shelf is mine. A bunch of technical journals I didn't think I'd need, but a couple of them aren't online yet, if you can believe it. Now I've got a statistical analysis problem I can't put off solving any longer, and the answer is somewhere in these boxes."

She pulled a heavy box halfway off the shelf and was standing up on her toes trying to peer in when it tipped and slid toward her. Rice lunged forward, his forearm bumping her shoulder as he caught the box and pushed it into place.

The elbow to his head came fast and hard. He might have dropped to his knees if he hadn't caught himself with his hand on the shelf. At first he thought it was some kind of accident, but when he'd recovered enough to look up, Sara had backed against the wall, as far away as she could get in the closet, a black plastic stun gun in her hand.

For just a beat, two beats, their eyes locked: predator and prey. She was wild-eyed, her easy self-assurance gone. He saw himself in her face: monstrous, deadly, looming over her and stinking of man-sweat. Something else there too: the raw certainty of to-the-death resistance. He thought of that yellow timber rattler on the fire road, the urgent warning fizz of its rattle.

"Oh, shit, I'm sorry." He raised his hands in what he hoped was a peaceful gesture. The two pointy silver electrodes on the stun gun weren't arcing, so she hadn't actually turned the thing on, which he had to think was a good sign. He retreated through the doorway and rummaged in the desk in the office, returning with a red Sharpie. She was still pressed against the wall, eyes closed and weapon lowered, looked like she was concentrating on her breathing, maybe something a therapist had shown her. He leaned in and set the marker on a shelf.

"Just put an X on the boxes you want, and come get me when you're ready. I'll make us some coffee." He left before she could reply.

TWELVE

He dumped ground coffee into a filter, poured eight cups of water in the machine, and pressed the rocker switch. His ability to interact with other human beings in a civilized manner had obviously atrophied. Should've been more careful, he told himself, shouldn't have been fooled by her I'm-okay act. After a while, the machine started sputtering. No Sara. He opened cabinets, banging around so she'd know he was busy here in the kitchen and not lurking behind a door somewhere, normal domestic activity, pulling out sugar, mugs, a glass jar of local milk from the fridge. She must've had that stun gun in a holster of some sort, hidden under her shirt tail. He felt like an asshole.

The coffee machine had spat out the last of its water and he was almost ready to go looking for her when she appeared in the doorway, leaning a little into the door frame.

"That smells good." The skin of her cheeks and forehead looked damp and she'd brushed her hair back into a ponytail; she must've stepped into the bathroom. She seemed drained but composed.

"It's a vice." He pulled a chair from the table for her, but she stayed where she was. "I drink too much coffee. You want a beer instead?"

"No, coffee's perfect. And I am so sorry. You were trying to help and I think I may have hit you in the head."

Rice waved her apology away and stepped to the sink to wash his hands, realizing that he might have done this before he'd started making the coffee. He was also pretty sure a goose egg was raising up just over his left temple, but it would be hidden in his hair, which was, now that he thought about it, long and scraggly and not very clean.

"You probably saved me from a broken back," she said. "I can't predict what's going to freak me out. It just happens."

"I shouldn't have rushed you like that." He started to compliment her on her reflexes, her self-defense technique—clearly she'd had training—but decided it would be insensitive. "I'm just glad you didn't get me with the stun gun."

"Me too. My instructor said he's seen guys lose control of their bladders when they got hit with those things."

Rice grinned, drying his hands on a dish towel. "That would've been embarrassing."

She watched his face long enough to make him uncomfortable. "Starr said you're sweeter than you look."

Rice had no idea what to say to that, but she didn't seem to expect a reply. She took the chair he'd offered, leaned back, and crossed her legs. Her long Nordic face was pale in the indirect light. "She told me about the bear carcass that guy showed you."

He guessed this was Sara's heroic effort to make ordinary conversation, which he appreciated. It made him feel a little less like the kind of guy who terrifies women. He pulled the pitcher and poured two mugs. Sugar and milk were on the table. "You ever see anything like that? Dead bears? One-armed mushroom pickers?"

"Thanks, black is fine. No, I didn't. But I have a story for you."

He sat in the other chair across from her, poured a shot of milk into his coffee.

A good friend, she said, a wildlife biologist at Tech, had been working with the state game department on a bear study, looking at ways to manage interactions between rural residents and the growing bear population. They'd radio-collared a bunch of bears over in the Blue Ridge Mountains, but last winter most of the subjects were killed in a three-week period. The poachers apparently tuned into the frequency of the collars and walked right up and shot the bears where they were hibernating. They cut off the paws, cut out the gallbladders, and left the carcasses.

"Once the researchers saw what was happening, they went out and tranked the bears that were left and pulled their collars, but two more were killed before they could get to them."

"How many?"

"He didn't say exactly. I know they had maybe twenty-five bears collared at one time. It was on TV last fall."

Sara's energy seemed to have come back. Maybe it was the coffee. The game department, she said, had made a big deal out of publicizing the study while it was going on, and local TV stations had sent crews out with the researchers. The TV people wanted a guaranteed bear, so they only went out when the researchers were tranquilizing collared bears to take blood samples and measurements. The producers liked the high-tech radio collar angle, and it got to be part of the story, how they used the radios to find the bears. The poachers must've seen one of those shows and come up with the idea.

Rice thought about this. It wasn't far-fetched. "You'd need a programmable high-frequency scanner and some clue about how to use it. That stuff's pretty easy to get. Military surplus."

"I was imagining an evil electronics genius."

He shook his head. "Probably just a local with skills. If they killed twelve bears, and they sold the gallbladders for a couple hundred each, that's a lot of money around here."

It wouldn't be enough to interest the mafia, he thought, but the organized crime guys wouldn't be out there shooting bears anyway; they would be the buyers, the exporters. More money in that. He would try to find out tonight. He'd driven out to a truck stop on the interstate where they still had pay phones—he wasn't going to risk any more calls from the lodge—and called the number from the Beer & Eat again. Now that Rice had some galls to sell, the unpleasant buyer was willing to talk. They were meeting sometime after nine. Rice was supposed to call him again around seven and find out where, which was a pain in the ass, but the guy had insisted.

"It'd be a lot of money to me," Sara was saying. Her lips compressed and she raised her mug and finished the coffee, returning the heavy mug to the table with emphasis. "Assholes."

Rice found this reaction interesting. He stood and offered a refill. "I've met one guy who seems okay, a bear hunter from . . . around here." He'd almost said *from Sycamore Hollow* but remembered at the last second that that was where she'd been raped. "He's the guy who came up and vacuumed the bees in the cabin. He's pretty upset about the poaching himself. The fact that they just leave the carcasses seemed to offend him."

Sara was nodding, staring at the coffee he'd just poured.

"He also says the bears up here have no respect because they're not hunted enough. He knows locals come on the property, though, and I got the impression he does it himself. Seems to be part of bear hunter culture. Property boundaries and state regulations are for other people." Rice felt guilty about pushing, but he asked the next question anyway. "Did you ever catch any bear hunters up here?"

"Couple times," she said. "They drove ATVs around the Forest Service gate, came down the fire road. It was before Starr had the fence put in. When I ran into them on the mountain they acted like I was on *their* land. I asked them to leave and they got belligerent, made a point of showing me their guns, said they were looking for their dogs. Apparently that's what they always say. I called the game warden on my cell and they got in trouble, had to pay fines." She shrugged as if to say it was no big deal, probably had nothing to do with anything. "You make good coffee, for a bachelor."

"Thanks. The secret is to use enough." His antennae were a-tingle but it was pretty clear she was changing the subject.

"Most bachelors are cheapskates," she said. "They make watery coffee."

"Not me."

"You're living high on the hog up here."

The conversation flagged uncomfortably. They drank their coffee. Rice wondered what "high on the hog" really meant, where the expression came from. Maybe the best meat comes from up on the shoulders? But bacon comes from the belly, and everyone loves bacon. He thought about asking Sara, but she seemed tense. She stood and walked to the sink, looked out the kitchen window. He watched her still silhouette, and he wondered about bear hunters who would brandish their weapons at a woman out in the woods by herself, and what they might do to get back at her for calling the law.

Outside, the clouds had lowered and darkened. He had hoped to be on the mountain by now. He'd walked up there every day this past week, looking for boot prints, cigarette butts, sardine tins, ATV tracks, anything. He wanted to put in a couple of hours before he drove to the truck stop to call the buyer.

Still looking out the window, Sara asked, "What are you going to do if you catch those bear hunters on the property?"

"I told Starr I'd take their picture. Then we can call the law, like you did."

She turned and smiled at him like she knew him better than that. Shaking her head, she said "That's just lame."

SHE'D MARKED SIX HEAVY BOXES IN THE CLOSET WITH RED X'S, AND THEY moved them out to the car in two trips, Rice carrying two, Sara insisting on carrying one herself each trip. Four fit in the cargo area of her car after removing the UPS box she said was from Starr, and

Rice slid the last two onto the messy back seat, shoving aside a pile of junk mail, biology textbooks, student papers, workout clothes, empty grocery bags.

The box from STP had been mailed to Sara's address in Blacksburg from a company in Wisconsin. Apparently she'd had it sent to Sara because she was worried UPS would just leave it at the locked gate to be stolen. He cut the box open with his pocketknife. Inside were five "digital wildlife cameras" with cable locks, a bunch of memory cards, rechargeable AA batteries, and a battery charger.

"You got Starr worried about the bears. I hope it's okay. You're kind of a whiz with the data." She sat on the steps to the cabin with one of the cameras and started trying to pry apart the plastic blister pack. "Starr asked if I thought you could use these to document the bear population, keep track of it over time. I told her you could use sites on the existing habitat survey grids, so the integration of the data should be seamless. You'd pick up a lot of data on other species, too, not just the bears. I'm really sorry, it was partly my idea, and it means more work for you."

He lifted another of the boxed cameras and slit the otherwise-impenetrable plastic with his pocketknife, held the camera in the light, opened up the back. The copy on the package said *Professional high output covert infrared*. This was high-quality equipment, much nicer than what he'd used in Arizona. He'd always called them trail cameras—you usually set them up along a game trail to take pictures of the animals that walked past.

Sara gave up on her blister pack and handed it to Rice, launching into what he was afraid would be a long explanation of why the additional data would be worthwhile. She said bear numbers had been stable on the preserve throughout the twentieth century, even when bears were scarce everywhere else, which he knew from the old logbooks. Her bear biologist friend suspected that the long-term isolation from human disruption and the uninterrupted availability of dead and dying large-diameter den trees, the kind you only find in old-growth forest, might have fostered a unique bear population here. For one thing, the biologist predicted they would find a lot of older bears on the preserve, but more interestingly, he'd said the bear "culture" would be intact. While not social in the manner of wolves or lions, black bears could live forty years if no one was trying to shoot them, they were smart and omnivorous, and their ranges typically exhibited a high degree of overlap and mutual use. A complex social network could arise in a protected place, where decades-long reciprocal relationships would develop among a large number of bears.

He was intrigued by the concept of bear culture. It wasn't something he'd considered before, and he wondered if shared knowledge particular to a population could reside in the oldest bears and persist over time, and maybe even be communicated across generations. Sara's disquisition veered off into statistical analysis and he interrupted, told her the idea for the cameras was fine, that he didn't mind the extra work. He asked if she'd like to see inside the cabin.

Bare bulbs hanging from the ceiling lit up when he hit the wall switch. He realized it didn't look like much. The smell was earthy from the open crawl space and woody from the plywood and the sawdust left by the plumbers and electricians drilling through the old joists. His pistol was in a box in the back, but he didn't think she would see it.

"The kitchen and living space will be one room. Full bath next to the kitchen. Bedroom's back there." He pointed toward the west end of the cabin, feeling like he was selling the place. He suspected Sara was STP's secret agent, here to check on his work, which was reasonable, given that STP had left him here unsupervised for more than six months, and the Traver Foundation was pouring money into the remodel without STP or the board having seen so much as a photograph.

She nodded and made perfunctory noises of approval, walked

across plywood sheets into what would be the kitchen area, glanced around as if imagining cabinets, appliances. Then she turned to face him, took a deep breath, and put her hands on her hips. She looked nervous. "I have to tell you something. I hope it's not going to be a problem."

He waited.

"I've applied for the first fellowship."

It took him a second to realize what she was talking about. "You mean with the foundation, to live here. Why would that be a problem?" The thought of someone else—anyone else—living up here still gave him jitters, but Sara seemed reasonably tolerable.

"Well, I used to have your job. You might think I'm horning back in on it, like I'm watching you, or judging whether you're doing it right."

He started to grin but stifled it, not sure how sensitive she was. "I don't worry about things like that. I bet you have a good shot at the fellowship. Starr seems to think highly of you."

She reddened, and he saw her realize that her rehearsed speech, her concern about his reaction, had been misplaced, that it was, or should've been, pretty obvious, and she should've figured it out over the past hour or so. She tumbled into an overexplanation of her own motives, her reluctance to take advantage, her decision driven by the fact that it would be hard to finish her paper any other way.

"Easy access to skinks," he said. "Skinks out the back door."

"You got it." Her smile was grateful. She turned and gestured dramatically at the gutted interior of the cabin. "So, what are you thinking for the paint in here? A nice light eggshell might look nice."

"I hadn't really thought about it."

"Now I'm messing with you."

"But you're right. I guess I figured it'd be white." He looked around with new eyes. "Shit, Starr's gonna want to see paint chips." He imagined conversations about color shades and the moods they evoke.

"Don't worry, they have that stuff online now. On the In-ter-net? Once the drywall is up, you email her pictures of the interior and she can do a mock-up with the different colors. She can decide what she wants and order it herself. You pick it up at the paint store and Bob's your uncle."

"Ah. Good to know." He walked out onto the front stoop. Sara, he guessed, had been the intended recipient of the first fellowship from the beginning, maybe even the main reason for its creation. Rice's job was to build a new living space for Sara and relieve her of the caretaker duties.

She stood beside him. They gazed amiably up at the weather. The rain was still holding off, but it wouldn't for much longer. "I promise if I get the fellowship you'll hardly know I'm here."

"Who's Bob?"

"What? Oh. It's an expression. British, I think." She paused. "You know, I don't have a clue who Bob is, or why exactly it would be a good thing to have him as your uncle."

"You can look it up. On the In-ter-net." Fearing he might've triggered a lengthy extension to their conversation, he stepped down from the porch and headed for the car, willing her to follow. She got the hint but stopped with her hand on the car door handle.

"One last thing." She opened the door and turned to look at him. "Have you seen a cat?"

"You mean that black house cat?"

"You didn't shoot her."

He shook his head. He'd glimpsed a small black cat two or three times but never got a good look at it. "Is it yours?"

"Not really. She was feral, I saw her on the side of the road a few times, I thought she was a weasel at first, so skinny, linear. She was in the bushes by the mailbox one day, and I spoke to her, I don't know what I said, but the next morning she showed up here, and started following me around, she would just appear, like a spirit or something, sitting up in the rafters on the porch, or under the steps, absolutely still, and watch me. It was a little spooky. If I tried to pet her she would come alive and slip away, disappear."

"You're supposed to shoot cats up here. You know where the rifle is as well as I do." He nodded toward the lodge and saw her grin. After her miscue earlier, she was reading him better now. "Think of the wood thrushes," he said, "the meadowlarks, the skinks."

"I know, I just couldn't do it. I tried to trap her in that big Havahart in the shed, I was going to take her to the vet and get her spayed, talk my brother into adopting her. But she wouldn't go near it. I bought a can of wet cat food and put it in the trap. She didn't even seem tempted. Never acted hungry, just interested, watchful."

Sara seemed likely to continue the cat conversation, but Rice had a meeting with a bear gall buyer tonight and there were some things he had to do first. He paused long enough that she went ahead and sat in the driver's seat, looking up at him.

"I'll keep an eye out for her," he said. He hadn't seen the cat for a month or so, and he wouldn't be surprised if the coyotes had killed and eaten her—at least two good-size packs spent time on the property—but he didn't say so. "What's her name?"

She shut the door and started the car, rolled down the window. "How do you know I named her?"

THIRTEEN

Driving across the old bridge at the west end of town, he glanced through the spaces in the railing without slowing: a street and a dimly lit public parking lot eighty feet down, a few scattered cars parked overnight. He turned right at the far end and drove several blocks into a residential neighborhood before parking on the street. He'd called from the truck stop, and the buyer had made him wait there for half an hour and call back again for the location.

As he opened his door he reached into the slit in the side of the passenger seat cushion with his right hand and hooked his fingers on the grip of the .45. He paused, hand on the pistol, the foam pressing down on his knuckles. He'd left his holster at the lodge, but he could Mexican-carry, he'd done it before.

On the other hand, he had a record now, and if he got caught carrying the thing concealed without a permit he would certainly go to prison. Besides, he didn't need to be armed, it was just old habit—grabbing the gun for a clandestine meeting in the middle of the night. This wasn't going to be dangerous. Local toughs like the Stiller brothers embraced a kind of residual Confederate bellicosity and would welcome the escalation of a shouting match into a shoot-out, but—he hoped—they weren't going to simply murder him if he was unable to produce a firearm and defend himself. Besides, his investigation of the bear poaching was unofficial preserve business, and according to his only slightly self-serving interpretation of his employment agreement, he couldn't carry when he was working. His hand slid from the slit in the cushion, left the .45 where it was.

What his agreement actually said was that as caretaker of the Turk Mountain Preserve, Rice was prohibited from carrying a pistol on the property, probably because the trustees were afraid a pistol-packing caretaker might shoot a trespasser and they'd get sued. Poachers were trespassers who were armed by definition, though, and he'd considered carrying the .22 target rifle when he was up on the mountain looking for them. The Winchester was a hell of a rifle—when he'd found it in the closet back in March he'd sighted it in at a hundred feet, and if he was careful the thing could put seven shots into a single ragged hole—but it was heavy and unwieldy, not something he wanted to hike with. Instead, as he'd told STP last week, he carried the point-and-shoot digital camera she'd mailed to him in the spring for documenting plant species he couldn't identify on his surveys. He'd read somewhere that photo-graphing trespassers was more effective than just ordering them to leave the property.

That camera was buttoned in his shirt pocket tonight. A pic-ture of one of the Stiller brothers looking stupid with a bag of dried gallbladders in his hands might give Rice some leverage, a way to keep them off the preserve.

Cracked concrete steps led down from the near end of the bridge to a handful of unmetered parking spots underneath. Wa-ter from an evening thunderstorm dripped and echoed in the dark cavernous space, invisible pigeons up in the transoms cooing at his footsteps. Scant ambient light shone from the hazy sky. He moved into the darker shadow of a bridge pillar.

The night was chill, clearing after the rain, the smells of wet concrete and faint garbage. Crickets chirped, their rhythms slow, sleepy. He exhaled a gray backlit cloud toward the faux-antique streetlamp at the far end of the parking lot. The soft nylon cooler hanging from his shoulder was light, but he set it on the pavement.

He watched for five minutes, ten. No car pulled into the parking lot. The guy was probably here already. Rice had his flashlight, held it ready in his right fist, thumb on the switch. He thought of flashing the light into the shadows but didn't want to give himself away: the beam you got with the first push of the switch was unsubtle, something like two hundred lumens. When you pushed the button a second time it switched to a dim but useful light that didn't drain the batteries as fast. The little flashlight, a gift from Apryl just before everything went sideways in his old life in Arizona, had been weaponized with a sturdy scalloped metal bezel jutting out at each end, one around the lens and one around the push-button switch in the tail cap.

Fifteen minutes. The buyer was out there somewhere, doing exactly what Rice was doing: waiting and watching, not showing himself.

Off to the right, a momentary reddish glow in a little picnic area past the parking lot. No streetlights there. He watched and the glow came again, showing a man in a dark Carhartt work jacket— the square white label on his chest was conspicuous—sitting at a picnic table. Rice pulled the bill of his baseball cap down to shadow his face and walked over with the cooler.

The man stood, a bunched shadow unfolding as Rice approached. He wasn't a Stiller.

"Where's your vehicle? You were supposed to park down here." He spoke in a quiet voice, his accent not as pronounced as it had sounded on the telephone.

"Where's yourn?"

He was shorter than Rice but still tall, probably six feet. Medium build, strong-looking, tense. His movements were emphatic, like he could barely contain his own energy. He was making a point of keeping his back to the streetlight. Rice set the cooler on the table and punched the switch on his flashlight twice with his thumb, swept the beam across the man's face backhand—he was fortyish, dark red hair and short beard. The skin was tight across his cheekbones and forehead, like it had been stretched, an intense face, with close-set blue eyes that squinted as his arm came up to block the light.

"Shut that thing off."

The man had his own light, a foot-and-a-half-long metal police light with a red filter over the lens. It cast a dull red glow, what he'd seen earlier, inconspicuous at a distance and easy on dark-adjusted eyes.

"Raise your arms."

"What, you holding me up here, buddy?"

"I'm patting you down."

"The hell you are."

"You want to do business you put your fucking arms up."

Rice shrugged and held his arms out like a scarecrow, glad he'd left the pistol in the truck. The man stepped behind him and swatted Rice under the arms, around his waist, thighs, on both ankles. Rice had been patted down before, and this one was quick, almost perfunctory.

"I got your number from this old boy who's in business with the Stillers, DeWayne and them? I guess you and them—"

"Unzip the cooler."

"All right. Okay. See I hear them Stiller boys're into a lot of different shit around here. Maybe once you got everybody patted down we could all do some business together." Rice stepped back as the man shone the red light into the cooler.

"Where are the paws?"

Shit. He'd thought this might be a problem. "You didn't say nothing about no paws."

"Everybody knows you need the paws."

"What d'you do with 'em?"

"I don't do anything with them. Some slant in Korea makes fucking soup with them, what do you care?"

"You send 'em all the way to *Ko-rea*?"

"Yeah, I FedEx this shit to my buddy Moon Dung Bin in Seoul and he PayPals me the money."

Rice paused long enough before laughing to seem like he was trying to figure out whether it was a joke. "Well, hell. I can get you a lot more of these."

"Uh-huh. You're a big-time bear hunter, are you?" There was a tension in the man's voice now that Rice didn't like.

"Me and my cousins, yeah. We got people in West Virginia, too. They kilt eleven bears up there last year. We got eight. We all been saving the galls."

"But not the paws."

"We didn't know."

"Are you a stupid redneck?"

"Fuck you, buddy. You want these galls or not? I'll take a hunnerd each, since I ain't got the paws."

The man made a show of reaching into Rice's cooler and lifting the quart plastic Ziploc bag with the three shriveled gallbladders. Held it up to the red flashlight. He was grinning without much humor and his teeth looked bloody in the light.

"I'll give you five bucks for the three of them if you throw in the cooler."

This wasn't going well. Rice sputtered a "Bull-*shit*" and snatched the bag from the man's hand, tossed it back into the cooler. His questions about the Stillers hadn't even generated a denial, and this guy was way too serious to put up with photography. Rice was zipping the cooler shut when the man swatted it off the table with his flashlight.

"You don't have any paws because these aren't even bear galls, are they?"

He held the light close to Rice's face and Rice threw his arm up, pushed it away. He turned to pick up the cooler from the ground and, trying to maintain his ruse, started to say something about how some assholes didn't know a good business proposition when they was looking right at one, but the man came around the table fast and smacked the big flashlight hard into the back of his knee. His leg buckled and he started to roll to the right but the man caught him with his arm around his neck in a rough one-armed headlock.

"Do you have any idea how goddamn frustrating this is?" He wrenched Rice backward, the thick forearm clamping on his carotid, trying to choke him out. Rice tucked his chin and shrugged his shoulders, protecting his neck. The man's violence was sudden, confident, the moves of someone used to physically dominating others. "I'm sick of ignorant, stupid, dishonest hillbilly fucks."

Rice felt the flashlight come down again, this time on his ankle, but his boot cushioned the blow. He still had his own flashlight in his hand and he jabbed the crenelated bezel into the guy's elbow, three quick stabs, finally hitting the funny-bone notch with the third try, the guy's ulnar nerve lighting up, drawing a surprised "Ah!" as the arm went limp. He sucked in a big lungful of air and grabbed the paralyzed arm, reached his other hand behind the man's knee, and stepped under his center of gravity all in a single motion, lifting him from the ground in an improvised fireman's carry. He was about to break him in half on the picnic table when he felt cold metal pressed against his temple.

"Okay, that's enough. Put me the fuck down."

Rice set him on his feet, shook him off, and stepped away, keeping his hands visible. The man stood bracing his hip on the table, silhouetted against the distant parking lot lights. In the red wash from the flashlight on the ground, Rice could make out a medium frame semiauto in his right hand. He was breathing hard but the gun was steady. Body language said a shot was possible but not imminent. Rice squatted slowly, eyes on the gun, and retrieved his own flashlight and his baseball cap, reached for the strap of the cooler, and swung it over his shoulder. The bag with the galls had fallen out. Quick look around, no sign of it. Didn't matter.

"Who the fuck are you?" the man asked. His voice was calm, the temper tantrum apparently over. "What are you up to?"

Without answering, Rice turned his back on the gun and walked to the steps under the bridge, pins and needles up and down his spine. When he looked down from the railing, the man was gone. He walked around the block, making sure he wasn't followed, limping a little, favoring his right knee, glad the guy hadn't whacked him on his glass kneecap. He was angry at himself for getting into a fight on his very first attempt at undercover investigation. Near where he'd parked, he leaned against an old black maple buckling the sidewalk with its roots. The town was quiet except for distant music from a college party somewhere. After twenty minutes he walked to his truck and drove away.

FOURTEEN

Standing next to the spring box, Rice drew the .45 from its holster and shot holes in homemade cardboard head-and-shoulder silhouettes. He shot singles, pairs, double taps; he practiced head shots, center mass, Mozambiques; he shot two-handed, right-handed, left-handed, standing, sitting, lying down, from behind trees, walking. He tried running but his leg was still stiff from the gall buyer whacking it with his flashlight. He worked on his magazine changes, shooting to slide lock every time. Guys who had been in an egregious number of firefights had told him to train that way because in the real world nobody counts their shots, you just keep shooting until you realize you're empty and you have to reload in a screaming panic.

He'd bought a bunch of lead-free ammunition for the .45—wouldn't want to pollute the drinking water—and every month or so he would drive up here to this small, steep-sloped hollow to run through this backwoods Travis Bickle routine. He used the holster his father had kept with the gun, a pancake design handmade by a guy in Boise. It held the pistol high behind his right hip where you wouldn't see it under an untucked shirt, the butt raked forward and snug against his side. The holster had been almost new, but Rice had used it for two years in the desert and now the leather was sweat-stained and molded to his body.

His decision not to arm himself in his dealings with the locals had come easily, but he was starting to reconsider. The gall buyer last night had spooked him, just a little, the way he'd handled his pistol, drawing it as he was being lifted off his feet, the steady hand. Probably ex-military. Not some bumpkin you'd expect to write his number on the wall in a public bathroom, who would misspell *ginseng* unless it was on purpose. Crime organizations in Arizona—the Mexican cartels, street gangs, bikers—had been actively recruiting military personnel, combat vets rotating out of the sandbox and getting dropped into a crap economy. He wondered if the buyer was working for an East Coast gang, somebody with Asian connections.

He wasn't sure what to try next. The simplest approach would be to catch the poachers on the property. He'd been spending more time up there, but it was a big mountain, and according to Boger they used crossbows, so he shouldn't expect to hear gunshots. He thought about calling Boger again, asking him for some names of other bear hunters he could talk to, but when they'd spoken the other night, Boger had been unfriendly, like he'd decided Rice wasn't someone he wanted anything to do with.

He picked up his brass and loaded his frames and targets in the truck, repaired the divots in the earth, and raked fresh leaf litter over the top. When he pulled his earplugs, the water rushing from the spring box sounded preternaturally loud. The Traver family had built a stone and masonry spring box about the size of a minivan on top of the cleft in the limestone bedrock, and they'd buried pipe to the lodge, several hundred feet lower in elevation, so the whole system was gravity-fed, no pumps. An eight-inch pipe protruded near the top of the box for the overflow, and the water pouring out constituted the headwaters of Perry Creek, a brook trout fishery that tumbled toward the Dutch River Valley—part of Rice's job was to seine the creek twice a year and count the bugs he caught.

He was climbing into his truck when he saw something on the spring box, an animal perched there, absolutely still, watching him. The creature was inky black, dark as a hole in the world, slender, and he thought *black weasel*, then he remembered that was how Sara had described the feral cat. He was surprised the shooting hadn't scared her off. More like it had attracted her. He eased back out of the cab and walked closer.

"So you're Mel." The name didn't suit her. He'd asked Sara if it was short for *melanistic* and she'd shrugged and said she was a scientist, not a poet.

The cat blinked at him. Then she disappeared without seeming to move. He climbed up on the box to look, but she was gone so completely that he wondered if he'd imagined her. He would bring the Havahart trap tomorrow just in case; he couldn't leave her up here in good conscience.

He cleaned his pistol at the desk in the office and forced himself to sit there afterward and make some calls to arrange supplies—nontoxic laminates for the subflooring, recycled insulation, some special kind of wallboard, all per STP's specs. Replacing the notebook he used for cabin remodel notes in the desk drawer, he noticed a small stack of Sara's Virginia Tech business cards tucked in a corner. The phone was still plugged into the wall. He dialed her number before he could change his mind.

She didn't seem surprised that he'd seen the cat. "I knew she was a survivor."

"Well, she's not supposed to be surviving on the preserve. I'm going to try the trap in the shed. Maybe I'll have better luck than you did."

Sara asked if he'd installed the trail cameras, and he demurred, having forgotten about them altogether. Then she was inviting herself for another visit Wednesday. She would drive up first thing, help him set up the cameras, and pick up the cat if he managed to trap her.

He didn't reply right away.

"Rice, is that okay? You see I just went out on a limb there, asking if I could visit? Help me out."

"I think I'm free Wednesday."

"You're free every day. Why don't you invite me to stay for dinner. We can see if we're going to be able to stand each other."

FIFTEEN

outhbound, deep in the Tohono O'odham Reservation, Rice and Apryl made their way by moonlight in a dry wash. This route was comfortable, and they'd used it half a dozen times. The banks on either side were fifteen feet high, making a trench through which they could pass invisible to anyone watching the surrounding country. They'd picked up two twenty-liter dry bags at a stash house in Phoenix, sealed with a special kind of tamper-proof tape the cartel had started using. Rice was still new enough at this that he wasted mental energy speculating about What Was in the Bags. The math was easy: if it was bulk cash, and if it was all hundreds, it could be around $2 million in each. That would be heavy, though, forty-some pounds per bag, and these weren't quite full. But still. And it might be something more interesting than cash, maybe uncut stones, bearer instruments, prepaid $9,900 cash cards. He had been shocked at the amount of value Apryl routinely carried for the cartel.

Three months ago, on that stone ledge overlooking Baboquivari, he'd told Apryl she should have someone on overwatch, that her counterparties would expect her to, and maybe she'd faked it so far, feigned the kind of confidence you have when you know, and you know the other guy knows, that there's someone who cares about you, someone armed, someone hidden nearby and watching. But eventually, he said, word would spread that she was all alone, and someday some asshole was going to take advantage of that.

She'd been taken aback. He hadn't done it intentionally, but by challenging her tactical chops he had got her mind off shooting him in the head. They argued, and she put her pistol down on the sandstone, sat cross-legged behind it. Later she pulled a knife and cut his zip ties. She admitted she couriered packages—she didn't call it smuggling—to help buy meds for her schizophrenic little sister who had run away from their parents to live with her. He laughed at that because he thought she was joking, but she was altogether serious. Her dealer had talked her into carrying when he'd found out she made her living hiking around in the backcountry along the border. She knew a lot of the Border Patrol agents; they all thought she was an eccentric tree hugger. The dealer's Mexican supplier was a comer in the cartel—she wouldn't say which one, though Rice could guess—and he'd liked Apryl, liked her grit and reliability, and as his star had risen, so had hers. It was an unusual arrangement. Apparently he preferred a multimodal approach to smuggling, and he had come to rely on Apryl to move low-mass, moderate-to-high-value assets both ways. She filled a niche.

After doing it for eighteen months, she was making enough that she could pay for her sister's meds, salt away some cash for her sister in case something happened to Apryl, and fund a few biological studies she thought should be conducted. Her way of giving back to the border country. According to Apryl, the border mountain ranges were the only "real" places on the continent, grown increasingly anarchic in the past decade as the Border Patrol had forced the northbound cross-border traffic into more remote, difficult terrain, deadly geography with poetic names: the Perillas, the Pedregosas, the Dos Cabezas. Apryl loved the Chiricahuas best, a gigantic, rugged sky island of staggering biological diversity, haunted by the ghosts of her kin Cochise and Geronimo, they afforded barely plausible routes north for hundreds of desperate migrants conveying their hopes, dreams, and plastic water containers into the "pristine" wilderness. Apryl was half-Apache, a fact he thought she sometimes made too much of, adopted as a toddler in hyperconservative Mr. and Mrs. Whitson's spasm of open-mindedness amid a middle-aged reproductive panic, followed within the year by Mrs. Whitson's pregnancy with sister Tracy and—all of this according to Apryl—a growing buyer's remorse as to the little dark-skinned girl with behavioral problems.

Tonight, whispering as they snuck through the dry wash, she'd told him about the planned border wall along most of the Arizona–Mexico line, and her idea to fund a major study showing how it would fuck up the cross-border migration of threatened and endangered megafauna. He was thinking about that, wondering if they were likely to get good data on any endangered species, as there were only so many that had been listed, and Homeland Security probably got to ignore the ESA anyway. He let himself become a little distracted in the heat that was stupefying even in the middle of the night, and when two coyotes bringing in a bunch of illegals came around a bend he was too stunned at first to react. The illegals, quick-witted survivors that they were, turned and ran back down the wash. One of the coyotes fired a shot as Rice and Apryl scurried behind a boulder. Rice shot back once with his .45, nearly blinding himself with the muzzle flash, and the other guy opened up with an automatic weapon of some sort, bullets ripping past, ricocheting off the rocks, sounded like a 9mm submachine gun.

While Apryl crouched beside him with her .22 in her hand, cursing, Rice experienced a sensation of detachment, thinking here he was in his first firefight, and that instead of a scientist he'd become some kind of ridiculous desert outlaw—a dilettante Clyde to Apryl's only slightly more credible Bonnie, and that the bullets going by sounded sibilant, like insects.

They weren't completely naïve. They'd tried to prepare for something like this. Neither of them had any knowledge of gunfighting beyond what they'd seen in movies, but at Rice's insistence they would drive way out in the desert to an old dump once every week or so and shoot rusty kitchen appliances with their pistols. It was a forbidding, postapocalyptic place where someone—they imagined gang members working on their drive-by marksmanship—had cut down every saguaro in sight with what looked like machine-gun fire. They knew they would probably be outgunned in any violent encounter, but they had built their success on stealth, their innocent-scientists cover, and their knowledge of the remote border country, and so far they'd been lucky. Now here they were out in a remote part of the Sonoran Desert, a small, or possibly large, fortune in their backpacks, being shot at by criminals with a submachine gun.

He asked Apryl to hand him her pistol, and when she refused, surprising exactly no one, he reached over and pried it from her grip. The second coyote stopped shooting to reload and Rice leaned out with a pistol in each hand and emptied both magazines in the coyotes' general direction, firing seventeen shots as fast as he could pull the triggers, lots of noise and flash and more ricochet, hoping they would think he and Apryl were better armed than they really were. He slapped his second magazine into the .45 and dragged Apryl twenty yards up the wash to a rock outcrop, pushed her down behind it, and fell on top of her. The coyotes fired off another thirty or forty rounds on full auto, shooting at nothing while Apryl squirmed under him like the cat in the old Pepé Le Pew cartoons and hissed in his ear to get the fuck off her and give her back her fucking pistol.

Eventually the coyotes seemed to run out of ammunition and retreated to round up their charges. They all must've climbed up out of the wash because Rice and Apryl didn't see them again. Apryl's take on the incident had been pretty typical. After threatening to shoot him if he ever tried to take her pistol away from her again, her pronouncement was simply "We need to gun up." He couldn't disagree, and a few weeks later the two of them attended a three-day tactical rifle training course near Phoenix. Three days of rubbing elbows with genuine Arizona gun-nut subculture. Their co-trainees were all decent-seeming citizens, many of whom openly admitted they were preparing for (a) the Islamic or socialist insurgency the new socialist-Muslim president was about to unleash on the country, (b) the narco insurgency the Mexican cartels were going to mount across the weakly defended border, and/or (c) the always-imminent black-helicopter takeover of the United States by the United Nations.

Based on what they'd learned, Rice and Apryl decided they needed to carry one military style semiautomatic rifle when they were working along the border. Apryl researched the subject with her typical thoroughness, weighing the relative merits of various calibers, of piston mechanisms versus the "direct impingement" design, tactical optics, slings, and so on. He told her she was acting like the cartel loonies and mafia poseurs she despised, but he knew the paramilitary Zetas had changed the game in the past few years. As Apryl put it, "this military shit is de rigueur anymore."

Rice used to think he'd developed a reasoned approach to the use of weapons, neither hair-shirted pacifist nor wild-eyed operator wannabe. He enjoyed shooting, but he'd never been a full-on gun nut, and he was at least ambivalent about the wisdom of stirring a bunch of highly lethal weapons technology into the soup of everyday human society. Apryl, when condemned by her vegan pacifist friends for owning and carrying not just a gun but a handgun, would respond that there was little point in eschewing the technology, that by doing so you only put yourself at the mercy of mean stupid people who had no such compunction. "This particular technological cat," she would say, "is out of the fucking bag." The technological cat she referred to included, Rice supposed, everything from sharpened sticks and steel blades to .22 pistols and semiautomatic carbines with high-capacity magazines, but did not include—yet, anyway—your .50-caliber machine guns, RPGs, MANPADs, Hellfire missiles, Apache attack helicopters, and so on. He told her it was just a line-drawing exercise, like so much else. For him it had come down to a practical approach, a kind of arms race: if the violent thugs he might have to face carried a particular weapon, then he wanted one too.

A few weeks after the course, they drove back up to Phoenix and met an obese white guy with a New Jersey accent who sold gray-market firearms out of his pickup truck, blew three grand on a desert-tan FN SCAR 16S. An upmarket rifle, according to Apryl, would send a signal, and this one was the shit, a new Belgian carbine in 5.56mm with a folding stock, easy to hide in a backpack and handy in a close-quarters firefight, but still accurate past three hundred yards. They also bought a bunch of expensive magazines and a sling and a compact Trijicon scope that cost half as much as the rifle. It was a hell of a weapon, and he carried the thing in his pack for most of a year—taking it out to watch over Apryl's solo meetings with cartel reps—and though he never had to shoot anyone with it, he did grow disturbingly fond of the confidence it gave him, the sense of invincibility. Near the end, when he'd started to suspect Apryl's new friend Mia Cortez wasn't what she claimed to be, he'd buried the rifle way up in the Chiricahuas in a sealed PVC pipe like a good prepper, thinking if he was wrong about Mia he could always go back and dig it up.

SIXTEEN

Rice was half-listening to the news on the clock radio in the kitchen, hoping for a weather forecast, when he remembered this was the morning Sara was supposed to show up. A sports report followed the news. He switched it off and watched out the kitchen window as the sky changed from not quite black to a dark, noncommittal gray. Cloudy, felt like rain.

He told himself again it had been a mistake to call Sara the other day. He was still surprised at himself. After all these months of contented solitude, what, he was suddenly lonely? Nothing to be done about it now. He started a second pot of coffee and decided he'd better shower. When he'd dressed, he found her sitting outside on the front steps, writing in a spiral notebook, her hair in a thick blond ponytail that hung down her back. A blue plastic chest cooler on the porch.

He pushed the screen door open and stepped out. She turned at the noise and smiled.

"There's coffee," he said.

"I smelled it." She held the door while he picked up the cooler. "So where's my cat?"

"I caught a possum instead. He wouldn't get out of the trap. I had to shake him out."

In the kitchen, she transferred several plastic containers and a glass casserole dish from the cooler to the refrigerator. Two bottles of Australian Shiraz appeared on the counter. When she took off her jacket, she caught him looking for the stun gun.

"I left it in the car," she said.

"Leap of faith?"

"Something like that."

They made peanut butter and honey sandwiches to bring for lunch. The sandwiches went into her pack because Rice would be carrying the trail cameras and mounting hardware in his, and he didn't want that stuff to smell like peanut butter. Trail cameras caught enough hell from bears without smelling like food.

Rice kept his pace moderate on the way up the mountain, but Sara had no trouble keeping up. She watched quietly while he attached the first camera to a tree, but he could tell she was restraining herself, and as soon as he reached behind his neck and rubbed some of his own sweat on the case, she started to object. He explained that black bears liked to destroy the cameras, and he'd had to figure out ways of securing and concealing them so you could get some decent data. A little bit of man-scent wouldn't scare them off but might keep them from biting the camera housing. Depended on the bears; some trial and error would be required no matter what.

She asked how he knew this and he explained that he'd worked on a science tech contract for a conservation group deploying and monitoring trail cameras along the Mexican border. This was the study he and Apryl had partially funded, through Byzantine channels Apryl had come up with, to assess the impact of the planned border fence on large mammals that crossed back and forth between U.S. and Mexican habitat, especially the rare ones like jaguars, jaguarundi, and Sonoran pronghorn. They'd nearly finished it when everything went to hell last year, but Rice hadn't seen a published study. Probably got buried by the Homeland Security types.

None of these details were things he would pass along to Sara, of course. Instead, he described the pictures: scores of immigrants, a few smugglers carrying weed in huge improvised backpacks, deer, coyotes, raccoons, coatis, javelinas, the occasional lion and jaguarundi, and a lot of blurry close-ups of curious black bears. During the months they worked on this study, out of thousands of usable fauna images, they'd taken three confirmed jaguar pictures.

Sara deferred to his expertise after that, walking back and forth in front of the cameras so he could adjust the motion detectors and providing an almost unbroken narrative about subjects ranging from the indigenous lizards and salamanders to Zoology Department politics. She talked about her skink project, which compared the genomes of the preserve's coal skink population with those of populations in less protected areas. She'd apparently spent a lot of time chasing the lizards around with nail clippers, snipping off scales or pieces of their tails or toes for DNA samples.

She said she'd been the caretaker for nearly two years, but her teaching schedule had required her to spend a couple of nights a week in Blacksburg during the fall and spring semesters. It was much better, she thought, to have someone at the preserve full-time, especially now, with the bear poaching. He waited for her to elaborate on her story about catching the bear hunters on the property last year, but she still seemed reluctant to talk about it.

By the time they finished with the cameras, the clouds had thickened, a low drizzling overcast, cooler than it had been and threatening real rain. They decided to leave the transect and walk to the cliff overlooking the inner gorge, and they stood near the edge for a while without talking. The view was compelling: a hundred feet down, the ragged, uneven canopy of true old growth filled the canyon. Towering crowns of hemlock, red and white oak, hickory, gum, ash—at least a dozen species, all giant specimens, all shuffling in the wet breeze, hazy with mist. Here and there, bare snags thrust from the canopy like bony fingers. While they watched, the cliffs on the far side disappeared behind low clouds coiling up from the river several miles downstream. The energy coming off that forest, so close now, thrummed in Rice's chest, like he was standing next to a pipe organ.

Sara unpacked their sandwiches and they ate leaning against one of the car-size limestone blocks that lay scattered along the top of the cliff like giant dominos. Rice walked around one of the boulders and into the brush to have a piss, and on the way back he snapped a stick underfoot. A ruffed grouse roared straight up from the rocks nearby and then set its wings, gliding down into the gorge until it flared and dove behind the top of an enormous white pine.

"You're not very stealthy." She produced an apple from her pack and offered it but he shook his head. "We've been scaring wildlife all day," she said.

She was right. They'd seen animals, but only as they fled: a big gang of turkeys had flushed off the fire road, a few deer had thumped away with tails flashing, then near the spring a large animal they couldn't quite see had crashed through thick brush ahead of them, probably a bear. He refrained from mentioning that he didn't have the same experience when he was alone, but it did happen from time to time, and it occurred to him that spooking animals could give away his position to lurking poachers.

She watched his face.

"What are you thinking about? You just lit up."

"Do you know what a ghillie suit is?"

She shook her head.

"Ghillies were Scottish shepherds; they got so good at stealth and camouflage that rich landowners started hiring them as gamekeepers and wardens, they'd prowl around the estates catching poachers. They invented these camouflage suits, big bushy things with leaves and sticks woven into them, and they stink, to mask your scent. Military snipers still use them. If you know what you're doing with a ghillie suit, you can disappear. It's like magic."

"You're kind of a ghillie yourself. If you had one of those suits maybe you could catch the bear poachers." She bit from her apple and after a moment she spoke from behind her hand. "What makes it stink?"

"Anything with a strong scent, I guess. Possum shit, cedar branches. You leave it in the woods for a week, let the bears piss on it."

They were silent for a while. Rice stared at the spot in the forest where the grouse had disappeared and imagined how he would construct a ghillie suit. Sara finished her apple, wrapped the core in a plastic bag, and tucked it into an outside pocket on her pack. The drizzle turned to rain and they pulled their hoods up to shelter their faces.

"Have you ever walked around down there?" Her voice was muffled by the hood. He looked over, watched the rain running in little rivulets down the back of her blue rain shell.

She turned back to look at him. "Rice?"

"No. No, I haven't."

"You're kind of out of it."

"Sorry. I don't sleep much anymore. Usually it's not a problem." He blinked and tried to focus. "I've walked all the way around on the ridges, but I've never climbed down to the bottom. I was told to keep out."

"They told me that, too."

Except for the one habitat survey transect through the northwestern end where the cliffs were lower, the inner gorge was off-limits. In the so-called Anthropocene epoch of global warming and ubiquitous invasives, the idea of keeping any place "pristine" had fallen out of vogue with conservation biologists, but the Traver family had been protecting the place for so long that this most remote part of the preserve served as a practical baseline, a rare—possibly unique—fragment of primordial Appalachian forest where most of the pieces were still in place.

The no-humans-allowed policy was strict, and had become more so over the years as the importance of minimizing intrusion by invasive species had become better understood. You had to apply to the foundation's board of trustees for permission to enter the inner canyon, and you had to have a good reason. As far as Rice knew, no one had applied yet during his tenure, but he'd seen in the logs that one or two individuals or groups were granted access every year. They were mostly scientists, but the foundation had also admitted poets, musicians, painters, photographers, Native American groups, and "spiritual seekers." If Sara's database was successful, he expected they'd start to get a lot more requests. The preserve would become a popular and important research forest. Maybe that's what everyone wanted.

Sara grinned at him from the blue cave of her hood. He didn't think this hard rain could last much longer, and on cue it began to slacken.

"It's only a little after noon," she said. "We can climb down and make it to the river before it gets dark."

He hoped she wasn't serious. All the way to the river would be a hell of a hike. He pictured the maps from the wall of the office, followed the broad creek bottom as it narrowed to a deep cleft after another mile or so, the contour lines in the lower gorge smashed so close together they merged into solid brown shading, the blue line of the creek twisting and turning. Even on a 7.5-minute topo, it was impossible to tell exactly what was there.

A hard breeze moved through the gorge and pushed against the crowns of the giant trees, heaving them back and forth in slow motion. The air was calm where they stood, and the rain had stopped. He pulled his hood back from his head, the usual minor revelation: new sounds, big sky, peripheral vision. After a few moments Sara did the same. She shook the rain from her arms.

"I've always wanted to see what herps are down there. Starr said she could get me permission to go in and do a survey, but I was afraid. I know that sounds strange."

He thought about that. It did seem strange, and he almost asked her what had changed her mind before he caught himself. He hadn't been through a tenth of what she'd experienced, and he felt sometimes like his DNA had been scrambled.

Pale sheets of rain blew in again and obscured the far green slope of the gorge, then the opposite cliff, wind thrashing the tree-tops below them. The sky overhead was a dense swirling gray. He figured it was going to rain off and on all day.

"It's spooky down there," he said. "Ancient." He stood and lifted his pack. "Let's go if we're going."

SEVENTEEN

They found a steep chimney, somewhat less vertical than the cliff face and anchored with big solid rhododendron bushes. Rice descended first, facing the cliff. He tested each foothold and handhold with his weight, but the rock was craggy, with plenty of easy holds, and the springy trunks and branches of the rhododendron were like the rungs of a ladder.

The light changed when they descended below the top of the forest canopy. They paused to rest on a ledge, leaning back against the lichen-crusted rock and gazing out into rain-dripping leaves and great wet reaching branches. The air was cooler, sharp with the scent of hemlock growing along the creek, but something else was different as well. Neither of them spoke. To Rice it seemed they'd crossed into another country, dark and green and primeval. Even the sound of water rushing another hundred feet below sounded unfamiliar and exotic.

When they'd climbed the rest of the way and stood at the base of the cliff, Sara asked in a whisper, "Do you feel that?" He just nodded.

She crept along the creek, peering under stones and pawing

through piles of old leaves, naming unusual species of plants, bugs, herps. With her phone, she began photographing the animals she found. Still whispering, she called him over and pointed out a small black salamander she said was a Jefferson salamander. She covered it back up with leaves, led Rice to a rotting stump where she moved a chunk of rotted wood and pointed out another, larger salamander with vertical stripes on its body, an Eastern tiger salamander.

"I've never seen either one before in the wild," she said. "*Jefferso-nianum* is uncommon, *tigrinium* is rare, it's endangered in Virginia and only found in a few places, certainly not here."

She crawled around some more on her hands and knees, scribbling in her notebook. He leaned against a tree and let his mind drift through the old forest. Now that he was actually in the canyon, the effect seemed less powerful, but only because it was more spread out here, distributed among individual entities. The giant trees were like dormant gods, vibrating with something he couldn't name, not quite sentience, each one different from the others, each telling its own centuries-long story. On the forest floor, chestnut logs dead since the blight had rotted into chest-high berms soft with thick mosses, whispering quietly. Something called out and he turned to face a looming tulip tree, gnarled and bent like an old man, hollowed out by rot, lightning, ancient fires. His skin tingled.

Sara brought him a small snake, about a foot long, khaki-colored with black spots. It slid in no particular hurry from one hand to the other until it gave up trying to get away and coiled around her wrist.

"Mountain earth snake," she said. "*Virginia pulchra*." When she raised the snake up to eye level, Rice reached out, held his forefinger under the snake's cream-colored chin. It rested its head and its tongue flicked in and out, running a sophisticated chemical analysis of his skin.

"I've never seen one of these before," he said.

"You wouldn't have. They're rare, and fossorial. Not even supposed to be in this part of the state. It's like the Lost World down here." The snake became restless again and slid to her other hand. "So many people hate snakes," she murmured, as if to herself. "I think it's because they threaten people's worldview—they're alien, limbless, impossible, black magic: a stick come to life. But maybe we're all sticks come to life." The snake wrapped around her thumb and she addressed its impassive face. "We want to think we're exceptional, ensouled, angel fairies or God's special children. The magic of being animate matter isn't enough."

She paced off a twenty-meter square, marking the corners with sticks, and asked Rice to use her phone and take pictures of what she found. She wanted to do a quick and dirty survey so she could show Starr something relatively systematic when she presented their research proposal. Rice would have to help her, she said. They could do the field work in the spring, and coauthor a paper.

He smiled. "You can't tell Starr about this. We're not supposed to be down here."

"I'll say you got us lost."

Their paper, she said, would establish a new standard for forest vertebrate diversity in the middle Appalachians. She said people had forgotten over the generations what a forest was supposed to look like, that they had come to accept the degraded second-, third-, fourth-growth harvested forests as normal, and the paper would radically disrupt the shifted baselines of complacent conventional perception. A few more places like this might escape the chainsaws. Maybe people would stop being such assholes.

He shook his head at her optimism but she didn't notice. He was beginning to enjoy her company, her idealism, her enthusiasm, even her talkativeness, so he didn't say what he was thinking, didn't say that despite its resilience over millennia, and despite the sentience and power that even now was shaking Rice to his bones, the hard truth was this forest, undimmed since the last glacial, was going to disappear in the not-very-distant future. He'd read those scientific journals that used to sit on the shelves in the office, and the science had seeped into his subconscious, feeding his innate pessimism. First the hemlocks would go; the adelgid wasn't in the gorge yet but it was coming. Without the year-round cover, the creek would heat up, the gorge would become more xeric. Around that time the macroclimate would be seriously destabilizing as multiple feedback loops kicked in, shit nobody's even thought of yet. In his mind he saw the great crowns on fire, a catastrophic, soil-killing burn. Only weeds would grow in the desolate canyon, invasives, r-selected plants taking over. Species homogeneity in a geological eyeblink. Not just here. Everywhere. Wait seventy million years. Repeat.

When Sara offered him the phone, he smiled and took it from her. He said he'd be glad to help with the paper. He said he hoped it would make a difference.

TWO HOURS LATER AND A MILE DOWNSTREAM, RICE CROUCHED AT THE HEAD of a hundred-foot waterfall and drank creek water from his cupped hands. After hesitating, Sara did the same. A few yards away the stream, grown powerful after gathering dozens of tributaries in the canyon, rolled over a sharp stone lip and dropped to the foaming white pool below. A dull roar drifted up and surrounded them. Slick, moss-covered cliffs reared on both sides. A gentle, steady rain pattered on their hoods. The light was failing in the gorge, and they were wet to their thighs from walking in the cold water. Sara had begun shivering. He handed her the fleece pullover from his pack. She demurred but he insisted she put it on, under her shell. A touch of hypothermic clumsiness at the wrong moment could kill them both.

This was the third large falls they'd encountered. They'd had to climb down cliffs alongside the other two, and each time the rock faces had become more dangerous, more sheer, with more lethal exposure. Sara waited with their packs while he scouted a route around this one, edging out along a game trail that led to a foot-wide ledge that he followed until it vanished. He backtracked and climbed down a vertical crack. Twice he lost his holds on the rain-slick rock and skidded to the next ledge where he could stop himself, but there were stretches where a slip like that would have been fatal.

He felt rushed, worried about climbing in the dark, so he only descended far enough to eyeball a route that would get them close to the bottom. Back at the top of the falls he found Sara staring at the water where it bowed into a translucent, green-tinted lens and fell over the edge. She was more exhausted than he was, and she wasn't talking. When she noticed him she took out her phone from its plastic bag in her pack and showed him the screen.

"What am I looking at?"

"No service," she said, smiling.

"You're surprised? Down here?"

She shook her head but didn't elaborate. He rigged a simple belt harness with a nylon strap from his pack, explaining that the exposure was a little scary in places. He asked if she knew how to rappel and she shook her head, which surprised him. It might be better if he just belayed her while she climbed down anyway. He only had the twenty-five-foot rope he kept in his pack for emergencies, so they would have to keep the pitches short.

At the first exposed stretch, he leaned back into a wide vertical crack and braced his feet, paying out the rope as she descended. When she made it to the skinny ledge he'd pointed out, she called "off belay" like he'd told her and gave a thumbs-up. Then she sat with her back against the cliff, passing the rope behind her lower back, around her hips, and called out "Okay," intending to belay him, imitating what he'd done for her. He called back that he was fine, she didn't need to belay him. She gave a taut shake of her head. In the faint light she looked surprised, then outraged. He dropped his end of the rope and climbed down.

When he joined her on the ledge, she shook the coiled rope in his face.

"What the fuck was that?"

He pointed out that they had no chocks or pitons or any sort of protection to anchor her in a belay, and there was no way she could hold him. "If I fall," he said, "I'd pull you down with me."

"Forget it, then." She untied the makeshift harness from around her waist and handed it to him, still attached to the rope.

Her irrational stubbornness was making him weary. "Sara, think. If I belay you it reduces the risk to both of us, to the team . . . to our partnership. But it only works one way. It makes no sense to put you at risk just so you won't feel guilty."

"Guilty? You think I don't want to feel guilty?" She was shouting now, gesticulating, and she nearly lost her balance. She paused when she saw Rice shifting his weight, getting ready to lunge for her. Her hands fell to her sides.

"Your eyes are bugged out," she said, and leaned back into the cold, wet stone of the cliff face, laughing quietly.

The rain had finally stopped, but a brisk wind was ripping up the canyon as the sky cleared and they both were shivering now. He described the signs of hypothermia and asked her to watch him for slurred speech, blue lips.

"We should use the rope here," he said, but she didn't reply. In the weak gray light she peered past her toes at the next stretch of climbing and then started down. She climbed slowly, carefully, but without hesitation. He watched, stowing the clammy wet rope in his pack. He cupped his cold, scraped hands close to his face and breathed on them. How had this all started? They were supposed to set up the trail cameras and hike back to the lodge for dinner. Then their transgressive descent into the forbidden gorge—how Freudian!—his disorienting awareness/hallucination of individual forest spirits, Sara's excitement at finding rare species. A stubborn push downstream, obstacles gradually morphing from fun to exciting to scary. Their situation was such a classic textbook fuckup he was almost embarrassed: overextending on a whim, reckless momentum carrying the victims past several points of no return. Getting dark, growing cold. Dread settled heavily in his gut, a familiar, leaden organ nestled somewhere near his liver. It occurred to him that he and Sara might not be good for each other.

When he caught up he saw they were checkmated, that when he'd scouted their route he'd mistaken the distance to the base of the cliff. The ledge where they stood was still at least twenty feet above the roiling pool at the base of the falls. He couldn't have seen it from above, but the cliff below them was undershot and unclimbable. They stared down at the water.

"It's not as high as an Olympic diving platform," she said.

"But you don't know how deep the water is." The water looked dark, maybe deep, maybe not. Impossible to tell in this light. The other pools they'd bypassed had been five feet deep at most, and five feet wouldn't be enough. "There could be rocks or logs hidden in the water, under the froth. Maybe I can lower you with the rope."

As he said this he looked around and realized it wasn't going to work. The ledge was barely wider than his boots and it sloped downward. No way he could hold her weight just standing here. There was nothing at hand he could use as an anchor, no root, no knobby outcrop. Twenty feet back, the cliff was split by a big vertical crack where he could wedge a leg and a shoulder to brace himself. But his rope was too short for that to work.

It made no sense to stay there, but they waited long enough that his quadriceps began to quiver. Sara's legs were shaking, too. They had to retreat to that crack where they could rest. Then it would be a climb in the dark, returning to the top of the falls, going back the way they'd come down. They would have to use his headlamp. He could lead, slide the headlamp down the rope, belay her as she climbed. If she would even let him. It was just two short pitches. Then they could find some shelter from the rain, spend the night.

He could build a fire. They would try the other side in the morning. At the very least they had to backtrack off this ledge, right now. But he remained paralyzed.

She turned to look at him, gave a tired smile, and jumped, her ponytail lifting from her back and waving above her head as she fell.

His first reaction, lasting only an instant, was that Sara might be more messed up than he'd thought. This was followed by several strobe-flashes, elements of a plan: first assess her consciousness, her injuries, how to get to her without killing himself, make a splint for a broken leg, maybe a tourniquet for a compound fracture—but then his mind went blank and before she had even hit the water he said *fuck it* and jumped off the cliff after her.

The laws of physics limited his fall to a little longer than a second, but his experience didn't square with physics, and he was a long time dropping through the cool wet air. Sara splashed into the pool to his left and went under. He took a deep breath and crouched into a loose cannonball as his boots slapped the surface, trying not to knife through to the bottom. Cold water closed over his head and his pack jerked hard against his shoulders and he was still in a crouch when his feet slammed into the creek bed. It was deeper than five feet, but not much. He pitched backward, his pack cushioning the impact, but most of the breath expelled from his lungs in a big silvery bubble that broke apart and floated away from him. He reached his arms up to the sheen of the surface. The deep thrumming bass note of the falls was a loud voice in his ears and the water was colder than he'd thought possible, the broken plane of light above him like an ice ceiling. He hung there, suspended, listening to the voice, trying to understand it. Then his hands cut through the surface and he pulled himself up, spitting water and inhaling a great raggedy breath and looking for Sara.

He was sure she would be hurt, a broken leg, an ankle. She hadn't even aimed for the deepest part of the pool. But as he swung around to face downstream, drifting with the current toward the shallows at the end of the pool, Sara was there, pants slicked to her legs, pack dangling from an elbow, stepping out onto wet gravel and looking around, shivering and dripping, hair hanging flat and wet down her back. Her eyes were wide, and in the last bluish light of the afterglow she looked rapt, exhilarated. She smiled at him and raised her arm to point at the first man-made object they'd seen since they'd left the lodge—a heavy rusted iron pipe protruding from the far side of the pool. It was the water intake for a small summer camp on the Dutch River someone had run back in the twenties. The place had folded during the Depression and the Traver family had acquired the property to add to the preserve.

He found his feet and waded out to stand beside her. "I know where we are," he said.

EIGHTEEN

They sat side by side at the kitchen table stabbing with forks into an open container of cold lasagna. It was after 1 A.M. The first bottle of Shiraz was almost empty.

The hour of walking from the river to the lodge in the dark, using trails Rice knew well, had passed in exhausted silence. Sara had carried a bag into the unused bedroom to change into dry clothes and hadn't come out. Rice had changed and then fallen asleep on the sofa, waking after midnight from a dream of falling in the canyon. He'd knocked on Sara's door to see if she wanted to eat and she'd come out bleary-eyed a few minutes later.

The lasagna wasn't authentic but Sara had gone to some trouble to make it healthy, with whole wheat pasta, spinach and mushrooms, pine nuts, ground turkey. It was the first decent food Rice had encountered in a long while and he overate spectacularly.

"I can't fit any more," he said, setting his fork on the table.

Sara peered into the glass dish. "This was supposed to last you a while."

When she stood, her chair tipped over, and before he could stop himself he reached out to catch it. He froze, remembering her reaction in the closet that first day. He held the chair, waiting for the elbow, but it didn't come, and after a moment she smiled. "Your face," she said. "You look like you're waiting for a grenade to go off."

He mumbled something about not wanting to spook her.

She crossed her arms, seemed to find him amusing. "You know, I've got pretty good radar, and I can tell you're not going to hit on me."

He raised an eyebrow at the abrupt conversational turn but couldn't think of a response. This wasn't comfortable territory.

"I get hit on a lot, I think guys decide I'm right there in that sweet spot of moderately good-looking but not beautiful and undoubtedly oh so grateful for the male attention. Guys who know I was raped have managed to restrain themselves recently, but with you, it's not even on the table. I'm not complaining, it's a big part of why I'm okay being alone with you. But I'm curious. You're hardly a eunuch, and you're not gay."

"Nope. Are you?"

"Some guys think I am. I've sure tried it."

"Really?"

"Oh, great, suddenly you're interested."

He started to object but she bugged her eyes and said "Men!" and went back to watching him. The wine had disinhibited her, and this scientific inquisitiveness made him squirm. He felt some sympathy for the skinks she studied. He watched her hands, half-expecting her to draw nail clippers from a pocket and come at him for a DNA sample.

"So am I right? How's my radar?"

"You're right. I'm taking a break from all that." He stopped, thinking it hadn't been a year, that it seemed impossible the world could actually circle back to November again. All that shit last year should've unsprung the calendar, slinging him in a straight line through unfamiliar seasons toward whatever hell or oblivion waited for him.

"Oh, no. I'm sorry." She must've seen it in his face. "Nasty breakup?"

"Yeah."

"It's okay if you don't want to talk about it."

He didn't reply. The investigator's phrase "sexualized torture-killing" came to mind, and he knew if anyone was qualified to hear him talk about this it was Sara. Maybe someday.

She replaced the top on the depleted dish of lasagna and opened the refrigerator, her face composed and pale in the yellow light from inside. He couldn't tell if she was disappointed. When she turned back she frowned at him.

"Now you're staring at me."

She was right, he was staring. Making a decision.

"The bear hunters you caught on the property, when you called the game warden. Big stocky guys, red hair?"

"Uh-huh. Their dad runs that store in Stumpf."

"Did they threaten you?" He was afraid this might put her off, but she seemed to trust him now and didn't hesitate.

"Of course they did. They're assholes. I told the sheriff, and sure enough they all had alibis the night I was attacked. He said he had to cross those guys off."

"Alibis can't be hard to come by around here. The Stillers are bush-league drug dealers with violent inclinations. If they're selling bear parts, too, poaching up here and selling the parts, they had a motive to want to hurt you, run you off."

"Ha," she said, not really laughing. "That sure backfired."

"How?"

"They got you instead."

He thought about the dead bear the mushroom picker had showed him, his failed undercover adventure with the gall buyer. "So far I haven't slowed them down much."

She didn't respond but her look was challenging, and just a

little bit fierce, like she wished she could catch those guys on the mountain again. Self-Defense Sara taking them down with flying elbows and crackling stun gun. Bear poachers pissing their pants. They might be better off with Rice as the caretaker.

"I'm going to have a talk with those guys," he said.

"Who, the Stillers?"

He looked at her. Shrugged.

"They're not going to talk to *you*," she said.

NINETEEN

Just south of the Camino del Diablo and the southern edge of the Cabeza Prieta Wilderness, a few hundred yards into Sonora, Mexico, sometime after 4 A.M.

Rice held his flashlight in his teeth and pulled on a pair of leather gloves. Watching for scorpions, he pulled flood-packed trash, brush, and cholla pieces away from the northern end of a culvert under Federal Highway 2, eventually uncovering a lattice of welded rebar. It looked solid, but he tugged on it once, then rared back and kicked it with his boot, setting off a rattlesnake some ways into the dark culvert. He kicked again, but the grate didn't budge. He cut his light and stepped away from the concrete abutment, into the light of a waning gibbous moon.

"Fuck," Apryl whispered behind him.

A tractor-trailer roared past overhead. When the sound of the truck had receded, the rattlesnake was still buzzing. Must be a western diamondback, Rice thought. He'd brought a snake stick, but they had no time or tools for the rebar, and they were going to have to cross the highway. He preferred the rattlesnake. Behind them, past the bollards lined up along the border, was one of the most remote and forbidding areas of the continental United States. But here in Mexico, well before first light, the machinery of commerce was surprisingly busy.

Apryl was peeking up above the abutments, watching for the next traffic. He decided to try her one last time.

"It's a sign," he said. "We have to back off."

She didn't even look at him. "Mia said it might be blocked. It's not a big deal, the surveillance here is broken half the time. Let's go."

Bent at the waist, she ran up to the tarmac and sprinted across. Feeling like an armadillo, Rice followed, noting headlights a quarter mile off, coming from the east. Truckers probably saw lots of people scurrying across this highway. Mostly going the other direction.

Mia Cortez, their cartel contact on the U.S. side for the past few months, had set up this meeting, supposedly with people who were important in the narco-government of Sonora and who had need of Apryl and Rice's unique services. Mia had risen to some sort of management position in the cartel's Chicago operation, and she was smart, and she knew a lot of people on the Mexican side. She even helped launder Rice and Apryl's money to fund the border wall study. But Rice had always had a bad feeling about her, and he and Apryl had nearly broken up over Mia Cortez. The only part of the argument about this meeting that he'd won was his insistence that they leave their firearms in the United States, buried up in the Chiricahuas. You seriously did not want to be arrested with a gun in Mexico.

They'd camped last night near Quitobaquito Springs so they could arrive at the meeting place early enough to have a look around. Mia had planned to drive down from Phoenix. Rice's certainty that today's plan would be disastrous had bordered on premonition even before Mia had texted Apryl after midnight, saying she was held up in the city and wouldn't make it in time. They couldn't miss the meeting, she texted, couldn't be late, so Apryl and Rice had to go without her. Rice had said absolutely not, this is fucked, we abort, but Apryl asked him to trust her judgment the way she had trusted his for the past year, and he'd decided that if he couldn't talk her out of this debacle, he would walk right into it with her.

South of the highway, they had to cross a half mile of mostly flat ground to the tamarisk thicket along the nearly dry Rio Sonoyta. They walked fast through nothing but knee-high saltbush for cover, due south by Rice's compass, hunched over and finding what shadows the land gave them. In the tamarisk, they searched by moonlight for twenty minutes before they found the big stone cairn, river stones piled in a neat pyramid up out of the riverbed. It had been there for a while; Rice imagined some kid with stonemason skills marking the place he first got laid. Or maybe it was someone's point of departure from old Mexico, headed for the promise of el Norte.

The clients would be watching for them at the cairn. They might or might not be asked to carry one or more dry bags back across the border. Mia would know what to do with the bags.

Apryl watched the cairn while Rice headed out to scout a perimeter. It didn't take him long to find what he'd expected: two rattletrap topless Broncos with big tires, four federales lounging in each, whispering and smoking. He could have found them with his eyes closed.

At the cairn, he took Apryl by the hand and led her deeper into the cover of the thicket.

"Federales," he whispered in her ear. "Quarter mile downstream."

"That's who we're meeting, Rice."

He stared at her.

"It's the feds, on both sides. Off the books. I can't tell you more than that, not now. The police are probably here for security."

"Wait, what?" He was apoplectic. Mia Cortez had stolen Apryl's brain. "She told you that? I knew she was a fucking cop. Come with me."

At the riverbank downstream, they crawled to the edge of the thicket, and he handed her his binoculars.

"These guys are not our clients. They're here to arrest us."

She watched them for a while. She handed the binoculars back to Rice without speaking.

"We have to go back," he said. "Now. It's going to get light soon."

They backtracked to the edge of the tamarisk. The highway looked clear in both directions, and they were jogging across the bare flats, halfway to the culvert, when four police cars approached in the eastbound lane, lights flashing.

"Might not be for us," he said, knowing they were. He and Apryl flattened themselves on the sandy ground behind a small rise.

The police cars slowed and pulled off the side of the highway, two on each side of the culvert. A big black SUV pulled around in front of the lead police car. Back in the river bottom, a poorly muffled engine cranked, then another. They wound up, whining and protesting, as the Broncos climbed the riverbank in low gear.

The takedown was perfectly civilized, probably in part because two DEA agents had come along to assist. Rice was glad he and Apryl hadn't brought their guns, as there was really no reason to arrest them, but then the DEA guys turned to face the United States of America and the Mexican captain produced two condoms filled with something, presumably cocaine, and dropped them into Rice's backpack. The captain ushered Rice into one of the Mexican vehicles while the two agents put Apryl in the Suburban and sped off toward the border crossing at Lukeville.

TWENTY

ilton Stiller ran his general store in a hundred-year-old painted clapboard building crouched on a low bank above the Dutch River. Inside, a single wide room tilted slightly from the front door to the back, where a small porch cantilevered out over the riverbank. Too-bright fluorescent lights hung from the ceiling, humming and flickering. In that light the deer and bear heads watching from the walls looked shocked, interrogated. A walk-in refrigerator filled with Stiller's impressive stock of beer was in a more recent addition to the old building—in the summer it felt like a little cube of Antarctica magically transported to the mountains of Virginia. On the doorjamb at the store's entrance, dates were stenciled beside faint watermarks from past floods. The highest was level with Rice's chest: November 5, 1985. The oldest was waist high, from October 17, 1927.

The girl working the register looked high school age to Rice, but really he couldn't tell anymore. She was talking to a tall, languid fellow leaning over the counter, their heads close together. Blurry blue prison tats on his arms, though he seemed young for that. They both smiled at Rice when he came in, plenty friendly, must not recognize him. He asked if they knew where he could find DeWayne or his brother.

"Which one?" the kid asked, grinning.

Rice grinned back. "The one that's not in prison."

"Nardo," he said, and looked at the girl.

"I ain't seen 'em all week. They party over at Ape Hanger if you want to check later."

"Didn't know they had bikes."

She laughed. "They don't, yet. They hangaround with a guy in—" Her boyfriend said "Hup" without looking at her and she stopped with her mouth open. Then she shut it.

The boyfriend spoke to Rice. "Mister, if you're lookin' to score I can help you with that."

Rice shook his head, said he had to talk to DeWayne and them about something in particular. He left, and drove the forty minutes to Clifton, and found the bar on a side street not far from the interstate. Parked outside were two Harleys and a dualie Chevy pickup with those exaggerated woman-silhouette mudflaps— secondary sex characteristics of the female human as imagined by juvenile males. Neon signs in the bar's blacked-out windows advertised cheap beer. The girl at the store had said "hangaround" as one word, the stress on *hang*, which meant the Stillers were hoping to join a club. If they were looking to expand their drug business, which he assumed they were, the club would be one of the so-called outlaw motorcycle gangs.

Again he left his pistol in the truck. There wouldn't be any trouble in here. Rice had never had a problem with bikers, and whenever he'd ventured into their world they had always treated him reasonably well. He disliked the decibel level of their bikes and he found the complicated high-school-for-grown-ups social structure of the clubs a little ridiculous, but even the outlaw gangs were less psychotically violent than the cartels, and the fight-the-mainstream ethos of their subculture suited him just fine.

When he sat at the bar he got a few slow glances but he was more comfortable here than he'd been at the Beer & Eat, certainly more at home than he was at the coffee shop in Blakely. Sometimes the students in the Bean looked up glassy-eyed from their phones and stared as if a grizzly bear had come through the door.

The pudgy bartender had an open, guileless face, young, not the biker-bar stereotype. He greeted Rice like a regular and Rice ordered Bud in a bottle and a shot of Wild Turkey and turned on his stool to check out the other patrons. A slow afternoon: a couple of two-tops and three guys and a young girl together at the bar. The music was headbanger metal but not too loud, not yet.

He'd had no reason to care about the motorcycle clubs in the area, but now he was curious. The bartender hadn't tried to make conversation, maybe he'd learned not to, and Rice had to wave him over.

"So what are the colors around here?"

"You out of state?"

Rice nodded. "I wrecked my bike couple years back and ain't been riding in a while. Finally found my next ride, sent the deposit today. I'll be out there on my own and I want to know what's up."

"It's bones and pistons but you don't see 'em much. More guys are in the support clubs. You'll be okay."

Rice knew the club; he'd dealt with them a few times in Arizona. Definitely an outlaw gang, one of the bigger ones, generally well organized and deep into the usual criminal shit.

"I'm not worried," he said. "It's a matter of respect."

"Hear that."

The bartender set up another beer and shot without Rice asking. This would be the most whiskey he'd had in a long time.

"What's the ride?"

"What?"

"The bike you're gettin." He was watching Rice sidelong. The little shit is testing me, Rice thought. He almost laughed.

"'81 Shovelhead. Needs some work." This was the exact bike Apryl had bought and promptly wrecked soon after Rice started working with her. Her one indiscretion.

The bartender brightened at this. "'81 Shovelhead," he repeated. "That sounds all right to me."

"I'll be glad to get back out there," Rice said.

"Just watch out for the tourists."

Rice shook his head, not understanding.

"You know, the *SOA* fanboys. They roll up in here weekends, act like they're into bikes and shit, they're scouting for 'one per-centers.'" He made air quotes and shook his head, the world-weary insider with a baby face. "They see some dude with a beard and cuts and they're trying to sneak pictures with their phones. I got to throw them out so they don't get the shit beat out of them."

"Fuck is *SOA?*"

"It's on TV. It's about a club, you ain't seen it?"

"No, I don't get to watch much television."

"Hollywood bullshit." He shook his head, but then he paused and glanced over Rice's shoulder at the tables, lowered his voice. "Sometimes it's okay." He pulled out his phone and pressed and swiped at the screen with his thumbs, handed it across the bar. A promo shot of a strong-looking brunette in sunglasses: streaked hair, middle-aged, sexy. A little trashy, enough to prompt the imagination.

"That's the club president's old lady. On the show. She's like sixty but tell me you wouldn't hit that."

Rice looked again, feeling out of touch, and handed the phone back. "Shit, son, that woman would fuck you to *death*."

"Ho!" the bartender said. "Yes, she would."

He said it again as he left to take care of the increasingly rowdy kids at the other end of the bar. They were drinking draft beer, pitchers, getting after it at three in the afternoon. Then again, so was Rice. His head was expanding like a balloon, what liquor did to him. Should've had something to eat before he left the preserve. They didn't seem to serve food here. When he'd finished with the others, the bartender drifted back to Rice, rolling his eyes. He seemed to think Rice was the real deal.

Rice looked at his watch. "I was supposed to meet someone but I guess I'm too early. You know the Stillers? DeWayne, Nardo?"

"I know of 'em. They come in here. Them and their buddy."

"Skinny fucker?"

The bartender laughed. "Yeah that's him. Jesse. I wouldn't mess with him though."

"They said they were joining a club."

"Shit. They're too good for the support clubs, got hooked up as prospects with this one local full patch, probably the only one in the county."

"Who is that?"

But the bartender just shook his head and smiled, and Rice smiled back. No hard feelings.

"I figured they were just hangarounds."

"They say they're prospects. They're pretty tight with this guy." He shrugged. "Might be bullshit."

As Rice understood it, if you wanted to be in one of the clubs you had to start by hanging around in places where the members and their entourage went to party. You did what you could to ingratiate yourself, and if they liked you they'd take you on as a "prospect," a probationary status involving slave labor and a rougher version of fraternity hazing. It could go on for years, but if you were fit to join, eventually they let you into the brotherhood. It was all deadly serious, life-and-death for some folks.

He was still feeling the whiskey and figured he'd better get out of there before he wanted a third. He paid, left a good tip, and as he was walking away his new buddy called out that he had to bring that Shovelhead by when he got it. Rice nodded and pushed the door, squinting at the bright afternoon. Maybe he should buy a bike. The caretaker of the Turk Mountain Preserve ripping up Turpin County on a Harley, frightening the wildlife. STP would love it.

When he got to his truck, the driver's-side window had been smashed, glass shards on the seat and in the gravel, glinting in the sun. He tried the door but it was still locked, so he used his key. Nothing inside was disturbed. His pistol was still in its hiding place. Wasn't really anything else to steal.

He walked all around the truck but found no other damage. The hot parking lot was empty, the same bikes parked in the shade, the big pickup. Quiet except for traffic noise from the interstate. He found a hammer in the junk behind his seat and knocked out the rest of the window, brushed the glass from the upholstery. Sat and shut the door and waited a moment before turning the key, beer and whiskey coloring this new development. He felt giddy, thinking it didn't take much to get people's attention around here.

TWENTY-ONE

The skeleton had been disarticulated by coyotes and stripped clean by smaller scavengers. With no skin in the way, it hadn't taken long. Dark red bones lay scattered among the pine needles; the spine had been dragged away from the tree but was still partly intact, still connected to the ribs arcing up from a drift of fallen oak leaves. The remnant of some viscera even the vultures wouldn't eat hung desiccated from the rack of the rib cage like foul jerky.

Rice squatted on his heels beside the big pine tree, remembering the day the mushroom picker had shown him the bear. It seemed a long time ago, but could only have been a couple of weeks. He was sleeping less and less and the passage of time had become dreamlike, hard to track. He had come here partly to make sure his afternoon with the mushroom picker hadn't been a hallucination.

The sun felt warm on his neck but the light was watery and autumnal, the dusty carpet of pine needles glowing in sunlit patches. Today was Saturday, so he and Sara had walked down the canyon just a few days ago. He reached his hand down and dug through the duff to the soil. It was cool, not quite moist. All that rain had dried up fast, still droughty in this part of the state. A high-pressure system had settled in and the sky in the north held a deep, impenetrable blue. Cottony balls of cumulus decorated the western horizon. Last night had threatened frost, and with no moon the Milky Way had swarmed bright and animate across the sky.

Yesterday he'd found a junkyard north of Clifton with a window that would fit his truck, and they only charged him fifty bucks plus another fifty to install it. Usually he would put off fixing something like that but he couldn't afford to be pulled over. The junkyard guy said that kind of daylight vandalism would be quick, in and out: probably they pulled up alongside and the passenger reached out the window with a hammer, didn't even get out of the vehicle. He asked Rice if he had enemies and Rice had said not that he knew of, but he was sure those kids at the store had called the Stillers the minute Rice walked out the door. On the way back from the junkyard he'd stopped off at the store looking for the young couple, but old Bilton Stiller was ensconced in his usual spot at the register and refused to give Rice their names or tell him where his boys lived or much of anything else. After that, an uneventful hamburger dinner at the Beer & Eat, which was packed again on Friday evening. He'd sat at a table by a window so he could keep an eye on his truck. His several attempts at conversation had gone nowhere. He'd waited until near closing, nursing a third beer, but the place had remained bereft of Stillers.

He pushed off the pine trunk and stood. When he tugged on a rib, the bear's spine and rib cage lifted from the leaves in a piece, surprisingly light and releasing a weak stench of rot. He considered the other bones lying on the ground, thinking he should choose one to carry back with him, add it to his collection in the office. The skull would be best, but the poacher had taken the head with the skin. He kicked around in the leaves and pine needles for a while, looking for a femur or some other large bone until he began to feel a distinct queasiness. It occurred to him that pilfering bear bones might not be altogether appropriate. He wondered why, but was no less certain for not knowing. Now that he acknowledged it, the old feeling of judgment was powerful, raising the hair on his arms. He glanced around at the thicket, half-expecting to see a black bear face peering at him. He told himself for the hundredth time that he wasn't becoming superstitious so much as submitting to an undeniable blurring around the edges of so-called reality.

He was pushing through the brush, headed back toward the fire road, when he first heard it: a thin, drawn-out cry behind him, far off, somewhere down in the canyon, down in the ancient forest. He caught his breath and listened, stilled his feet in the noisy leaves.

Not a familiar sound. He waited, tried to replay it in his mind, but he had no idea what it might have been. He breathed, and cupped his hands behind his ears to help him hear. It had been a still day, and for the first time all afternoon the air began to move, a warm breeze on his face, lifting up out of the gorge like the exhalation of a god. It smelled of moss and decaying leaves, astringent pine and hemlock. The sound it made in the pine boughs was low and sad. It died, leaving behind a faint white noise from the waterfalls. Then the high falsetto he'd heard before, modulating into a second, deeper syllable—a hound's mournful bay. Another, farther away.

He tripped once on a cat's claw vine, but laurel branches broke his fall and he pushed to his feet and ran on. The slope steepened, laurel and rhododendron thicket giving way to open pine and oak forest, and soon he was running too fast, out of control. He knew he should stop, lean against a tree, take a breath, and reimpose his will over his body, but his legs seemed to have achieved independent volition, as if he'd grown a secondary, sauropod brain in his lower back that had chosen today to stage its coup and now the rest of him had to go along.

A fallen log appeared in his path, and he stutter-stepped and leaped over it, sailing in the air before he touched down again, sliding in the soft loam and fallen leaves, nearly falling. He regained his balance, stutter-stepped, jumped again, flying another ten feet, landing in a controlled slide. In this way he flew down the side of the mountain, contorting his body in midair to avoid the tree trunks that flashed past his face. He lost any sense of time or distance, though he knew he was approaching the forbidden heart of the preserve. The hounds' voices were louder here, and over the crash of his feet in the leaves they echoed like sirens, screams of agony, now an underwater sound like whales singing. Finally, inevitably, his foot landed on a slick root hidden in the leaves and slid out from under him. He went down hard on his butt, bounced once, skidded and tumbled over and over until he slammed into the trunk of a hemlock.

The impact knocked the wind out of him and he lay still for a moment, trying to breathe. The hounds had gone quiet. His ribs hurt where he had hit the tree, and something from his pack had poked him in the back, but nothing seemed to be broken, and he felt none of the lightheaded shocky nausea that came with serious injury. He sat up and hyperventilated to oxygenate his blood, and after a while his head cleared. The trees were big here, nearly as big as they were in the inner gorge, and the light was subdued, crepuscular, the air moist, earthy. The stream rushed somewhere farther down.

His knee ached and his thighs quivered as he stood, turned to look around the other side of the hemlock, toward the sound of the water. There, ten yards farther, was the cliff, a leaping green distance falling away to thick forest in the gorge. He shambled weak-legged to the edge, peered over at sheer limestone, the streambed way down there, water in silvery skeins among tiny moss-covered boulders. This place was just upstream from where he and Sara had climbed down into the canyon. Butterfly wings tickled his gut as a giant hand swept him from behind, urging him forward, and he backpedaled away from the cliff, sat back down in the leaves. If he hadn't fallen when he did . . . he saw himself running off the edge like a character in a cartoon, legs kicking and arms spinning windmills as he fell in a graceful arc. He might never have been found way down here. He would have died, broken on the rocks, and his carcass would have polluted the water for months, probably sickening the trout downstream.

A red squirrel chattered nearby. His pulse quieted in his ears, but another rhythmic sound, off-kilter with his heartbeat, was coming from the slope behind. He turned. A dog peered at him from behind a tree trunk, panting with its tongue out and lips drawn back in a dog smile. It barked twice and started downslope toward him. A female with a wavy white-and-liver coat, she looked more setter than hound. She wore a collar with a red, fist-size cylinder waggling a short wire antenna. He called and she crept to him and rested her head on his leg. He stroked her neck, her soft white cheek splashed with chestnut. While he examined her collar and the transmitter, she sniffed daintily at his hands, his pants, his ears. The brass tag said *Dempsey Boger, 221 Sycamore Creek Road, Wanless, VA.* There was a phone number.

"What the hell, Dempsey?" The setter looked a question at him. "Not your fault," he said. He unbuckled her collar, not sure what he planned to do with it. There was actually a law against removing radio collars; he'd come across it during his research session at the Bean. It had been passed, he imagined, at the behest of some unholy alliance between bear and raccoon hunters on one side of the room and natty fox hunters on the other, each group trying to pretend the other wasn't there.

The setter perked her ears and turned upstream. A faint clamor of growling and barking, a pack of dogs squabbling somewhere off to the west. He stood and headed toward the noise, the setter quartering back and forth in front of him with her nose to the ground as if they were grouse hunting. Before long, they walked into bad air, a throat-closing stink, nastier than the usual carcass smell, decaying flesh overlaid with cloying sweetness. It was nearly visible, and he headed toward the source as surely as if he were following a plume of smoke.

Two animals appeared from the right, black-and-tan hounds running with their noses high. They shied when they noticed Rice, but then they sat down to watch him. "Com'ere, boys," he said. They wagged their tails. One bayed brokenheartedly. Three more lighter-colored hounds loped fast across the slope, nearly falling over the first two. They all ran off together toward the stench. All wore transmitter collars.

Licorice. That's what the sweetness was. He realized he was smelling bear bait. Dempsey had said the dead bears he'd found had been baited, and Rice had looked it up online: hunters would haul a sack of rotten food into the woods and hide nearby to shoot hyperphagic bears drawn by the stink of megacalories. He crouched behind a big shagbark hickory on the crest of a ridge and scanned the forest below. The growls and barking grew louder, and the setter hovered close by. She seemed slight and timid, and he wondered how she survived in a pack of bear hounds.

There they were, a dozen hounds milling around, agitated by something hidden behind a small rise. In the foreground, an enormous cow head buzzing with flies and yellowjackets hung fifteen feet in the air, a dirty white Charolais with a short section of iron rebar driven through its eyes and suspended from a wire. It twisted slowly in the light breeze: left, right, left, as if searching for something in the canopy overhead. Directly underneath, deadfall logs and branches had been gathered into a loose square enclosure where three of the hounds scratched and snuffled in the bare dirt. Most of the dogs were farther uphill. He backed down below the crest of the ridge and jogged to the north, the setter following behind like a co-conspirator. They crawled up to hide behind a limestone outcrop and watch the scene downslope.

The dogs had quieted, and he wondered if they'd scented him, but none seemed to be looking his way. This time he saw it, past the cow's head, a black bear carcass lay in a little clearing, the rest of the hounds gathered around.

"Fuck me," he said, and the setter gave him another look.

"Not your fault. I guess."

One of the hounds, a huge, fawn-colored male with a black head, was biting and pulling at the bear's ear, bracing all four feet and hauling backward, dragging the stiff carcass a few feet, stopping to turn and snap at any of the others that got too close. The dog looked as big as a steer and had the heavy skull and jowls of a mastiff. Another knot of hounds were worrying a second, much larger bear carcass another hundred yards or so past the first.

Nobody was around, no humans with the hounds. He stood and walked down the ridge to the first carcass. The big yellow hound noticed him and woofed and stood glaring with his black head low, heavy lips like black curtains pulled away from his thick yellow canines. He growled in a voice so deep and portentous that the back of Rice's neck actually tingled, the residual hairs lifting in a lame imitation of the dog's spiky ruff that stood up in a ridge all the way down his back. They stared at each other, two mammals facing off at a kill, until one of the other hounds saw an opening and lunged at the carcass. The mastiff roared and bowled into it with his shoulder, sending it tumbling, but all in the same motion he whirled back to face Rice, apparently having decided the human was the primary threat to his possession of the dead bear.

"All yours, big fella." Rice walked past him, toward the other carcass. Several of the hounds slunk to him for attention, whining and rolling over on their backs, sliding downslope in the dry leaves. He scratched their bellies and removed their transmitter collars, which he stowed in his pack. A few of the dogs were Dempsey Boger's, but most wore no ID tag at all. They all smelled faintly of skunk.

Neither of the bear carcasses had been skinned, but the paws were missing and their abdomens had been slit open. Looked like they had been dead awhile, so the hounds had nothing to do with this. The second carcass was a big male, 350 pounds or better, and it might've been dead a day or two longer than the smaller one. The entry wound was high on the rib cage, consistent with a shooting vantage up in a tree. Rice opened his old Buck lockback and scratched at the wound with the blade, picking away the blood-matted hair. Some sort of white powder was mixed in with the dried blood, and the wound was a gaping X shape rather than the neat entrance hole made by a bullet. He tried to remember what the wound had looked like on the skinned carcass the mushroom picker had shown him, but he hadn't even thought to look for it.

He stood next to the carcass, the setter and three other hounds gathered round him. While he'd been out chasing buyers and bikers and redneck gangsters, someone had come on the preserve and killed these bears. He'd neglected his job, failed to meet his responsibilities.

Inside the rough log bait structure, three hounds were snuffling up crumbs from some sort of pastry, smears of white sugar frosting, sticky residue of honey on packed dirt licked smooth. The licorice smell came from a dense, dark oil that had been smeared on several tree trunks about six feet off the ground, some of the smears gouged with claw marks. A hound stood up on his hind legs and gave a perfunctory leap in the direction of the cow's head. Hung that far up, it was inaccessible and must have driven the bears mad. More searching turned up marks on an oak trunk from climbing spikes. They led to a thick horizontal branch, where the shooter had waited.

The poachers must be using night-vision scopes or goggles so they could kill the bears in the dark with quiet crossbows, and they probably only came onto the property after midnight. Rice usually stayed out after dark but not all night. Not every night. That's why he hadn't seen or heard them. The equipment wasn't as expensive as it used to be. In southern Arizona, the Border Patrol folks had military-grade night vision and drove around at night with their lights off hunting illegals. The better-heeled vigilante groups had civilian stuff that was nearly as good, and recently the narcos and some of the coyotes had it, too. Only the poor illegals and lower-echelon mules were blind in the dark. He and Apryl had been planning to buy a scope when they were arrested.

He didn't disturb the bait structure, and he used a stick to obscure his boot prints in the dirt underneath the cow head.

The hounds seemed to have lost interest in the carcasses—live bears were presumably more fun—and they started wandering off. These hounds must have stumbled on the bait and the carcasses; they had nothing to do with the poaching, though he was sure some of the people running them were involved.

Rice followed mindlessly for a while, walking along behind the setter. She led him upstream to where the cliff guarding the inner gorge wasn't as high, then past a screen of chest-high laurel to a steep game trail. He clambered down after her to the stream, where a few of the others were already drinking.

He lay on a flat boulder at the edge to dip his face in the current and drink, his teeth nearly shattering from the cold. Thick moss covering the rocks felt soft and cool on his belly, and the air was wet with spray from a small waterfall plunging a dozen yards upstream. All of the hounds—even the standoffish mastiff—had followed and were drinking with him now, as if the presence of a strange human absolved them of any further need to look for bears. Or maybe finding the carcasses had made the whole enterprise seem moot. Who knew? He rolled over on his back and stared up into the thick, dark tangles of hemlock arcing over the stream and, far above, green-gold poplar leaves brushing the blue roof of sky. The leaves up there seemed remote as stars, incidental to the massive trunks and branches supporting them.

The setter curled up next to him, and the others settled in pockets of hemlock needles among the rocks. It was easy to lie there without thinking—the world was cool rock, rushing water, dogs panting. None of them were supposed to be down here, of course. He had to get the hounds out of the canyon and off the property. He got up and removed a few more of their radio collars and put them in his pack—if he couldn't find the bear hunters, he could make them come to him.

TWENTY-TWO

He sat with a beer on the front porch steps, watching the driveway. The setter and five of the hounds lay in the shade, the others having run off with the mastiff on the way home. Rice had put out a bucket of water and he'd fed the dogs an old can of Vienna sausages he'd found in the pantry. Eleven radio collars lay interlocked in a pile at the top of the steps, silently transmitting their whereabouts. He'd left his .45 in the drawer by his bed, sticking to his gun policy even though an angry mob of bear hunters should be traipsing up the driveway any minute now. He hoped the three-mile climb from the front gate would take some of the starch out.

He'd marked the bait station on the map in the office. It wasn't close to any vehicular access, which puzzled him, and scuttled his assumptions about where to look for the bear poachers. The slope above the bait was steep and thick with deadfall in places, not suited for an ATV. On the other hand, it was a smart place for bait because it was close enough to the inner gorge to attract the bears that sheltered down there. The poachers could effectively hunt the most remote and protected part of the preserve without having to climb up and down the cliffs.

To his right, the sun hung close above the lower flank of Turk Mountain, shooting out tiny rays like quills when he squinted. The sun had reached the horizon, and the crickets slowed their chirping as the air began to cool. Sunset and sunrise, he thought, the edges of the day, were the only times you could see the sun move. It touched the top of the ridge and began to disappear. He reminded himself that it was the earth's rotation, that the sun itself only seemed to move, but what difference did that make? He felt he was watching time itself pass. The last bright quarter shrank to an eighth, a six-teenth, a point, and then nothing, the sun's dark negative lingering on his retina.

Jesus, did it move that fast all day long? He imagined the sun rushing across the sky, trailing a tail of fire like a gigantic comet, and no one looking up, no one noticing. Out in the valley, the moun-tain's shadow crept inexorably toward the Blue Ridge, a spreading blue shade that consumed the geometric patchwork of rolling farm-land and woodlots. A crow he couldn't see called from the woods in couplets. Caw-caw, caw-caw, caw-caw. Like some kind of code.

Above the lodge, the resident chimney swifts whirled in a twit-tering gyre. Had to be a hundred of them, all roosting at night in the big stone flue. The juveniles were strong flyers now, and the birds would leave soon on their trans-hemispheric migration. The flock spun faster and faster. Rice imagined they were gathering centrifugal force, enough to hurl them seven thousand miles south to the Amazon basin. Feeling hopelessly provincial, he toasted the flock's safe journey with the last of his beer, tossed the can toward the screen door behind him, and reached over to grab number two where he'd left it beside the railing post. Popped it open, still cold and sweating. He liked this time of day, the sun gone and the world in a melancholy bluish cast. The calendar said tomorrow would be the autumnal equinox, day and night in nearly perfect balance as this part of the world tilted farther away from the sun, ending the fecund riot of summer.

The dogs all leaped up at once as if the ground were suddenly electrified and stood in the fire road baying in the direction of the mountain. When they paused for breath Rice heard the throaty putt-putt-putt of two-stroke engines, ATVs making their slow way down the overgrown switchbacks. The arrogant bastards must've cut down STP's new fence at the end of the fire road. They couldn't have breached the Forest Service gate: the steel posts were set in concrete, and a welded steel box protected the padlock. You would have to reach your hand up into the box, remove a big active wasp nest, and feel around with the key to open the thing.

Three four-wheelers drove past the cabin and into the gravel parking area. The dogs had backed into the mowed grass in front of the lodge, still baying, declaring their new allegiance to the caretaker of the Turk Mountain Preserve, provider of canned lunch meat. One of the big red-faced Stiller boys he'd seen at the Beer & Eat that night in Wanless—DeWayne, not Nardo—drove the first machine, and the skinny guy Jesse drove another. Three hounds stood on a metal platform mounted behind the seat of Jesse's machine. Two older men rode double on the third ATV. They wore baseball caps embroidered with *Black & Tan* and the figures of hounds. They looked like twins, with bloodshot blue eyes and identical short beards, grizzled and tobacco-stained. The one in back had a lever-action carbine propped on his hip. He must've seen the pose in an old Western, some crusty character actor riding shotgun on a stagecoach.

DeWayne dismounted and caught one of the hounds by the scruff of its neck as the other five shied away and trotted past the porch, out of reach, where they sat on their haunches in the grass to watch. No one seemed to have noticed Rice, sitting on the top step, obscured by the railing. He stood and walked over to the middle of the porch, where they couldn't miss him. The exhaust from the three ATVs stank of burning oil.

"Where's 'is fuckin' collar?" DeWayne complained. He turned

and said, "Hey, Jesse, didn't they—" but stopped when the other pointed at Rice.

Rice tossed the hounds' collars, all strapped together, out into the yard toward DeWayne. Then he retrieved his beer from the top step and set it on the flat top of the railing, leaned forward. Waited. The others shut off their idling machines. DeWayne swatted the reluctant hound open-handed on the side of its head, dragged it over to the bundle, picked one out, and buckled it around the hound's neck. He rifled through the rest, discarding several, and hauled the dog over to his four-wheeler. It sprang onto the platform behind the seat like a cat and waited for DeWayne to clip on a short leash. DeWayne shut off his motor.

In the sudden silence, DeWayne said something under his breath and Jesse's face broke into a brief, horrifying smile, showing a row of crooked brown lower teeth.

"I reckon you fellows know you're trespassing," Rice said.

"We got a legal right, asshole." DeWayne spat juice from the snuff swelling his lower lip. "We can come on anybody's land to get our hounds, and you've done committed a misdemeanor taking them collars."

"Section eighteen point two dash ninety-seven and one-thirty-six of the Code of Virginia." Rice smiled. "But you can't have a firearm with you when you go after your dogs, and you can't use vehicles without the permission of the landowner. And since this is only the hound practice season, you're not supposed to have a firearm with you anyway. So I guess we're even." He wasn't going to ask about the bait, didn't want word getting out that he knew it was there.

Jesse smirked but DeWayne ignored Rice's recitation entirely. "Where the rest at?"

Rice shrugged. "They ran off with the big yellow sonofagun. You might find 'em with your radios—that big one wouldn't let me take his collar off."

The two old men, still sitting double on their machine, laughed at this in ridiculous, high-pitched voices. Rice wondered if they were simple.

"Cain't nobody but ol' Bilton git near 'im!" one of them screeched. DeWayne snarled some sort of insult and they quieted, but the one sitting in back frowned and shouldered his rifle, taking his time, and aimed it at DeWayne's head. Rice thought he was about to witness a murder, but the man hissed "Pow" in a quiet voice and lowered the rifle. The others paid him no attention.

DeWayne moved a few slow steps toward the porch. He seemed to be fighting an urge to charge up the steps and strangle Rice to death but after a few seconds he managed a taunting grin.

"We heard you were lookin' for us. Heard somebody messed with your truck."

Rice smiled back. "Breaking windows and running away is pretty chickenshit for wannabe outlaw bikers, DeWayne." The man frowned at this but seemed unable to think of a reply right away.

"I like your dogs," Rice said. "How much y'all want for these ones that followed me home?"

"Ain't but one ourn," DeWayne said. He stood in the yard and watched as Jesse, who still hadn't said a word to Rice, fiddled with a radio receiver, and climbed up on the seat of his vehicle, reaching overhead with an H-shaped wire antenna. "And he ain't for sale."

"What about the others?"

"They Dempsey Boger's hounds. We don't hunt with that black sumbitch. You call him if you want to."

Jesse was waving the antenna back and forth in a wide, diminishing arc, listening to the receiver's high-pitched beeps, as if he were dowsing for water. When the waving stopped, the beeps coming fast and regular, the antenna pointed south, toward the Dutch River. He picked up a walkie-talkie and spoke with someone, the other voice loud and angry and completely incomprehensible. Jesse looked at Rice.

"You gone let us out that goddamn gate of yourn or you gone

make us cut the lock?" He had small, close-set gray eyes and skin so pale Rice could see the blue veins branching in his temple.

Rice considered the question. He sure as hell wasn't going to let them out, but he hadn't called the game warden or the sheriff, and he assumed the lock-cutting threat was not idle. He wondered if there was some way he could keep them from cutting the lock on his own. He glanced at his truck, imagined driving down there in front of them, parking the truck to block the gate. But then what? Then they'd have to drive back up the mountain, go back the way they came. That might teach them some sort of lesson, but he didn't want them driving their stupid machines through the property again. It was a conundrum.

"You shouldn't of messed with them collars, motherfucker." DeWayne had edged closer and closer to the porch, and now he stood in the grass directly below Rice, glaring up at him. His scalp was pink underneath his spiky red hair, sweat dripping down the flushed, freckled skin of his wide, frowning forehead. He reminded Rice of a snapping turtle, dim and single-minded, pale greenish eyes underwater, looking up from the bottom of a murky pond.

"Come on, DeWayne." Jesse had started the engine of his four-wheeler, but DeWayne wasn't finished yet.

"We hunt up on that mountain whenever we want. There ain't nothin' you can do about it."

"You're wrong about that. I'm up there all the time, and there's lots of things I can do. You're not going to like me."

The older men cackled at this. "Thar's a neeeuw sharf in town!"

DeWayne's face had turned a deeper shade of red, and Rice knew what was coming before he even said it.

"Then you better watch your back when you're up in them woods."

Rice felt a perverse thrill. This guy was breathtakingly stupid.

"DeWayne, I believe you just threatened me."

He was already on his way down the stairs, not sure what he was planning. DeWayne tensed and took two steps back, clenching and unclenching his thick, red-freckled fists. He was heavier than Rice, not as tall. Funny him being so nervous. From what Rice had heard about the Stiller boys, beating people up was pretty much standard practice.

"Remember the old caretaker, Sara? Did you threaten her too? Did you show her what a big man you are?" Walking straight at DeWayne, he watched for a reaction and what he got was pretty ambiguous: a pause, a flash of surprise, maybe, or DeWayne's guard coming down for an instant. It was enough.

"What the fuck? We never did nothing to her." After a moment, he added, "She didn't steal no fuckin' collars."

"We got to go, DeWayne," Jesse called. "They down by the fuckin' river."

DeWayne seemed to grasp Rice's intention before Rice himself, and he reversed his retreat, deciding instead on preemptive aggression. He was shouting, spittle gathering in the corners of his mouth, but Rice couldn't hear what he said, couldn't hear anything but a high-pitched whine, a sound like the beehive had made as he broke away the paneling in the cabin and there was that pause before the bees attacked. Now a familiar and not unpleasant sensation of tipping forward, submitting to gravity, like jumping off that cliff after Sara. DeWayne rushed him with his fist raised, elbow cocked behind it. Rice feinted right and slipped left as DeWayne's forearm shot past his ear, then he stepped in close and torqued a left hook into the side of DeWayne's face. In his imagination his fist seemed to pass through DeWayne's skull and out the opposite temple. DeWayne's head snapped over his shoulder and a wet brown turd of snuff popped out of his mouth. He took a step back and sat down hard on the ground.

Rice forced himself to break off, to leave DeWayne sitting there, not really hurt. He glanced at the old man with the rifle, he and his twin on the ATV both grinning and nodding their heads as if this were all a farce Rice had staged for their entertainment. He walked to DeWayne's machine and unclipped the leash from the hound.

His left hand wasn't working very well, should've used his elbow like he'd been taught. The hound wagged and panted and hopped off the platform, looking up hopefully at Rice's face. Was he stealing bear hounds now? There were three more to free, but when he stepped over to Jesse's ATV those hounds didn't know him and they crouched back on their haunches and barked. They had big, angry voices that drove into his head like steel spikes. The setter and Boger's other hounds started barking, too, nervous, alarmed, milling around in the yard. Rice no longer felt like he was in control of the situation. He looked at Jesse, who backed away, holding his radio receiver out in front of him like a shield, then he turned back toward the lodge just as one of the old men—still grinning—came down on his forehead with an oaken club from the firewood pile.

While Rice lay stunned in the gravel drive, DeWayne staggered over and kicked him once in the ribs, not very hard, he didn't seem to be feeling too good himself. He leaned down to pick up something, Rice couldn't see what, probably the old man's club, but there was a metallic click and someone said unh-unh in a high mocking singsong. DeWayne cursed but he tossed away whatever it was and lurched out of Rice's field of vision.

The four-wheelers drove off. He tried to stand but his head felt like it had been split open and he started to black out so he lay there with his eyes closed, trying not to think about anything, until it was nearly full dark. One of the dogs came and snuffled his ear, but he didn't open his eyes to see which one. When he finally got up, they had all disappeared. It made him unaccountably sad. His left hand was swelling, the first and second knuckles throbbing. Dried blood in his eyes, ears ringing. He washed down six aspirin with the warm beer from the porch railing and lay on the sofa with a towel on his head to soak up the blood. He sensed there would come a time when he would laugh at his performance today, but the pain leaping inside his skull stole his sense of humor. When the aspirin started working he promptly passed out.

TWENTY-THREE

CERESO Nogales, Sonora. Visiting day, number five. He had become a counter inside just like everyone else. Two months, four days in, who knew how many to go, five visiting days, five visits from Apryl. She's there today in tight jeans, scuffed Docs, and a leather jacket over a black T-shirt. Standard uniform. She was smiling, which meant she was hiding stress. He knew better than to try to extract the source. Before, she'd worried about the danger she'd brought to her sister, but she'd convinced Tracy to move back in with their parents in Scottsdale, a place of at least relative security.

They sat at their usual table in the corner. The guards along the walls staring straight ahead. Other prisoners at other tables with lovers, wives, families. Low murmurs in Sinaloan Spanish, Rice catching about three-quarters of it. News from home, mostly. What you wanted to hear when you were inside.

"How you doing?" She watched him closely, smile gone, her concern for him pushing away whatever the other thing was.

"Healthy as hell. No beer, no tequila, nothing to eat but nutritious prison food. All I do is work out. Raoul is teaching me the way of the sicario."

Her eyes widened. He wasn't supposed to say his cellmate's name out loud, the one who'd loaned him the knife his first night inside. "God-dammit, Rice. Please don't expect me to fucking joke about that."

"We're getting along fine."

"Stop it!" She'd leaned forward and said that a little too loudly. Heads turned toward them. A few glares, blank stares. She sat back, breathed. "You're being naïve. I've asked around. Fucking DEA had them put you with him on purpose. People don't get along with him. They survive him, survive contact with him, or they don't. Usually they don't."

"I'll survive. Really, the man is misunderstood."

He didn't want her to cave to the DEA and make herself a target of the cartel, so he'd already told her Raoul Fernandez was protecting him. He'd told her to stop worrying. Fernandez was important to the Juarez cartel, and with the Aztecas watching their backs, Rice was a lot safer in CERESO than Apryl was out there in southern Arizona, caught between the DEA and the Sinaloas.

Naturally, she found his story far-fetched, and now she glared at him long enough to justify a change of subject.

"I slept with M.," she said. She didn't look away, didn't look down. She raised her left eyebrow.

"Really?" he asked.

She nodded. She seemed pleased with herself. They knew now that undercover DEA agent Mia Cortez had infiltrated the cartel in Chi-cago but recently transferred to the Tucson office. According to Apryl, she swore she wasn't responsible for Rice's situation, that it was her bosses who'd insisted on using him as leverage. Apryl was frustratingly cryptic in their visiting-day conversations, but as best he could tell, she'd been playing along, parceling out a few juicy but insignificant tidbits in her role as confidential informant, hoping to co-opt Cortez in some grand plan she wouldn't talk about, working both sides in a dangerous balancing act that drove him mad with worry.

"And how did that go?" he asked.

She gave a little impatient shake of her head, grimaced. "You know what this means."

"You're going to have to put a rainbow sticker on your jeep?" He had to admit he was a little jealous. Then, naturally, he started wishing he'd been there for the act. Mia Cortez was an attractive woman, about Apryl's height, curvy. His imagination started firing.

"Rice." That purple gaze again. She knew what he was thinking.

"Yeah, I know," he said, acting like he should have a clue what the fuck she was up to. "It's good news."

TWENTY-FOUR

He dreamed of snakes: thick, arrogant vipers in the lodge, coiled listlessly on the furniture, under the bed, on the kitchen counters. Their heads were grinning ceramic snake skulls and they seemed deadly and invincible as gods, ignoring him as he crept about, trying to live in a place that had never belonged to him. Eventually he realized they ignored him because he was already dead, had been for a long time, he was only a ghost and the snakes were waiting for something that had nothing to do with him. The realization woke him up and he lay for a while on the sofa in the gray predawn, wondering how much his head was going to hurt when he sat up. He'd been having death dreams more often of late. Sometimes he felt like he was rehearsing, as if his subconscious had decided he needed practice, as if we learn how to die in our dreams.

Dempsey Boger drove up around seven and leaned on his horn once, long and angry. The Stillers must've followed through on their threat to cut the lock on the gate. Bolt cutters would be standard equipment for those guys. Boger had turned his truck around so the bed was facing toward the lodge. With his back to the porch, he lowered the tailgate and reached in, pulled the stiff carcass of a dog toward him to rest on the tailgate. Two other hounds watched through the wire doors of their box kennels in the truck's bed.

Rice hooked his thumb through Boger's radio collars and walked out on the front porch barefoot. He shivered. It was only late September, but the crisp morning had the feel of autumn rushing into winter. He'd taped a wad of gauze to the cut on his head, which probably needed stitches. The pain and blood loss left him mildly nauseated and lightheaded. He felt permeable, uncontained; the breeze blew right through him.

"Dempsey." The man turned at Rice's voice.

"I brought you somethin'." He lifted the carcass and laid it on the ground at his feet. "We called this one Monroe, on account of his voice."

Rice looked at the dead dog lying in the gravel, its mouth slightly open. *Monroe*, with the emphasis on the first syllable. High and lonesome, no doubt. The dog's coat was muddy and spotted with blood.

"What happened?"

"Well now, Monroe here," Boger said, "looks like he done got hisself run over after you took the goddamn collars off the goddamn hounds. Found him this mornin' on the road through the pass. Vet said somebody'd dropped off another'n that got hit, a little setter cross. Some more was wanderin' along the river." He paused, staring at the carcass. He had a smoker's rasp, but the modulation of his voice was smooth and rhythmic, a storyteller's voice. "One's still missin'. They ain't used to cars, roads. I try to keep 'em away from roads."

Rice decided he couldn't stay on the porch. He wondered how much Boger knew about what had happened with Stiller and the others. Walking down the steps, he felt none of the anger, none of the eerie power that had propelled him yesterday. The breeze was chilly, but the sun felt warm on his face. The gravel path dry and cool on his feet. Far down at the south edge of the meadow, a grove of fencepost locusts shed tiny leaves winking soundlessly to the ground like rain.

He squatted to examine Boger's dog, which he recognized now—it was one of the males that had followed him home. He ran his fingers along the rib cage, feeling the peaks and valleys, the cold, wet fur. The dog had been lean, fit. He looked up at Boger, who was close enough that Rice could smell the cigarette smoke on him. He wanted to say he was sorry, that if the old man hadn't knocked him out he'd have hung on to Boger's dogs until he came to get them.

With his hand on the dog's chest, he said, "Your dogs were on this property, and you knew it, and everyone knows bear hunting hasn't been allowed here for about a hundred years. You can't run your dogs on Turk Mountain *without* them coming on this property, and I won't put up with that." He stood and laid Boger's collars on the truck's tailgate.

"So if I start hounds up on the national forest, and they run on y'all's property, you're gonna steal the collars?"

"Might not try that again, but I'll fuck up your hunt one way or another." Boger didn't seem the type to press charges under the statute DeWayne Stiller had mentioned, but Rice wasn't going to push his luck. A court appearance to answer a Class 1 misdemeanor charge was all he needed.

Boger reached inside his jeans jacket, fished his pack of Kools from a shirt pocket. He knocked the pack twice on the heel of his hand, shook out a cigarette, and lit it with a wood match, turning to shield his face from the fresh breeze in the lee of the cab. He shook the match out and tossed it in the truck bed, drew on the cigarette. Squinted at Rice through the smoke.

"And that don't seem unreasonable to you?"

"It's completely unreasonable. It's my job."

Boger's glance flicked to the bandage on Rice's head. "Your job's gonna get you killed you keep beatin' on Stiller boys."

Rice imagined he saw the slightest hint of a grin, or maybe just an amused tightening of the lips under the man's usual skeptical squint. Clearly there was some animosity between Boger and the Stillers. Might be the only reason Boger was speaking to him at all.

"Nearly got me killed yesterday." He said it matter-of-factly, not making a joke.

A furry white head rose up in the cab. It was the setter bitch, his companion from the mountain. When he walked over, she poked her nose out the open passenger-side window to sniff his hands and forearms. Her left hind leg was encased in a bright blue fiberglass cast. She rested her head on the door and closed her eyes while he scratched behind her ears.

Holding the cigarette in his lips, Boger picked up dead Monroe and placed him back in the truck's bed, slammed the tailgate. Then he stood there and smoked and watched Rice and the setter.

"It's a bad break," he said.

Rice didn't look up from the dog's peaceful face. "You're a tough old girl, aren't you."

"She ain't but three."

"What's her name?"

"Sadie."

"She looks more bird dog than bear hound."

Boger didn't respond to that. He said, "Bilton Stiller still can't find three of his hounds. One of them was his best dog, or so he says, some big-ass yellow hound."

"I remember him. That dog was unfriendly."

"Bilton's saying you killed them hounds, left 'em up in the woods. Took the batteries out the collars." Boger didn't sound like he thought much of the accusation.

"Well I hope you told him different."

"Ha!" Boger's smile was broad, a real smile it seemed, but his dark brown eyes were level, reserved. "I don't tell Bilton Stiller much of anything." He watched Rice's puzzlement. "I'm not his kind of people."

"What's wrong with you?"

"You really that dumb, or you just pretending? Some politically correct California bullshit?"

"I'm from Arizona."

Boger just looked at him, expecting an answer. Rice stared, starting to feel dumb indeed, noticing the lines radiating out from the corner of Boger's eye, fanning above his high cheekbone, those dark, dark brown eyes, the sclerae not quite white, more an eggshell shot with red, like he'd been up all night looking for his dogs, which he probably had.

"So you're saying it's a race thing?"

"Yeah it's a race thing. Us Negro-Cherokee half-breeds what live up Sycamore Creek ain't good enough to wax Bilton Stiller's monster truck."

"Hunh." Rice hadn't realized the social dynamics of northwestern Turpin County were so complicated.

"You don't know what that means either, do you?"

"I know what a monster truck is."

"It means people like the Stillers need to believe there's somebody they're better than. You also didn't know they was messing with you at the Beer & Eat when they sent you up to my place looking for a bear hound."

"You heard about that."

"Sent that ol' boy up Sycamore Holla, yuk yuk yuk, he might never come out. It was quick thinking, you talking to me about honeybees. If I'd known you were gonna accuse me of bear poachin' I might've shot you and buried you behind the kennel. I would've for sure if I'd known you was going to kill Monroe."

He pinched the butt of his cigarette, tossed it in the bed with the match and the box kennels and Monroe's carcass, and pulled out his soft pack. Rice wondered if the guy was a heavy smoker or if he was just worked up.

"That big yellow hound still had his radio collar on the last time I saw him. They should've been able to find him. You think I ought to stop by the store and have a talk with Mr. Stiller?"

"Might be an interesting conversation. From what I hear, old Bilton's a fool for his hounds. One thing he has on his boys. They could give a shit about the hounds. Or anything else."

"Would they use bait?"

"Bait's only good if it gives you a place to start your hounds, where they can pick up a scent. You got to set up your bait in different places, keep adding popcorn and rotten apples and whatnot. It's a lot of extra work on top of everything else. I don't know any houndsmen who do it."

"What if you're not using the dogs, what if you put out your bait and climb up in a tree with a crossbow and sit there until the bears show up. You said yourself you'd found dead bears that'd been baited."

"That's different. You find another one?"

"I found two. You all's dogs found them yesterday." Sadie whined and Rice looked over. She was asleep, her cheeks puffing out as she half-barked, half-whimpered. Dreaming. He swept his palm from her eyebrows back over the top of her head and down her neck. He'd read that dogs like to be petted because it reminds them of their mothers licking them when they were young. Her eyes half-opened and then shut again. She must be on pain meds. "It was way up in that canyon, near the top of the cliffs. The bears were missing their gallbladders and paws, and like you said before, the wounds were broadhead cuts, some white powder in 'em."

"It ain't a canyon. Nobody says 'canyon' here."

"What do you say? It looks like a canyon to me."

"It's a holler."

Rice nodded, waiting for him to pick up the thread of their conversation again, but Boger just looked at him through a cloud of fresh cigarette smoke.

"So what do you think?" Rice prodded. "About the bait? Will the Stillers come back, add more bait like you said?"

"Somebody'll come back."

"Not the Stillers?"

"Stiller boys ain't that enterprisin'."

"You think it's somebody else?"

"I've heard some things."

"But you're not going to tell me what you've heard."

"Not sure I like your attitude."

Rice shook his head but didn't respond.

"What I think," Boger went on, "is you've decided you're gonna take care of this little problem yourself. Maybe you figure you can *handle* these redneck poachers dumpin' moon pies and stale doughnuts in your precious *old-growth forest*. Shootin' them pet bears."

"Yeah, I'm pretty interested. I don't see why you'd protect them."

Dempsey glared at Rice like he was about to tell him to go to hell, but the moment passed and he cleared his throat, which turned into a cough, a smoker's hack forcing him to turn away from the truck and hold his fist to his mouth.

The setter was awake again, probably reacting to the tension in the men's voices. She stood in the seat and turned around in a circle, knocking her cast against the dashboard, and lay down on her side and scootched her hips out, rolled onto her back. With her cast sticking straight up in the air, she didn't look comfortable. Rice reached in and rubbed her belly. He tried a shift in subject. "How are those bees doing?"

"They're all right."

"I've been eating a lot of that honey. It will fire you up."

"Wild honey will do it." Boger slid in behind the wheel and the setter put her head in his lap. For a moment he looked down at her like he'd never seen a dog before. "You eat enough of it, you'll turn into one them bears you're so worried about. The Stillers'll come after you for real."

He shut the door and started to speak through the open window, but another, shorter coughing fit took him. He pounded his chest and examined the dwindling cigarette in his hand. Didn't know where it had come from. Didn't want it anymore. He reached it forward to the ashtray, stubbed it out. Looked up at Rice with watery eyes. The man needed to go home and get some sleep.

"You and them folks own the place got to remember there's families around here been hunting bear up on that mountain ever since their great-great-granddaddies run off the Real People two hundred years ago, and there ain't a thing in the world you or anyone else can do to stop 'em. You keep on like you are, it'll turn into a war, one you won't like much."

"Maybe. I was told pretty much the same thing yesterday," Rice said. He was cold, and he crossed his arms over his chest. "What about the Cherokee? Did they hunt bear up there? Before they got run off?"

"Not much. That mountain's haunted—they called it *ooh joo teeah nee sew ee ohdah*. Many Others Mountain." He snorted and turned the key in the ignition. He was grinning, without much goodwill in his eyes. "I know you know what I'm talking about."

Then he put his truck in gear and drove slowly down the driveway.

TWENTY-FIVE

Rice found the blister pack of same-key padlocks and opened the last one with his key. The second lock was way up on the mountain, protected by wasps inside that steel box on the Forest Service gate. Later this week he would hump a half roll of barbed wire up there and repair the fence he was sure the Stillers had cut on their way in.

He laced his boots, poured a whole pot of coffee into a big plastic convenience store mug, and walked down the driveway. A leisurely hike, he hoped, would help clear his head. The day was quiet except for a weak breeze that rose occasionally to a gust, shuffling branches. His boots crunching in the gravel. The ubiquitous crickets; crows cawing in the distance. A few dead leaves came off and blew overhead, translucent, backlit and glowing briefly in the sun.

Many Others Mountain. Boger had to be making that shit up.

At the entrance, the gate was shut—probably the Stillers had left it swung wide but Boger couldn't bring himself to drive away from an open gate, no matter how mad he was. Rice opened the mailbox, thinking maybe the Stillers had come back and put a live rattlesnake inside, but it was so full of junk mail there wouldn't have been room anyway. Must've been a while since he'd last emptied it: mass mailings, free local newspapers, nonprofit solicitations for Sara that didn't get forwarded, thick booklets of coupons for shit he didn't want. He left it, promised himself he'd clean it out soon. Nothing in there would be addressed to him. Any mail sent to his old address in Tucson had been forwarded to P.O. boxes he didn't intend to visit again.

A red pickup with a lift kit and straight pipes roared around the turn just past the driveway. Rice stepped back onto the shoulder as the driver nearly clipped the mailbox and gunned it down the straightaway, headed toward Stumpf. The passenger turned to look out the back window, laughing, white teeth in a sparse black beard. No one Rice recognized. A translucent sticker across the top of the window read *FEAR THIS* in bold letters, a twist on the *NO FEAR* stickers the local teenagers seemed to like. Rice wondered if those boys could know anything about fear. He wondered if they had any idea what their stupid stickers were saying.

He pulled the gate shut behind him and locked the chain with the new laminated steel padlock. After some searching, he found the old lock in the weeds, its shank cut. It wasn't a small lock, but now its twin, or triplet, looked flimsy hanging there against the latchpost. The chain that had felt so reassuring every time he'd wrapped it around the end of the gate seemed insubstantial as well. He could buy some better hardware, a new lock and chain, though if he did he would have to mail keys to a list of folks who were supposed to have access: STP wanted one in Tucson for some reason, and both the sheriff and the game warden were supposed to have keys. The fire department too. Also, as he'd already seen, Sara apparently got one.

He dropped the broken lock in his empty coffee mug and started back up the driveway, walking fast, then jogging, which made his head hurt worse than it already did. The lock rattled in the mug. He pushed himself harder. Boger was right: Rice intended to handle the poaching problem himself, but he'd been completely ineffective. Two more bears had been killed. The Stillers were driving ATVs through the preserve with impunity. He'd relinquished his precious self-control and started a fight with DeWayne that had ended with Rice knocked into semiconsciousness with his own firewood. He'd let Boger's dogs run off to be killed and injured, and now the one local he thought he'd connected with, his one ally, was telling him to back off.

He jogged all the way to the meadow, where he stumbled and almost fell, then bent over and vomited his coffee in the grass. He sat in the driveway for a while. He gently pressed his fingertips against the swollen cut at his hairline; a dark bruise had already spread from the cut to the right side of his forehead. He'd hacked away the hair with scissors and razor, washed the cut with soap and water, then dabbed it with isopropyl alcohol. When the bleeding stopped, he'd applied two butterflies and smeared it all with Neosporin.

After the two kills at the bait station, the poachers might stay away for a while, or they might start restocking the bait again right away, but sooner or later they were coming back—the preserve's bear population had to be irresistible. And that's when he would catch them. He would be out there at night, haunting the mountain like one of the ghosts Dempsey had mentioned. Dempsey had warned Rice about his excessive tactics, but what the man didn't realize was that Rice had been holding back, and his holding back was the problem. One of the few lessons Rice's father had managed to pass along before he died was that when you slack off, what you're really doing is choosing to fail because you didn't try hard enough. It was a rational choice, his father had said, for people who would rather fail on purpose than risk finding out they're not good enough, but if you made that choice you should at least be honest with yourself about what you were doing.

His shirt was sweaty, clammy, so he took it off and tied it around his waist. Instead of continuing up the driveway he walked north along the edge of the forest, eventually coming to the open locust grove visible from the front porch of the lodge. The trees sheltered an old livestock graveyard, bleached white cattle bones partly hidden in the grass, glowing in the sun like the remains of some ruined miniature city. He had no idea where they had come from. There was nothing in the old logbooks about anyone running cattle in the meadow.

He picked up a cow skull, peered into the shaded eye sockets lined with green lichen. The thin bone at its nose was chipped and cracked. Another totem for the office. He set it down with his coffee mug. A pelvis bone tangled in the grass came free with a little tugging. He brushed it clean and turned it over in his hands. Bleached white in the sun, it was intact, symmetrical, curved gracefully and shaped like a helmet. In the front were two oval holes that seemed to stare. He set this next to the skull.

Moving into the sunstruck meadow, he stooped to pick up a rib from among the other bones, two feet long and curved like a sickle, square-stemmed at its base where a knob came out at a right angle. The inside edge of the rib was surprisingly sharp. He swung it at a tall thistle. The top half of the plant lifted, trembling, and tumbled into the grass. He swung the rib again, harder, cutting the thistle closer to its base.

He was falling into one of his trances, an angry version. His senses sharpened, the bright sunlight clanging around him, a breeze bending the hairs on his skin. For a long time he'd stepped on any hint of the violent part of himself that had caused so much trouble last year. But what could he hurt here? He stalked through the meadow until he found a copse of twelve-foot-tall pokeweed, where he lay about with the rib like Samson with his jawbone. A desperate and frenzied rage took him, his cutting strokes growing more violent, the soft, juicy stalks bursting in a spray of sap, the big plants heeling over to fall in slow motion, purple berries raining down. When he'd exhausted himself, he stopped and regarded the shattered pokeweed stalks, the green and purple carnage. It was just vegetation.

In the shelter of a small rise he found four oval impressions in the grass where deer had bedded. He curled up in one. The deer had made the ground comfortable, and no sticks or pebbles poked into his bare flesh. He would rest here until he felt better. The meager warmth from the sun was not enough to offset the chill of the breeze that puffed over his skin, raising goose bumps.

His dream was a nondream—he simply was aware of what happened around him as he slept: he knew the slow, inexorable movement of the sun, the wind's gentle swish in the grass, the musty metal smell of warm soil. He watched three deer approach, stamping their front hooves and snorting at the strange sleeping human until their nerve broke and they bounded away, stark white flags floating and twitching over their backs. A silent raven circled him once and flew on over the forest. Ants crawled on his legs, a mosquito bit his arm.

Violent shivering woke him and he sat up, chilled but calm. The cut on his head had seeped blood to dry in the hair over his temple while he slept. He stank of old sweat. Even so, those deer had come close. They'd known what he was and they'd come so close he probably could have killed one if he'd wanted. He thought about that, what it might mean.

The sun was well past its zenith now, and he stared at it for a while, trying to see it move as he had in his dream and temporarily blinding himself. He walked back to the locust grove for his mug and bones. He tried to fit the cow pelvis over his head to wear it like a ceremonial Pleistocene headdress, but several fused vertebrae at the sacrum got in the way. He laid it on the ground and broke off part of the sacrum with a rock, and this time it fit, resting on his crown, and he could see through the holes.

Halfway through the meadow, he stopped to rest. The view was better from up here, and he rotated slowly, panning like a camera, the world reduced to two oval windows. Turk Mountain leaning over the lodge like an old threat, the valley bright in the sun, the Blue Ridge edging the eastern horizon. All this light. Equinox. From now on, the nights would be longer than the days.

He turned his back to the sun and saw in the grass his own grotesque shadow, the shadow of a man wearing a bone helmet. A massive-headed monster with short, thick horns. A minotaur. *Fear this*, he thought. His heart moved in his chest, the usual rhythm. *Fear me.* A roar in the trees on the mountain: the wind reaching the meadow in a moment, harder and colder than before, ending the afternoon. He waited, and felt the sun's light slowly enter his body. He had nothing but these old bones; he was made of light and air, water and earth. He shivered again, shivered over his whole body like a bear.

TWENTY-SIX

CERESO Nogales, Sonora. She'd visited less than a week ago. She'd been more preoccupied than usual, and if he hadn't known her to be fearless he would have thought she was afraid of something. But what could be worse than what she'd already lived with for the past eight months? When he'd pressed her, she'd paused, measuring what she could tell him, which wasn't much. "I'm going to be okay," she said, speaking slowly, as if trying to invest her words with more meaning than they could carry. "No matter what you hear. I'm okay."

Somehow Fernandez got the news before anyone else and he took it upon himself to tell Rice. The official line was random drug violence; she'd been doing a rare plants survey for the Coronado National Forest near Lochiel. Border Patrol had found her body hastily buried in Antonio Canyon, like something a mountain lion would do, a lion meaning to come back later and finish. But it wasn't a mountain lion, and it wasn't random. And she wasn't okay.

Rice felt something slip inside, like stepping on black ice. Nausea swept up from his balls to his throat, one wave, then another. His skin tingled and chilled. Translucent indigo lobes appeared in his peripheral vision and threatened to flood the bright Sonora morning.

She pulled onto a jeep road north of Sells and drove up into some godforsaken mountains in the reservation, explaining in a disconcertingly offhand manner that there was a remote crag she'd wanted to climb, and that she wanted him to spend the night with her up there. On the mountain they cooked enchiladas with prosciutto on his little camp stove, drank a bottle of cheap caber-net, partook of one line of cocaine each. Just one—she'd told him early on that she wouldn't work with a fucking addict. Later, in the moonlight, they screwed on a foam backpacking mattress until the coke wore off.

So that was how it started: the one chaste white line of coke and the waning gibbous moon coming up late, bare feet and warm sandstone, coyotes going off nearby, a low moaning wind out over the desert. Trying to sing and laughing because they didn't know any of the same songs, her careless laugh he heard for the first time, a girlishness he'd never seen in her. He figured out much later what it all meant, how much it meant, her trusting him like that. She was not a demonstrative person, and for Apryl that night was a consummation, a seal on some private commitment. Nothing else was required. She'd made up her mind.

By the end, Apryl had taught him that love was the same thing as courage. He didn't understand until he'd been locked up in CERESO for a while. He wished he'd figured it out sooner.

Rice shook off the fugue and found himself in the prison's courtyard, still seated on a concrete bench beside Raoul Fernandez. He stood and stepped away, as if the man were throwing off radiation.

Fernandez called him Rice-Moore, with the emphasis on his first name, like "Rushmore."

"You are sicario, *Rice-Moore."*

He said this gently, smiling, as if the preposterousness of bestow-ing the title on someone like Rice was apparent, the pronouncement clearly an act of extreme generosity. Rice knew what Raoul was imply-

ing, and the apparently genuine show of compassion from this sociopath who tortured and killed people like Apryl for a living was so perverse and complicated and surreal that it pushed Rice over an edge he'd been skirting for months.

The next morning he began to train in earnest.

TWENTY-SEVEN

Rice spent his nights on the mountain, waiting in the dark for the Stiller brothers to show up, headlamps flashing: a procession of grim-faced men laden with bags of cast-off baked goods and baskets of bruised apples, road-killed deer carcasses slung over their shoulders, long-barreled revolvers in their belts, men who will not welcome interference from the likes of Rick Morton.

He waited, but they didn't come.

He watched the bait station, climbing the tree the poachers had used, skulking there against the trunk as the light failed and the bait station transformed into something more sinister, remnants of a savage ritual gone haywire: tattered bear carcasses, a log cage haphazardly built for some unspeakable purpose, the ghastly cow's head witched into the air, keeping its vigil.

Other nights he stalked along the ridges, listening for voices, engines, footfalls, but hearing only the insects' waning symphony, three species of owl, hoarse barking of foxes, a pack of big eastern coyotes that howled like wolves, and once, a bobcat scream so desperate and feral it made his eyes water.

The crescent moon thickened to a bright oblong eye that fell behind Serrett Mountain a few minutes later each evening. Rice found he could make his way around the preserve even in scant starlight, and he always knew where he was, placed precisely on a three-dimensional map in his head. He wondered about this. The months he'd spent typing a century of logbook data into Sara's spreadsheets, obsessively locating every observation on the maps, must have built a kind of synthetic memory in his subconscious, a bone-deep knowledge of the preserve, as if he'd lived there for generations.

During the days, he worked on the cabin, but he was sleep-deprived, anxious, and distracted, worried he was missing the poachers returning unexpectedly by daylight. He considered calling Sara, telling her about his encounter with the bear hunters. She would probably be disappointed that he'd only punched one of them. He knew he should call STP too, report the trespass, the cut padlock. But he could never quite bring himself to plug in the phone.

Soon he began neglecting the cabin, preferring tasks that required him to be on the mountain. He repaired the fence the Stillers had destroyed at the Forest Service boundary, and he hiked the survey transect through the top of the gorge, switched out the data cards and batteries on the five trail cameras. The cameras used infrared light to take pictures in complete darkness, and the first ten images he uploaded to the laptop showed a young bear the size of a big Labrador drinking at the high-elevation spring at night, its humped body jet black against the gray leaf litter, the bright white foliage. He'd programmed the cameras to take a burst of five images of whatever tripped the motion detector, then wait three minutes before resetting. The delay ensured the memory card didn't fill up with hundreds of similar images of the same animal. The next five images were in the daytime, ten hours later, a handful of white-tail does sniffing around the spring. Then two more bears the next night, both much larger than the first one. A raccoon, opossums, a fox. Another bear, a huge male, moving fast through the frame. It disappeared after the third image.

He loaded his pack with metal Posted signs and fencing materials and walked the preserve's seventeen-mile back boundary, replacing faded and lost signs and repairing fence as he went. He explored the adjacent national forest, walking the logging roads, the ridges and spurs on Serrett Mountain. But he found no trace of bear poachers or anyone else.

By the end of the first week, he returned to the lodge less frequently, and he didn't stay long. On the mountain he drank from creeks and springs seeping out of limestone cliffs, and he ate overripe pawpaws and handfuls of tiny wild grapes. He shat in catholes, cleaned himself with leaves, swam in the river at midday. He was always hungry. The nights were chill and damp and he no longer noticed his own constant shivering.

The animals, though, were still aware of him as an interloper; he still vibrated at a disturbing frequency. Deer fled; ravens watched him with silent disapproval; jays and squirrels scolded him. Just after dawn on a particularly foggy morning, a yearling female bear came to sniff around the empty bait station and quickly detected Rice perched in the poacher's tree. She shied away, trotted off a dozen paces, then sat on her haunches and, with idle, almost dismissive curiosity, watched this strange arboreal ape trying to hide in a tree. Rice felt ridiculous. When he climbed down and hiked to the edge of the inner gorge, the bear followed him for a while before losing interest and wandering off.

The fog burned off and the morning turned breezy and sunny. He rested on the cliff where he and Sara had eaten peanut butter and honey sandwiches in the rain. He dangled his feet over the edge. He remembered the grouse he'd flushed gliding out over the forest. Sara had been right, he needed a ghillie suit.

TWENTY-EIGHT

At the lodge, a couple hours' rifling dusty storage rooms and closets gave him the basic materials. A pulpy decoction of black walnut hulls, yarrow, milkweed, nettle, sumac, blue food coloring, and a few shriveled blackberries in boiling salt water made a thick green dye. Empty burlap sweet feed bags and loops of sisal baling twine he sank with rocks in the biggest pots he could find. He set the pots to simmer on the stove.

He cut pieces from an old disused badminton net and glued them to a leaky green rain poncho with dollops of epoxy, laid the poncho in the grass so the glue could dry in the morning sun. The dyed burlap and sisal emerged from the pots in variegated shades of green, darkening in places to greenblack. He set the material out to dry beside the poncho while he tried to catch up on his work in the cabin through the afternoon.

Later, he started the coffee machine and went looking for the last few items he needed: several undyed burlap bags, scissors, and a big sewing needle and the spool of monofilament fishing line he'd used to hang the pig galls in the shed. The corks he'd saved from the wine Sara had brought. A pair of brown gardening gloves, threadbare brown dishtowels, and a tan cotton T-shirt that had always been a little small. He put these things in his backpack.

On the mountain, he headed for a big boulder where he could keep an eye on the slope above the bait station while he engaged in the tedious and time-consuming work of cutting the burlap into strips, tying them onto the netting, and shredding the ends. He cut up the towels and T-shirt and sewed the lighter cotton fabric in among the dyed and undyed burlap and twine. When the gorge darkened around seven thirty, he spread his tarp behind the boulder and worked in the light of his headlamp, listening to the forest. Dew fell through the night, wet as a light rainfall.

When he'd attached all the fabric he'd brought—he could add more burlap later—he cut clumps of grass and leafy branches and tied them in among the burlap and cotton on the shoulders and hood. This part of the process he would have to repeat every day, discarding the old stuff and weaving in new foliage to match his surroundings at the time. Finally, he thumbed his butane lighter to flame one end of a wine cork. The cork caught fire and he held it upright to burn for a few seconds before blowing it out. After it cooled, he rubbed the burned end over his nose, cheekbones, chin, brow, blackening all of the bright protruding surfaces.

The poncho settled over him, draped like an animal skin, the bunched fabric thickest on his back, shoulders, and hood to erase the head-on-shoulders human profile. He found he could walk without making much noise if he moved carefully, slowly, and when he knelt or sat, he knew he would disappear, his outline hidden by the dark, soft-edged mounds of disorganized fabric. He'd read that if you were caught out in the open in a ghillie suit, with no cover to blend into, you could just crouch down and hold still, and a deer or an antelope or even a person could look right at you, maybe give you a curious double take, but never recognize you as something dangerous.

By the time he'd walked down to the bait station, wearing the poncho and carrying his pack in his hand, it was nearly first light and his shirt was soaked with sweat. He'd known this would be a problem. The poncho was waterproof and he was going to get sweaty if he walked around in it. He sat in the leaves with his back against a tree trunk and waited. The canopy opened to starlight in the west, a gap where a giant tulip tree had fallen years ago. He'd noticed it before but now he wondered if that's why the poachers had picked this spot, whether they wanted the light for their night-vision gear. He sat there in his ghillie poncho and concentrated on being invisible.

Two barred owls moved through the forest, calling to each other in otherworldly voices. A large bear ignored the old bait and snuffled at what was left of the two bear carcasses for so long, Rice decided it was either mourning or feeding on the carrion. Later, two does passed by, and a raccoon climbed around on the bait structure at dawn. The sky in the opening overhead turned to hot gold. He shaded his eyes and could make out a pair of ravens circling hundreds of feet up, quorking to each other, glinting like chips of obsidian in the sunlight.

As he waited, time ebbed and flowed—a black spider wasp took several minutes to fly past his face, but the sun cleared the spine of the mountain in seconds. By now he was used to this kind of distortion—if that's what it was—and he didn't fight it. The scientist in him resisted the notion, but he knew he was being drawn closer to some new understanding. The sun rose higher and morning light filtered through the foliage. The cow's head hung motionless, not enjoying the daylight—it had grown ragged and hollow-cheeked, suffering from the depredations of crows and maggots, six inches of rebar protruding from each eye socket caked with chalky bird droppings. He'd watched crows perched on the rebar, one on each side, reaching around to dig with their bills in the cow's open mouth.

A guild of small woodland birds appeared in the understory: noisy chickadees, titmice, juncos, downy woodpeckers, red-breasted and white-breasted nuthatches with their tiny nasal bugles. A brown creeper scurried up and down tree trunks like a feathered mouse, quiet except for an occasional high-pitched peep, trying to hush the more boisterous species. The birds were hungry and feeding, but they didn't seem desperate—instead they projected a relaxed workaday industriousness.

A pair of chickadees landed on Rice's chest and began pulling out threads of burlap. His stifled laugh rustled the fabric, perplexing them, but they didn't leave. One seemed to realize Rice was a sentient creature and hopped up on the hood to peer into his eye. Sara had pointed out that chickadees possess certain cuteness factors that tend to make humans adore and anthropomorphize them—the protuberant rounded forehead, the short bill, their tiny feathered bodies, the big eyes. Rice looked into this bird's face just inches away. One shining black eye regarding him. Not so cute up close, he thought. It looked wild, other, merciless. He felt a thrill of recognition.

He blinked and the chickadee flew away. Soon the little flock had disappeared downslope, headed into the inner gorge, carrying their birdy perspectives with them. A connection of some kind remained, and without moving, without meaning to, Rice followed. He found himself acknowledging at a cellular level, as if for the first time, that these creatures would not vanish into nonexistence as soon as they lacked a human audience.

The birds were in the cliffs now, feeding desultorily as they hopped and fluttered through the laurel rooted among the rocks. They were clear in his mind as he moved among them. Was he imagining this? Maybe it had to do with the ghillie, the perfect camouflage, or too many sleepless nights watching in the forest. Or maybe it was something else entirely.

He reached out to the birds, moving closer in his imagination. It felt like he was asking permission to join them. The chickadee was sharp-eyed, quick, a pounce and a small black beetle was in its beak, legs flailing, the exoskeleton crunching, an oily taste. A sip of dew from a drop suspended under a blade of grass. When the birds flew from the cliff, Rice flew with them, swimming impossibly through the vast invisible air, a moment of vertigo as the creek flashed by far below, the treetops, clouds in the endless sky, then a gathering pause—a syncopation, a skipped heartbeat, an intake of breath—and some great cosmic valve opened, a vision of the gorge exploding in his mind, all of it at once, in every color, infrared through ultraviolet, everything was alive, speaking in a billion voices, a phantasmagoria of undreamed presences, the planet's magnetic field itself vivid and pulsing around him.

He screamed and jerked awake. Still in his spot near the bait station.

The forest was quiet again, warming in lambent sunlight, the air still. Had he really screamed? His head began to throb, not unpleasantly, like a tiny hand, a bird claw, had reached into the healing cut where the old man had hit him with the firewood and was gently squeezing his frontal lobe in a one-two-three rhythm.

He'd crossed over some frontier and come back, but traces of the other place clung like mud. He breathed and settled into the ground, feeling Earth's motion in his bones, the slow spin of the planet, ponderous on its axis, traveling in its accustomed arc around the sun. Continental plates ground and shattered. Far away the sun lifted water from the oceans and rained it back onto the land. Life squirmed and sprouted, inhaling, exhaling, it spoke and wept, hatched and died.

He waited another hour. When he stood, his ghillie camouflage rustled softly. He felt steady and strong.

TWENTY-NINE

After he started wearing the ghillie poncho, the other animals' reactions had ranged from curiosity to acceptance, but mostly they ignored him. Rice, for his part, had turned predatory. He'd been hungry for days, but now, like the wolf in a cartoon, he began sorting the animals he encountered according to their delectability. A turkey walking through the forest appeared in his mind's eye plucked and dressed, fresh from the oven, skin browned and still crackling. Cottontail rabbits turned on a spit over charcoal, glistening with bacon fat. Deer he mentally butchered into their various cuts: hams, ribs, tenderloin. Without thinking much about the implications, he made a spear, nothing more elaborate than a long sharpened stick, and began to hunt.

When he finally managed to pin a big fox squirrel to a maple trunk, it didn't expire quietly as he'd hoped but chittered and flung itself about, trying to get away. He drew his knife in a panic to kill it, to end its suffering, and it bit his finger just before he severed its spine at the base of its skull.

He awoke from his predator's trance, his chest clotting with regret. He lifted the warm, furred body, held it close to his face, peering into the eyes. No one home. There had been life, a conscious presence, then in an instant it was gone forever. Where did it go? How could the universe possibly work this way?

Thinking it might help, he apologized to the squirrel the way he'd read Native Americans would when they killed an animal for food. It didn't help, though he understood the key was to love and respect the squirrel species and accept the gift of meat and sustenance that came in the form of individual squirrels. Which was hard, in that it still entailed a predatory suspension of empathy, an objectification of individual others, centers of perception, their own universes surely very different from his own but nonetheless significant and demanding consideration. He'd spent enough hours watching wild animals to be incapable of forgetting that.

He wondered, had he hardened his heart? To harden one's heart would help to avoid pain but, he was sure, it also impaired one's consciousness. At some other time he might have sat longer puzzling this out, but he was hungry. He built a tiny fire of dry hickory twigs in a crevice in a boulder, skinned and gutted the squirrel, and cooked it on a green-stick skewer over the coals.

His kills grew cleaner as his hunting prowess developed, but a quick death was death nonetheless. An alert, self-willed creature going about its business, transformed with a stab of Rice's spear into an inert corpse he could eat. He found it strange, and more than a little heartbreaking; certainly it rubbed his nose in his own mortality, all of this adding up to the price of meat, of causing the deaths that sustained him. Despite his misgivings, he soon broadened his prey base beyond fox squirrels to include gray squirrels, cottontail rabbits, and grouse. They were all small animals, and he was only able to spear one every couple of days, not enough to quell the hunger. He started thinking about turkey and deer. He might need a better weapon.

This thing that was happening would help him catch the poachers, he was sure. But there was more to it than that. He knew he was no longer altogether in control. Memories he'd long shut off, now seeped through. Buffers were being stripped away—scientific detachment, language, story, self-consciousness itself. He tried not to worry.

THIRTY

Rice stood in the cabin, looking up at Sara's black cat perched in the loft over the bathroom like an owl. He had no idea how she'd got in here.

Wait. She must've snuck in when he'd brought the flooring. He'd forgotten about the delivery—he'd ordered it weeks ago—and they'd unloaded down at the locked gate, so he'd hauled the floorboards up here in his pickup, nearly a thousand board feet of tongue-and-groove salvaged from a nineteenth-century warehouse somewhere in Pennsylvania. STP had found a company that catered to people like her, people who wanted to know the provenance of their building materials the way others cared about what farm their tomatoes came from, the name of the pig that gave them their pork chops. It was beautiful wood, heavy and whiskey-dark, hard as iron.

He'd intended to rent a table saw and an electric floor sander from the place in Blakely, but he didn't see them in the cabin. Not out back either. Had he forgotten that too?

Power tools might not be what he needed right now anyway. The world seemed to lie at a remove as he walked through it, as if he were piloting someone else's body, the controls mushy and imprecise. He functioned well enough in the forest, but now that he'd come out he'd begun to falter. At the edge of the meadow he'd hesitated, reluctant to return to this world. The forest seemed to hold him, to discourage him from returning to the lodge, as if only through enough time away from the human-built world would the accreted layers of self-deception dissipate like condensation evaporating from a fogged window. Or mirror. He had no idea which. He'd removed the ghillie camouflage and buried it in leaf litter and dirt because he didn't want it to pick up any civilized odors.

He watched the cat and she watched him back, her black face featureless in the indistinct light, as if she wore a veil hiding everything but her bright green eyes.

"Hello, Mel."

She showed no signs of distress, though he was afraid she might've been shut in here for a while. He wasn't sure what day of the week it was. It could be any of the seven. He couldn't rule out a single one of them.

It might even be October now. He should check in with STP.

"You know I'm supposed to shoot you."

Mel blinked at him. This is weird, he thought. He should get her down from there, encourage her to depart the cabin. She might've taken a shit somewhere. He couldn't smell it, though, just the turpentine tang of the heart pine floorboards. Should he get the ladder? He found he couldn't move. Maybe he was dreaming. He'd been dreaming intensely, furiously, desperately, he didn't even have to shut his eyes. He'd given up trying to untangle dream from experience.

Something tall and heavy began to tip in his subconscious, he saw it now, an antique hardwood hutch stuffed with precious china heeling over. He'd always stopped it before, pushed it back into place, but now that didn't seem so important. He backed away—best not to stand underneath something like that, best just to let it fall, to let it come crashing into your day.

The kid, he was skinny, taller than he'd expected. Younger, too, maybe nineteen, twenty-one at most. He dressed the part of the narco, if not the sicario, dressed it self-consciously. That had bothered Rice for a moment, the pathos of the retro outfit, the silk jacket, big silver belt buckle, snakeskin boots. Tattoos winding around his wrists, his neck. Snakes, it looked like. Buzz-cut dark hair, wide mouth, fleshy lips, heavy eyebrows. Eyes far apart, dark, frowning at the noise Rice made, a rustling as he drew the pistol and stepped out from behind a defunct Telmex booth. The kid started to react, fast but sloppy from drinking, he reached under his jacket, cross-draw, like he had a shoulder holster, but Rice was shooting, landing double taps and walking toward him, remembering what he'd learned from Raoul Fernandez, you are dead if you hesitate, and no head shots, no fucking Mozambique, the cabrito is too cocky for armor, you shoot him in the chest, shoot him as many times as you can, so he shot the kid in the upper torso eight times with the 9mm, not missing, and the kid was down, bleeding out in the packed dirt alley, gurgling and moving his right leg in slow spasmodic kicks.

Rice only had a few seconds before someone showed up.

He toed open the jacket. In the shoulder holster was a big European 9mm, an HK. Spendy, a status weapon. On his upper arm, the obligatory Santa Muerte tattoo, not what he was looking for. He rolled him over, and there was a sick-spinning horror, like maybe he'd been played, that this was somebody else, this was not the guy, he'd been tipped to murder some kid who had nothing to do with anything, but then there it was, the Mayan mask screaming on the other side of his neck, hidden beneath his collar.

The liquefaction of his internal organs reversed, firmed, every cell of his body resolute. This was not a boy dying in the street but a psychotic, sadistic murderer. Apryl's murderer. Rice's proper prey.

The mask tattoo was the family sign. The older brother, the one who would be coming for Rice after this, had one on the back of his head.

He wiped down the burner Beretta, placed it on top of the phone booth, and walked north.

He looked up at the cat still peering down from the rafters. Her inclement gaze. He could kill her with his spear, take away her life, too. Like another squirrel, another rabbit. He was a killer, he could do this. But his eyes were wet.

The horror at what he'd done to the kid in Juarez hadn't ever come back. He had worked hard at never doubting. What was this now? Which was worse? Feeling it or not feeling it? Apryl had called his pet maxim the Rice Moore Universal Paradox and Source of All Misery: "individual organisms don't matter at all, and individual organisms matter a great deal, blah blah blah." He did his best to live within that paradox, denying neither the first truth nor the second.

"I don't care," he told the cat.

"Yes, you do," the cat said.

"I don't want to."

No reply. He shook his head and stood, brushed the seat of his pants. Took off the gloves and dropped them on the floor. Glanced at the cat one last time. She sat without moving. The hallucinations were becoming routine. He left the door open.

THIRTY-ONE

He stepped quietly in the leaves, a long, slow stalk upcanyon along the eastern slope of the gorge. The gibbous moon sailing high in a clear sky lit the forest floor with patches of soft white light. He hadn't slept. His diet of squirrel meat and overripe paw-paws had upset his stomach, so he'd fasted as well. He wasn't sure how long. Three, four days. Going without food had made him woozy at first, and then came the hunger cramps, which he ignored until they went away. Now he moved through a waking dreamscape.

His thoughts had become inarticulate, the talking man-voice inside his head silenced by hunger and sleep deprivation, by too much time alone in the woods, by whatever it was that had been gradually possessing him for months. This morning, walking among the old trees of the inner gorge, he'd felt something clutch the back of his neck and lift him like a kitten. It carried him alongside the columnar trunks and up into the lower branches. Below, a bedraggled man in ghillie camouflage, dim green light falling around him, his blackened face childish and lost.

Farther up the mountain, a great horned owl hooted five times.

The night air moved over his face like water. The forest was quiet for a long while, and he felt like he must be one of the few animals awake at this hour. As if to answer his thought, a fox barked twice, somewhere behind him. He wasn't sleepy. He had become at least as comfortable in the forest at night as he had been in the daylight.

He lost some time to one of his fugues and when he came to himself a bear was walking up the slope toward him, passing through light, then shadow, then light. It was a big male, old, grizzled, limping. It seemed to be aware of his presence, able to see him despite his ghillie camouflage. Rice waited, wondering, unafraid. The bear moved into shadow, and a man came out into the moonlight. It was the mushroom picker, carrying his backpack, climbing the steep slope.

In his current state, Rice didn't find the transmogrification terribly surprising. He thought it was more important to explain that he was hunting the poachers who had killed the she-bear, but the man shushed him. He dropped to one knee and removed his pack. He laid it down between them in a moonlit patch and untied the top flap. Rice squatted on his haunches to see. The man reached in, felt around, and removed a dead bird, a male kestrel. He set it gently on the open lid of the pack, arranged just so with its wings folded and its head turned to the side, its sharp, curved beak pale yellow shading to black, the blue of its flight feathers and the deep red on its back too bright and saturated for moonlight. Its eye was a shiny liquid black. Was it really dead? Rice stared, moved by the beauty of the bird, wondering what it meant.

The mushroom picker reached inside the pack again and pulled out a plastic bag, a colorful antique Rainbo bread bag with its open end loosely knotted. Holding the bag against his chest with his stump, he untied the knot and pulled out three pale dried mushrooms the size of his thumbnail, offered them on his open palm. Rice hesitated. They looked like magic mushrooms, psilocybin. He didn't have time to get high.

"I have to be able to catch the poachers," he said.

The man nodded and reached the mushrooms a little higher, as if that's why he'd brought them. Another time dislocation occurred, the mushrooms held there motionless in front of Rice's face while he worked through a decision, the reasoning part of his mind grown slow and unaccustomed to structured thought.

Rice was unclear exactly how the shrooms were going to help him find the bear poachers. A trip might finally push him past the threshold he'd been straddling. Maybe he could simply disappear, merge somehow with the forest, finishing the process he felt had already begun. Another ghost haunting Turk Mountain. Eventually Sara would come looking for him, and she would find his clothes collapsed here in a pile, the ragged ghillie poncho no longer needed. He would be a vengeful, badass ghost, and he would torment poachers and other interlopers. They would fear him.

He expected the mushroom picker to ask what he was grinning at, but he didn't seem to notice. He was oddly intent, insistent. Making this offer to Rice seemed to mean a lot to him. Rice glanced down at the kestrel, alive now and perched on the canvas pack, regarding Rice with its head canted.

He took the mushrooms and placed them on his tongue. He chewed and swallowed. They left an unpleasant bitter taste. The mushroom picker smiled then, his teeth bright in the black shadow of his beard. He gathered up the kestrel—dead or sleeping again—and replaced it inside his pack, refastened the top, shouldered the pack, and walked away without ever speaking.

Soon three large bears appeared near the empty bait station, rearing up to snuffle and scratch at where the sweet oil had been smeared on the trees. It seemed to Rice that he was seeing as the trail cameras saw, in infrared: the bears were featureless black silhouettes against a shimmering white background. They moved in slow motion as they began to play, fighting and wrestling. More bears came, all of them huge, both boars and sows, greeting each other, familiars. Eventually they settled down, gathering for some common purpose, a council. A dozen bears formed a loose circle in the open area underneath the hanging cow's head. Several of them turned to look at Rice expectantly. He understood they were offering some sort of invitation. He felt compelled, but also, now that he came right down to it, afraid. If he joined them it would mean a kind of death. If he crossed over again he wouldn't come back. Wasn't that what he wanted?

They waited. He felt himself starting to drift again.

Sometime later he rolled to his side and sat up, dry leaves clinging to his sleeves. The ghillie poncho was tangled around and underneath him. He stood, stretched his legs, his back. He wasn't near the bait station. The ground sloped several hundred yards to a band of space and bright moonlight where the forest gave way at the top of the cliffs. He guessed he was a half mile northwest of where he'd met the mushroom picker. Could he have walked here in his sleep? He used to sleepwalk as a teenager, after his father died, but he hadn't done it in a long while.

The moon shone through the canopy behind him and to his left. It would be setting soon, had to be close to midnight, maybe past. He'd been asleep, sleepwalking, whatever, for at least an hour. The most sleep he'd had in a while. He started to rearrange the poncho on his shoulders, but then he stopped. He held his breath, listening.

A low growling sound, faint but distinct. He remembered the bears, waiting for him. This was not a sound a bear would make. He felt like his perceptions had been tuned, that he knew instantly what was out of place. The sound came from higher up the side of the gorge, off to the east, and it wasn't an animal but an engine, muffled, coasting downhill against compression. He jogged toward it, moving laterally across the slope. Not an ATV, and the slope was too steep for one anyway. A dirt bike would be louder, and high-pitched like a chainsaw. This sounded unlike any motor he'd heard.

A faint red glow appeared above him, appearing and vanishing among the trees. He remembered the gall buyer's red-filtered flashlight. He stood in his poncho and waited as the light crossed back and forth, slowly descending. A man on a motorbike of some sort, with a big black bag on the back, making his way down the steep slope in long, sweeping switchbacks. He rode thirty yards to the left, then a careful turn, maybe trying not to kick up duff, like he didn't want to leave an obvious trail, then forty yards in a shallow angle to the right, then another turn, back to the left, a patient, fully controlled zigzag down a slope Rice would've thought too steep for any vehicle. The bike would have to climb back up the same way.

Rice made a quick calculation and moved a hundred yards to his left to crouch under the branches of a big rhododendron. The rider passed through a patch of moonlight off to the right. It was a Honda trail bike with fat knobby tires, soft and partly deflated. Bulging from the side of the bike was an oversize muffler extension. It looked homemade and was about the size of two paper towel rolls end to end, raised up so it wouldn't contact the ground on the steep switchbacks. Up close, the engine sound was a low, throaty cough.

On his next turn the rider brushed past Rice's rhododendron on the uphill side, so close, his face lit red by the headlamp. Rice didn't know him. Not a Stiller, not the skinny guy Jesse. It wasn't the gall buyer from beneath the bridge. This guy was younger, bigger, nearly Rice's size. Trim beard, light skin and dark hair, deep-set dark eyes, chiseled cheekbones. Serious-looking. Military rucksack on his back, a crossbow with a quiver and a big night scope strapped on top. He'd lashed what looked like a contractor's heavy-duty trash bag to a vertical U-shaped metal bar behind the seat. The bag looked full but it couldn't be very heavy—stale pastries and popcorn for the bait station.

Rice was invisible, even in the glow from the headlamp. The guy didn't glance at him. As he passed, Rice reached out and touched the metal bar, the backside of the trash bag brushing slick against his cotton glove. He felt an upwelling of power, the undeniable, intoxicating power of invisibility, of the unseen hunter. His whole body quivered from it.

The rider turned again, and Rice turned with him and followed, stalking thirty yards back, moving in a wavy downhill line bisecting the bike's wider zigzag path. The stinking exhaust from the engine caught in his throat. They were closer to the inner gorge now. Three more turns, Rice guessed, and the rider would reach the top of the cliffs, where he would have to head down-canyon to reach the bait station.

Without knowing he'd decided to do it, he lifted up onto his toes and sprinted downslope in the ghillie poncho, his feet quiet, barely touching the ground, a dark formless monster flying over the moon-dappled forest floor.

THIRTY-TWO

The distant growling noise came again. He tried to wake up. A pleasant weight of fatigue lay on his chest like a sleeping housecat, holding him down. This was a soft, comfortable place but the thing making the sound was getting closer. He forced his eyelids open. He was in his bed, the room bright from the open window.

He squinted at the white ceiling, vague shadows cast by curtains moving in the breeze. His head hurt, and he had some trouble lifting it from the pillow. Adrenaline began shooting into his bloodstream.

Tires on gravel, coming up through the lower meadow.

He rolled and put his feet on the floor, opened the drawer in the table, pulled out the .45. He started his press-check drill but something was wrong with his hands. The fingers on his right hand wouldn't close all the way, and he couldn't make his left hand grip the top of the slide. He laid the pistol on the wool blanket beside him.

Cocked and locked.

What the hell was wrong with him? He sat on the edge of the

bed. He was dressed in loose canvas pants, filthy and torn, stained with mud and something darker splashed on the tops of his thighs, blood maybe, a ripped green T-shirt, funky wool socks. What he'd slept in.

His ghillie poncho lay in a lumpy tangle on the floor next to his pack. That was stupid. He shouldn't have brought it inside. He glanced at his pillow, the pillowcase smeared with dark dried blood, soaked through and still wet-looking in a couple of places.

Boots, over by the door. When he tried to stand, his right knee gave way and he stumbled forward to land on his hands in a hunched push-up position but his left palm split open and he collapsed to his elbow.

Frustration edged toward panic. Left knee to chest, pushing with the right hand, he stood up on the left leg, testing the right, reaching down, feeling the knee swollen and spongy, glancing at his palm, weeping watery blood and plasma from a single deep cut. The right hand wasn't much better, knuckles swollen and scraped, part of his thumbnail torn off. New pain signals arrived from other parts of his body, ribs on his right side firing up, something burning under his left arm, nausea and a headache kicking in now, a headache that made him wonder if he'd ever had a real headache before. The pain was almost audible. A convulsive retch snaked through his torso but nothing came up.

He squinted out the window, bright sunlight gouging like fingernails at the backs of his eyeballs. Dust rose in the still morning air, light flashing off a windshield, driving fast. He limped out the back door in his socks, carrying the pistol in his hand, registering the bright sun, the warm humidity, the birdsong and insect buzz. He knew his dreams had been vivid and disturbing but nothing specific came to him.

He walked past the shed toward his hiding place at the back of the cabin, but Sara's Subaru was suddenly there, pulling into the parking area. Her brakes locked and she skidded in the gravel. Sara in big sunglasses looking at him through the windshield with her mouth open.

The pistol. He reached it behind him, pushed it under his belt in the small of his back, ice on his skin. Limped to her car.

"Good morning," he said, but "good" barely qualified as a whisper, and "morning" was more like a groan. He must not have used his voice for a while. When he tried to smile, the skin under his jaw stung, flesh tearing there, another wound reopening. He touched it with his fingertips, wet, a smear of blood.

Sara stared, the engine running. Then she shut it down and got out, closed the door and leaned back against it, the engine ticking, heat coming off the car. She pushed her sunglasses up onto her head. Squinted at his face, made a move like she was going to lift her hand up and touch him, stopped and folded her arms under her breasts.

"Jesus, Rice."

He looked down at his grimy shirtfront, his left hand hanging at his side, watched with dreamy detachment as he rubbed his bloody forefinger dry against his thumb. Blood oozed from the cut in his palm and ran down his pinky finger. A drop fell to the gravel. He leaned to the side, trying to see his reflection in the car window, and there he was, distorted, dark with smeared carbon and mud, the remnants of his homemade camo face paint. He had a beard. He felt his chin to confirm, yep, a beard, which he didn't grow all that fast. Felt like several weeks' worth. Some of the darker streaks on his face looked more like blood than burnt cork.

Sara was watching him, no longer amazed, more analytical now. He tried to smile again, tried to claw his way out of his self-fascinated stupor.

"Rough night," he said.

"Rough two and a half weeks, I guess." She seemed irritated by this.

"It hasn't been that long."

Another lengthy pause. Studying him. "Starr asked me to come check on you. Apparently you two had an interesting conversation the other day."

He frowned, shook his head.

"Do you remember talking to her?"

"Um." His mind was pretty much blank on that score.

"Rice, what the hell happened? What's with the pistol? Did you find the poachers? Is that it?"

He saw a bearded face in the red glow of a headlamp passing within arm's length. There was the low-throated growl of a muffled engine. The stink of exhaust in his face. He tipped forward and flew, fast and silent, an owl dropping on its prey. This made him dizzy and he staggered, the right knee starting to fail, but he caught himself.

"Rice?"

"I don't know. I think so, maybe. The pistol's not . . . I don't carry the pistol up there."

She shook her head. A detached observer in his brain noted the thin screech of a red-shouldered hawk somewhere nearby. Perception of the world around him came and went, and like a wave washing over him he felt again the hot sun pressing down, heard the background trill of crickets. Sara's light blue eyes had gone from alarmed to worried to aggrieved in less than a minute, but as he watched, some of the usual humor crept back in. She blinked in slow motion.

"They didn't let you take their picture, did they?" Her mouth stretched into a grin but stopped short of smiling. He appreciated the way she was handling this. It occurred to him that she'd been through some shit herself, enough very serious shit that more of it happening wasn't much of a surprise. He liked that about her, it was something they had in common.

"Did you get beat up again?" she asked.

At first he wasn't sure what she meant by "again," but then it came to him, the old bear hunter whacking him with the firewood. He must've told STP about it.

Then she did smile, though she remained in that disapproving pose, resting against her car with her arms crossed.

"Starr thought you were tough. It's why she hired you."

He shrugged. "You should see the other guy?" He made it a question.

Her smile got stuck, turned rueful. She sighed.

"Did you hurt somebody this time?"

"No. I don't think so."

"You don't think so."

"I think I ran away."

They stood without speaking. He gathered she was disappointed in him. A blue jay screamed like a hawk at the edge of the forest. Probably harassing the red-shoulder, mocking it.

"You smell like a goat," she said.

He gave himself a sniff. Nothing. Must have got used to it.

Sara breathed another sigh, possibly enjoying this a little bit. "Starr said you weren't altogether coherent—her phrase—when you talked on the phone."

"I bet."

"Are you on something, Rice? Something serious?"

"Coffee and honey. Serious sleep deprivation. I think I did shrooms last night."

A skeptical look, but playing along. "Where'd you get those?"

"The mushroom picker." The patent absurdity of what he was saying tickled him, and he grinned and said "Who else?" but Sara's expression didn't change. "The guy who showed me the bear," he added.

"You saw him again?"

"I think so."

"Can you tell me what happened?"

He thought about that. He tried to remember, but concentrating made him woozy.

"Not really," he said.

THIRTY-THREE

She insisted on driving him to the quick-care medical clinic in Blakely. They knew her there and would bill the Traver Foundation. Before they left the lodge, he stood at the bathroom sink and washed the blood and mud and cork black from his face, applied deodorant, changed into cleaner dirty clothes. His whole body hurt but he dozed in her car on the way, sleepy in the hot sun, half-dreaming surreal snatches of what felt like memory from the night before: the mushroom picker offering him drugs, bears wrestling underneath the hanging cow head, the red glow of a headlamp moving through the forest. A man he didn't know buried a knife in his side and he lurched awake with a yell. Sara looked over but didn't comment.

At the clinic, a nurse led him to an exam room and got him into a gown, started an IV. She made notes on Rice's injuries, asking questions he couldn't answer. He said he didn't remember much about what had happened, and repeated the somewhat far-fetched story he and Sara had cooked up, that he'd been collecting samples on a steep rocky slope, using a sharp knife to cut away tiny pieces of a rare plant for analysis. He'd fallen and must've cut himself on the way down, hit his head on the rocks. He felt unaccountably content as he dozed off, thinking they must've put something in the drip.

A couple of hours later he was ready to leave, and when he'd dressed he found Sara in the waiting room, working on a small laptop computer. He felt stronger and more clearheaded now, so much so that he'd commented on it and the nurse said IV rehydration was the closest thing in medicine to a miracle cure. His palm had been stitched, as had his jaw—they'd shaved a patch out of his beard—and a deep cut in his left latissimus dorsi. There was a new abrasion on the side of his head and he'd suffered a mild concussion. The old wound from the guy with the firewood had mostly healed, though it should've had stitches and would leave a scar at his hairline. He'd bruised some ribs, but no fractures. His knee was bruised and sprained and he should make an appointment at the orthopedic clinic if he still couldn't put his weight on it after a day or two. Other than that, he was severely dehydrated, anemic, and fatigued. They sent him home with a handful of Tylenol 3 and told him to eat something and go to bed. To stay hydrated, to force liquids and keep his urine clear. He and Sara stopped at a deli in a strip mall on the outskirts of Blakely and she bought him two turkey sandwiches, which he ate on the way back to the lodge. He got in bed and fell asleep listening to her on the phone with STP, relaying a version of events that made him seem dedicated to his job.

When he woke the first time, he found a note from Sara on the kitchen table saying she had to get back to teach, but to please call her, to use the telephone that she had left plugged in and sitting on the desk in the office. There were smart-ass instructions on how to operate the rotary dial, how to hold the handset. She also noted that if he didn't do this, she would have to drive all the way up from Blacksburg again tomorrow, which she didn't have time to do; in fact if she did have to drive back here she would miss a deadline for a grant proposal for their study of the inner gorge, so if he had any respect at all for her work, he would pick up the goddamn phone and call her or Starr or both. Also, he should think about a trip to the grocery store because he was completely out of food.

He called and talked to Sara's answering machine, told her he was fine, that he was getting some rest, drinking his water, pissing clear.

Everything hurt, much worse than before: head, ribs, back, knee. All three cuts throbbed like they were alive. He shook three of the prescription Tylenols into his fist and washed them down with a big glass of water. He got back in bed and lay there listening to far off thunder, and after a while heavy rain came drumming on the metal roof, sifting through the screen window to fall on his face like sea spray. Sleep crept up on him, and along with it the beginnings of a dream, a scarred, ancient bear standing in a patch of moonlight, right in front of him, close enough to smell, to touch. He jerked awake. Sat up and tossed his sheet and blanket aside. Cool air smelling of rain-wet grass washed across his bare back and shoulders.

He couldn't remember what had happened in the forest. Something serious, serious enough to short out his memory. Certainly a violent encounter, and a mental episode of some sort, maybe a psychotic break. Fragments came to him but he couldn't tell what was hallucination and what wasn't. He sat on the edge of the bed with his feet on the floor and his elbows on his knees, hung his head, closed his eyes and focused, thinking back, digging for the last thing he could remember with any clarity.

Nothing but a vague smear of being in the woods, feeling invisible and amorphous, not quite human . . . whatever that meant. He strained to clasp a memory, something he could hold, some coherent thread of narrative, but he got nothing but vivid, untethered sensation. For a long stretch, who knew how long, he'd wandered the forest day and night in his ghillie camouflage, and his head had grown quiet. He seemed to have lost for a while the incessantly talking presence that he had thought was himself. Then, clearer than before, a sequence from last night: the mushroom picker, the kestrel, the mushrooms. The gathering bears, their invitation to join them, his mysterious transport to another part of the gorge, the poacher on a muffled trail bike passing close, the exhilaration of his wild swoop down the mountain. Then it shut off. Nothing. He could almost see the blank white screen, hear the broken end of the film slap-slap-slap in the film projector.

He got up and shut the window, wiped the sill dry with a towel. The codeine had kicked in and he lay back, feeling pretty good, and drifted off. A man with a knife lunged at him through a patch of moonlight and he woke up again with a start. The same image he'd seen in Sara's car. He thought about that. It was vivid, real; it corroborated a snatch of memory that he pulled into focus now, just a second, half a second, a crouched dark form thrusting fast, catching him in his left side, not a knife but an arrow, a crossbow bolt with a nasty black four-blade broadhead on the tip. That explained the wound under his arm. But he thought of the white powder he'd found in the entrance wounds on the two bear carcasses. They hadn't run far. Why wasn't he dead?

THIRTY-FOUR

The rain had stopped the next time he woke. A dim light outside, felt like early morning. If he'd dreamed again, he didn't remember it. No more memories from the other night came to him. He showered and shaved, careful of the stitched cut on his jaw, and in the kitchen he turned on the radio long enough to hear the weather forecast. The line of thunderstorms that passed through yesterday was just a taste of what was coming—a Class 3 hurricane named Julia had made landfall on Florida's panhandle and was already drenching north Georgia, the mountains of North Carolina. Flood warnings had been issued for the entire mid-Atlantic region. It was Tuesday, October 7. He'd slept for a day and a half.

He checked the fridge and the cabinets, but Sara was right, he was out of food. In the freezer a crumpled paper bag with the last few ounces of coffee. He was out of milk so he drank it black. The wild honeycomb in the freezer was gone. He wondered what he'd done with it. No way he could've eaten it all. Could he?

The coffee went down more easily than he'd expected, the caffeine helping him to focus. On the front porch, sitting on the steps where Sara had sat with her notebook, he finished his cup and watched the gray predawn. He still felt a neurotic pull to be up on the mountain looking for the poachers, and this afternoon he would hike up there and walk around near the bait station, try to jog his memory, decide what to do next. First, though, a trip into town for supplies. A list started to form, a trick he'd used in school: imagining a crumpled envelope, seeing his hands flattening it out on a table, then a pen in his hand, writing down what he needed to remember. Whatever he wrote down would be there in his head, as sure as a paper list in his pocket. Before he left he checked the cabin, where the floorboards he could barely remember stacking were still waiting to be laid. He swept up, reordered his tools and inventoried his supplies, added a few things to his mental list.

Early fall had arrived cool and clear after the thunderstorms, a few scattered maples and oaks wetly red high on the mountains, the forest pale green in the lower elevations. When he was close enough to Blakely to pick up the public station on the truck radio, he heard another report on Hurricane Julia, now a tropical storm, and the potential for an official end to the summer's drought. Rice had never been in a hurricane, and he found it hard to imagine, especially on a bluebird autumn morning. Julia must have sucked away all the moisture from this part of the world, leaving blue skies and dry, gentle breezes.

In Lowe's, his facial cuts and contusions got some looks from the shy, heavyset checkout girl, who must've assumed he was another bar-brawling construction guy. At the rental place he picked up the table saw and floor sander.

Saving the grocery store for last, he filled a shopping cart with his usual supplies: beer, bread, peanut butter, oatmeal, cereal, canned tuna, coffee, milk. A big block of white cheddar on sale. A dozen bags of various frozen vegetables, fresh local apples, bananas. He'd lost at least fifteen pounds, and he needed to regain his strength. A hungry man in the grocery could be dangerous even under normal conditions, but after his weeks alone in the forest, Rice felt like a hunter-gatherer tumbled into a bizarre cornucopian paradise. Where had all this food come from?

At the meat counter he ordered five pounds of ground turkey. While the guy wrapped the meat, Rice stared through the glass at the neat cuts of bloody beef, the pale chicken breasts, suddenly remembering for the first time the animals he'd killed. Squirrels, rabbits, grouse. Every hunt came back to him in detail. He saw deer glide past, unaware of his hunger, his hankering for venison. He recalled he'd spent a day trying to make a bow and arrows, a childish effort that failed miserably, the bow twisting when he drew it, imperfect arrows flying out on random vectors. His problem was he had no elders to teach him, and now he resolved to look on the Internet and figure it out. He'd been a good shot with a bow and arrow as a teenager. He would make his own tools and kill a couple of does during the archery season before the local deer hunters arrived for the nuisance hunt. He wouldn't have to buy meat again.

All that would come later. Now he was in the store, where the pickings were easy. Possessed by gluttony and a little vertigo, he foraged under the fluorescent lights, filling his cart and jostling politely with extra-large matrons hollering emphatic local dialect into their cell phones. Stocking up before the storm, they piled milk gallons and diapers and juice boxes and bags of frozen tater tots into their own groaning carts and ignored Rice altogether.

He drove west out of town, taking the long way home through a series of pastoral valleys, eventually turning onto a gravel road that followed the south bank of the Dutch River. The road wound around tiny deserted hamlets on the higher ground, in and out of long narrow hayfields in the floodplain, through small woodlots where old trees reached their branches out over the road. The air gusting through the open windows of his truck was cool and smelled of wet leaves, dry grass, and gravel dust. The sun seemed to be drifting away, exhausted. Overhead, a flock of migrating grackles moved in a coordinated cloud, the inky iridescent feathers and fierce yellow eyes invisible at this distance. A broad-winged hawk rose up out of the river bottom and the grackle flock veered toward it in a point, harassing it downstream like a cartoon bee swarm. He'd been out of CERESO now for longer than he'd been inside, but even a short incarceration could change the way a person sees the world, and almost a year after his release, the pleasure and novelty of driving alone through open country had not abated.

When he pulled into the entrance to the preserve, the gate was shut but the padlock was open on the chain. For a moment the old panic flashed through him, but clearly it was someone with a key. Not Sara—she felt the same way Rice did about keeping the gate locked—which left the fire department and law enforcement.

He ran through the possibilities on the way up the driveway. The game warden might have heard about the poaching and stopped by. There could be a fire at the lodge or on the mountain—maybe the poacher had retaliated—but he hadn't seen any smoke on his way out from town. The poacher might've complained to the sheriff about being attacked on the preserve by some psycho in a ghillie suit. Of course, then he would have to admit he'd been trespassing, on his way to stock his illegal bait station, and that he'd stabbed Rice with an arrow, poisoned or otherwise. That kind of escalation to deadly force would at least raise eyebrows in the sheriff's office. Who else? Maybe the Stillers were making trouble.

Topping the final rise, he found two vehicles parked in front of the cabin, a dark blue Ford Expedition with *Sheriff's Department* in white on the driver's door, and beside it a big Chevy pickup towing a trailer with two ATVs chained down side by side. He reached down and made sure the .45 was tucked all the way into its hiding place in the seat. If they'd somehow got a warrant and searched the lodge, what would they have found? Nothing. He didn't own anything illegal or incriminating other than his pistol. A couple thousand dollars cash in the fireproof box in the attic wouldn't look good, but these folks weren't revenuers. He didn't think they'd climb up there on a routine search anyway. You had to know where the trapdoor was, and get up on a chair to pull the short cord, duck the ladder that came sliding down at your head.

Two men and a woman leaned against the end of the trailer, one of the men in a brown uniform, clearly the sheriff, trim, not a big guy, with close-cropped gray hair, maybe in his late sixties. He was older than Rice had expected, though STP had said he'd been sheriff forever. The other two were both short and stocky, strong-looking, could've been brother and sister. All three carried Glocks on their hips in black plastic holsters. The woman was talking into a handheld radio. She turned away from the breeze coming off the meadow, listening to the radio. She had a long dark ponytail hanging down her back over her bright green jacket. On the rear window of the pickup cab was a sticker, the black silhouette of an M4 military carbine.

He parked beside the sheriff's vehicle. When he got out, the sheriff walked up and stuck out his hand. "Mr. Morton, I'm Sheriff Mark Walker. Sorry to barge in on you like this, but we're looking for a missing person up on your mountain."

Rice swallowed, returning the man's handshake. Walker had a firm grip—Rice's hand still hurt like hell and he had to fight not to wince—and he hung on for an extra beat, watching Rice's eyes. Rice had seen law enforcement folks who were so stupid you couldn't believe their spouses let them leave the house alone, never mind carry a firearm and the power of the state. Others were as smart as anyone he'd ever encountered. This Sheriff Walker had a smart look to him. He'd obviously noticed the stitched cut on Rice's jaw and he was studying him without seeming to.

"Nobody's seen this fella for three days. Couple witnesses say he was driving around with a dirt bike in his truck either Friday or Saturday. This morning search-and-rescue found his truck parked at the end of a Forest Service access road over the other side of Serrett Mountain, somebody'd vandalized it, smashed the windows, slashed the tires. No bike, but they saw what might've been tracks going east. Course after the rain there wasn't much left. Some of the search-and-rescue folks—I'm sorry, these are my deputies, Bayard Stimson and Janie Broad."

Rice nodded, they nodded back.

"The search-and-rescue folks have been riding around on the logging roads with dogs, working east from the truck, but they haven't found anything, no more tracks, no bike, no missing person. We were wondering if you might've seen anyone?" That last sentence was a question, gentler than a declaration, eyebrows up, his face still holding an official, apologetic smile. Like the sheriff was still giving this Rick Morton out-of-towner the benefit of the doubt. Though he might've heard about his scrape with the Stillers, and that he was an eco-Nazi hermit who lived up here all alone, and hell who knew what else, and here Rick was, looking freshly beat up from yet another scrape, and there was this truck vandalism, this person gone missing on or near the Turk Mountain Preserve.

Thinking all this, Rice hesitated. It was only for an instant but in that instant he saw the sheriff's eyes change. They sharpened, and his body shifted, a subtle tensing, and just like that Rice was a *person of interest*. Walker's smile never wavered. Rice had seen this before. Without another word spoken, the air had changed, roles had been assumed, and in the face of that kind of suspicion, the truth—or as much of it as possible—was the only thing that was going to work.

"I saw a guy on a motorbike, an old trail bike with a souped-up muffler, to make it quiet. He was way up in the woods, in that big gorge on the other side of the mountain. It was Saturday night, or maybe Sunday morning early."

"And—"

"We've had some poaching, dead bears left in the woods."

"I've heard of that. They sell the gallbladders."

"That's right. I found where someone had been killing bears over bait, at night, and I was up there watching. A guy rode down on his bike, he had a crossbow with a night-vision scope. I accosted him"—he flinched inside at the euphemism—"and he went crazy, tried to kill me with an arrow from his crossbow." Rice cocked up his chin to show the cut on his jaw. "I got away, and I guess he took off."

Rice held the sheriff's now one hundred percent skeptical law enforcement gaze, but in the long pause he could see he'd thrown him with his story. It was shit you wouldn't make up. You wouldn't want to, under the circumstances. You'd make up something less incriminating. In his peripheral vision, the deputies gave each other a look.

"How come you didn't call our office about this? If he attacked you like you say. An assault with a weapon like that is something most people would report."

"I'm all right. And I was more worried about the bear poaching anyway. I thought about calling the game warden, but there wasn't much he could do. I figure the poacher fellow knows I'm onto him now, and maybe he won't come back."

The sheriff just looked at him, poker-faced as hell. "Why's that?"

"I might've spooked him some. It was night and all. I think that's why he attacked me."

"So you don't blame him for trying to stab you with a arrow."

"Well, I wouldn't say that. But what was I going to tell the police—you all, your office—about it anyway? He was long gone. It was night . . . I didn't get a good look at his face." Rice pictured the chiseled face in the red headlamp. He reached up and grasped his own chin with thumb and forefinger. "He had a beard, a short beard. He sure never told me his name."

"And now he's gone missing. And somebody messed up his truck."

"I don't know anything about that."

"Uh-huh." Walker turned and nodded to the other two and they jumped up and started unfastening the ATVs, moving them down from the trailer. "You mind showing us where all this happened?"

THIRTY-FIVE

The four of them rode the ATVs up the fire road, Rice on the extended seat behind Bayard, and Sheriff Walker riding behind Janie Broad. Rice had suggested the others start up the mountain without him while he put away groceries in the freezer and fridge. He could leave the heavy sander and table saw in the truck for now but he couldn't afford to let all that food spoil. Walker had given him a quizzical look and said they'd wait. Like Rice might try to escape in his truck, or maybe he couldn't catch the ATVs on foot. Now they were steering the unwieldy vehicles through the pine saplings grown up in the road, barely beating his walking pace, but he didn't think hopping off and jogging ahead would impress the Sheriff's Department. His knee had swollen some during his morning in town anyway, so he told himself to relax and appreciate the ride.

Bayard had introduced himself with "Call me Stoner," not a friendly gesture but, Rice surmised, a declaration that no one but the sheriff was allowed to call him by his real name. He was a muscular, energetic guy with a buzz cut, smelled of cologne and clean sweat. Rice wondered about the nickname. Maybe it was ironic. The guy was wound up and squared away, either ex-military or wished he were. Before they'd mounted the ATV, Stoner had drawn his Glock from its holster and locked it in a small plastic vault underneath the handlebars. Rice had grinned at this and Stoner, smiling back, had said, "It was up to me you'd be in handcuffs." He offered no more conversation on the way up the mountain. He seemed to have decided the missing motorbike rider had stumbled upon Rice's meth lab, and Rice had offed him and buried the body on the mountain.

In fact, Rice was acutely aware of the fact that he didn't remember *not* killing the poacher. The truck vandalism didn't sound at all familiar, but who could say? There had definitely been a fight—his wounds were real, and his recurring visions of the guy stabbing him were too vivid to be imagined. It was at least plausible that Rice had won the fight after all, that he'd injured or killed the poacher before wandering off in an amnesiac rage to beat on the guy's pickup truck. He considered leading the search party to a completely different part of the gorge and then coming back later by himself to scout the real scene, just in case. But he'd already mentioned the bait station, the bear carcasses, and they were going to want to see that. And if he had killed someone, he knew from experience he would feel something in his bones no matter how hard he tried to forget it, and right now he just didn't.

They parked the ATVs on the fire road at the spot where Rice usually turned off to drop into the gorge. Janie had been talking the other searchers in on the radio, and soon four more ATVs with five searchers and three dogs motored into sight, coming down the fire road from higher on the mountain. Rice had repaired the fence next to the Forest Service gate where the Stillers had come through, so these folks must have the fire department's key to the padlocks. He thought about asking how they'd got past the wasp nest, but everyone was acting uptight, eyeing him with open hostility.

Two of the searchers' dogs were Labradors, one yellow and one black, both wiggly, happy-looking females, trotting ahead of the vehicles. The third was a big male German shepherd riding on a platform like the Stillers' bear dogs, his collar clipped to a thick leather leash held by a tall woman riding behind one of the drivers. The drivers were shutting down their engines when the shepherd noticed Rice and charged, yanking the leash from the woman's hand. She and the guy driving her ATV started yelling, "Derek, no!" but Rice crouched, his knee firing with pain, and held out his hands, palms down, thinking who names a dog Derek? The dog skidded to a halt and sniffed his fingers, swept his big tail back and forth in a graceful arc. The tall woman walked slowly toward them, speaking in a calm, low voice, saying things like *whoa there* and *just hold real still mister* and *hey Derek big buddy*. Two ATV motors were still going but their drivers just sat there, frozen. Everyone else stood where they were and watched Rice and the dog.

The sheriff's voice, quiet but firm: "Get your dog, Sue Ann."

"Hello, Derek," Rice said. "Everything's fine." He thought these people were overreacting just a little bit. The dog looked him in the eyes, stepped forward and began licking his chin, working his way over to the cut on his jaw and licking more insistently there. Derek's breath was hot, humid. Smelled of dirt and dog kibble.

The woman stood in the fire road, her hands loose at her sides. She stopped trying to coax the dog and stared.

"Shit," someone said.

Rice reached up and scratched the lush hair behind Derek's stiff ears. This was the biggest shepherd he'd ever seen, nearly as tall as Bilton Stiller's yellow bear dog, and he could fit Rice's whole head in his jaws if he wanted. After a few seconds it felt like Derek's tongue was starting to rip the stitches from his flesh, but when Rice tried to gently push him away, Derek braced his feet and kept licking. Rice pushed harder but Derek was immovable, so he gave up and endured the dog's attentions, hoping dog slobber was somehow therapeutic.

"That dog has put four perps in the hospital, Mr. Morton." This was Stoner speaking. "You're a lucky mo."

"I like dogs. They can tell." Rice rose, wincing again at his knee, and handed Sue Ann the end of Derek's leash. He turned to face Stoner. "And I'm not a perp."

He led the way through the rhododendron and laurel thicket and down the steep forested slope toward the bait station, keeping the pace slow. Everyone in the group had trouble keeping their feet, slipping in the wet leaves, hanging on to saplings, sliding down on their butts. Derek wanted to walk up front with Rice and the other dogs, and his handler was glad to hand back the leash. Apparently the two labs were "air scent dogs" and worked off-leash, while Derek was more of a trailing dog.

Rice could tell the searchers were warming up to him—Derek must be known as a good judge of character—and now they all seemed to trust him as their guide, descending into the gorge. The two labs looked to him for direction now, and he held the leash of the trailing dog. If he led the group straight to the body, he was going to look like the stupidest murderer in history.

THIRTY-SIX

The walk down to the bait station took nearly an hour, and by the time they got there the sky in the canopy opening had a greenish cast, milky with high clouds, and the treetops were beginning to shift in a fitful breeze. These folks were slower than Sara had been, less sure-footed. Most of them, anyway. The big woman who handled Derek seemed to be having less trouble, and Stoner was half-killing himself to make sure he kept up with Rice. The group was quiet, probably thinking of the climb back up to the vehicles.

At the bait station, Rice showed them the hanging cow's head, the scattered and desiccated remains of the bear carcasses, and the scars in the oak where the poacher had used climbing spikes. From there they quartered another half mile up the south slope, and after a short search Rice found the big rhododendron where he had waited as the poacher rode past him.

He stood next to the twenty-foot-tall shrub. The others gathered around, looking at him. Here's the last place I remember, he thought.

"I was hiding here, and the guy on the bike was switchbacking down the slope, I could hear the bike, a low-pitched compression, motor noise, then I saw his red headlamp."

"You use red 'cause it won't ruin your eyes at night," Stoner said.

"Yeah, I thought he'd be using night vision, but the NV scope was on his crossbow and I guess he got around using that headlamp. I didn't see him until he was pretty close, maybe up there, he went past that big white oak." He pointed, and saw in his mind the red glow disappearing as the bike passed behind the trunk, reappearing on the other side, slowing for another turn. "He came right toward me, couldn't see me at all." He hesitated. They would find it later if they searched the tractor shed, so better to get it out now, when he could manage the story. "I was wearing this old poncho I'd done up as kind of a ghillie suit."

"A ghillie suit?"

"My homemade version." They all seemed to know what a ghillie suit was. Sheriff Walker's face didn't give away much, but Stoner and a couple of the others were starting to smile, trying not to seem eager. *Of course* you were wearing a ghillie suit.

"I'm supposed to keep track of the wildlife here, keep records of what I see and where. I figured good camouflage would help. I got in the habit of using it when I'm out in the woods." He shrugged. It was time to start making shit up anyway. "So I was kind of crouched here by the bush, in the poncho"—Rice pointed—"and he was right there when I just stood up. I startled him, I guess. He slid his bike down hard on his leg, but he got right up. I was starting to tell him this is posted property and he was trespassing and what was his name, I don't know how far I got before he . . ." Rice paused, distracted. The night was coming back to him now, just a trickle at first, but vivid, real. As he stood there, he felt himself rise and fly down the mountain.

"You okay?"

"Yeah, sorry. I'm trying to remember exactly what happened. It was a little disturbing. He pulled one of his arrows from a quiver on his crossbow and tried to stab me with it."

"Bolt," Stoner corrected.

"I bolted all right. I took off down the hill, that way." He pointed to where he'd followed behind the poacher after he'd ridden past. He started moving downslope, following the memory as it came to life in his mind. At the same time, he was struggling to make up a more palatable story for his audience. He took big steps, sliding in the leaves on the steep slope, and the others followed, slipping and sidestepping, trying to keep up. His stomach flipped and sank, reliving the roller-coaster drop of his final wild sprint at the poacher.

Fifty yards down, he felt the impact, the deep compression of the guy's ribs under his shoulder, heard a retching expulsion of breath. His momentum lifted the poacher from the bike, the plastic bag of bear bait bursting, a sick rotten sweetness in his face, Rice and the poacher airborne together, the poacher relaxed, almost limp, must be knocked out. He held on to the guy's pack, holding it away from his face, the crossbow strapped there swinging wild. They hit the slope hard and slid in the deep leaf litter.

He stopped in the spot where they'd landed, waited until the others caught up and were standing around him again. No one said anything.

"I ran down here, but he followed on his bike." Even after yesterday's rain, the forest duff was obviously disturbed in a broad, twisting path leading toward the cliff overlooking the inner gorge. "He ditched the bike somewhere around here and came at me on foot. He had a big plastic bag on his bike, with the bait, and I could smell it, I think it must've broken open." He bent over and pawed through the rain-wet moldering leaves. "Critters probably ate most of it by now, but there should still be some of the crap that spilled out."

Derek and the other dogs found it, scratching in the leaves

themselves, sniffing and wagging at the soggy popcorn, fragments of glazed doughnuts. The tall woman stooped to look at what they'd found, praising the dogs.

Both legs felt wobbly when he stood; the fight was coming back to him in real time.

They rolled twice, three times, fast, the red headlamp went dark, and Rice started to push away, meaning to roll clear to his feet, but the poacher came to life, strong hands ripping at the poncho, reaching back to claw at the back of Rice's head, pulling, trying to flip him forward. When Rice threw his leg around to clamp the other man's thigh and brace himself, the man's head jerked back in a wild head-butt. Rice turned to the side at the last instant but the glancing blow above his ear was still hard enough to set off a bright orange flash behind his eyes. The guy had too much fight left and Rice wanted to finish him. He unhooked his leg but hung on to the pack, twisted it to tangle the guy up in the straps, then he levered to his feet, and pivoting, using what was left of their momentum, he slung the poacher as hard as he could into a tree trunk.

That should have been the end of the fight. What came next should not have happened. Surprise, a touch of admiration, a little fear flushed through him in the remembering. He knew he should say something to the sheriff and the searchers—they were standing and watching him, waiting—but he closed his eyes and saw the guy bounce off the tree with a grunt, spinning, moving fast and low like a wolf spider in the broken moonlight, shedding his pack and pulling a bolt from the quiver on the crossbow in one impossible motion, lunging at Rice with the glinting black blades on its head. He felt the point catch in the layers of burlap on the poncho and he threw himself backward, twisting away from the attack, the other man pursuing and making short, efficient thrusts with the bolt.

"He's got the bolt in his hand, it has a broadhead, I could see that in the moonlight." He fought to control his breathing so he could speak, his body responding to the memory, injecting his blood with counterproductive adrenaline. "I thought it was poisoned. He'd been using poison on the bears. I thought he was going to kill me. If I hadn't been wearing the ghillie with all that thick burlap, he would've killed me." He backed along the path of torn-up leaves he and the poacher had made, half-mimicking in slow motion his part in the fight. He didn't have to make this up. "He kept stabbing at me, and he got me a few times, not deep. I was scrambling, backing up, trying to get away from him."

He remembered backing up fast, dodging behind tree trunks, feeling in the leaves for a stick, a rock, anything. The poacher was wheezing hard, couldn't catch his breath, but he kept pushing, not speaking, a relentless shadow, anticipating Rice's movements, denying him time to find his footing or come up with a weapon. Rice knew he had to try something or die so he faked a stumble, shifting his weight to his left foot and setting up a round kick with his right leg. The poacher bought it and moved in close, the four-blade tip whistling in the air as he swiped it at Rice's face, trying to blind him. Rice blocked it with his hand and threw the kick low, connecting with his shin on the outside of the poacher's knee, buckling it, but at the same time the broadhead bit through the cotton glove into his palm and he thought of the poison, the realization coming in an instant, thinking, Now I'm dead, this asshole just killed me.

He was only vaguely aware of the sheriff and the others. This immersion in his own memory was a version of his usual fugue and at some level he understood he was probably acting oddly, but he also knew that if he resisted it he might never know what had happened. He let it come, a little afraid of what he would find out, stepping along in the leaves, watching the end of the fight unfold in his mind.

He caught the poacher's wrist to hold off the bolt and stepped close enough to pound with his other fist, hammering the side of the guy's head, his face, but the poacher was strong and even with Rice's hand locked onto his wrist the bolt smacked his jaw, stabbed his left side where the burlap wasn't as thick. It didn't matter. He didn't care about the poison now. He grabbed the man's head with his thumb jamming into an eye socket and the man cursed for the first time as Rice wrenched him to the right, forcing him to put his weight on his left leg, and while it was pinned there he slammed the knee with another round kick. This time something cracked and he went down, a controlled backward roll, pulling Rice down too, trying to pull him onto the bolt, to impale him, but Rice pushed with his legs, jumping forward at the last second, somersaulting over the broadhead, and it was as if he had dived into nothingness. The man's grip on his poncho failed and the ground fell away under him until he smashed feetfirst through a rhododendron bush and slid on his ass another fifty feet, grabbing at branches ripping past, pain spiking as he struck rock with his knee, his ribs, his head.

He stood at the edge of the cliff where he'd fallen. He was lucky; the slope down to the ledge where he'd fetched up wasn't absolutely vertical, and it was thick with brush. Leaves had begun to wilt on the branches he'd broken on his way down. The others had followed, and when he turned to read their faces, Stoner was the only one still skeptical. Rice's story was true, true for the sheriff and the others. He wasn't acting. They didn't know he'd been remembering it for the first time—what they saw was a man recalling a traumatic experience, and it gave his account authenticity that went beyond good acting.

"I fell down there. I didn't mean to, but it's what saved me. The brush broke my fall. I was out for a while on that ledge, and by the time I climbed back up and dragged my ass over the edge here it was quiet. He was gone, back up that slope, I guess." Rice made a zigzag motion with his hand to describe the guy's path, the way he could get a trail bike in and out of that steep gorge. "He probably figured he'd killed me."

"He cut you. You must've been wrong about the poison."

Rice looked at Stoner. "I guess so."

More remembering: a dead man, vengeful and impotent, he clawed his way back up the cliff, his own right leg nearly useless, nausea sweeping his guts, nausea and a seething, disbelieving wrath. He tried to run up the slope to follow but his knee was bad and wouldn't hold him. The pain rushed in and he leaned against a tree, vomited some watery bile, all he had. The poison was starting to work. He hoped he'd at least done some real damage to the guy's knee. That left eye would be sore for a while, too. He staggered to the edge of the cliff and sat there on a rock. His pulse still raced, but his breathing quieted. He didn't experience vivid memories from his life. He felt tired. He dry-heaved a few times. No more hallucinations, no transcendent experiences. Just pain, bad but not yet so bad that he couldn't handle it. He wondered how the poison would kill him. Convulsions? Internal bleeding? Would he start vomiting blood? He hoped he wouldn't shit himself. A panic attack threatened briefly, but he quelled it.

He waited to die while the moonlight failed, moonset darkening the forest in the inner gorge. At least this was a good place to do it. But the minutes passed, and he didn't get worse. In fact, after twenty minutes he felt a little better, the nausea passing the way it usually did when he injured his knee. He'd always had glass kneecaps, and he'd had to learn to manage pain at an early age. Eventually he decided he wasn't dying after all and began the long, excruciating hobble back to the lodge. No detour to smash up anyone's truck, though; no way, not in his condition. He'd gone straight home.

"You know," Stoner was saying, "it don't surprise me Mirra come at you like that, with the bolt. That fucker can go off like a grenade."

"Shut up, Stoner," Janie said.

"You all know him?" The poacher, so long a frustrating mystery, had a name. *Mirra.* Rice wondered why they hadn't mentioned it before.

"What does surprise me," Stoner continued, ignoring both of them, "is you still breathing. He's a scary mother barehanded, but a guy like that comes at you with a weapon of any kind, he comes at you with *a ballpoint pen*, and you are a fucking ghost."

"Bayard." This was the sheriff. Stoner shut up.

Rice nodded, agreeing with Stoner. He would dream of it again: that quick spidery shadow, stabbing, black blades in the moonlight.

"I'm breathing," he said, "because I ran backward as fast as I could and fell down the damn cliff."

They all laughed at this, even Sheriff Walker, even Stoner, after a moment.

Rice grinned, playing the part, but he didn't feel like laughing. He was wondering where this Mirra had gone. It made him nervous that no one knew where he was.

THIRTY-SEVEN

t the lodge, the sheriff answered a call on his cell and sat in his SUV to talk while Stoner and Janie drove the ATVs back onto the trailer. They planned to drive around to the far side of the mountain and up the Forest Service road to join the rest of the search party. They'd all agreed that if they were going to find Mirra they had better do it before the storm hit, so the group had split up in the gorge, and two of the guys had used ropes to rappel to the bottom with the smaller Labrador so they could search along the base of the cliff. Rice had told them they would be able to climb out a mile or so upstream. He was uncomfortable with their intrusion into the inner gorge, but under the circumstances there wasn't much he could do about it. The others, with Derek the shepherd and the chunkier Lab, had set off on the trail of the motorbike, though apparently rubber tires didn't leave much of a scent for the dogs to follow, especially after a hard rain.

Rice put away the rest of the groceries, and when he checked, Walker was still on the phone but Stoner and Janie had left without him. The sheriff had asked Rice for his driver's license, and by now he'd had someone run his license and plates, which was a problem.

Supposedly the top cartels had got IT religion a few years ago and hired a bunch of elite hackers out of Eastern Europe to quietly infiltrate computer networks used by U.S. law enforcement agencies. Now simply querying his name in the Arizona MVD database was like sending up an electronic flare: *Rice Moore is in Turpin County, Virginia.* Or maybe it wasn't that precise. Or maybe the whole story was another tall tale, his pals in CERESO messing with him.

He was about to start the coffee machine when he heard the Explorer's door slam and then Walker's boots slow and loud on the front steps. Rice met him on the porch. He was frowning and his lips were pressed in a tight line like he was biting back his temper.

"Is Rice a family name? It's unusual."

Shit. "My mother's middle name. Not sure why they gave it to me as a first name but they did."

"And you've been using 'Rick Morton' because you're hiding out from the Mexican drug gang you testified against last year."

"I never had to formally testify, but yeah, to them I'm a loose end. Or maybe more like a hangnail. I think if they could find me they'd try to take me out."

"But you're not in WITSEC. You're hiding on your own."

Rice nodded. Walker was mad but didn't seem mad at him. The wind was gusting oddly from the south, warm and wet. Rice could feel it plainly now: a dramatic, unfamiliar change in the weather.

"You want to come inside? I'm making coffee."

Walker's face relaxed a bit. Rice thought he saw the start of a slow grin. His primary suspect in a potential homicide offering him coffee. "Out here's just fine, Mr. Moore." He stepped over to the railing and leaned forward with his hands on the top, looked out at the big view. Nearly everyone who spent more than a few seconds on this porch seemed to do the same thing. Rice had done it a few times himself. Today the valley was soft and far off in the weird light coming from those high green clouds. He watched Walker sidelong.

"So what now?"

"Well, I have an ex-con who was the last person to see Mirra and who admits to being in a life-or-death fight with him the night he disappeared."

"Life-or-death for me. Not so much for him."

Walker didn't say anything. He seemed to be working through a decision-making process even as Rice watched. Might be a good time to argue his case a bit.

"Sheriff, I told you the truth up there. And my record, the thing in Mexico, it was all completely nonviolent. No reason to think I'd hurt anyone. All that mess, that whole world, it's behind me. I've made a new start here."

"Right, well, I talked to your boss and she sure vouched for you. But now here comes the real interesting part. I also just talked to someone who insists you *are* violent, a dangerous hombre, and he wants me to lock you up."

This made no sense. Rice frowned but didn't reply.

"He thinks you killed Mirra and hid the body. He's a fed." Walker's voice was flat, but it conveyed his feelings about federal law enforcement officers telling local sheriffs what to do.

Rice shook his head. Still made zero sense. He hesitated. "I didn't kill the guy. You know I didn't."

"I don't know anything. If we find Alan Mirra dead up on that mountain of anything other than a rattlesnake bite, Bayard'll be back up here with his handcuffs." He turned away for a moment like he was hiding the grin that had finally taken over his face. Probably picturing Mirra chasing Rice over the cliff. "But I believe your story. Most of it."

"Thanks." He supposed he should start praying to the mountain gods that Mirra turns up drunk somewhere, nursing a sprained knee, a black eye. Busted ribs. A swollen ear. Shit. "This fed, how does he know me?"

Walker shrugged. "He's the one who flagged Mirra going

missing in the first place, and he's been bothering me—bothering Suzy—about him since yesterday morning. I owed him an update. When I mentioned your name, your real name, and the fact that you're the caretaker up here, he 'bout had kittens. He knew your record. Said he's run your prints. I don't think he likes you much."

"Where in the hell did he get my prints?"

"Didn't say."

"I have absolutely no idea who this guy could be, or how he knows me, or where—why—he would've picked up my fingerprints."

"I can't help you with that." Walker started down the steps, speaking back over his shoulder, careless, more casual than how he'd come up, which Rice took as a hopeful sign. "Meet me at my office in an hour. Your DEA friend will be there. We'll figure this out."

Rice watched Walker's vehicle back out and turn and roll down the driveway. DEA. He must've let that slip on purpose. Rice stood there thinking for a long while after the sheriff's brake lights disappeared into the forest, but he failed to come up with even the most far-fetched theory to explain why a DEA agent in Virginia had developed a grudge against him.

THIRTY-EIGHT

He parallel-parked in a two-hour spot on Main Street and found the sheriff's office in the basement of the old brick courthouse. The lady at the front desk was on the phone, talking to someone about the hurricane, explaining without much patience that if the water comes up to the house then they ought to get out of the house. She held up a finger and gestured toward a line of plastic chairs along the wall. When she hung up he approached the desk and told her he had a meeting with Sheriff Walker. She rolled her chair forward and gave him a singles-bar once-over.

"He'll be here in a minute, had to stop off at his house and change. You don't look like a drug mule."

"Thanks. You must be Suzy."

She typed a few keys and looked at her monitor. "You don't want me to process you into custody, do you?"

"How'd you know?"

"Sheriff said you were paranoid." She smiled and picked up a plastic pen, leaned back in her chair, laid the tip of the pen between her teeth. She was a little heavy but pretty, buxom and dressed to show it, probably not much older than he was.

"I didn't think I was going to be arrested anyway."

"You're not. Did you have to swallow condoms stuffed with heroin?"

He grinned. "It wasn't like that."

"I'm so glad."

He knew she was flirting and it flummoxed him. Must be his sexy scars and bruises. Now that he checked, no wedding ring. He didn't have one either, of course, and they were of an age. Had he lost all of his instincts for this stuff? He used to be a relatively normal guy.

"You look like that actor, Viggo Mortenson? But not in a good way. You know, like in *The Road*?"

He wasn't sure what to say to that. He hadn't seen the movie.

Still appraising him, she said, "You look like you're not getting enough sleep."

Walker came through the door, looking harried. He'd changed into jeans and work boots and a blue short-sleeved shirt untucked. A Virginia Tech baseball cap, tan golf jacket under his arm.

"Anything on the missing guy?" Rice asked.

Walker shook his head. "No, but I am getting tired of hearing your name. Names. Bilton Stiller called to accuse Rick Morton of murdering three of his bear hounds. Said they went missing a couple of weeks ago on Turk Mountain. He'd heard about Alan Mirra, and he figures you've gone crazy, killing men and dogs too up on that mountain."

"Mr. Stiller has been watching too much television."

"Mr. Stiller's an asshole." This from Suzy.

Walker ignored her. "I asked him how many beers he'd had so far today and he laughed and hung up. You ready?"

"We going somewhere?"

"We have to sneak out to an old motel on Route 22 to meet this character. You'd better drive. Everyone knows my truck."

"Is he undercover or something?"

"That he is, Mr. Moore. Agent Johns is an undercover pain in my arse."

"Y'all have a nice time," Suzy said.

Outside, darker clouds were piling up in the south, with heavy arms and wispy tentacles reaching northward, the storm reconnoitering. Rice drove, and Walker pulled his hat down low and slouched in his seat. The county sheriff's ass on his illegally concealed .45 gave Rice some shortness of breath, but he'd tried sitting on it himself when he'd started hiding it in the seat. Rice had fifty pounds on the sheriff, and if he couldn't feel it, Walker couldn't feel it.

"I'm too old for this cloak-and-dagger crap. I hope you appreciate it."

"I do appreciate it, Sheriff." A light turned yellow and he accelerated through it. Who was going to stop him? "You know the Stiller family pretty well?"

"I know 'em better than I want to. Bilton's all right."

"But the boys?"

"What are you getting at, Mr. Moore?"

Best out with it. "I think they raped Sara Birkeland. Them and that guy Jesse who's always with 'em."

"And what makes you think that?"

"They had a motive, to intimidate her, run her off. The bear galls are worth a lot of money. They threatened her."

He glanced over at Walker. He was shaking his head.

"And I asked one of them about it. He acted fishy, guilty."

"Ho. I'd best lock those fellas up."

"Sara said they supposedly had alibis."

"I'm not talking to you about this. Take a right here."

On Route 22 north of town, they pulled into a weedy parking lot fronting on an abandoned strip mall. At one end of the mall was a little motel and Walker told Rice to drive around behind it, where the vehicle wouldn't be visible from the highway. A dark blue F-150 was already parked, and the door to one of the decrepit rooms was open. When they walked in, Rice realized he was in some little bit of extra trouble.

THIRTY-NINE

I guess you recognize me," the man said, interrupting Walker's attempt at an introduction.

Walker shut the door behind him with a hollow clack and the room fell dark but for an orange glow seeping through the drawn curtain. Rice whirled and put his back against the nearest wall, sank into a defensive crouch. It was just reflex, but his sudden movement startled Agent Johns, who said "Hey!" and sidestepped fast to the window.

Walker asked what the hell was going on, the question directed at both Agent Johns and Rice. He sounded annoyed. All he'd done was shut the door. Johns swept open the curtain and the room brightened. He had his pistol in his other hand, pointed at Rice. It looked like the same one from before, a compact SIG with an intimidating .45-caliber hole in the end of the barrel. No one said anything for a moment. Rice held up his hands and grinned, wondering if his life could get any more absurd.

"The plastic bag," he said.

Johns lowered the pistol but didn't holster it. His beard was trimmed and he looked showered and generally cleaned up, but he wore mud-specked jeans and the same dark Carhartt jacket. "You obviously weren't some redneck bear hunter. I was curious. I got more curious when I saw your record."

"But you couldn't find me."

"I sure wish I had."

Walker had recovered from his surprise and he moved between the two men. "Put that away, Johns. He's not armed."

"You sure?"

"I'm not armed," Rice said.

Walker stared at Johns until he reached the pistol back under his jacket, behind his hip. The sheriff seemed to want Johns to explain, so Rice kept his mouth shut and glanced around the room. The brown carpet was torn and stained and stank of mildew. In the back, a counter and a sink, a cracked mirror reflecting the window and the parking lot outside.

"My cover," Johns said. "Black market in bear parts. It's just an entry. Mr. Moore tried to sell me some pig galls, fakes. I called him on it and he got rough."

Walker turned and looked at Rice. Eyebrows up, not smiling but maybe not far away from a smile.

Rice shrugged. "He started it."

Johns ignored him. "A small-time drug mule from Arizona selling fake bear galls in Virginia made no sense until you told me he's the caretaker at that nature preserve. Now I get it. He was trying to figure out who the bear poachers are. Takes his job a little too seriously, thinks he's one of those rangers guarding rhinos in fucking Zimbabwe. He's delusional, convinced he's got shoot-to-kill orders. Found a poacher in the woods and shot him in the back."

Rice laughed. "How about I found a poacher in the woods and he nearly killed me."

"Sheriff Walker told me your story. If Mirra had attacked you, you'd be dead."

"That's what everyone says." He held up his bandaged palm.

"You want to see stitches? Here, in my side? Look here." He tilted his chin up. "I thought he'd been using poisoned bolts on the bears. When he cut me I thought I *was* dead."

"He does use poison. But it's not like in the movies where the Indian dips his arrowhead in fucking curare. He stuffs powdered Anectine—suxamethonium chloride—into a rubber pod behind the broadhead. The rubber peels away when he shoots a bear. If he was coming at you like you say, stabbing and whacking you with the broadhead, the pod would've burst, and you would've got some of that shit in your cuts. Again, you'd be dead."

"I guess I'm lucky."

"No one's that lucky."

"A little Sux in a cut won't kill you," the sheriff said to Johns. "You're being ridiculous."

Johns started pacing back and forth in front of Walker, the taut skin of his cheeks and forehead flushed. "Doesn't change my point. Alan Mirra is a vet, ex-marine, four tours in the sandbox, he saw more combat than most, got tapped for MARSOC, top five percent of his ITC class. He's not just tough, he's an expert." He wheeled on Rice, pointed his finger in his face again. "You surprised me that night under the bridge, and I had to stop the fight, so sure, okay, you're competent, violent, you can handle yourself. But I'm not a genuine badass. Mirra is. You do not walk away from a fight with that guy, *especially* if he has a weapon and you don't."

Rice was quiet, remembering how the poacher—Mirra—had absorbed a tackle that should've knocked him cold. Rice had come out of nowhere, a complete surprise. He must've cracked some ribs. Seven seconds later he was in full retreat, wondering if he was going to survive.

Johns made a show of looking Rice up and down. "Are you a genuine badass, Mr. Moore?"

Walker was leaning back against a rickety veneer desk in a corner next to the window, watching Johns with his arms folded.

There was no bed in the room, but you could see where it had been, the rectangle where the carpet was darker.

The sheriff turned to peer out the window. "I knew Alan Mirra when he was younger," he said.

The desk creaked as Walker hitched himself up on it, feet dangling. The room was uncomfortably stuffy and for a moment it looked like he was going to try to open the window. But he took off his jacket and leaned forward, resting his weight on his palms on the front edge of the desk. His underarms were dark with sweat. He started telling a story that Rice assumed must be pretty familiar around here, the abusive, alcoholic father, the young teenage son finally standing up to him. Except instead of getting himself killed, Mirra had put daddy in the hospital, told him not to come back.

"Can you stop that?"

Johns had been pacing back and forth in the little room. He stopped and looked at Walker.

"What?"

"Just hold still for a minute."

"Okay. Whatever." He started bouncing from foot to foot. Dude was seriously wound up. Rice thought he might be on something. Undercover cops got hooked on shit all the time.

Walker stared and then gave up and resumed his story. Rice walked to the back of the room and sat on the counter next to the sink. It sagged but held his weight. In the poorly lit bathroom to his left, the toilet bowl was dry, crusted with mineral deposits. A broken shower curtain rod lay on the floor.

Mirra had dropped out of high school as soon as he could, Walker said, and got tangled up with bikers from up north. Eventually Philly PD caught him stealing cars, and a judge must've seen something in his character and offered him an ultimatum: military or prison. He picked the military, and found his calling.

"In a few years he's a genuine war hero, headed for Recon, like you said. But then he gets hurt, and suddenly he's back home, a decorated vet with an honorable discharge. I keep an ear out, hoping he's shaped up for good. For a while it's quiet. Then rumors start coming in, violent, erratic behavior, he's quit his job at the plant in Coalville, he's back in with his old motorcycle gang, getting by with no obvious source of income."

There it was. Rice felt a satisfying click in his mind as the connection between Mirra and the Stiller boys fell into place. Mirra would be the full patch the bartender at the Ape Hanger had mentioned. Like Boger had said, the Stillers weren't enterprising, not on their own. But as foot soldiers for a honcho like Mirra? He recalled Sara's story about the radio-collared bears. Mirra would know how to hack the electronics.

Johns tried to interrupt, but Walker wasn't finished, held his hand up and kept talking. "Now he disappears, and you start calling, taking risks to get in touch with me, meeting out here in broad daylight, hell, you're about to wet your pants. I understand, he's your CI and you're worried. But like Mr. Moore said, Mirra probably thinks he killed a man. Even the DEA can't protect him from that. Maybe he panicked when he saw what happened to his truck, took off on his motorbike."

"What, you think he rode off on that fucking bike?" Johns seemed not to have considered this possibility before, and when confronted with it he was outraged, let his voice get a little louder than was absolutely necessary. "You want to disappear you don't roar off on a bike like that. People notice you. I gather nobody's called in saying yeah I saw Alan Mirra hightailing it for Mexico on his dirt bike?"

Rice thumped his heels against the loose cabinet door under the counter. "You don't go to Mexico anymore," he said. "I wouldn't recommend Mexico."

The others looked at him like they'd forgotten he was there.

He pointed up, indicating north. "Canada."

"He's resourceful," the sheriff said. "Probably carries a burner phone, called one of his biker buddies. He's a thousand miles away." He hopped down from the desk. "Or," he continued, "maybe he wrecked his bike in the woods and fell on one of his arrows. Someplace we haven't looked yet." He walked to the door and opened it, stood there looking out. Like the claustrophobia had gotten to him. The wind snatched at the door and he reached up to hold the bill of his cap. A Styrofoam cup clattered across the parking lot.

"What about Moore?" Johns asked.

"What about him?"

"Can you just hang on to him until we find out what happened to Alan? Forty-eight hours?"

Still facing out the door, Walker spoke like he was explaining to a child. "I don't have a body, Agent Johns. You find me a body and maybe I'll arrest someone."

Johns smacked his open palm on the desk where Walker had been sitting. Rice figured it must be a new thing, the local sheriff standing up to him.

"You sure he's not going to take off on you, Sheriff? I called around in Tucson, talked to some people who knew him when, and I wouldn't be so quick to trust him."

"Who'd you talk to?" Rice asked.

But Johns just looked at Rice with that smug face. Rice wondered if he could land a punch before the guy drew his damn pistol. Probably not.

"Agents? CIs? Did you tell them where I was?"

Johns still didn't answer. Rice felt sick. This was much worse than the electronic flags from the plates and the prints. There were cartel moles all over the place down there, CIs switching allegiances when the weather changed. Until this moment, despite all the attention from Sheriff Walker, Rice had managed to maintain a faint hope that he would be able to stay on at the preserve.

"Thank you, Agent Johns. And the Sinaloa cartel thanks you too."

"Bullshit, it's not the cartel who's after you. What I heard, your girlfriend was the player, she was working with us, and the cartel had her hit while you were locked up in Mexico. Sinaloa would've forgotten all about you, but you did a bad thing in Juarez after you got out." Here Johns started to cheer up. "Who cares, right? It's a fucking war zone. What people do over there is off the radar. But what's so beautiful is you managed to make a mortal enemy of just about the last guy on the planet I'd want pissed off at me." He barked an unattractive laugh and asked Walker if he knew what Los Ántrax was. Walker didn't answer.

"They're the enforcers for the Sinaloa cartel, like mafia special forces." He was grinning at Rice now, shaking his head in mock pity. "Anyway, maybe it's all bullshit, or maybe Mr. Moore is a vigilante who murders people he thinks deserve it."

"Mr. Moore isn't going anywhere," Walker said. "He'll stay in Turpin County. He'll check in with me every day. If Mirra doesn't turn up soon I'll have some more questions for him. You're free to add your own. We can do this again. Just not in here."

Rice was still sitting on the shelf against the back wall, hesitant to leave without knowing exactly when Johns had "called around in Tucson." It mattered, but he was unwilling to give Johns the satisfaction of his asking.

Another gust of wind pushed through the open door. Walker put his jacket on and looked at Rice like it was time to go.

"Come on, Mr. Moore, I need you to drive me back to the office before Suzy has herself a breakdown. She's not good at natural disasters."

FORTY

He found the aisle with the padlocks and picked out the biggest one, read the packaging to see if it would defeat bolt cutters. Didn't say, but it was half again as heavy as the lock on the front gate now, with a thicker hasp. He nearly dropped it. The swelling in his hand had subsided, nothing broken, but the knuckles were still stiff, the fingers clumsy.

The store was about to close, and a skinny teenager with short black hair watched him from the customer service counter. Thorny vines snaked up out of his T-shirt and wrapped around his neck. Not the kind of ink you would expect to see in the Turpin County Farmers' Co-op. He padded across the store and peered over Rice's shoulder. Rice turned and glared at him.

"I see you're looking at padlocks," the kid said. "That Master in your hand is the best in the store." He seemed nervous, like he'd been told to work the floor but it didn't come easy to him.

"Seems sturdy enough," Rice said. The kid had a plastic name tag pinned to his black T-shirt. "You know how to work that chain cutter over there, Damien? I'll need about five feet of the thickest one."

"You locking up anything important?"

"Just a gate. Somebody cut the old lock with a bolt cutter."

"You think they'll come back?"

It seemed an odd question. "They might. Or somebody else might." The image that had compelled him to stop at the co-op after dropping off Sheriff Walker came again: a dusty crew cab with Sonora plates pulling up to the gate, a lithe *sicario* sliding off the seat and inspecting the locked chain, the Mayan mask tattoo staring insanely from the back of his shaved head.

"'Cause a guy with a forty-two-inch bolt cropper could cut that lock without even trying. Or he could spray it with Freon and smash it with a hammer, or he could pick it or bump it if he knows what he's doing."

Rice hefted the substantial lock in his palm. It cost $37.99. He raised his eyebrows at Damien. "You're a hell of a salesman."

"A shrouded Abloy and a sixteen-millimeter boron composite motorcycle chain would be better. But then he'll just walk over to the other end and knock the gate off its hinges with a hammer."

"No, son, we got that top gudgeon reversed."

The kid smiled for the first time. He had good teeth, and piercings in his left nostril and right eyebrow. These were just holes without anything in them, probably a concession to the clientele at the co-op.

"You some kind of security geek, Damien?"

"My dad's a locksmith in Pittsburgh. We do some consulting." Rice must've looked incredulous. He explained he was a mechanical engineering major at Tech, taking a semester off, living with an uncle in Blakely to maintain his in-state residency.

Rice folded his arms. The kid had steady brown eyes, a look of engagement.

"You have to keep all this to yourself."

He described the Turk Mountain Preserve, the poachers coming in on ATVs, the long driveway. The gate at the front entrance was welded steel and opened out from the latchpost, which was made from an old telephone pole, same as the hinge post. Most of the road front-age was a steep bank, a new woven wire fence and salt-treated posts at the top. It occurred to him that the Traver Foundation must've put in the gate and fence when Sara started as caretaker. They'd had couples before, but as far as he could tell from the logbooks, she was the first single female caretaker the foundation had hired.

Damien thought for a few moments, nodding, scratching his belly. "I should look at a map."

Someone was locking the front door, but Damien said not to worry about it, and Rice stood behind the counter watching him create a map of the Turk Mountain Preserve on his laptop, down-loading tax maps from the county website and superimposing them on a topo. He pulled traffic estimates for Route 608 from the DMV site and downloaded aerial photos from a USDA site.

"This the house, in a big open pasture?" He zoomed in and pointed to the black rectangle representing the lodge. Two smaller squares for the tractor shed and the cabin lay nearby in the appro-priate spots. "Who else might want to get in the front gate? Is it just poachers?"

"Let's just say it might be somebody more serious."

Damien leaned back, away from his laptop, and cocked his head a little to the side, showing off the elaborate tattoo on his neck, the bright green leaves, the long, curved black thorns. Rice had decided it was a fantasy plant, resembling nothing that occurred in nature.

"Say there's a woman living there by herself," Rice continued. "Somebody's threatened her."

Damien nodded and hit a few keys and pulled up a blank table, typing as he spoke. "The first thing to understand is there's no way to stop someone from getting in if that's what he really wants to do."

Rice already knew this but it still made him a little sick to hear it. Consequences of Agent Johns burning his DIY WITSEC pro-gram kept tumbling into place. Sara was going to win the fellow-ship at the preserve, and she planned to move to the cabin as soon as classes were over. She would have to face the Stillers and various other local hostiles by herself, but that wasn't what worried him. The new Sara could handle those clowns. It was the other thing. He planned to make his departure somehow conspicuous, hoping to take the cartel-related danger with him, but someone might still show up to search the preserve. When they didn't find Rice, they would interrogate anyone they did find.

Damien was describing the tools available to the "determined intruder": Freon spray, manual bolt croppers, pneumatic bolt cropper, hacksaws, angle grinder, cutting torch, lockpicks, hammers, drills, cable cutters, chainsaw, even a bull-bar on his truck so he can ram the gate itself. In a rural setting, he said, the best you could do is turn away casual trespassers and create a delay for the bad guys.

"The length of the delay depends on how good your overall design is, how much inconvenience you can put up with getting in and out, and how much money you're willing to spend. You get to the point of diminishing returns pretty quick, especially given that somebody who's extremely motivated will just walk in, or cut the fence and ride in on an ATV, or two guys could lift a dirt bike over and ride in on that."

"A dirt bike. Shit." Assassins in Mexico used motorcycles all the time, two guys on a bike, the shooter riding pillion. It was something they'd picked up from the Columbians. "So far you're not doing much for my peace of mind."

"You can still control the situation." Damien started typing again, explaining how to fix weaknesses at the entrance. He asked about the driveway, how long it took to drive up to the house from the road. Rice kept it in good shape with a blade on the tractor, but the water bars that controlled runoff also acted as speed bumps. Ten minutes, he figured, even if you were in a hurry.

"Okay, that's your best feature, ten minutes is plenty of time to get ready. A driveway alarm will give you time to load the shotgun, make a phone call, get in the safe room, whatever. They're cheap and effective, we got 'em in the store. Picks up the magnetic field of a vehicle and you get a warning if someone breaches the gate and drives in. We can order you a strong padlock and chain that'll deter your poachers. Then if the alarm goes off you know you got a different kind of problem."

Or someone with a key, Rice thought.

He drove home fast in the spitting rain and arrived at the entrance just before dark. Low, scudding clouds enshrouded the mountains, and the world steamed and glowed in the failing greenish light. He'd decided Damien was a good salesman after all. They'd loaded a bundle of thirty-six-inch rebar in the back of the truck, along with a new mattock and a supply of PVC piping and conduit. On the front seat was a driveway alarm that would sense a vehicle driving over it and send a radio signal to a small walkie-talkie receiver. The receiver and the battery pack for the transmitter were plugged into the cigarette lighter, charging. He'd also ordered the fancy padlock and motorcycle chain with expedited shipping, so he could set them up before he left. It meant STP was going to have to swallow a significant charge on the foundation's co-op account, which she wouldn't mind once she understood the extra security was for Sara. She was going to be less excited about the prospect of finding a new caretaker.

Working with the mattock, he buried the sensor under the driveway in a length of PVC pipe about a hundred yards up from the gate, far enough so that any off-road vehicle that drove around the gate would be back on the driveway by then and would set off the alarm. He dug a shallow trench and buried the wire from the sensor in the flexible conduit running fifty feet to the transmitter box, which he bolted on the far side of a big white pine where you couldn't see it from the driveway. He installed the batteries and propped the PV panel out of sight—he would tell Sara to come back on a sunny day and find a better spot for it—adjusted the frequency, and turned it on. When he drove across with his truck, a peremptory male voice spoke from the handheld receiver on the seat beside him: "Alert, Zone One." It repeated until he hit the reset button.

Soaked with sweat and rain, he drove back to the entrance and turned his truck around so his headlights lit the gate. Damien's prescription to discourage would-be trespassers from chainsawing the gateposts—and the first few fence posts on either side—was to drive three or four lengths of rebar into the ground alongside each post, then staple them to the post with big fencing staples so they'd be a pain in the ass to remove. He hesitated now, wondering how that was going to look. STP cared about aesthetics. The rain had abated temporarily and he walked out onto the wet pavement. The gate and the fence were set back about twenty yards from the road, with a wide gravel entranceway where the gate swung out. He didn't think you would notice the rebar from the road.

The sound of an engine, diesel, high-beams shining down the straightaway. Feeling jumpy—even more than usual—he went for the pistol in the truck, tucked it in his pants, stood so the engine block of his truck was between him and the oncoming vehicle.

The vehicle slowed, hesitated, then Dempsey Boger's pickup pulled off the highway. Sadie the broke-leg setter stood up on the front seat and poked her head out the open window. Rice came around the front of his truck.

"Dempsey. Sadie." He stepped over to pet her and she wagged and sniffed his hands. Boger finished a cigarette and stabbed it out sparking in the open ashtray under the dashboard.

"She's out of her cast," Rice said. "How's the leg?"

"It don't seem to hurt much. But the vet said it'll always be a little stiff."

In fact her left hind leg stuck out toward the dashboard.

"She seems pretty content. Gets to ride around in the truck with you."

Boger peered toward the shut gate. "You lose your key?"

"I was about to work on the gateposts, put some rebar on 'em." He figured it wouldn't hurt for the local bear hunters to know he was beefing up security. "Ordered a new lock and chain too."

"I reckon you did." Boger chuckled and turned off the ignition, cut his headlights. He opened his door and slid out, left the door open, the yellowish interior light spilling into the bed. He stretched and walked around to the back, stepped up on the bumper with one boot, leaned forward to lay his heavy forearms on the top of the tailgate with his big calloused lumberjack's hands hanging loose, resting. He tilted his head up to the black sky, the trees tossing in the warm wind.

Rice figured here comes some weather talk, but Boger peered at him in the light from the cab. "You don't look so good," he said.

"Thanks." Rice left the setter with her head hanging out the window and leaned on the edge of the bed just behind the diamond-tread aluminum toolbox.

"You jumping ex-marine bear poachers in the middle of the night now?"

Rice thought he sounded a little bit happy about it, like the episode confirmed his dire predictions, his suspicions about Rice.

"Naw. That's just crazy talk." He reached up to feel the stitched cut on his jaw. It was still sore from his encounter with Derek the friendly police dog. He let the long silence hang, wondering if he should approach Boger about keeping an eye on Sara after he was gone. If he could see past their philosophical differences. Rice was about to explain that he would be leaving soon when Boger spoke again, his voice losing its lazy rhythms, like he was struggling with what he had to say.

"Somethin' you oughta know. Stiller boys been running their mouths, they're scared, must be what you done to Alan Mirra. They say Mirra's biker gang is fixing to get rid of you."

Rice almost laughed, but Boger clearly wasn't joking. "Get rid of me? In what sense?"

"Hell should I know. That gang they're in, you could just use your imagination."

"He turned up yet? Mirra?"

"Not that I've heard."

"You don't seem surprised he was poaching."

Boger was silent. A violent gust shook rainwater from the trees along the road. It occurred to Rice that Boger didn't just happen by, that he'd come to warn him. That he should take this seriously.

"I think Mirra and the Stiller boys were in on it together," Rice said, "setting up bait, shooting the bears at night, selling the gall-bladders. Did you know about that?"

They both stared into the empty bed of the pickup. Dented and scraped, swept clean except for some grease-caked sawdust in front of the wheel wells. No reply. Rice suppressed a grin. Boger simply ignored you when he thought what you were saying was asinine. Pretended you hadn't spoken. It was pretty effective.

"I need to talk to those stupid bastards. Do you know where they live? Bilton wouldn't tell me."

"They used to rent somewhere out near the interstate, but they was laid off at the sawmill back in July, got evicted. Heard Alan Mirra let 'em move into a old trailer on his place." Boger held Rice's eye for a moment: he might withhold information or he might give information and Rice was going to have to deal with that. What he'd done just then was he'd let loose some information, a gift to an outsider, which was, despite the animus between him and the Stillers, against his usual inclinations, and Rice had better be paying attention. Then he stepped around his truck, yawned, put his hand on the open driver's-side door.

Sadie whined at Rice. He rubbed her throat and she lifted her head, leaned into his hand. He smiled through the cab at Boger. "And Alan Mirra's place. Where might that be?"

FORTY-ONE

Heading south out of Wanless, he turned on Cougar Lane, wondering about the road-naming process, and what complicated, contradictory psychology had led to the locals requesting the name of a predator intentionally hunted to extinction 130 years ago. Did they think they'd seen a mountain lion here? You heard reports all the time, though the sightings usually turned out to be big housecats, bobcats, or golden retrievers. He'd wondered if a lion might be hiding out in the gorge on the preserve, but he'd never seen any sign.

The Stillers' place wasn't hard to find—he only had to follow the Harleys and pickup trucks. He'd sort of planned to just knock on the front door and see what happened, but a party was ongoing in a ratty-looking trailer lit by a yellowish security light on a pole. A second trailer a quarter mile deeper in the wooded lot, windows dark, lit from above by another security light, was likely Mirra's. At the near trailer they'd set up a couple of big blue tarps lashed on a metal scaffolding out front, a kind of awning that snapped in the wind, Christmas lights strung across the top.

Rice paused to watch from the end of the driveway. Rainwater dripped from white extension cords onto the unconcerned heads of a half-dozen large bearded men in shiny wet black leather jackets. Orbiting around them were a handful of eager-looking younger men fetching beer and lighting smokes. Women of various shapes and ages stepped in and out of the trailer, where more people moved behind the windows. Three tapped kegs lay askew in tubs of ice. The rain came down hard, quick violent sprays going crosswise on the windshield. He got the wipers flapping faster. He needed to think of a new plan. No one paid him any attention, and he drove on up Cougar Lane until he came to an old logging road. He backed in and got out, pulled the hood of his rain shell up over his head. Walked back toward the party.

Out back of the trailer they'd built an old-fashioned wood-frame outhouse, likely not to code. Another string of Christmas lights ran from the trailer on a couple of metal poles to the outhouse. The string of lights passed under the eaves of the outhouse and lit the space inside. While Rice watched from the forest, two skinny girls emerged, one in a red puffy down jacket, and ran cursing through the rain to the back door of the trailer. The music was loud inside but all he could hear was the bass. Sounded like 1970s and '80s southern rock, and some classic metal he couldn't quite place. Laughter, harsh voices raised over the music. Maybe three dozen men and women packed inside and under the shelter out front. A guy walked around from the front and pissed in the weeds grown up at the edge of the forest not ten yards from where Rice stood. He gave his dick two quick ungentle shakes, like he didn't want anyone to think he was whacking off, zipped and turned, and walked back to the party.

Rice returned to his truck and grabbed a roll of duct tape and a length of old climbing rope from behind the seats. He released the magazine from his pistol and ejected the round from the chamber, thumbed the seven rounds from the magazine, reached back into the cut in the seat cushion for the spare magazine, and emptied it onto the passenger's seat as well. He took off his boots and damp socks, put his boots back on, and dropped all fifteen rounds into a sock. He fit that sock inside the other and wrapped them with duct tape to hold the ammunition in a tight ball at the toes. A knot tied at the other end would serve as a stop for his grip. Holding just below the knot, he swung the heavy weight in a short horizontal arc, smacking into his palm.

Waiting again in the woods behind the trailer, he bet himself that Jesse would be the first of his three potential targets to come out for a pisser. He waited with a quiet mind, motionless, placing himself in the focused fugue he'd learned over the past few weeks in the forest. The predator's patience is not an act of will, of holding oneself in check, but one of faith, of an absolute certainty that prey will come. For Rice, a little more than an hour passed altogether pleasantly in the storm before DeWayne opened the back door and took one step into the grass before stopping to make his water. Too lazy to walk to the woods.

"Hey, DeWayne!" Rice moved to the edge of the yard and played his flashlight in the dark weeds behind the outhouse. He laughed, trying to sound drunk. "There's some bitch lying in the bushes back here!"

"Who's that?" Zipping up, squinting into the rain. Christmas lights flickering and blowing back and forth in the wind.

Rice knew this wasn't fair play. As if he were imitating the scream of a dying rabbit to lure coyotes and bobcats, he spoke in a slurred Turpin County accent, describing a nonexistent female biker helplessly inebriated, a woman who took her pants down to piss and passed out, her imaginary genitalia exposed to DeWayne's eager gaze.

FORTY-TWO

Rice faced in the direction of the trailer and watched the dark forest. He had his knife out and was absently whittling by feel a point on a thin green beechwood stick. The music from the party was barely audible over the rain and wind. No hollering, no crashing through the brush, no stabbing flashlights. He turned back to the beech tree and pressed the switch twice on his own flashlight. DeWayne Stiller hung there, his hands and arms duct-taped to his body, dancing on his tiptoes, trying to take the tension from the climbing rope noosed around his neck. A dark goose egg had raised up under his ear from the improvised sap. In the light he started screaming into the tape over his mouth and snorting wet, bloody tendrils from his nose.

A memory intruded, DeWayne and the others sitting sour-faced with their beers in Wanless back in early September. The day the mushroom picker had shown him the first dead bear. The day all this started. He'd assumed they worked at the sawmill, but even then they'd been laid off for weeks. No seniority. He'd seen DeWayne at his father's store but he didn't seem to work there. He was an unemployed delinquent who had bloomed into a small-time drug dealer and wannabe outlaw biker. He poached bears and he sold the galls. Rice doubted he'd finished high school. He wondered if he had a girlfriend, maybe one of the girls in the trailer.

Rice hadn't spoken since DeWayne had come to, and he hadn't bothered with a blindfold because of the pitch darkness. He stepped closer and stripped the tape from the man's cheek. DeWayne spit snot and blood onto the ground and spoke in the strained, high-pitched voice of a man teetering on the edge of a complete breakdown.

"You fuckin' greasers! Fuck you!" A string of partially coherent curses and promises of retaliation followed.

Rice paused. Greasers? He had expected confusion, anger, fear, but DeWayne was spasming with terror.

"You gonna cut my fuckin' head off?" The question had started off defiant but ended on a whimpering, plaintive high note. Now he was hyperventilating, struggling to balance on his toes.

Rice still didn't speak, wondering who DeWayne thought had captured him. He'd never heard of any Latino gangs active in this part of the state. It was possible the MC had been buying wholesale from one of the cartels, but a nobody like DeWayne wouldn't be involved. Unless he'd tagged along with Mirra for some reason. It seemed far-fetched. After a pause, DeWayne found his voice again.

"You fuckers think everyone's scared of you. We ain't. Diddy coulda shot you, he almost did. He got a good look at you. We told the club. They're on their way."

"You told the club what?" Rice asked his question in a harsh whisper, but on second thought, he didn't care if DeWayne knew who he was, so he followed up in his normal voice.

"You little boys been putting out hits on people, DeWayne?"

"No! Mirra said not to. He said not to do anything till he got back."

"You talked to Mirra? Where is he?"

DeWayne didn't reply. If he'd recognized Rice's voice, he hadn't shown any surprise. He was about to pass out anyway. He bobbed on the rope, leaning and righting, shuffling his feet in the leaves. Rice was curious about Mirra, but he didn't have much time. Someone might see his truck and wonder about the Arizona plates. It was even possible, though unlikely, that they'd notice DeWayne was missing from the party and come looking for him. DeWayne was a hoss, had to be pushing 240, and Rice had only dragged him so far into the forest.

Rice took a breath, let it out with his eyes closed, steeling himself, then he shouldered DeWayne against the trunk, pushed his head into the smooth bark with his forearm. In this position the noose was tight and DeWayne probably couldn't breathe at all, but Rice cupped his hand over the man's mouth anyway. He fit the point of his sharpened stick into DeWayne's left ear and stabbed twice into the wall of his ear canal. DeWayne jerked like a fish and his high-pitched scream went on for a while, muffled by Rice's hand.

Rice leaned in and spoke close to the other ear smashed up against the bark. He said something to the effect that if DeWayne didn't tell him who raped Sara Birkeland, next time he was going to keep pushing until he poked a hole in his walnut-size brain.

He pulled the stick, made sure the bleeding wasn't too bad, and let him swing back to where he could take his weight on his toes again. DeWayne nodded spasmodically, moaning and whimpering. His calf muscles were starting to fail. He stank from shitting and pissing himself.

Rice walked back to the stump where he'd set up STP's camera, pressed the button that started the video recording. He shone his flashlight on DeWayne's face—his eyes scrunched shut against the beam—so he could be identified. After that it was mostly going to be audio. Rain dripped steadily from the leaves overhead but he understood the camera was more or less weatherproof. STP had said she was afraid he'd drop it in a creek.

He backhanded DeWayne across his mouth, prompting a quiet, high-pitched keening. Then he was weeping, shaking his head, trying to say something. His voice was hoarse, whispering, his larynx in spasm against the pressure of the rope.

"They'll kill me."

"Who'll kill you?"

"Mirra and them. The club."

"You saying Mirra and the bikers did it?" He opened his knife near the man's good ear, a loud click, and whittled a rough wedge point onto a new beech branch. "I think it was you."

"No! I didn't have nothing to do with it."

Rice waited a few moments, walked away, whittled on the stick some more, came back. Softened his voice. "Or maybe you just watched, D. Maybe it was that ugly Jesse fucker down there at the party wondering where your lost ass ran off to? Or was it your brother? Alan Mirra's your fucking hero, did you do it to impress him? Was he there? Did he tell you to do it? Maybe it wasn't your fault. Was it some stupid initiation for the club?"

Rice laid the point of the sharpened stick gently on DeWayne's good ear and he twisted away and slipped so that the rope tightened on his throat, shutting off his air again. Rice let him scrabble in the dirt, righting himself, getting some slack in the rope. The knots must have loosened. While he waited for DeWayne to stop retching, he considered whether he should tighten the rope. Probably not. He was nearly out of time. It was going to work or it wasn't.

"DeWayne, this is easy. You tell me the truth and I let you go. And you know damn well I can't go to the law with what you say. It's just for me. Was it them? Mirra and Jesse and your brother?"

"It wasn't us. They was staying at Mirra's place."

"The rapists were Mirra's houseguests?"

DeWayne panted and swallowed before trying to speak again. "Me and Jesse swore not to say nothing, Mirra made us swear, he said if we told anyone they'd kill us."

"DeWayne, *I'll* fucking kill you. Look at yourself. You think I won't?"

DeWayne sagged into the rope. He'd given up. In the light from the flashlight his face was dark, turning blue. Rice stepped over to the branch where he'd tied off the end of the rope and gave him enough slack so he could lean back against the tree. With the pressure off his larynx he hacked and wheezed. Rice waited. DeWayne would talk now. In between retches he said Mirra had been hiding out in Philly the past couple of days, with the club. "He didn't even tell us he was alive till tonight." He said he and Nardo and Jesse used to hang out at Mirra's place, back before they moved up here. Mirra gave them meth to sell when he could get it, and they helped with the bear poaching. Using bait was his idea, crossbows at night, poison pods, killing all those radio-collared bears. Mirra had a guy, Jonas, who bought the galls, paid good money.

DeWayne and Jesse showed up at Mirra's one day last fall and these three bikers were there, "badass fuckers, enforcers, officers way up in the club, bragged about killing people, blowing away cops."

They were pushing Mirra about training club members in military tactics, and Mirra was bargaining, wanted the club to take over the bear parts market, export the parts to China or someplace, make a bunch of money. DeWayne was fuzzy on the particulars. He and Jesse were trying to impress the guys from the club and had got pretty messed up sucking on the meth pipe they were passing around. Jesse bragged about killing bears, and the three enforcers were from the city, they were interested. They said they wanted to go hunting with the hounds, shoot a bear out of a tree.

"We said we could take 'em up on Turk Mountain, lots of big bears there, but we had to watch out for the caretaker 'cause she'd called the game warden on us, we had to wait till she left that night, we knew her schedule. These guys called us pussies for worrying about her, they start asking questions, where the place was, if she lived by herself, shit like that. They said they'd help us teach her a lesson, we could all go and wait for her to drive out. Mirra told us to shut up. Kicked us out."

The next morning, DeWayne and Jesse went over to see if the bikers still wanted to go hunting, but they were gone, and Mirra looked like he'd been up all night. They'd heard about the girl and asked Mirra if he and the enforcers had done it. Right then "Jonas" drove up and he and Mirra started yelling at each other like De-Wayne and Jesse weren't there, he was mad about the enforcers and the girl, wanted to know why didn't Mirra stop them, Mirra said they stole his truck, they punked him for trying to tell club officers what to do. Mirra'd been out all night on his Harley looking for them, and when he came home he'd found his truck there and the enforcers and their bikes gone.

"Jonas asked all of us where we'd been, said to make sure we had alibis, witnesses. He knew what all to do, he'd brought a vacuum cleaner and made us vacuum inside Mirra's truck while they took a hose and washed the outside, underneath. They changed the fuck-ing tires. Mirra made us swear not to tell anyone, not even Nardo, said he'd kill us if we did, the club would find us and kill us. Me and Jesse swore we'd keep our mouths shut and we fucking meant it. That's all I know, I swear it."

"I need their names. The three bikers."

"I don't know. They never said!"

"Are you ready to die for those fuckers, DeWayne?"

"Y'all are gonna kill me anyway."

"There's no one else here, D. I'll just let you go back to your party."

"That Mexican's here, I can fuckin' smell 'im."

Again with the Mexican. "DeWayne, you're delusional. You're smelling your own damn self."

DeWayne was frustrated now. "We know what y'all are doin'!

You think we're stupid? We always knew you was in with them, we knew you was gonna try and take over the county."

"Who is 'them,' D? Who the fuck are we talking about?"

"Diddy *saw* him. He come by the store looking for you. Diddy run 'im off and called me and Nardo."

Oh hell.

"You're full of shit. Nobody came looking for me."

DeWayne's certainty about what was happening finally started to drain away. For the first time he sounded confused. "You go ask Diddy. He's still at the store movin' shit up to the loft."

Yeah, Rice thought, feeling weary. I'll do that.

"I need those names."

"They never told us their names!"

He smashed his forearm into DeWayne again, pinning him against the tree, and hauled on the rope, taking up the slack, lifting his head and torqueing his spine. He held the flashlight in his teeth and laid the flat of his knife on DeWayne's cheekbone, pricked the lower eyelid with the point, lifting it away from the eye. DeWayne made no sound, his air was cut off, but his legs began scissor-kicking. He let go with another long, blatting bowel evacuation.

Rice let the point of his knife pierce the lid but kept it away from the man's eye.

"You know what they called each other."

FORTY-THREE

Ahead in the gloom, the warm yellow lights in the front windows of Stiller's Store looked homey and welcoming. He pulled off the highway and parked in the gravel lot, got out, and looked through a window. Mr. Stiller was carrying a heavy-looking blue plastic bread box stacked with canned vegetables up a set of steep retractable steps to a loft. He looked exhausted. Wasn't much merchandise left downstairs, but he seemed to have saved the heavy stuff for last, maybe hoping his sons would come help.

DeWayne sure wouldn't be coming, though Rice had cut most of the duct tape away before leaving him propped up against a wet tree trunk, and he was probably back at the trailer by now.

Rice had promised DeWayne that if he kept his mouth shut Rice would make sure the Sinaloa cartel stayed out of his motorcycle club's territory. He'd also promised he would show the club his recording of DeWayne ratting out the three enforcers if DeWayne had the temerity to do any one of a long list of things, including reporting Rice's assault on his person to the sheriff or anyone else in the world, attempting any sort of payback against Rice, harming or threatening, or allowing anyone else to ever harm or threaten, Sara, or ever again setting foot on the Turk Mountain Preserve without Rice or Sara's explicit permission. He suggested DeWayne tell everyone back at the party that he'd been pissing in the forest and had fallen over drunk, hit his head on a tree.

The *Closed* sign was facing out but the glass-paneled door was unlocked. Rice pushed it open as the wind blew up again outside. Rain spattered on the metal roof and on the south-facing windows. When he saw Rice, Stiller widened his eyes and faked a big grin, like it was a pleasant surprise to have Rice walk into his store. Stiller was a stout man, not tall, probably still strong in his late fifties. A balding, scaled-down version of his sons: the ruddy freckled face, the close-set, suspicious eyes. Rice knew him as a reticent, hostile fellow mad at the world, especially outsiders like Rice, upon whom he had to depend for a large part of his business.

"Lookee who's here." Dumb happy expression on his face, his voice flat. Bilton Stiller was doing irony.

"Hello, Mr. Stiller. It's been a while. I've been meaning to stop by."

"I bet. Too bad it's goddamn past midnight and we're closed."

"You need a hand?" Stiller had disappeared through the hole in the ceiling and didn't reply. A small television on a shelf behind the counter played a news program; a satellite loop of eastern North America's weather showed a broad gyre spinning north from the Gulf of Mexico, Hurricane Julia crashing into the Florida Panhandle and engulfing parts of Alabama and Georgia, losing some of its coherence but not much speed as it rode northward up the Appalachians into Virginia.

Stiller spoke, coming back down the steps. "That shit is here already," he said. "Gonna knock down all them big old trees up by you. They'll lay on the ground and rot, doin' nobody any good at all."

He said this with a kind of resigned certainty, as if he didn't have much to show for his life besides hard-earned wisdom. Rice had been in the store a dozen times, but this bit about the storm was the most the man had ever said directly to him. When he turned around, Stiller was coming slowly off the bottom step, grinning and carrying an old short-barreled pump shotgun alongside his leg.

Rice smiled back when he saw the gun. "Hope not," he said. "You sound like Dempsey Boger. He hates seeing all that timber go to waste up there."

Rice watched to see if suggesting that Stiller had anything in common with Boger would stir him up, but he just stood at the bottom of the steps with his shotgun, the portrait of redneck swagger.

"You need to leave now, honeybun."

Instead, Rice lifted a case of Mrs. Fearnow's Brunswick stew and carried it up the steps, realizing he was hungry, had hardly eaten all day. A bare bulb in the loft showed a clean-swept inventory room that was larger than he'd expected, boxes and bags and crates stacked on the floor and arranged on shelves against the far wall.

Bilton came up behind, glaring now, leaning forward, up on his toes, the shotgun canted at an angle so it would cut Rice's legs off if he fired. Rice saw another similarity with his big son DeWayne, an innate violent reflex: when in doubt, pick a fight.

"The hell are you doing?"

"I'm helping." He set the case down. "How come your boys aren't here?"

"'Cause they're allergic to work."

"They seem to be having a hurricane party up at their place. Is that your beer they're serving?"

Stiller frowned but didn't answer. Rice brushed past him and headed back down the steps, loaded up again with big cans of fruit cocktail, the contemplation of which quelled his appetite. When he turned around, Stiller was lifting a case of various soups in serving-size cans with pop-top lids. The shotgun leaned against the wall at the base of the steps.

"I hear Alan Mirra went a-hunting up on Turk Mountain and

jest disappeared off the face of the earth. They cain't even find his motorbike."

"I heard the same thing." Apparently DeWayne hadn't shared with his dad the news of Mirra's resurrection. Just as Walker had guessed, Mirra had holed up with some club members in Pennsylvania.

"You got you a secret cave where you put the bodies? Anybody gets close to your drug patch or what-all you got going on up there gets bushwhacked? You got Alan Mirra laid out in the mud next to my hounds?"

Rice decided Stiller was only half-serious. "You called Sheriff Walker and accused me of doing something to your dogs. I think it's pretty funny that you called about the dogs but didn't say anything about me knocking down your son."

That seemed to surprise him. "Hell. That boy needs a knocking down ever' now and then. An ol' Michum done give you some knocking down right back."

"So we're even?"

Stiller shrugged, sealing their agreement. They were square when it came to knocking folks down. Until tonight, anyway. Impatient to be done with the charade, Rice stacked and lifted a ninety-pound armload of juice boxes and condensed milk and cases of assorted cans he couldn't identify, stuff that might've been on the shelves since the last big flood.

He grunted as he limped up the steps, his bruised ribs nearly shattering in protest, hoping his knee wasn't about to give way. "But you're mad at me because some of your dogs are still missing, and you think I shot them."

"You did *somethin'* to 'em."

"No, I didn't." He deposited his load against the wall and straightened, promising himself not to lift anything else that heavy for a while. Stiller came in behind him with an armload of canned energy drinks. "Here's the thing, Mr. Stiller. I *like* dogs, even big-ass yellow dogs that growl at me like they're fixing to bite my leg off. I like dogs a lot better than I like people. I can't have you all hunting on the preserve, but I don't blame the dogs. Next time I'll tie 'em up so they don't run off."

Stiller looked away and mumbled something about how next time he'd better let them dogs be if he knew what was good for him. Rice wondered if he'd heard about the incident with the big German shepherd up on the mountain.

"That big yellow one was your dog?"

"Mack. He's still missin'. Gone this long he's dead or stole." He didn't show any emotion. Stiller's heart didn't seem to be in a confrontation about the dogs.

"I'm sorry to hear that." Rice seriously doubted anyone could have stolen that dog. Mack. Mack the scary giant mastiff. Seemed like someone would've called the dog catcher if they'd seen him.

The next load Rice carried was the last of the heavy stuff, and when he came down from the loft, the shotgun had disappeared and Stiller was seated behind the counter watching the TV.

"You got any cold beer for sale?"

Stiller rolled his eyes, jerked his head toward the refrigerator. "No discounts, I don't care if you helped out."

Rice opened the walk-in and, as usual, the door slammed shut behind him when he stepped into the cramped space. The light was dim and cold, dry air caught in his throat. All of the inventory from the coolers in the store was stacked in here along with kegs and cases of beer. The sign on the inside of the door seemed particularly appropriate today: STOP! DONT PANIC! in large clumsy letters. Underneath it read Push bolt to get out.

On a whim he picked up a six-pack of Corona and pushed the bolt on the door with his hip. When he came out, Stiller gave him a nasty sneer—Mexican horse piss, should've guessed it. He rang up the purchase, and Rice was handing over a twenty when the man came out with it.

"Your Mexican friend ever find you?"

Finally. "Excuse me?"

"Some old boy come around looking for you."

"Yeah, DeWayne mentioned that. When was this?"

"Right after lunch, I believe."

"What'd he look like?" He tried to act nonchalant, laying the money on the counter.

"Said he was your friend. Buncha tattoos on him but he dressed good, had new clothes anyway. Had a accent but not like them greasers over by Marshalton what sound like a goddamn Fritos commercial. He showed me your picture, wanted to know if I knew you, said he was your old pal from out west, passing through on business."

Shit. Stiller made change, and Rice fumbled two quarters. They fell to the floor and rolled in opposite directions. He squatted down to pick them up.

"I don't know anybody like that."

"Said your name was Rice Moore, not Rick Morton. He knew you lived around here, said he wanted to surprise you. Now, this fella looked to me like he was in the drug business, and I got to thinking, maybe you and him was in the same gang. Figured y'all might be looking to move into some new territory."

"I'm not in the drug business, Mr. Stiller."

Stiller was puffing up now, having some fun. "Rice Moore's your drug name? You're 'White Rice,' and your buddy is 'Brown Rice.'"

"It was just one guy? What did you tell him?" He was sure Stiller had gleefully sent him straight up to the preserve. Probably sitting on the porch of the lodge with an AK right now.

"Got a dago in your gang named Rice-A-Roni?"

Rice stared, vaguely aware the man was mocking him. He let the silence hang. A car passed by, tires swishing on the wet road. Rice listened for it to slow down but it kept going. He waited while Stiller's playground bully belligerence spent itself.

"Yeah, it was just him. I said I didn't have nothing to do with no out-of-state drug dealers, and he could take his greasy Mexican ass straight back out the door. I reached under the counter here and I got my hands on the twelve-gauge so he'd know I wasn't messing around." Pleased with himself, Stiller leaned his head back and actually looked down his nose at Rice.

Rice wanted to hug the unpleasant old man. He wondered what he would say if he knew how close he'd come to dying.

"And how did he take that?"

"Just looked at me smiling for a while—"

Deciding whether or not to kill you, Rice thought.

"—then he turned and walked out, drove off in a new black Tahoe with Arizona plates. When you come in I figured you wanted to make some trouble. Thought maybe your Mexican fella had got his feelings hurt."

FORTY-FOUR

He'd opened a beer before pulling away from the store, and he was seriously considering a second one now, driving on Route 608 toward the entrance to the preserve. His reloaded .45 lay on the passenger seat, but the beer was doing him more good than the pistol would. The beer was cold, as advertised. The pistol looked puny and ridiculous—he wished he had that FN SCAR he'd buried in Arizona. His eyes flicked to the rearview: nobody following. Ahead, between intermittent slashes of the windshield wipers, the road looked treacherous in the headlights, rain-smeared, pregnant with black SUVs nosing out of tree-lined driveways or gravel side roads.

His own laugh surprised him. Fucking Agent Johns. He'd found that guy's number on the wall of the bathroom in the Beer & Eat. Johns must've blown his general location weeks ago. He wondered how long the "Mexican fella" had been in the area.

He accelerated and blew past the driveway at sixty-five, no sign of anyone waiting, hit the brakes, and screeched around the curve that came up fast, drove another mile before he turned around. Nothing out of place, nothing suspicious, no black Tahoe. He pulled up to the gate and leaned forward over the steering wheel, flicked on his high beams. The rain had slackened, but wind still gusted in the trees. Didn't look like anyone had tried to get in. He carried the pistol with him when he opened and then closed and locked the gate, but no cars passed on the road and, when he checked with his flashlight, no tracks around the gate, no footprints, no tire tracks coming in. Of course, any tracks more than an hour old would've been washed away, but Rice didn't sense any intrusion, not yet.

The receiver on the seat startled him when he drove over the sensor, dutifully informing him of a breach in Zone One. When he came out of the forest he killed the headlights and nosed along with the running lights. Heavy rain began to fall again, and he was almost to the parking area when he simultaneously saw lights on in the lodge and the reflectors on a car parked in his usual spot.

Lights off, ignition off, pistol in his hand, sliding out of the truck before he'd formed a conscious thought. He pushed the door closed clicking too loudly and hid behind the truck. Knelt in the wet gravel and watched. The rain ran down his neck. Nothing happened. By now he'd started wondering why an assassin would leave his car there in the open and turn lights on in the lodge, and when he crept forward he confirmed the car was Sara's. The hood was cold. STP must have called Sara after she talked to Sheriff Walker today, might have even asked her to drive up here and check on him again.

Fighting off a mental newsreel of murder and mayhem, he snuck fast up the front steps and peered through the window to the left of the door. In the great room she lay on her side on the couch under a wool blanket from the unused bedroom. As soon as he could breathe again he called her name and tapped on the glass, wondering if her timing could possibly be worse.

"Hey, it's me. Be right back."

She sat up and regarded him. Didn't look like she'd been all the way asleep. Worried. Mad, a little.

He waved and ran back to his truck, parked it next to the Subaru, and slid the driveway alarm into his jacket pocket. Pistol in the small of his back. When he opened the front door, Sara was still sitting on the sofa, blinking at him. He took off his jacket and hung it dripping on a peg beside the door, faking a calm he didn't feel. He looked at his watch. Almost one thirty.

"How long have you been here?"

She yawned and tossed off the blanket, got her feet on the floor. "I don't know. I got here, it was after nine I guess. Would it be intrusive if I asked where the hell you've been?"

He couldn't calm down. He felt hot, jittery.

"No one's showed up?" he asked.

"No. No one ever shows up. Were you expecting someone?"

He wasn't sure how to answer, and before he could start, she spoke again.

"Starr called, told me about that missing guy, the poacher. She'd talked to Sheriff Walker."

He nodded, glad to have something he knew how to talk about. "He's okay. When we fought I fell down a cliff and he thought I was dead and he took off, hid out with his biker pals in Philly."

She looked confused but didn't say anything. He realized he'd been speaking rapidly, and tried to slow down. There wasn't time to talk, but he sat in a chair, left knee bouncing.

He and Sara both looked at his knee. He tried to make it stop.

"It all sounds kind of crazy." He stood up again. "Look, Sara—"

"They said his name, the guys who raped me. When they thought I was unconscious. *Mirra.* I must've thought they were saying 'mirror' so it seemed to be nonsense at the time. Then when Starr said it as a name it triggered these memories." She stared at her hands, concentrating, forcing her mind back to that night without drama, without so much as an eye twitch. It made Rice feel like a coward. "I don't think he was there, but they knew him. Mirra this, Mirra that. They were talking about him and some other guy, or guys."

"Okay, yeah, that makes sense." He moved closer, sat on the edge of the coffee table, leaned forward, palms on his thighs. He couldn't quite hold still. "Um . . . shit." She looked at him. She'd just dropped what should've been an informational grenade and he knew his reaction was off.

"A lot happened today," he said. He knew that what he was about to tell her would be like a punch in the gut, but he didn't have time to make it subtle. "I think I know who they are. They're in Mirra's motorcycle club. Not the Stillers, three guys from out of state, serious criminals. I'll find out for sure, I promise, and we'll do something about it."

Now her mouth opened but no sound came out.

"Sara. Jesus. I'm so sorry, there's something else."

Lightning flashed outside. In the pause before the thunder rolled in, he felt detached and overdramatic, like a kid who'd been talked into a role in the high school play.

"We have to get out of here."

FORTY-FIVE

top."

He'd left her sitting on the couch while he stuffed his clothes, most of them dirty, into a trash bag, but now she stood at the bottom of the attic steps, waiting for him. He carried his heavy fireproof cash box under his arm. He made it to the bottom step before she put a hand on his chest.

"Why is a guy coming to kill you?"

He saw she wasn't going to let him off the steps unless he gave her something. "You know I was in prison last year, right? My partner and I carried stuff back and forth over the border for one of the cartels. The tech jobs for the agencies were our cover, a reason to be down there. Border Patrol ignored us. One day we were supposed to meet some new clients across the border and federales arrested us, planted drugs in my pack. We'd been set up, I still don't know why. They turned my partner over to the DEA but they hung on to me, threw me in a prison near Nogales. The cartel tried to kill me inside but it didn't work. After I got out I took this job and disappeared." There was a hell of a lot more to it but he hoped that would be enough.

It seemed to make her angrier. "I thought you were just in for, I don't know, possession or something. What *stuff* did you carry?"

"They never told us what was in the bags but we figured it was mostly bulk cash, prepaid debit cards, shit like that. Drugs sometimes, going the other way. It was small-scale compared to the tunnels, the trap cars and trucks and all that."

"And what, you think they're after you now?"

"They've been after me all along. Now they know where I am. All that business with the sheriff, Mirra going missing. There was a DEA agent running his mouth to people in Tucson."

"We'll call him, we can call Sheriff Walker."

Rice was shaking his head as he raised the steps and shut the trapdoor, but she'd reminded him of something. He laid the cash box by the front door next to his backpack and the big contractor's trash bag with his clothes in it. Other than his truck, this was pretty much everything he owned. "Sheriff Walker is busy."

Sara followed him to the office, where he'd left STP's camera. "What, the storm? Isn't this more serious than the weather?"

He suspected she was playing along, didn't quite believe him. Probably thought he'd snapped again. He couldn't blame her.

"Walker isn't ready for this sort of thing, and I don't want to get him killed. It's safer if we leave." He pulled the data card from the camera and sealed it in an envelope, wrote "Sheriff Mark Walker" on the outside. Back at the front door he opened the combination lock on his box, pulled out his modest cash hoard, and stuffed it into the top pocket of his pack. He dropped the envelope inside the box and relocked it. "I'll put this in your car, and if something happens to me—meaning I'm dead or disappeared—give it to Walker, tell him there's important evidence inside. He'll be able to get it open."

"Evidence of what?"

He told her it had to do with the three bikers, but it was complicated. They could talk about it later. He started describing his plan: he would drive out first, she should hang back several hundred yards. Low beams only. If it was safe at the entrance he would open the gate and wait for her. The weather would give them some cover. He was making plans on the fly and he didn't like it.

"If something happens on the driveway, if you see lights, another car, anything—they might be waiting at the entrance—you back up, turn around, drive back here, hide somewhere you have service and call 911. Hide in the woods. They're not going to waste time looking for you. Do you have a weapon? Besides the stun gun?"

She nodded, but he was distracted, remembering the preserve's .22 rifle. Better bring that. In the office he unlocked the closet, made sure the magazine was loaded. When he leaned the rifle against the wall beside the front door, Sara had disappeared.

"We should go," he called out.

"Wait." She was in his bedroom, stripping the sheets from his bed. "We can make it look like you moved out. We'll shut off the power. You go dump everything in the fridge and the freezer into a bag, we'll take it with."

"There's no time."

"It'll take five minutes. If they think you're gone for good they'll leave you alone."

No, he thought, they won't. He won't.

"Go," she said. She'd opened a drawer in the empty dresser and was folding his dirty sheets into it. "Kitchen trash, too."

In the pantry he pulled out another big trash bag from the roll and opened the refrigerator, started tossing the food he'd just bought into the bag. The storm came on with more rain, heavier than before, wind booming in the metal roof. He told himself he wasn't just humoring Sara. That maybe she had a point.

He carried the last bags to his truck at a run, came back up the front steps two at a time, remembering he should bar the back door when they shut off the power at the breaker box. Everything else was loaded. Sara waited for him in her blue rain shell, holding a towel to wipe up their wet boot prints on the way out. He'd just inserted the steel bar into the brackets on the back door when the voice began speaking to them from his pocket.

"Alert, Zone One. Alert, Zone One."

He checked his watch while Sara looked at him, frowning.

"What's that?"

FORTY-SIX

They turned right just past the cabin and drove their vehicles up the fire road. Exactly eight minutes after the alarm went off, they disappeared into the forest. Rice was confident the heavy rain would hide the glow from their running lights—he'd warned Sara to keep her Subaru in the lowest gear and not to hit the brakes. He pulled off into the wet forest duff and coasted to a stop, shut off the truck, got out in his rain shell, and jogged back to Sara's car.

She moved her laptop bag and he sat in the front seat. He reached up to turn off the interior light so it wouldn't come on again, laid the driveway alarm receiver on the dashboard. They drove on another hundred yards, out of sight of his truck, nosing into the thick pine saplings at the first switchback, before she shut her engine off. The darkness was total, and he felt the dense forest enclose them protectively, like coming home, giant trees thrashing in the wind, to his mind now a sound of sword-rattling. She would be safe here, so long as the storm didn't drop a big branch on her car.

"Do you have a signal on your phone?"

She hit a button so the screen light illuminated. "One bar. It's usually better than that up here. Must be the storm. You want me to try 911?"

"Not yet. It's almost three now. If I'm not back by nine, call the sheriff, tell him everything. Tell him to be careful, he can't come alone, he should bring Janie and Stoner."

"If you're not back from where?"

"I'm going back down, to the lodge. I have to see what happens. Who it is. I need to make sure they don't come up here."

"Rice," she began.

"I know this is happening fast. I'm sorry. I promise I'll explain later."

"It's just so far-fetched. And suddenly you've got this alarm system installed?" She grabbed his rain-wet hand, held it for a moment, peering at him in the light from her phone. "Remember what you were like when I drove up here Sunday? That wasn't even three days ago. I probably shouldn't have left you alone. Just stop and think for a minute. Is it possible you're overreacting?"

"You heard the alarm. Someone's coming up the driveway. I locked the gate behind me."

"Maybe it's malfunctioning. Maybe someone from the sheriff's office is driving up here, something about the storm, or something about that Mirra guy."

Apparently she'd been thinking things over on the short drive up here. "I promise I'm not as batshit as I seem. Just please wait here until nine."

"I'll come with you." She felt around underneath her seat and produced a can of bear spray. "I can help."

"Bear spray?"

"My father bought it for me. I have the stun gun too." She reached under her jacket but he put his hand on her arm. She saw his face, surely ghostly in the dim uplight from her phone, and froze.

"You're not even a little bit scared, are you?" he asked.

"I'm not scared. I'm pissed off. You can't just park me up here like a goddamn mannequin!"

He knew being brave sometimes entailed preferring physical danger to whatever psychic distress would come from avoiding that danger. Sara would rather face the real or imagined danger coming up the driveway than sit here and stew. He didn't blame her, and he loved this about her, but she didn't understand what was coming. He felt a surge of incipient panic and squashed it. For a moment he considered duct-taping her to the steering wheel. Instead he tried to explain about the kind of people who were after him, not rednecks with shotguns, not rapist bikers from hell, but professional killers.

"If you come with me, I'll be distracted. They'll kill us both." He tapped the alarm receiver. "This will tell you every time someone drives in or out. If you have to move around, lose the blue jacket, it's lousy camouflage. It's important that you not call Walker before nine, but if you have to call him, don't show yourself until he calls you back and confirms he has everything under control."

He squeezed her fingers, antsy and impatient, his mind racing ahead of him toward the lodge. She was quiet, and he guessed she was angry, still struggling with her doubt. He asked her again to please not call anyone before nine. He checked his watch in the light from her phone. Eighteen minutes since the alarm. He tried to smile, said something inane and perfunctory like he'd be okay, he'd be careful. When she didn't reply he reached down and flipped her phone over on its face, got out, eased the door shut, and returned to the truck for his ghillie poncho and the target rifle. The .45 was in its holster behind his hip.

He unrolled the ghillie and put it on. Carrying the rifle with the muzzle pointed at the ground so the bore wouldn't fill with rainwater, he walked blindly down the fire road, blundering into the tall grass on either side. There should have been a hint of light overhead once he was out of the forest, but he couldn't tell up from down.

He stopped, tried to slow his mind. If he kept going like this he was going to make a mistake. Whatever power he'd felt those days in the forest, whether it came from some mystical sylvan entity or his own twisted psyche, he could use some now.

The grass hissed as the rain fell in sheets, warm and tropical, smelling of sea salt and coastal marsh, scents Hurricane Julia must have carried all the way from Florida. He leaned his head back and closed his eyes, the big raindrops coming so fast and thick he could barely breathe, spattering on his face, thunking on his forehead, on his eyelids, slipping through his lips, pooling in his eye sockets, overflowing to spill like tears down his temples. Where had this water come from, the Gulf of Mexico? The Caribbean? He imagined it tasted like the ocean. Julia had traveled thousands of miles to flood Turpin County with evaporated seawater. Some of it landed on him but that was just happenstance. These were large forces at work.

Half-afraid he might drown himself, he stood with his face tilted to the rain and let his mind clear. After a while, the first sketchy outlines appeared, a sense of where he was, the way the fire road lay below and behind him, an open path through the grass to the rain-drenched buildings downhill, then the sloping contours of the land all around were filling in, he felt it as surely as the topography of his own body, felt the mountain rising behind him, all the trees in the forest leaning away from the wind.

FORTY-SEVEN

No lights, no vehicle, nothing but wind and rain. At the edge of the driveway, gravel underfoot, he crouched down and felt for tire tracks in the mud where he and Sara had driven onto the fire road. They'd already washed away.

He knelt in the meadow, opened his knife, and began cutting clumps of grass and weeds, fitting them into the hood and shoulders of the poncho, tucked under the netting, tying them off with hanging strings of baling twine. He felt the pocket for the burnt cork and the dyed gloves, but they had disappeared, so he dug into the earth and smeared mud on his face and the backs of his hands.

Holding the rifle in his arms, he crawled toward the lodge, following the gentle incline and fighting the pain in his knee. When he came to the edge of the yard he backed up a few feet, arranging the grass in front of him so it would allow a line of sight that would encompass the lodge and the shed. He drew his .45 and tucked it inside his jacket, under his chest. He draped wet grass over the rifle barrel and lay prone to wait.

The rain came down, a staccato patter on the roofs of the buildings, splashing in puddles under the eaves. He guessed thirty,

thirty-five minutes had passed since the alarm, plenty of time for whoever it was to drive up here, but they would stop at the edge of the forest and cut their lights as Rice had earlier, creep along using the vehicle's running lights, the heavy rain providing cover. A team would deploy from the vehicle, spread out and approach from different directions, hit the place fast and hard. A single assassin would take more time, use more stealth, patience. The fact that they hadn't showed up yet argued for the one guy.

He lifted the rifle and fitted it to his shoulder, swept it left and right in a short arc, then he rested the fore-end on his left fist and waited. After a while, the rain diminished and the wind picked up, cooler than before. He wasn't sleepy but he began to shiver as his body heat seeped away into the wet earth. No sound of a car engine, no tires in gravel. Only the metronomic drip-drip-drip of rainwater from the roof.

He pulled the pistol from his jacket and laid it in the grass where he could reach it.

The dark bulk of the lodge appeared above his tunnel of grass, or rather there was a moment when he understood he'd been seeing it for a while. The sky grew lighter, and now he could see the outlines of the other buildings. The shed was to his right, and between it and the lodge he thought he could make out the dark wet gravel of the parking area and the lighter grass beyond that. It was too early for first light, but the full moon would still be up, falling toward the mountains in the west. The clouds must be thinning, the bulk of the storm passing to the north, its remnants beginning to clear. The cool wind gusted, swishing in the tall, wet grass for a long while before it receded, leaving only the sound of dripping water, its tempo gradually slowing.

Someone was there. Rice couldn't see him, but his whole body tingled with certainty.

A dark blob appeared beneath the window to his bedroom. It slowly elongated, standing to peer inside the dark room. No flashlight, so he must be using night vision. That was why he'd waited—most NV tech is useless in heavy rain. The figure was still for a few seconds, then it retracted, crouching, and moved to the next window, the office, and repeated. Rice raised the rifle up a few inches and pointed it, though he couldn't see the sights. Moving again, the intruder rounded the near corner, looked in the kitchen, crept up on the back porch, looking in all the windows, then disappeared around the far side of the lodge. Rice rested the heavy rifle and took long deep breaths. Five minutes. He would be inside now, would've picked the lock on the front door, or he could cut the screen from a window on the front porch, use a glass cutter to quietly remove a pane, reach through and unlock the latch.

Another ten minutes passed. He would be stalking through the lodge, searching every room, all the closets. He would check the attic. Nothing but bare mattresses on the beds, the power switched off, empty refrigerator and freezer propped open, defrosting in a puddle on the floor. Sara had even poured some bleach into the toilets. They'll smell it, she'd said. They'll know you're long gone.

There. He was walking between the lodge and the shed. In profile, his face seemed to have a long beak, the night-vision goggles.

Rice followed with the rifle until the man disappeared on the other side of the tractor shed. A rattle as he slid open the big door. A few minutes later, the door banged shut, then quiet. He must be checking the cabin. It would look like a work in progress, waiting for carpenters to return.

A Carolina wren began to chip and buzz, warming up for its predawn chorus. The man didn't come back. Ten minutes, fifteen. Rice waited, thinking no way he's gone. Twenty minutes. Then, a big engine in low gear, coming up the driveway. No headlights, must be using the goggles, driving with his lights off. The vehicle crossed the gravel parking area and pulled around behind the tractor shed where it would be hidden from anyone else coming up the driveway.

The driver's-side door opened—no interior light came on—and he slid from the seat and shut the door quietly, Rice watching his dim shape over the barrel of the rifle. He leaned back against the door. He'd taken off the goggles and was peering idly around at the dark mountain, the horizon and the silvery moonlit meadow, facing Rice but not seeing him. The storm was still breaking up, the moon in the west a quick brightening and dimming, clouds moving fast in a high wind. He was tall, slender. He wore a dark knit cap and his face seemed pale, but that might just be an effect of the moonlight.

The man no longer believed there was any danger here, and because of that, he was helpless, and Rice would kill him.

He realized this had been his plan all along. Without ever consciously making the decision to do so, he'd been hunting this man ever since he'd left Sara in her car. He wondered at that for a moment, but the question was fleeting, barely disturbing the calm surface of his focus, then it was gone. His thoughts flew ahead, analysis and decision, one after another without slowing down for articulation. There was no more talking to himself.

He strained to see through the rifle's aperture sights, but they'd been designed for shooting NRA fifty-foot small-bore targets in daylight and were useless right now. He'd learned to shoot with both eyes open, and by a kind of dead reckoning he knew he could put the little bullet somewhere in the man's torso, maybe clip his spine, his heart.

But he also knew who this almost certainly was. Unless he made a spectacularly lucky shot, the man would be on the move and returning fire before Rice could work the bolt.

The .45 was ready, near his right hand. If he could manage a solid hit with one of those big slugs, the man wouldn't be shooting back, at least not accurately. Tough shot though, at this range, in the dark, and the guy might be wearing armor anyway.

He would have to wait for better light. He'd brought the rifle for a reason. His pistol was more powerful but it wasn't a sniper's tool; the rifle would be precise enough at this range for a head shot. In good light, he wouldn't miss.

He could wait. A deadly patience settled his bones, molded his body to the earth.

Then, as if in response to Rice's complaint about the shooting light, the man reached into a pocket once, twice, then brought his hands to his face and a lighter flared and went out. The cigarette glowed orange as he inhaled, illuminating Rice's sight picture: centered in the rear peep, the circular metal insert in the front sight framed the orange face, at thirty yards a high-confidence shot into the ocular cranial cavity. Even if the bullet deflected off the skull, it would stun the man long enough to allow follow-up shots.

He slipped the safety off. The cigarette flared, dimmed. Flared. The round stamp of the front sight was locked on the man's face.

Wait. The voice spoke inside his mind so clearly, he worried the man leaning against the truck must have heard, and his first reflex was to shush it. But it spoke again. *Can't just murder him,* the voice said.

He hesitated, his hunter's trance broken. His own voice started blabbing away in his consciousness again. Suddenly you give a shit, he thought. You torture a poor unemployed backwoods drug dealer whose greatest hope in life is to join a fucking biker gang, but you won't put down a psychopathic multiple murderer who came here expressly to kill you?

Then the man was grinding out his cigarette on the sole of his boot. He tucked the butt in a pocket and switched on a small flashlight, disappeared around the front of the lodge.

FORTY-EIGHT

Rice was trembling, knees and elbows numb, his hands clumsy on the rifle. He shifted his weight around, had to get some circulation going, but too much movement might be visible from inside the lodge. He realized he was afraid, for the first time in a long time.

Agent Johns had been right about one thing: of all the bad guys in the world, this was not the one you wanted hunting you. If you got lucky and had a chance to kill him, you took it. You didn't try to capture him, or intentionally wound him, shoot him in the leg or the shoulder like the honorable hero in a bullshit Western. He's been shot like that before, he can function at close to a hundred percent with peripheral gunshot wounds that would have you curled up screaming on the ground. If he hears a voice telling him to put his hands up or some stupid shit like that, the man is moving and shooting in an instant. You could have your weapon right on him and as he slips away you might get off a shot, you might even hit him, but not well, and he'll kill you long before he bleeds out.

Rice should have shot him when he had the chance, should have shot him in the face when he was lighting himself up with his fucking cigarette.

But he still had the advantage. The man still believed he was alone. His guard was down. He was walking around like he was on vacation or something. Rice could still kill him.

Dawn wasn't far off. Only a few clouds now, moonlight giving way to first light. Off to his left, the eastern horizon was brightening, washing out the stars. He could let the man go. Sara's plan might work. The man might believe Rice has moved out and is on the run again.

He was inside the lodge for a long time. Light from his flashlight jumped around in the bedroom window, the office, the kitchen. This would be his more thorough search, looking for scraps of correspondence, notes, an answering machine with undeleted messages, anything to show where Rice had gone. He would look for a phone so he could hit redial and call the last number Rice had called, and he would find that antique green thing with the rotary dial in the office. He would notice the bookshelves, all those animal bones, skulls, the skins, that cow-pelvis helmet. He would recognize them as totems, and they would make an impression, though Rice couldn't imagine what they would mean to this guy. The quasi-religious narco-cults made mainstream religions seem almost coherent by comparison.

On Rice's face, a light breeze, much cooler, drier. A dozen species of birds were calling, celebrating the weather, the storm's passing.

The front screen door slammed shut, footsteps on the porch steps, careless, there he was, headed back to the Tahoe, coming almost straight on. With both eyes open, Rice centered the man's face in the doughnut ring of the target sight. The safety was off. His body flushed hot and his pulse throbbed so violently the front sight veered completely away from the man's face with each heartbeat.

Even if he does just drive away, Rice thought, he won't stop looking. He'll be a threat to anyone who might know where I went. Sara. STP. Even Boger, Sheriff Walker.

Onetwothree, he breathed, four, five, six, settling down. By his twelfth heartbeat the rifle was steady. You have to shoot him, he told himself. There's no other way.

Wait for him. He's still too far out. He's coming to you. Wait till you're sure of the shot. Ten more steps.

Then, movement, something new, off to the left, a small dark animal. It was beyond the limit of Rice's peripheral vision but he saw it anyway, Mel the black cat stalking low to the ground just underneath the back porch, eyes fixed straight ahead, oblivious to Rice hidden in the grass, to the man about to come around the corner—oblivious to everything but her own prey.

She paused with her legs gathered beneath her, quivered, and shot forward, covering six feet in an instant, moving with unnatural speed, legs could not carry a body that fast, landing at the corner of the lodge. A panicked, high-pitched chirping, and she lifted her head with a mouthful of grass and squirming wet vole.

Mel and the man saw each other at the same moment. She turned and bolted, great full-stretch bounds to the tall grass, not the proverbial scalded cat but something less corporeal, a shadow, a trick of the mind, too quick for the eye to resolve. The man had already reacted, twisting on the balls of both feet and dropping into a half-crouch, a pistol in his hand, so fast, the arm nearly extended, the off-hand clapping into position, bracing.

Don't shoot the fucking cat, Rice thought. He recentered the man's face in the front ring of his sights. He exhaled, began his trigger squeeze.

Everything slowed down. Stopped.

The pistol was a chunky black thing, a Glock. Mel vanished into the grass. The man smiled and it sounded like he said something to himself about *el gato negro*. The pistol dropped a few degrees, shoulders relaxing, but the grin froze and his eyes changed and Rice knew what was happening: caution exploding in his mind—if a housecat is here, maybe he shouldn't be so sure Rice has left—the feelers switching back on, the *sicario* Spidey-sense tingling, some ancient reptilian subconscious proto-mind detecting danger in the innocuous disheveled chaos of the meadow. The almost imperceptibly too-dark shapeless bunching foliage that was Rice must be visible now, surely manifest at the periphery if not in his conscious mind, the part of his mind still busy with the implications of the black cat. Rice's perception of time picked up again, from stopped time to slow time. His eyes stung but he didn't blink. He watched the man's expression as he let go of the cat and answered the screaming Paleozoic core of his brain telling him something was in the meadow, something was wrong there, his gaze pulled Rice-ward as Rice himself tried to shrink, to evanesce, but his own unwilling gravity was palpable, tugging the man's eyes toward the lumpy nonshape of the ghillie there among the late-season grass, Rice-gravity hauling his attention on a rope now, hand-over-hand, pulling his head, shoulders, the triangle of his arms with the pistol at its apex, his hips pivoting, obeying the attraction, turning toward Rice in a slow arc, accelerating.

FORTY-NINE

The Glock went off in a burst like a submachine gun, two of the bullets slapping into the wet ground close enough to spray Rice with mud, but the man was falling as he pulled the trigger, unconscious before he hit the ground, everything limp, a small splash before settling into the saturated ground.

Rice dropped the rifle and picked up the .45, swept it slowly left and right. He was sure the guy had come alone but he waited anyway. Thirty seconds. A minute.

His mind fizzed like he'd been bombing speed. Those shots going off all at once, Rice's rifle and the burst from the guy's pistol, what the hell was that? Bullets in the ground right there. He almost got me.

Don't think about that yet.

Be patient, he thought, don't fuck this up.

Three minutes. He shucked off the rain-soaked ghillie poncho and walked into the yard and stood with his pistol pointed at the man lying facedown in the grass. Bloody exit wound near the hairline, below the hem of the knit cap. No pulse. He'd been standing slightly downhill from Rice, leaning forward in his gunman's crouch, and Rice's bullet had entered his skull via his left eye and passed through the lower part of his cranial cavity, disrupting the brain stem and shutting off consciousness almost instantly.

The sun was on the mountain. The day had begun: wet green grass bent low with the weight of water; bright turning leaves of yellow, red, orange; the storm's last southwesterly breezes shaking loud cascades of rainwater in the forest. Birdsong sounding far off. A quiet cool morning, the air washed clean. Rice thought he understood what had just happened, but it kept slipping.

He rolled the man over with his foot.

He didn't recognize him. He'd thought he might, that there might be some family resemblance, but he didn't see it. His lips were parted and his teeth shone bone white but his left eye was a bloody hole. The other eye, lovely dark brown, stared up at the stark blue sky, where compact cumulus clouds scudded fast in a high wind, passing over the sun the way they had over the moon, dark then light, a shutter closing and opening.

Information about the universe leaked from the open eye like poison gas. Stuff you knew but had to pretend you didn't, just so you could make it through the day.

He reached down and closed the eye with his thumb. It slowly opened halfway. He pushed it closed and it opened again.

Hysteria fluttered like a moth in the back of his throat.

FIFTY

is forefinger in the cutout over the three, pulling the rotary dial down and around to the curved metal stop, releasing, the dial returning to where it started. His finger over the eight, a longer pull, the long return. Then the rest of the sheriff's number, slowly, one by one. Ringing. Sheriff Walker himself answers, and Rice explains. The sheriff pauses. Hell, he says, I don't need the paperwork. Why don't you just take that body and bury it up on the mountain.

He stared down at the body, morning sunlight slanting in over the mountain now and warming the cool wet grass.

Another fugue, maybe a couple of minutes' worth.

Wouldn't be calling the sheriff. Yeah, it was self-defense, barely. But he wouldn't be calling the sheriff.

He flicked the safety on and pushed the .45 into its holster. Light nausea. Shallow, fast breathing. Hands trembling.

He'd just killed somebody. To make sure he wasn't missing the point, he said the words, not aloud, but he said them in his mind. This wasn't even the first somebody he'd killed. How many people in the world had killed other people? On purpose? Had killed more than one? Couldn't be all that many. Especially if you didn't count military and police. It was pretty fucked up that he was one of them. How did he turn into this person who killed other people? He needed to sit down.

Stop it. Focus. There would be time for the other thing later.

He needed a plan, something simple, a short-term plan, some way to organize the present chaos that kept pushing him into his fugues. He checked his watch, not even seven thirty, but Sara must have heard the shots, she might be scared, thinking about calling the sheriff. He had to run up there, stop her from worrying, from making any unfortunate calls. But she shouldn't see the body.

So, first: body in SUV, SUV in tractor shed.

He jogged to the Tahoe, thinking don't touch anything, no prints—he used his bandana to open the door. Keys were in the ignition, smelled like cigarettes inside. The night-vision goggles lay on the passenger seat. Using the bandana to turn the key, shift the transmission, and hold the wheel, he pulled forward between the lodge and the shed and backed up to the body.

The guy's boots were dull-black, crepe-soled, quiet. His jeans were black, loose-fitting, wet from the rain, and he wore a tight black T-shirt under a black stretchy jacket that was the kind of fabric that wouldn't make noise when you moved. Tattoos on his neck: skulls, roses, stylized Spanish script that Rice didn't have the wherewithal to decipher just now. The tight black watch cap. Time to make sure: he pulled off the cap and turned the head to the side, with his fingers pushed the short dark hair on the back of the man's head into a part, exposing brightly colored tats. He checked to the left, the right, yeah it was there: the crazy eyes, the open mouth.

He'd come to take Rice out himself. And he'd come alone. Rice had knowingly signed up to run from this hellhound the rest of his life, and now he was dead.

This might be over.

It was good news, better than Rice deserved. If he didn't do anything stupid in the next few hours, he might be able to stay at the preserve after all.

He patted the ankles, pulled up the right cuff—a little SIG .380 in an ankle holster—and ripped open the Velcro straps to detach the holster. He picked up the Glock where it had fallen in the grass. It had a hole in the top of the slide revealing compensator cuts in the barrel, and a lever that looked like a safety on the left face of the slide, nothing Rice had seen before. He would look it over later. He laid the pistols on the front seat next to the goggles, went back and found four spent 9mm casings in the grass, put these in his pocket.

A Spyderco folding knife in the man's left pants pocket; in the right, the cigarette butt he'd stashed earlier. The flesh of his thighs felt cold, felt like meat.

It hadn't been five minutes.

Rice stood, shut his eyes. Should he apologize, the way he had to the animals he'd killed in the forest? He took a few deep breaths, fought back the nausea.

Keep moving.

A Kydex holster on the man's belt, a phone in the vest pocket of his jacket. In one side pocket was a small flashlight similar to Rice's, a loaded extra magazine for the Glock, a half-empty soft pack of Camels, and a disposable lighter. In the other, a small black stun gun, smaller than Sara's, and ten heavy plastic zip ties.

He held the ties in his hand.

"What the fuck are these for?" The man lay there, his face slack. Not answering.

He tossed the stuff from the man's pockets on the front seat and, using his bandana, unlatched the big rear door to the cargo area. It rose up on pressurized cylinders, a great maw opening in no particular hurry.

Inside were the bolt cutters he'd expected, along with a new green plastic tarp, a big one, still folded and in its clear wrapping, and two Wal-Mart shopping bags. He stared at the bags for a moment before rifling them. In the first he found a pair of elbow-length rubber gloves, a box of blue latex gloves, a package of disposable hairnets, a pair of plastic booties with elastic cuffs, three rolls of duct tape, and the open package of zip ties. In the other bag, a cheap ice pick and garden shears, both still in their clear blister packs.

Of course. Plain assassination wouldn't feel like sufficient revenge to a guy like this. Too merciful. He wouldn't have even considered it. No, he would surprise Rice in bed, disable him with the stun gun, zip-tie him to the bedpost, and go fetch the Tahoe with the rest of the tools. In a remote location like this, there would have been no hurry. He would've had all the time in the world.

Rice knew what these items in the Wal-Mart bags were for, and how to use them. He knew what had been planned for him. He'd been well schooled. It had started as idle entertainment first for Fernandez, then several other bored *sicarios*, all of whom must have recognized something in Rice: a powerful will to survive, a latent capacity for violence, a willingness to kill. Some athletic aptitude. Certainly a good memory, though most of it he'd prefer to forget. His hold on what he'd always believed was right and what was wrong had grown fatigued, eventually warping to fit the contours of the world he inhabited. He'd also developed an appreciation for the depressing banality of professional violence. The *sicarios* were just guys—highly skilled, and unusually willing to visit violence on other human beings, but ordinary in so many ways. Not alien, not other. He'd decided he couldn't judge them. After Apryl's murder, the training gave Rice not just a survival strategy but a story to cling to, a vengeance narrative that animated him, that bound together the atoms of his body.

He'd learned, for example, that a sharp point could be used to inflict intolerable pain in the auditory canal without making a mess of blood, tissue, DNA evidence that would require cleanup afterward. The ice pick there in the blister pack in the back of the Tahoe also was ideal for bone-tickling: stabbing through the flesh to any large bone—femur, pelvis—and then dragging the point along the periosteum, scraping across all those nerve endings, which made it feel like the bones were being broken, over and over. Again: lots of pain, not much bleeding. If he'd had an ice pick in his truck, he wondered, would he have tried that on DeWayne?

And the garden shears, doubtless made in China, cost less than ten bucks. Why spend more? These were plenty sharp. If nothing else worked—or if you were in a hurry—what got to interrogation subjects most reliably was lopping off parts of the body. Here his instructor had shaken his head in mock wonder at the quirks of the human psyche. There was something about losing pieces of yourself. People couldn't tolerate it.

No, he wouldn't have done that. Of course he wouldn't have. No way.

Exhausted and worn raw by what he *had* done in the past twelve hours, Rice felt horror and relief, anger and shame all scrabbling for purchase in his mind. It occurred to him that but for DeWayne's warning about the Mexican, right now Rice would likely be missing various pieces of himself. And Sara, what would have happened to her? He made a mental note to be nicer to DeWayne in the future.

Okay, enough.

Body in SUV.

He shuffled his feet up close and sat into a squat, keeping his back straight, worked his right hand under the man's stiff black leather belt at the buckle, gathered the front of his jacket with his left, and lifted.

A giant rag doll filled with water.

All of the parts lifelessly slumping: head lolling back, arms and heavy legs hanging. He stood as tall as he could, raised up on his toes, shrugged his shoulders high, shoved the body forward with his hips. The head thunked against the chrome bumper. Boots dragged in the grass. His grip on the jacket started to slip, and for a desperate moment he watched what was about to happen, saw it from a point in the air above and behind his right shoulder, a grotesque, panicked wrestling match with the uncooperative body, grabbing an ankle, an elbow, tumbling into the back of the Tahoe, flopping limbs, bloody head twisting around on the limp tattooed neck, the man's face contorted against the rubberized floor, an outraged, one-eyed stare.

Wait. Wait wait wait. Think.

He set the body back down in the grass. A fecal stench, and a darker stain in the crotch of the black pants. A smear of blood on the bumper. He was going to have to wipe that off. Another wet dark spot of blood the size of a fist on Rice's pants leg. Did he want to get blood all over the cargo area? All that stuff in there. The Wal-Mart bags, the duct tape.

The tarp. The tarp that Rice's body was supposed to be wrapped in.

He laughed out loud. Couldn't help it. Irony, he knew, was a fundamental force at work in the universe, like gravity and electromagnetism.

"Rice?"

He ducked behind the Tahoe, his hand reaching back for the .45, but of course it was only Sara, she must have heard him laugh. She stood up from where she'd been hiding in the meadow. Carrying something, probably that can of bear spray. She wore one of his dark plaid shirts over her blue rain shell for camouflage. Her blond hair shone in the sun and he realized he should've thought of that, should've told her to cover her head.

"Sara, you need to stay back." He rounded the Tahoe and walked toward her, glad the body was hidden from her view.

"What happened? Are you okay? I heard shots." Her voice trembled but she ignored his instruction to stay where she was and came forward, pushing through the heavy wet grass to the edge of the yard, where she stopped. "Whose truck is that?"

"Did you call Walker?" he asked.

She shook her head. Good. He relaxed just a touch.

"Were you laughing?"

He wasn't sure he could explain, so he let her questions hang.

"I didn't really believe you."

"I know."

"It sounded like a machine gun. I knew you didn't have a machine gun."

"Nope."

She asked again what happened, and what he'd been laughing at, then she asked if whoever it was was dead, but he didn't respond. His shirt was too big for her and she'd buttoned it wrong and it hung lopsided off one shoulder. Her pants were soaked to the thighs from the tall grass. He thought about Sara hearing gunshots and deciding the best course of action was to leave the safety of the forest and sneak down here with her bear spray to see if he needed help.

"I'll call Sheriff Walker." She pulled out her phone. "Do we need an ambulance?"

"Hang on," he said.

Her eyes got a little bigger. Rice knew how this looked: he'd almost certainly just shot someone, in self-defense or otherwise, and he'd been laughing, and now he didn't want to call the sheriff?

He tried to soften his voice. "If we tell the sheriff about this, if we set the wheels of justice a-turning, I'll have the entire Sinaloa organization after me within forty-eight hours. I won't live long. It was bad enough when it was just one guy."

"That makes no sense to me."

"I know, I'm sorry." He was afraid the next bit wasn't going to go over well either. "I have to ask a big favor. I want you to walk back up to your car, drive straight out of here, go home. You could end up in jail if you stay any longer. As far as you know I scared off a bad guy and he hightailed it into the forest, left his vehicle here. I sent you home. You haven't seen anything to the contrary. I'll call you—"

"I'm not leaving."

He stopped talking. He realized he didn't have a plan for this.

"Are you going to shoot me too?"

He stared, his mouth open. "What? No. Sara, were you listening?"

"I'm really sorry, Rice, but you have to tell me what happened. Otherwise I'll call the sheriff and you can tell him what happened." She paused, sighed. They both knew she wasn't going to do that. When she spoke again the note of hysteria was gone. "You can't keep doing everything by yourself. If you're as smart as you seem to think you are, you're going to let me help you."

FIFTY-ONE

Sara walked back up the fire road while Rice tucked his hair into a hairnet and struggled to fit his still shaky hands into a pair of latex gloves. His knowledge of criminal law was rusty and superficial, but if Sara was going to be an accessory to the various crimes he was committing, he guessed it would be better if she never saw the body. It was irresponsible to let her stay, but she was a stubborn person and he told himself there was no way to make her leave against her will.

Under Sara's interrogation, he'd admitted to wanting to shoot the man at the first opportunity. He'd emphasized his crisis of conscience. He didn't admit that he probably would have killed the man in cold blood if Mel the cat hadn't interfered, converting a murder into a near-death experience of self-defense. When he'd pointed out, with studied casualness, the divots in the grass where the man's bullets had nearly hit him in the face, she'd asked where the other bullets had gone.

"He didn't shoot at Mel, did he?"

"No, Sara, he only shot at me."

"Good."

When he'd asked why she wasn't more horrified at what he'd done, why she wasn't running down the driveway and calling Sheriff Walker on her cell, she'd deflected with an offhand "I probably should be," but her look was hard to read. After thinking about it, he'd decided some of what he'd seen in her face was trepidation over her hard-to-fathom decision to trust Rice in an extremely sketchy situation, but the rest was a sheepish awareness that she was admitting to a hardness of heart that polite company might find abhorrent.

He unfolded the green tarp in the grass and weighted the corners with firewood from the stack behind the shed, careful to avoid the piece the old man had used to club him in the head—it was probably contaminated with his DNA.

The man's boot soles were muddy. The soil up here might be distinctive, so he untied the boots, pulled them off, and set them aside. More splotches of mud on the man's pants cuffs, on his jacket at the left hip, and on his shoulder, where he'd hit the ground. Rice used his own pocketknife to liberate the torture shears from their packaging. He cut vertically up both pants legs from the cuffs to just below the knees, then around the legs, converting the pants to shorts and revealing muscular calves wound round with barbed wire tats. He unbuckled the belt and removed the black Kydex holster. Finally he cut the jacket sleeves starting at the cuffs, up the arms, and across the chest to the zipper so he could skin the jacket away from the body. He tossed the jacket in a pile in the grass with the watch cap and boots and pants legs.

With the body centered at one end of the tarp, he folded the edges over the man's head and feet to overlap in the middle, taped them together, and started rolling, rolled the body up in the tarp, as tightly as he could, like rolling up a rug. He wrapped it with a whole roll of duct tape, round and round, triple-taping along the seam so nothing would leak out.

This time when he lifted the body, it was easier to manage and it slid neatly into the back of the Tahoe. He pushed it into a slight curve to make it fit without folding either of the back seats down. After he deployed the cargo security shade and shut the rear door, the wrapped body was invisible from inside or outside the vehicle. He fetched a contractor's trash bag from the cabin and stuffed the man's boots and clothes in, tossed it on the back seat.

Sara had parked her car in the usual spot and was on her way back to the forest for his truck. The sliding shed door stuck halfway and he had to wrestle it open, but the tractor started right up. He drove it out into the driveway near the cabin, pulled the lever for the three-point hitch to raise the bush hog up high, like it was time to sharpen the blade. The Tahoe fit in the tractor's spot in the shed. He locked the vehicle with the remote on the key fob and pushed the shed door shut.

Body in SUV, SUV in tractor shed.

One more thing before Sara came back: he dragged the hose from under the front porch and washed away the blood in the grass. By the time she pulled his truck around the cabin and parked next to the Subaru, he was in the office dialing the old phone, just like he'd imagined in his fugue. His call went straight into Sheriff Walker's voice mail, Suzy's voice, telling him to please leave a message.

THEY SWITCHED THE POWER ON AND MOVED RICE'S STUFF BACK INTO THE lodge. Sara replaced his food in the fridge and freezer—she didn't think it had spoiled—while he went back out to the shed and spent nearly an hour searching the Tahoe. Afterward he rinsed off fast in the shower. The clothes he'd been wearing went into the washing machine on a heavy-duty cycle with extra rinse.

They ate a quick breakfast, homicide having no effect on their appetites. The dishes were rinsed and drying, coffee grounds dumped into a new trash bag. Everything normal. Rice laid the items he'd found in the Tahoe on the kitchen table. From the glove compartment, a registration to 77th Avenue Services Corporation, Phoenix, Arizona. Possibly a cartel vehicle, probably not stolen. No hidden compartments that Rice could detect. Under the driver's seat he'd found two small Ziploc bags with a few dozen 9mm hollow points in one, .380s in the other. A black Nike gym bag contained clothes, toiletries, a folded copy of the *Turpin Weekly Record.* He dumped these in the trash and stashed the two pistols, ammunition, NV goggles, and the things from the man's pockets in the gym bag. The Glock was a G18C, which he'd never even heard of, and the part that looked like a safety was a selective fire switch, allowing the pistol to fire fully automatic bursts. The thing was radioactive—if he were caught with a full-auto firearm he would grow old in prison—but he couldn't quite make himself get rid of it, not yet. The future was still uncertain. He thought of Alan Mirra and his motorcycle club, and the possibility that the cartel would find out what had happened and retaliate against Rice. As dangerous as it was to keep the pistols, an argument could be made that it would be more dangerous not to have them.

Sara opened a thick manila envelope he'd found on the back seat and dumped out twenty-seven one-hundred-dollar bills in two rubber-banded stacks, a marked-up map of Turpin County, copies of Rice's mug shots taken after his transfer from CERESO, and a printed skip tracer's report showing the results of a months-long search for Rice's whereabouts. A slim leather wallet contained four more hundreds and some smaller bills, a prepaid Visa card, and an Arizona driver's license with the man's picture, name of Paul Martin, a Phoenix address.

She arranged the items on the table, inspecting each in turn. "You know this guy?"

"Never met him."

"But you know who he is. Was."

"I know his name's not Paul Martin."

"Uh-huh. And what makes you think whoever sent him isn't going to come looking for him?"

"I'm pretty sure he was hunting me on his own. Kind of a personal project. He hired that skip tracer himself." The report was addressed to Paul Martin at a P.O. box in Tempe.

"I thought the cartel was trying to keep you from testifying or something." She leaned forward in her chair. She was focused but seemed calm, and Rice knew having her there was helping to keep him calm too. "Rice," she began, "I'm being really patient over here, dragging the truth out of you like this. You appreciate it, right?"

"I do."

"So . . ."

"His name's Delgado. Andrés Delgado. I didn't testify against the cartel. I killed his younger brother."

"Shit, Rice, what in—"

"Crotalito. That's what they called him, the brother. He was a *sicario*, a low-level hit man for the cartel. I never knew his real name." He ran a hand through his hair, rubbed his face as if he were trying to smooth out wrinkles, or wipe off some foreign substance. These words he was saying, he hadn't even allowed himself to think them for so long. "When they couldn't kill me inside they sent Crotalito after my partner to make sure she wouldn't talk. It was his first real job and it was supposed to be a simple kidnap, assassination, and disappearance, but Crotalito was a sadistic shit, couldn't help himself, he raped and tortured her, then he panicked and left the body on the U.S. side. It made the papers. The cartel didn't like that."

Rice's friends from CERESO had made inquiries, pulled strings, utilized back channels. The plan appealed to the cartel because it would eliminate Crotalito without alienating the influential and highly effective elder brother. The price was that Rice's identity would be leaked to Andrés. The vengeful, grieving boyfriend had found his brother and killed him. It was very unfortunate.

RICE HID THE GYM BAG WITH DELGADO'S THINGS IN THE ATTIC, FIRST peeling off a few hundreds from the stack in the manila envelope. The Traver Foundation's innocent-looking .22 target rifle was now a homicide weapon, but the bullet that had killed Delgado was gone, somewhere out there in the grass, disappearing into the earth, so he'd simply cleaned the bore, oiled the rifle, and replaced it in the closet.

Sara agreed to hang on to the locked cash box with, as she put it, "whatever the hell secret shit you've stashed in there." She would take it home and keep it in her apartment in Blacksburg. The tractor went back into the shed, and he drove the Tahoe down to the entrance, Sara following at a distance. He left the gate open for her to close behind her. Delgado had cut the padlock, and Rice was fresh out, at least until the new Abloy he'd ordered from Damien arrived, but Sara had said she would wrap the chain so it looked locked to people driving by.

When he pulled onto Route 608, no one drove past. No one saw a Tahoe with Arizona plates leave the Turk Mountain Preserve. He wore a plain baseball cap, dark sunglasses, a canvas coat, and a pair of old leather driving gloves he'd found in the lodge. The digital clock on the dash read 10:52 A.M. The gas tank was three-quarters full. He left Delgado's cell phone turned on, the charger plugged into the cigarette lighter, so that on the outside chance that anyone was tracking it, they would see that Andrés Delgado had left the Turk Mountain Preserve and was headed north.

FIFTY-TWO

Sara appeared in the kitchen doorway soon after he started the coffeemaker. A foggy morning outside, scant gray light seeping through the kitchen window. Her eyes weren't quite all the way open, and her hair stuck out in wings and tufts. She felt with her hand and tried to pat it down, then gave up and sat in the chair across the table from where Rice was eating a bowl of cereal. He'd set a bowl and spoon for her and she stared at the two boxes on the table as if the decision between them was beyond her capability.

"I smelled coffee," she said.

The coffee machine groaned and she glanced at it.

"Give it another minute," he said.

Yesterday afternoon he'd abandoned the Tahoe in a southeast D.C. neighborhood infamous for its high incidence of murder, drug busts, burglaries, and car theft. It was a risk driving Delgado's vehicle into an urban area, but he'd been careful about the speed limit and had made sure all the lights and blinkers worked before they'd left. He'd found a quiet street that looked like it might be popular at night with the right sort of crowd and left the keys in the ignition. He'd worn gloves, but he still scrubbed everything he'd touched with wet wipes. On a whim, he'd decided at the last minute to keep Delgado's phone, pulled the battery and the SIM card, and zipped it all in his jacket pocket. Before walking away to meet Sara several blocks west, he'd wedged a flimsy metal handcuffs key chain in the latch of the rear cargo door and jammed it shut. Whoever accepted the gift of Delgado's vehicle would be taking Delgado along with it. Sara had objected to the plan, she'd said they were dumping their dead assassin problem on people who were by definition poor and desperate enough to steal a vehicle, but Rice felt they were also dumping a late-model SUV on them, that it was a more or less fair transaction with an unknown and admittedly unwitting counterparty. The Tahoe would make its way to a chop shop and, in return, someone would be obliged to get rid of the body, creating a gap of pure randomness in the sequence of events. The evidentiary thread connecting Rice with Delgado would fray, unravel, disintegrate.

On the way back they'd traded off driving every hour because they both kept getting drowsy. Near Woodstock they'd pulled off the interstate and found a diner: grilled cheese sandwiches, coffee intended to fuel the last leg, but what it had fueled was an argument. Sara had no problem with today's homicide, but she kept pressing Rice about his execution of Crotalito, asking how old he'd been, speculating pointedly about the unimaginable poverty he must have come from, how vulnerable his teen brain would have been to the temptations of the cartel, surely he idolized his famous older brother, how much coercion might have been involved, how culpable was he really, like a child soldier, and so on until Rice told her he wasn't going to talk about it anymore. The kid had raped and tortured his girlfriend. He was a sadistic killer. Rice had put him down. He started cooking up an argument based on what he remembered about hunting squirrels in the forest last week— something about the predator's necessary and adaptive suspension of empathy—but he was too tired to pursue it very far and he had the sense to keep his mouth shut. They'd agreed to disagree and gone straight to bed in opposite wings of the lodge when they got home. Rice couldn't sleep, so he'd spent most of the night in the office entering historical logbook data on the laptop.

Sara pondered the cereal boxes. She might've been trying to read the ingredients. Finally they watched her hand lift from her lap as if of its own independent volition and clasp the box of generic wheat flakes. She peered at Rice while she dumped cereal into her bowl.

"You called him already?"

He nodded. She poured in some milk.

"What'd he say?"

"I got Suzy. She's the receptionist, or dispatcher. I'm not really sure what she is. Sheriff's gonna set up a meeting." He'd told Sara a DEA agent was mixed up in all this and might be able to do something about the three bikers. He'd described their connection with Mirra and the Stillers, though not how he'd found their names.

"Suzy?"

"What?"

Sara's pale blue eyes rose up from behind the cereal box. His face must've turned red.

"You like Suzy?"

"She's okay. She's funny."

"Funny ha-ha?"

"Yeah. Funny ha-ha."

What Suzy had said was that Sheriff Walker was already out and about, dispensing justice in a waterlogged Turpin County, and he'd asked her to tell Rice when he called that Agent Johns wanted another face-to-face with Rice, that the names Walker had passed along to Johns had—and here she'd performed an uncanny imitation of Walker's voice—"got that SOB's attention." Then she'd asked Rice if he liked to dance. He'd said no, and she'd sighed like that was the answer she'd expected and asked how about dinner and a movie? He'd said sure but wouldn't she get in trouble with the sheriff and she'd said she was always in trouble with the sheriff.

"What are we going to do now?" Sara asked. She had to teach this afternoon and would be driving back to Blacksburg early.

He got up to pour their coffee. "I'll ride with you down to the gate on your way out, just in case. You probably should stay in Blacksburg till we can be sure it's safe here. Might be a week or two."

"Why?"

"Well, we don't know this is over, not yet. A cop might have come across the Tahoe before anyone took it. And I might be wrong about Delgado freelancing, going after me without cartel support. They could send someone else. If I'm still alive in a couple of weeks we'll know I was right."

FIFTY-THREE

The eighties-vintage A-frame stood in hemlock shadows on a low bluff overlooking the Dutch River. Rice knocked on the back screen door and Walker let him in, led him through a musty great room to a screened porch with a view down to a bend in the river. The place was owned by a friend of Walker's wife. It was private, he'd said, and less damn depressing than that abandoned motel they'd used last time. He'd set out a pot of coffee and mugs.

"This is civilized," Rice said.

"Not sure coffee is what Johns needs, but I need it." He poured two mugs, didn't offer sugar or milk, so Rice sipped the black coffee and watched the river. It was roiling and turbid but the flood had receded, exposing broad bars of muddy cobbles on the far bank, willow thickets and sycamore saplings still bent downstream. When he'd driven past Stiller's Store on the way, the front door was propped open and Bilton and several other people Rice didn't recognize were inside, mopping the muddy floor.

Walker stood beside Rice at the screen. "I can guess why you're interested in those bikers."

Rice nodded. He hadn't said anything about bikers but he'd assumed the sheriff would look into the names himself. "Unfortunately I don't have anything you can use. It's a little bit complicated."

"I'll bet."

He was about to ask after Suzy when they heard another vehicle pull up behind the cabin. Walker went to see, and Rice heard him say, "Well hell."

Rice smiled, realizing what Johns was up to. Low voices in curt greetings, footsteps, more than two people, creak of hinges and the door pulling against the rusty spring. Rice turned with his coffee.

"Mr. Moore," Johns said, looking belligerent and pleased with himself. "I think you've met Alan."

Mirra stepped through the door, limping but somehow still giving the impression of coiled violence, an elaborate metal and fabric brace strapped over his jeans on his left leg. He wasn't smiling. His dark beard had grown out some in the past week and his face, like Rice's, still looked like he'd been in a fight and hadn't slept much since. The sclera of his left eye was a deep red and the flesh around the eye was purple, swollen. Rice didn't think he'd hit him in the nose, but clearly he'd had it broken more than once. Probably in his late twenties, he looked angry, but he might always look angry. It was the kind of face you wondered what would happen to it if it ever did smile. The look he gave Rice was cryptic, but if forced to call it something, Rice would have said it was curious.

Rice watched Mirra's eyes for a moment, then he said, "You're the guy from those nightmares."

A long pause followed while Mirra seemed to struggle, dredging something up from inside until a barrier gave way and it happened, the guy did smile, shaking his head, and his face didn't break. Suddenly a more complicated sort of fellow.

"Back the fuck atcha," he said.

Johns glared at Mirra, disappointed at not wrong-footing Rice. "What, you two are buds now?" He took a cup of coffee from

Walker and turned officious, brusque. Business at hand. What he wanted from Walker was room to work, room for Mirra and him. Same deal he'd worked out with the game warden months ago. "You're here," he said to Rice, "because you're the local vigilante who gets a free fucking pass from the sheriff's office, so I have to negotiate with you, too."

Walker said if they wanted anything from him, they were going to have to say what they were up to, and what they were up to, it turned out, was acquiring bear parts for the motorcycle club to trade for drugs in East and Southeast Asia. The club was growing its operations there, securing cheap sources of large quantities of meth, opiates, and designer drugs.

"And these people want bear parts," Johns said. "*Wild* bear parts, not farmed, for some goddamn reason they're convinced there's a difference." A steady supply of bear galls and paws sweetened the deals and gave the club an advantage with the best suppliers. The agency had given Johns some seed money and now with funding from the club, he and Mirra had developed a significant bear parts market in Virginia, West Virginia, and Pennsylvania.

"Sounds like you're onto a good business proposition," Walker said.

"It gets Mirra and me into the upper levels of the club. That's where the organized crime is happening."

"Rank and file ain't involved," Mirra said. Rice had wondered about a guy like Mirra betraying the brotherhood. He must have a beef with the leadership. Happened a lot, the higher-ups got greedy and cut out the membership; Johns had probably promised him only the higher-ups would be prosecuted. Might or might not turn out to be true.

Johns said he thought the investigation had the potential to take out a significant percentage of the narcotics supply in the mid-Atlantic all at once. Leaving a vacuum, Rice thought, to be filled within six months by a Mexican cartel. They'd be much better off leaving the bikers in place. He couldn't imagine anyone still thought the whole war-on-drugs charade made any sense anyway. Johns didn't strike him as a true believer, so this was all about his career. Rice wondered where Mirra would be left after it was over. He'd seen what happened to CIs for the DEA.

"So it's for a good cause," Rice said. "Killing all those bears." The others looked at him. "They want our bear parts because their wild bears are pretty much extinct. You commercialize bears here and that's what you'll get, eventually."

"Bears ain't extinct here. Ain't even close." This was Mirra.

"It's only for another six months, a year tops," Johns said. "When we drop out the prices'll crash again. Besides, bears have turned into a goddamn nuisance in a lot of places. People aren't shooting enough of them."

"Well, you're not shooting any more bears at the preserve, not on my watch. Turk Mountain Preserve's off-limits. In fact, my jurisdiction extends as far as I can walk, so you'd better stay off Turk Mountain generally. Serrett Mountain too."

"Fuck you," Mirra said, amiably. "That's public land."

"And I'll be watching it."

Johns appeared more outraged than Mirra. "You realize you're threatening federal law enforcement personnel in front of a county sheriff."

Rice knew he was reaching. "Not a threat," he said. "I'm giving you information. Telling you how the land lies. I'm part of the geography. If you guys are poaching bears near Turk Mountain, I'll be there."

Johns stared at the sheriff, probably hoping for support, but Walker rolled his eyes. Mirra was still grinning, like once he'd started this new thing with his face, he just couldn't stop.

"What about my truck?" He was asking Rice.

When the guy focused his attention on you, Rice decided, it

was a little bit scary. Even if he was smiling. Rice had nearly forgotten about the damn truck.

"Come on. You know I couldn't have done that."

"Figured you had someone with you."

"Not that I know of. Maybe the bears did it." Actually he suspected the mushroom picker, whoever or whatever he was, but he wasn't going to mention it.

Johns, impatient with the subject, insisted. "You're paying for his truck, Moore. You're responsible one way or another. Either that or you pay for his knee surgery, which you definitely are responsible for."

In Rice's peripheral vision, Sheriff Walker's eyebrows shot up, and Mirra turned toward Johns, vaguely dangerous. "You said—"

"I know what I said. Agency'll cover your medical. But we can't do the truck. Moore pays for the truck."

There followed a surreal discussion about the deductible on Mirra's comprehensive auto policy and whether it was fair to ask him to make a claim. Eventually the sheriff promised the police report would make it clear Mirra was the victim of random vandalism, and the deductible turned out to be a thousand dollars, which Rice couldn't afford, but then he remembered Delgado's cash, and agreed. He would drop off the money at Walker's office next week.

Johns drove out first, Rice following. Walker stayed at the cabin because his wife was bringing out a picnic later. When they'd passed through the open aluminum gate and onto the rutted gravel county road that climbed away from the river, Johns pulled onto the left shoulder.

Rice stopped alongside and rolled down his window, cut off his engine. The air was warm and smelled of crayfish. Mirra watched him through Johns's open passenger-side window. He still seemed to be in a good mood, maybe because Rice had promised to give him a thousand dollars. Johns stared straight ahead, his forearms resting on the steering wheel.

"Where'd you get the names, Moore?"

"Only so many places I *could* get them, right? But what you're really wondering is whether I know you covered up Sara Birkeland's rape, and whether I have proof, and whether I'm going to give it to Sheriff Walker."

Johns didn't seem surprised. "You think you can blackmail me?"

"Only sort of. I want you to find a way to take those three fuckers down. If not for the rape, then for something else."

"You know damn well I can't touch those guys, not yet."

Rice spoke to Mirra. "You weren't happy about what they did, were you? Not your typical rank-and-file MC members. No loyalty. They set you up. If it hadn't been for Johns, you'd have done time for a rape you weren't involved in."

Mirra didn't answer him. He seemed only idly interested in the exchange.

"Why don't you two put your heads together," Rice said. "You'll think of something. We can talk again in a month, see how it's coming along."

Now Mirra perked up, like he'd been waiting to ask. "What about the Mexican?"

"What Mexican?"

Mirra turned and said something to Johns that sounded like *I fuckin' told you*, and Johns leaned over him to give Rice an outraged, incredulous look. The thought of Rice surviving an assassination attempt seemed to bother him more than the blackmail. "Los Ántrax, for fuck's sake." He cranked the ignition and Mirra raised the window as Johns floored the gas and spit gravel, fishtailing off the shoulder and around a curve, headed back toward the highway in some kind of hurry.

FIFTY-FOUR

Rice drove west over the Dutch River bridge at first light. He'd seen no traffic, so he pulled off the road on the far side and walked back to have a look at the river. The bright washed air and indigo skies that had followed the tropical storm hadn't lasted long. A fine misty rain drifted around him, a wetness more of the air itself than anything falling from the sky. Rain showers overnight had wakened him several times pounding on the roof of the lodge. He peered over the concrete railing at the river fizzing against the abutments, swirling on the downstream side in brown foamy eddies that trapped the usual floating detritus: milk jugs, bright yellow motor oil containers, bits of Styrofoam, plastic bags.

He'd called Boger last night to thank him for the warning about the Stillers and the biker gang, and he'd asked when would be a good time to stop by with something. Also he was out of the honey Boger had left him and would like to buy some more, if he could spare it. Boger said well if you ain't busy up there watching leaves fall off the trees you can stop by first thing in the morning and help me switch out a culvert. I'll give you the damn honey.

He drove slowly in the dense fog along Sycamore Creek. When

he turned onto the gravel drive, a yellow glow appeared at the edge of the forest, indistinct dog shapes milling in the kennel as Dempsey, lit by a bare bulb in the wood-frame run-in shed, scooped kibble into big round aluminum pans. The dogs triggered a memory, a nightmare from the night before, and he braked too hard, skidding in the gravel. He shut off the engine but didn't open the door. The windshield wipers stopped in mid-swipe, fine raindrops beading on the glass. They accumulated into larger drops, pregnant and then bursting to run down the glass and out of sight. He watched the rain on the windshield and then he was watching his dream, himself, walking along the base of a high cliff in the inner gorge, under a vast curving overhang where water seeped silently down the rock in slow glistening sheets. Someone's camp, lean-to shelters and a stone fire circle in an overarched cavity out of the weather, the dirt floor stomped smooth and swept; animal skins were stretched in rough wooden frames made from branches with the bark still on, a big one with tawny fur leaning up against a boulder black with woodsmoke.

Dempsey shut the door of the shed behind him and approached the truck. Rice got out and pulled on his rain shell. Dempsey wore a dark canvas coat, already wet on the shoulders.

"You mind a little mud?"

"No, sir."

Rice climbed up onto the skidder as Dempsey fired up the ferociously loud engine, drove past the house and onto a muddy logging road where he picked up speed. The skidder clearly wasn't meant to be a passenger vehicle, and Rice hung on as best he could, bracing his butt against the welded-on dog kennels as the machine bucked and roared up the mountainside, spattering him with mud from the big knobby tires.

At the first landing Boger stopped the skidder next to a flatbed trailer with a yellow Caterpillar backhoe and two big corrugated metal culvert pipes chained alongside. They traded the skidder for the backhoe and continued another half mile as the road followed the contour southwest and made a deep bend into a forested hollow. A bold creek flowed over the top of the road where the culvert had been plugged on the upstream end and then completely exposed by erosion. It was old, a rusted iron pipe that Boger's ancestors must've put in.

"This first one ain't so bad," Boger said.

They dug out underneath the pipe with long-handled shovels and lay in the mud to push thick chains under and around so Boger could pull it out with the backhoe. Boger had skill with the backhoe, performing improbably delicate maneuvers with a toothed steel bucket the size of a bathtub, but a lot of the work still fell to shovels and iron digging bars, sifting rocks from the fill soil, building sluices at each end of the pipe to protect the channel from erosion. Later, Rice figured in the course of the day he must have lifted and placed a ton and a half of rock with his hands. Boger was strong and fit and the work turned into a contest between the two of them, the older man refusing to be outworked by the sissy-pants caretaker from the nature preserve. Rice started to worry when Boger's gaze lost focus and he began tripping over his feet, but the stubborn lout clearly wasn't going to give up, so Rice asked for a break.

It was early evening when they rode the skidder back down the two miles of switchbacks to Boger's house. Rice hopped down and Boger looked at him.

"You didn't bring no clean clothes, did you?"

"Didn't occur to me." Both men were caked with mud from head to boots.

"Nothin' of mine'll fit you. Meet me over to the kennel and we'll get you hosed off. Still be wet but won't be muddy."

Boger tried the door of the house but his wife wouldn't let him in, so he stood there until she handed him out a heavy paper grocery bag. He came back carrying the bag and two Buds in his other hand, folded towels under one arm, and Sadie the setter trailing along behind. She ran to Rice when she saw him, favoring the back leg. He knelt down, scratched the silky tangled fur behind her ears. She sniffed at his mud-flecked face, whiskers tickling his ear while he cracked open his beer with his other hand.

The hounds in the kennel bayed at them halfheartedly while Boger sprayed the mud off Rice with the chrome spray nozzle. It was high pressure, probably what Boger used to hose off the concrete slab of the kennel, and it hurt like hell but he didn't say anything.

Boger tossed him a towel and he dried his face and hair. He took off his shirt and wrung it out, put it back on. A little water wouldn't hurt his truck seat any. He handed Boger a sealed envelope with "Turk Mountain Preserve" written on the front.

"This is a key to the new lock at the front entrance," he said. "If you lose your hounds on Turk Mountain, come on up the driveway and we'll go get them."

"Your bosses know you made a key for a bear hunter?"

"For a houndsman. Yeah, she knows. She and the board want to try a new approach to things. We're not allowing bear hunting, but we'll try to involve some of the folks who live around here in what happens at the preserve. We're starting with you because I trust you and I'm going to need your help with some projects up there. If you have time."

Boger grunted something noncommittal, which was better than Rice had hoped for. He'd opened the door of his truck to leave when Boger stopped him.

"You hang on just a minute. You and me ain't square."

Rice grinned. "You probably saved my life. It's going to be hard to square that."

"That's not what I mean. We ain't square on you killing Monroe."

The bear hound. Lying in the gravel that morning, the wet fur, legs stiff with rigor. Seemed years ago, but he should've known Boger wasn't over it yet. He waited.

Boger nodded toward the house. "Maryanne's got three retired hounds living in there already. She won't let me retire 'em proper, the .357 way." He didn't smile, but Rice suspected this was just tough talk. "Soon as one dies of old age, anothern comes out of the kennel and into the house. She goes and picks one out, the oldest and weakest, the one the others are pushing off the food, and then I got to find and train me up a new hound. It's three broke-down hounds in the house all the time. But I do draw the line. At three. There ain't no room for Sadie. You have to take her. In the bag you got a week's worth of kibble so she don't starve 'fore you go to the store. Your honey's in there too."

Rice felt a little stunned, like Boger had gone upside his head with an open hand. It took him a moment to reply. "You want me to take Sadie?"

"That's what I just said."

"I don't kn—"

"She gets around good but she'll always have that stiff leg. Remind you what a asshole you are."

"I'm not sure my situation is a good one for a dog."

"I didn't ask about your situation."

Rice breathed, feeling his situation change. The man had made up his mind. He nodded, and spoke to the dog sitting expectant on the grass between them as if waiting to hear a verdict.

"I reckon that's fair."

They arrived back at the lodge after dark. Rice opened the door for her, and Sadie hopped out of the truck and chased an animal, a fast, dark flitting thing that turned out to be Mel the black cat. Mel ended up in the rafters above the front porch, with Sadie standing underneath, pointing with her nose, frozen except for a slow sweep of her tail. When Rice turned on the porch light Mel gave him a look. "You got a *dog?*"

He called Sadie inside and shut the screen door and went and stood under where the cat was sitting, utterly calm now, mute, dignified, unflustered.

"You know you almost got us both killed the other day," he said.

FIFTY-FIVE

cold gentle rain fell most nights, and in the mornings thick fog crowded the mountain like giant batts of cotton. He worked in the cabin all day and into the moon-dark evenings while Sadie explored the edge of the forest or rested on the porch, staring out at things Rice couldn't see. He laid in the insulation and hung the drywall. A crew from an outfit in northern Virginia installed the antique cabinets STP insisted on. The floor was installed and sanded, and he'd applied the nontoxic finish that STP had ordered. At night Sadie slept on an old towel on the floor in his bedroom and stank of wet fur, waking him up when she whimpered in her dreams. She stopped chasing the cat, and the two animals practiced ignoring each other. Mel stayed around, possibly glad for the extra company despite herself. She lapped up the offerings of fish-smelly water Rice squeezed from his tuna cans into a cereal bowl on the porch railing.

Before bed, he sat outside on the front porch with Sadie at his feet and the skinny black cat grooming herself on the railing. He drank a couple of beers to settle himself and watched the distant lights in the valley.

Ever since the night of the hurricane, Rice had found himself drawn to water. Some mornings he and Sadie walked down to the river, where she liked to creep along the bank and point frogs as if they were quail. Rice sat and listened to the current rush and thrum over the cobblestone bed, watched the light come slowly onto the rippling surface, flat metal light from an overcast sky. After lunch he let the dog chase him around in the tall grass of the meadow. When she caught him she pawed at his calf and he fell on his back as if she'd knocked him down. She stood there wagging, her face leaning down to peer into his. A little puzzled. She probably had never interacted with a human in this way before. She probably thought he was insane.

He'd taken apart Mirra's bait station, buried the deliquescent cow head, and packed out the cable and the rebar he'd pulled from its eyes. The two bear carcasses had mostly disappeared.

Dempsey Boger had brought him three bodark staves from a cousin's farm in the Piedmont, and he'd been trying to carve a longbow. The first had failed but the second attempt seemed like it was going to work, and as soon as he figured out how to straighten arrows he would start practicing.

On several nights he was awakened by the same dream, the driveway alarm—*Alert, Zone One.* He sat up in bed, his hand already on the .45, but there was no sound but Sadie's soft snoring.

When he walked transect surveys, he kept Sadie on a rope leash so she wouldn't range and skew the species count. He made a scheduled water test and the last aquatic bug survey of the year in Perry Creek, switched out the data cards on all the trail cameras, and uploaded the images, recorded the data in Sara's spreadsheets.

He talked to Sara on the phone every few days. She was keeping an eye on the news, checking D.C. websites for any hint that Delgado's body had been found, though they both doubted something like that would even be reported. Delgado had been missing for a while, and the more time passed without incident, the safer they were.

He hid Delgado's phone in the attic, and planned to have a look at it someday when he was ready, maybe get someone to help him translate any texts that might be on there.

Two weeks turned into three. The cabin was almost ready for Sara to move in.

Then he found the newspaper clippings in the mailbox. He called Sara for directions and drove straight to Blacksburg.

She came to the door in gray and maroon Virginia Tech sweats, looking alarmed. They stood in her kitchenette while Sadie inspected the living area, daintily sniffing everything she could reach. They watched her the way adults will watch a child to avoid awkward interaction. Finally he took the rolled-up *Philadelphia Inquirer* sections from his jacket pocket and flattened them on the counter.

"What is it?"

What it is, he thought, is me owing Alan Mirra a great big ol' favor, and someday he'll come a-calling.

She read. A hit-and-run motorcycle accident left one dead, reportedly a member of a notorious outlaw motorcycle gang. The more recent clipping described a gang shooting, an attack by the same OMG on a rival meth lab that went sideways, the bikers walked into an ambush, one guy shot dead, the second was in the ICU.

"These are the guys who raped me."

He nodded.

"How did you do this?" Her voice had jumped in pitch. Sadie, curled up on the shiny oak strip floor with her back pushing against Rice's foot, raised her head to watch Sara.

He started to say he hadn't done anything, but that would've been a pure lie and now she was crying anyway, trying to stop but the tears were rolling down her cheeks and catching in the corners of her mouth before she wiped them with the back of her hand.

She didn't make any noise. Should he hug her? That might be presumptuous. He never knew what to do with a woman who cried. When he was younger he would go off and try to fix whatever it was that had made them cry. Except when it was him. He couldn't always fix that. His mother hadn't cried much. Apryl had been too goddamn tough to cry, and she'd only done it once, when they'd seen the first jaguar picture from their trail cameras, down in the Pajaritos. She'd refused to talk about it afterward, but he thought he understood.

He wasn't sure what to do with Sara. Wasn't sure what else he could do. He'd done more than he was telling her, more than he would tell her.

"You need to get out of here so I can cry by myself."

That worried him but she smiled and wiped her face with her sleeves, said she was fine. He would be back in a few weeks to help her move anyway. She pushed him out of the kitchen. He let her. Sadie got up and followed.

At the door, Sara reached up and kissed him quickly on the mouth, her hand on his elbow as if to make sure he held still for it. Not a passionate kiss, but not sisterly either. More like an old girlfriend, familiar enough to go for the lips but not trying for anything more than what they'd already had.

ON THE MORNING AFTER THE FIRST HARD FROST HE KNELT IN THE DRIVEWAY on a greasy square of plastic tarp and sharpened the bush hog blade, yellow-white sparks showering from the grinder, bouncing off the steel housing of the mower and down onto the gravel. Six five-gallon cans filled with diesel waited in a row along the wall inside the shed. Tomorrow he would start the slow circumnavigation of the upper meadow in low gear, standing at the steering wheel to watch for fallen branches, rocks, torpid rat snakes not yet gone to their hibernacula.

That night the quarter moon was waxing, and he hiked up the fire road at dusk with Sadie ranging ahead of him, a darting ghost in the pale moonlight. They walked all the way to the Forest Service pole gate at the back boundary, then swung west across the saddle another three miles over to the high eastern slopes of Serrett Mountain. Climbing irritated the knee he'd injured falling down the cliff nearly a month ago, so he rounded the mountain on a contour and dropped down a steep ridge south toward the Dutch River. Walking downhill wasn't much better than climbing, and by the time he got to the river his knee was sore and a little swollen. He waded into the cold water. The heavy push and swirl felt curative. He lay on his back and let the current take him. Sadie whined once and then understood, followed along the bank, sniffing for muskrats and the last of the bullfrogs. A mile or so downstream they would come to an old ford and an overgrown road that led back to the driveway and the lodge.

Soon he was shivering. The steep dark mountainsides rearing up north and south of the river framed the Milky Way and made it seem unfamiliar and preternaturally bright, like something in a Hubble telescope photograph, or what you would see if you were looking out the window of a spaceship. A few bats jerked and swooped against the stars, echolocating bugs. They should be hibernating by now and he wondered if they were sick with white-nose disease, staying out too long, desperate to build up calorie reserves that might or might not see them through the winter. No other creature perceived the world through echolocation in quite the same way as these microbats, and when they were gone, their umwelt would disappear forever. A universe snuffed out of existence.

This depressing thought triggered a memory spilling suddenly into his consciousness, a gift from those mysterious days in the forest before Mirra finally showed up: an early morning, peering into a tiny feral eye inches from his face, then a dream, or a vision, when he flew out over the gorge and knew everything, all at once. It had terrified him at the time, but now in the remembering it gave him a frisson of glass-half-full optimism, something that ran decidedly counter to his nature.

He suspected he had retained some of that morning's extra-human perception, though it might be more sane to call it hallucination. Just for example, a bear sometimes followed him in the forest, a very large particular bear that Sadie never noticed, which Rice took to mean the bear wasn't real. It was there now, he knew, watching from a bluff just above the river.

The bear's bright eyes shone in a scarred face: a mask, expressionless. He watched, but he always kept his distance. He was strong, fast even with the limp, the missing left forepaw.

"Must have lost it in a trap or something, huh?" Rice said.

Sadie paused at the sound of his voice, but she realized he wasn't talking to her. She splashed softly along the shore, keeping pace as Rice floated shivering down the cold river and talked to ghost bears. He slid with the current over smooth stones, watching bats feed overhead in alien light.

ACKNOWLEDGMENTS

Thanks first to my amazing agent, Kirby Kim, and the rest of the pros at Janklow & Nesbit. Besides wise counsel and the agenting miracle of finding the perfect publisher, Kirby—along with Brenna English-Loeb—provided transformative editing that made *Bearskin* a much better book than what they'd plucked from the slush pile.

Thanks to my equally amazing editor, Zachary Wagman, whose insights and suggestions quickly brought this book up to another level . . . and I don't think he has stopped to rest since. Thanks also to Dan Halpern, Miriam Parker, Sonya Cheuse, Meghan Deans, Emma Janaskie, Sara Wood, and Renata De Oliveira. Special thanks to Andy LeCount and the entire HarperCollins sales force. It's a surreal and humbling experience to work for years on a story, and then suddenly there's this smart editor and a whole publishing house who believe in what you've made and they're going to a great deal of trouble and expense bringing it into the world as a book. You all have my bewildered gratitude.

Thank you, Evelyn Somers, Speer Morgan, and others at *The Missouri Review* for giving Rice's story its first home, and for crackerjack early editing along with encouragement and affirmation when it was needed most.

Over the years I had important technical help from a number of knowledgeable, talented, generous people, only a few of whom are named here, and none of whom are responsible for my errors of fact and/or judgment: Wildlife ecologist Dr. David A. Steen. Elite federal agent Matt Boyden. Writer and naturalist William Funk. Cousin and renowned forest ecophysiologist Dr. Samuel B. McLaughlin. Author and former park ranger Jordan Fisher Smith. Poet, stonemason, and aboriginal skills teacher Alec Cargile. Attorney and multithreat know-it-all Paul Moskowitz. And cousin Peter McLaughlin, brilliant musician and part-time desert rat who first introduced me to southern Arizona.

Thank you, Dabney Stuart—favorite poet, mentor of several decades, generous reader, inspiration. Thanks, Michael Knight, for the years of unflagging support and smart reading, and the humbling demonstrations of how it's done by a real writer. Thank you, cousin Gee McVey, who provided *Bearskin*'s origin anecdote (among others) and more than a half century, and counting, of the best of friendships. And a mountain-size debt to my lifelong friend Taylor Cole—business partner, conservationist, and expert on all things rural Virginia. Thank you.

My family looked after this unpromising late-born and gave me good books to read early on. Most importantly you were the guides and companions with whom I first experienced and was captivated by the vast world outdoors. Thank you, LeeBo, Nancy, Ginky, Ham, Nelle, Dr. Busch, Rosy, Eric, Uncle Roy Hodges (1912–1994), and Ed Carrington (1944–1986).

They say you're not supposed to mention four-leggeds in your acknowledgments. Yeah, screw that. Thank you, Whiskey Before Breakfast, Big Fred, Barney, Habanero, Toso, Eight, Sam, Winifred, Odin, Little Bear, and Roman. I could not have persevered without you.

Nancy Assaf McLaughlin: Partner, co-adventurer, editor, best friend, wife. I will try, but I can never properly thank you for your patience and love and faith and support.

And thank you, Rosa Batte Hodges McLaughlin (1919–2016). You would have been proud, and you would have kept this book on the coffee table even though I'm pretty sure you wouldn't have liked all the cussing, because your love and generosity always surpassed understanding.

Thank you, all.

ABOUT THE AUTHOR

James A. McLaughlin holds law and MFA degrees from the University of Virginia. His fiction and essays have appeared in *The Missouri Review, The Portland Review, River Teeth,* and elsewhere. He grew up in rural Virginia and lives in the Wasatch Range east of Salt Lake City, Utah.